WARLORD

AFTER IT HAPPENED BOOK 10

WARLORD

DEVON C FORD

PRESS

Published by Vulpine Press in the United Kingdom in 2025

Cover by Volodymyr Volianiuk, Coverly Design Studio

ISBN: 978-1-83919-709-3

www.vulpine-press.com

"Every man is guilty of all the good he did not do."

- Voltaire (1694-1778)

PROLOGUE

"Easy, boy," Dan murmured softly as the dog fidgeted beside him. He knew Ash wasn't ill-disciplined enough to be moving out of boredom, not when they were both in work mode anyway, but more that the dog was feeling the same unease that he was and needed to communicate that to his master.

"I know," Dan reassured him, slowly stretching out his left hand to soothe his best friend. "I know."

Not once did he take his eye from the scope during the interaction. Not once did his focus waver from the distant fire – far too large from a tactical perspective in his opinion – and from the gang of men and women gathered around it.

Not even when another nauseating wave of pain flared up deep inside his lower jaw to make his right eye blur for a moment.

He held his breath until it passed, concentrating on a few people in turn ringed by the optic on his weapon, then let it out with a sigh of annoyance.

Count fifteen. All armed, but they've got the tactical discipline of toddlers on trampolines.

A group that size on the move was significant given how much food and water they'd need to carry or find to sustain them, but the fact that they all went armed with an assortment of weapons was less of a concern given how it wasn't sensible *not* to go far from home without a gun. He watched them for another ten minutes, or long enough for the throbbing around his troublesome tooth to make four more attempts at driving him insane enough to do something drastic.

Withdrawing from the vantage point, expertly chosen, save for the fact that it was beside a thorny bush which had left more than a few invaders in his left thigh, he moved slowly until he'd gone back far enough to rise to a crouch and walk away.

Ash followed at his heel, trotting effortlessly and looking up at Dan's face just waiting for the word. He received nothing but the frown that was so constant it may as well have been tattooed on his features.

They moved fast, covering almost a mile of gentle downhill over rough ground until they reached his ride which would carry him back to the safety of his high walls and impenetrable defences.

Chosen for a low noise profile and not comfort – *never* for comfort – he slid the long rifle he'd used to watch the unexpected guests into a padded sling fixed to the horse's saddle just in front of his right knee. He adjusted the sling of his carbine so that it rested over his back and not down his front where it would represent another unnecessary threat to the safety of his balls.

"Sit," he growled at Ash.

The dog sat and cocked his head, one ear up in confusion, as he feigned an unbelievable innocence that made his owner smile reluctantly. Dan hated being without the dog as much as he hated riding a horse, but the combination of Ash and this particular mare had left him on his back more than once.

"I mean it, you little fucker," Dan warned, earning an excited shuffle from the aging dog who fully intended to ignore him.

The horse turned its head back to fix Ash with a "go ahead, I fucking dare you" look.

Dan untied the bridle from a low branch and made soothing noises to the horse as he held the left stirrup still and seated the toe of his foot securely into it. He hopped on the spot twice and lifted himself up with a groan to swing his right leg over the saddle that rested at his face height, and Ash did exactly what he knew the dog would.

Just as his backside hit the worn leather the dog made a lunge for the horse's back foot nearest to him, which the horse saw coming and had learned from experience.

"You fuckin' *twat*!"

The horse took off with the sudden acceleration of a motorcycle, throwing him backwards and sending a sinewy crunch up his spine and into his soul just to flare up the toothache again. The force of his wrenched back combined with the pressure and pain in his jaw took his breath away. By the time the horse had slowed and he could speak again, he turned to hiss a string of abuse at his dog who just trotted along beside both man and horse wearing a look of satisfied amusement.

"*Wanker*," Dan cursed at him, adding a final word as both dog and horse had forgotten their conflict in mutual amusement at seeing him inconvenienced.

Dan reached into a pouch on his battered and stained vest, pulling out a pinch of small green leaves. He crammed them into the back of his mouth and bit down with another shudder of pain as he caught sight of his dog beside him again.

"Not funny. You're a right prick sometimes, you know that?" he asked through the mouthful of fresh mint leaves.

Ash was utterly unperturbed by the names he was called. Both he and the mare happily trotted along, side by side, making Dan even more annoyed that they only sough conflict when the risks of him breaking his neck were at their highest.

Turning the nose of the horse south he sat up straight and pushed his heels down, giving them one small jab backwards to urge his mount on, and set off for the coastal track that would lead him home, whimpering with the pain throbbing at the back of his mouth.

GRANDPAPA

Sanctuary
Five Weeks Earlier

"Say, *bonjour grand-père*," Leah cooed, jigging the girl on her knee.

"Oi," Dan said, aiming a gnarled finger at the grinning baby proudly sporting two tiny teeth in the middle of her lower gums, "don't listen to her. Say *Dan. Duh. Ahh. Nnn*."

The baby, Adalene, said nothing but let out a stream of stringy drool from her mouth and smacked her chubby hands together in delight. Her cheeks were blotchy and crimson, denoting that more little white pegs of unrivalled sharpness were on their way soon.

"How's it looking?" Leah asked, still jigging the baby up and down but turning her face to pure business in a second.

"All good. Setting off in the morning. Should be three days there, spend the night, three back. A week on the road, so no panicking unless we don't arrive by lunchtime on day eight."

Leah's lips tightened, conveying the fact that she felt Dan was leaving too wide a margin for error in his blasé assessment. Even with two laden carts she could easily make the trip to Andorra and back inside of a week.

"You'll send pigeons when you arrive and when you leave?" she asked, eyebrows raised as if her words were more of a reminder than a question.

Dan, cup already raised to his lips to slurp a type of tea he'd taken a fancy to since their supply of instant coffee had been used up, was robbed of the opportunity to respond by Marie.

"Like he always says," she explained with such sweet sincerity that it could only be sarcasm. "If he tells you he's going to do something then you don't need to remind him every three months."

Marie leaned down and kissed Dan on the cheek, making a small noise of repulsion afterwards to remind him that he should wash. He knew that wasn't something he could put off until the nagging intensified, not unless he wanted to sleep on his own.

"Morning, darling, light of my life, pain in my ass," Dan said with such feigned sweetness that the look she shot him bordered on dangerous.

He decided to double down, widening the smile and his eyes to make certain she knew he was joking. She relented, smiling on one side of her mouth to make her cheek dimple behind the wave of greying, ashen-blonde hair falling down her face.

"Still setting off in the morning?" Marie asked, sitting down and taking the baby from Leah amid the uncoordinated clapping of pudgy, dribble-covered hands.

Dan opened his mouth to speak but was cut off again, this time by Leah.

"He is. Allowing for three there and three back with one spent overnight."

Marie nodded her thanks to a young woman who brought over a cup of the same tea Dan was drinking, graciously thanking her in fluent French with a genuine smile.

Dan liked the mealtimes. They felt like a holiday resort, even after spending the better part of a decade in their coastal fortress, and the happiness of everyone seemed to swell up the big hall in the main castle.

Most people lived in the surrounding buildings or on the other side of the narrow docks in Sanctuary, but each breakfast, lunch and evening the majority of them would come to the main rooms of the castle and be sociable. Many of them stayed late into the night, and for half the year a fire would be lit in the grand room where recycled glass bottles of home-brewed alcohol would be consumed.

"First trip in spring can always be tricky," Dan reminded the two women in his life. "Don't know what the snows have done to parts of the road until we get there."

He didn't need to remind them, not Leah at least who had run her fair share of escort missions to their oldest allied township after her initial foray had inadvertently sparked a small war.

They'd won that war convincingly, and as a result the road for trade and friendship had been paved and they had been travelling there to trade from spring to autumn ever since.

"What's the haul?" Leah asked.

The way she spoke made it obvious that the months she had spent with her baby and recovering from what she called 'the most violent encounter of her life' was making her antsy to get back to at least a partial return to her true calling.

She was in her early twenties now, a mother, and so far removed from the small girl Dan had caught wearing earphones and eating biscuits in a car showroom a million years before. She had grown into a hard woman, a ruthlessly efficient killer when she had to be, but she still retained that playful, happy demeanour that made her Leah. He often caught himself just marvelling at her, unable to put into words how proud he was at the way she'd adapted to the violent new world and retained a loving, caring soul.

"Salted fish mainly," Dan said as he fumbled with a rolling paper and a pinch of very dry tobacco, "given how good our summer catch was, but there's some alcohol and other bits and bobs along with a personnel change."

"You mean you wanted to be on the first trade run because you're almost out of tobacco," Marie said, demonstrating where Leah learned how to phrase a question like an accusation based on pure fact.

Dan paused, half-rolled cigarette almost at his tongue which was sticking out ready to wet the paper, and shrugged as if to admit that she was completely right as always.

"Will they have any fresh produce available to trade this early?" Marie asked, eager for something varied in her diet after a winter spent eating the same foods.

"Victor says so," Leah answered, betraying that she'd been poking her nose into town business when she was supposed to be on that long-forgotten concept of maternity leave. She caught herself, having the decency to look sheepishly at her adoptive parents in turn.

Adalene took the opportunity to arch her back with a squeal and try to throw herself out of Marie's arms, adding a very wet raspberry for good measure when she was denied one of her many daily attempts at self-infanticide.

Dan had to lean away to save his half-rolled cigarette, bending his soggy attempt in the process and frowning at it to consider if he needed to start all over again.

"Well, I don't mind having this little one if you need to stretch your legs," Marie said, not looking at either of them to see which one responded first.

Leah's eyes met Dan's, twinkling with excitement and pleading with him to let her go. He smiled.

"If *Granny* here doesn't mind having the terrorist for a week, I could do with the company," he said.

Marie fixed him with a stern look that he knew was false but he smiled again in anticipation of what she was going to come back at him with.

"I don't mind at all, *dear*," she said coldly. "And don't call me Granny to show off in public, you said I'm a *GILF*, and tha—"

"*La-la-la-la*," Leah blurted out as she shoved the tip of her index finger in one of her ears to block out the evidence of what she called 'old people getting it on'.

"Will Lucien be okay with you going?" Dan asked her seriously.

"You're kidding, right? I'm pretty sure he's ready to go back to the watchtower and sleep for twelve hours a day."

Marie's face dropped and she leaned in closer, muttering to Leah with concern in her words, "Is everything okay? You're not…falling out or anything?"

"What? No! He calls me his *tigress encage*!" Her accent was as good as Marie's if not better, but her eye roll said more. "He knows I need to get back to work soon."

"You sure he's not talking about Nemes—*OW!*"

Dan frowned at Marie, whose foot had accidentally jabbed out to hit him in the part of his shin that seemed to be connected to all of his personal insecurities.

"That lazy bitch could do with the walk. She's put on more weight than I have," Leah answered.

Dan knew that was bullshit, the part about Leah gaining weight anyway, because he knew she'd resumed rigorous physical training when Adalene was only about six weeks old and had got herself back to the same way she'd looked when they were fighting pirates the summer before last.

Nem, the veritable fruit of Ash's loins, was as gifted and loyal as her sire was, but she seemed to suffer each winter and would spend a long time sleeping or just moping around in a perpetual depression caused by the outside world being shut off when the snows came.

"Sounds good to me," Dan told them. "Do you want to ask Sera for another horse or shall I?"

"You go and tell her when you've had that," Marie said as she pointed at the lumpy creation he held between the first two fingers of his right hand. "Leah can run me through little missy's routine."

Dan looked at the rolled cigarette, annoyed as it looked more like a *Werther's Original* than a smoke, wishing that he could roll them as easily as others could.

His eyes snapped to movement on his left as three boys ran through the hall chasing an older, taller one. He clicked his fingers and the one being chased froze, his eyes roving for the source of the summons and his face splitting as he saw his father. He ran over and did that thing which all young children do before they grew old enough to dislike other people; standing far too close so that Dan with his failing eyesight was forced to lean back to see his son's face.

"*Papa,* can I come with you tomorrow?" he pleaded, his accent more French than his parents'.

"No, son," Dan said apologetically, his tone changing to reflect the adoration he felt for their boy. "I'm taking your big sister this time, so I need our *bravest* men to stay behind and keep everyone safe."

The boy's sulk turned into an expression of pride and excitement and he stood taller, trying to puff up his small chest to bear the weight of such heavy responsibility.

"I get my own gun this time, *oui*?" he asked, eager to live up to his sudden promotion to manhood.

10

"No," Dan said in a whisper before looking over both shoulders conspiratorially. "We have enough people to just watch the walls...we need *spies*."

The boy fell for it completely and leaned in to hear his father's next words.

"I need my *best* people watching the kitchen to find out who's been eating all the fresh croissants before I get up in the morning..."

Ben paled, visibly swallowed, then nodded seriously and tried to pretend he didn't already know the culprit as well as he knew his own reflection. Dan smiled at him and stood, then ruffled his hair too roughly and walked for the exit as a streak of dark grey fur loped out of the shadows to follow at his heel.

BACK IN THE SADDLE

Dan didn't sleep much that night. The list of things going through his head before any kind of mission, no matter how safe it promised to be, was long and impossible to exhaust.

Every potential hiccup he imagined led to the creation of multiple contingencies to be thought up, and each of those led down another series of rabbit holes until he'd created such a web of things that could go wrong that he lost sight of the original problem entirely and had to start again from the beginning.

Finally giving up on thinking, he tried to sleep, but the nagging doubts seemed to contort in his fading consciousness and conjure all manner of enemies cropping up from their past to treat him to a semi-lucid nightmare, jolting him from his near-sleep one too many times.

With a sigh he peeled back the covers and slid from the bed to find his clothes in the dawn light peeking through the gaps in the curtains. Ash grumbled as he woke up to Dan's movement, earning a whisper of reassurance as he dressed ready for action quietly and methodically.

He put on clean but faded cargo trousers over a fresh pair of reinforced socks to save his ageing feet from the harshness of travel, adding a base layer under a shirt before the thin, breathable windbreaker was adjusted to allow his heavy plate carrier to sit comfortably over his upper body.

His boots were laced with care taken over every speed-loop, and he stood to tighten the vest and pick up the short-barrelled rifle before a soft snap of his fingers roused Ash from his watchful rest. Before leaving the room in silence he had a single, lingering look back at a sleeping Marie and leaned over her to plant a gentle kiss on her cheek. She woke, blinked one eye open then the other, and tried to sit up with a grunt of confused panic.

"Shhh, it's okay. Go back to sleep," he whispered.

Marie blinked again before her brain activated and she understood why he'd woken her.

She grabbed his vest and pulled him closer, kissing him hard on the lips before pulling him on top of her. He threw out his hands to support his weight, careful not to crush her under the sharp edges of his weapons and gear, and just let her hold onto him silently until she was done.

She let him go, not saying anything – no words of good luck or unrealistic demands of impossible promises to come home – just quiet reassurance that topped off both of their batteries.

Dan slipped out of their bedroom and poked his head around the door of the next room to see his son sprawled out on the bed facedown like his parachute hadn't opened.

Smiling at the warm thoughts of both people so close to his heart he stepped quietly down the carpeted stone corridor to walk down the stairs and out into the fresh spring air.

"You never could sleep before an op," Leah said in a conversational tone from the shadows nearby.

"And *you* never seemed to have *any* trouble," he answered as she stepped into the weak light dressed for war.

The two bumped fists gently, more affectionately than with any kind of bravado.

"You're joking, right? You think I've slept much in the last eight and a bit months? I'm not joking, I could literally lean against that wall and sleep *right now*."

Talk of babies and waking up reminded him of a logistical issue he hadn't figured out.

"Marie's still asleep…"

"I guessed as much. Lucien's going to bring Addie up later today."

Dan nodded to accept the details and file them away, then smirked about the thought of sleep deprivation before Leah demonstrated she was ahead of his mental curve again.

"You merely *adapted* to the sleeplessness," she said, adopting a deep, croaky voice and quoting something she'd heard Neil mimic. "I was *born* in it, *moulded* by it…"

Dan let out a small huff of amusement and bumped her shoulder, timing the move perfectly to her steps so she was pushed off balance. She aimed her own response, signposting it too obviously so all Dan had to do was stand firm and let her bounce off him before the two walked on in companionable silence.

Ben had been a blessing in that regard, he remembered fondly, and was sleeping through the night from about six months old to wake each dawn with a ravenous hunger. He was still the same, and from about four years old he was raiding the kitchens for the freshest pastries long before his parents were up.

Racing ahead of them with youthful exuberance was Nemesis, fussing at her father's face and bothering him enough to bring out a snarl of annoyance that sounded far worse than his mood truly reflected. There was no malice of aggression in it, simply the pack alpha correcting the behaviour of a younger member.

Dan watched the two dogs as he walked, feeling a stab of sadness as he recognised the first signs of Ash starting to age. Nemesis was filled with restless energy, having so much in reserve that she unnecessarily wasted it by putting extra bounce into the additional steps she took, whereas Ash moved with an economy of energy, only expending what he needed to as if wisdom had taught him to keep as much in reserve as possible.

Dan guessed Ash was over ten years old by that point, having not been certain of his age when he'd found the awkward, leggy jerk so long ago, and as far as working dogs went he was past the age for retirement, but then again so was he. Or at least he was old enough that he should be behind the lines issuing orders instead of insisting on being the tip of the spear, but he also recognised he had some issues surrounding trust and control.

Like Dan, Ash had taken a hard run at the brick wall of life more than once but carried far fewer injuries.

Their arrival at the stables was greeted by two distinct sounds. The first was Ash making a straight run at one of the mares he held a particular dislike for, and the other was a predictably annoying impression.

"*You never said anything about an android being onboard!*" Neil snarled in an American accent, hopping stiffly down from the large horse drawn cart loaded with their supplies.

Both dogs went to him, sniffing at his pockets as they always did because they never failed to get something from their bountiful benefactor.

"You need some new material," Dan goaded.

"Sure, I'll just nip down Hollywood and tell them to pull their fingers out, shall I? Get them making new movies again so I can learn a few lines."

"Tell them that the term 'military grade' doesn't mean what they think it means while you're at it," Dan told him, earning an unforced chuckle back.

Neil had spent enough of his life wearing, carrying and being transported in equipment made by the lowest bidder to know the bitter irony of how the term was misunderstood.

Neil was thinner than the previous year, having suffered a near-fatal injury the last time he ventured outside the walls with Dan, but somehow the self-appointed Sanctuary morale officer's exterior never wavered.

He hugged Leah awkwardly, reaching around the gear on her vest and her around his reduced bulk.

"Get away from her, you *bitch*," Dan muttered, ninety percent sure he had the right movie.

"*Noice.*" Neil chuckled, offering him a fist bump of approval and greeting.

"You good to go?" Leah asked Neil.

"All loaded up and ready. Got one of mine and three militia for rotating. What brings you along? We expecting trouble?"

"I need to get out," Leah admitted, shaking her head to alleviate any worries. "Get back in the saddle or something."

At the mention of the word saddle, Dan groaned internally. He'd argued to be allowed one of the two surviving quad bikes instead of being forced to sit on the back of an animal that hated him for simply living, but with the very last of their rough fuel supply being needed to run their remaining non-sail fishing boats he was forced to admit defeat.

"How's the biodiesel project coming?" he asked Neil, earning a confused look because he'd started the conversation thread in his own mind.

"Sorry, my train of thought was horse. *Ugghh.* Quad bikes. Fuel…"

Neil nodded, catching up instantly.

"It's happening, but it's not like we've got a lot of chippies and pub kitchens using galloons of cooking oil for me to work with. Best-case scenario is we can run the older boats for a few more years, but I reckon I'll need to have them serviced more often if we do."

Dan nodded sadly, not expecting to receive good news but hoping for it anyway.

He took Leah's bag and handed it up to the people in the back of Neil's wagon, nodding a greeting to the man around Leah's age who acted as a loyal understudy to Neil. That young man referred to Neil as *Monsieur Fix-it*, which always made him smile.

As if reading Dan's thoughts on the animals, Sera stepped forward leading a horse and smiled at him. It wasn't a kind smile, but more that she was gleefully anticipating seeing him in discomfort like she always did.

The two people were friends – more than that, in fact, as she owed him her life more than once – but they were genetically predisposed to fight on any subject regardless of their deeper feelings for one another. The result was that they joked about their "love/hate" relationship, and Dan always added that Sera loved to hate him, but those who knew them knew differently.

"This one's yours," she said. "Be kind to her and she *might* not throw you off."

Dan looked at the mare. Light brown fur and big, dark eyes that seemed to show as much disdain for him as the town veterinarian-slash-surgeon did.

"Remember to keep your heels down and your back straight," Sera added condescendingly, like Dan would do if teaching someone the art of driving a car fast. Not that he'd ever get to do that again.

"This one again?" he asked with a tone bordering on a whine. "This bitch hates me!"

"Mare," Sera corrected him, even though she knew exactly what he meant.

She pointed to Nemesis. "*That's* a bitch."

Nemesis looked up sensing she was being addressed and gave a few awkward, tentative wags of her tail to test the water in case she'd done something wrong.

"Just follow Leah," Sera added. "She knows what she's doing and the horses are smart enough to make up for your lack of...every-thing...if only they could shoot a gun, eh?"

Dan muttered darkly, making feeble attempts to soothe the horse at the same time as cursing Sera under his breath.

"Back off," he snarled at Ash, adding a pointed finger at the dog who began skulking forwards low to the ground ready to growl and snap at the horse's ankles, or whatever stupid name they had for their ankles, right when Dan was about to hop aboard.

The horse heard his words, sidestepping nervously to see both Dan and the dog while fixing one with a threatening look and ignoring the other entirely. Dan bounced again, steadying himself ready for the attempt to mount it, managing the movement just fine, but the gun hanging from the sling on his chest caught and caused him to drop his groin straight onto the end of the suppressor.

He issued a yelp sounding somewhere between being winded and a newborn baby crying.

Muted laughter rippled around the tired travellers, which only served to darken Dan's mood further as he stood up on his left foot and adjusted the weapon so that it didn't give him a blunt force trauma vasectomy.

"Shall we?" he asked stiffly, still not able to give his words their full volume as the pain hadn't fully subsided.

Leah handed up her heavy long gun case to Neil who nestled it beside the shotgun that rode literal shotgun next to him.

"All aboard," Neil said loudly, waiting for the universal double-thump on his transport before he clicked his tongue and urged the two horses in front of him to start moving.

Leah, left hand on the reins and her right hand hanging casually free, turned her horse effortlessly and trotted alongside the wagon with a hint of smugness adding to her happiness at being gainfully employed once again.

Dan, left behind with the horse who had both ears turned back to focus on him entirely, exchanged one last withering glance with Sera before he jabbed his heels back and told the mare to "get on."

It didn't move, making him jab his heels harder as if the damned animal wanted to compare sizes before they'd even taken one step. Sera shook her head with slow, patronising disapproval.

"Move, you bloody glue-pony," he growled, doing things his way.

The horse started, giving him a huff as if letting him have the first victory, and began walking intentionally slowly towards the town gate.

"Tell me again why we have to suffer this?" Dan called out as he caught up with the wagon and Leah.

She let out an audible sigh, communicating to him the same sentiments he'd felt when explaining something obvious to the younger iteration of his protégé.

"Because we've been reliant on fossil fuels for as long as possible, and *you* agreed we should be ready to be mobile without it. That was almost two years ago, but I'm guessing you've forgotten…"

Dan made faint noises, muttering so far under his breath that there was no chance of her even detecting a single word to take offence at, proving that living with Marie for so long had, finally, taught him caution.

He knew it was right, and he knew it was his idea, but the thought of adapting to a life on horseback in his late forties made everything ache just to think of it.

As they approached the main gate, three shapes stepped out from under the shadow of the tallest part of the wall under the ramparts. Dan could make out the new stones there, replacements for the ones blown down in the explosion years ago – an explosion he'd been so close to that he considered himself part of – and in the early dawn light their brighter shades served as a constant reminder that their safety was never a certainty.

"The next station is Andorra. Mind the gap," Neil announced like he was a London Underground recording.

The three members of the militia, all wearing a semblance of uniform and carrying the standard weapons of their force, spoke muttered greetings and climbed aboard while Dan silently assessed their gear.

Three Glock pistols and three HK-four-sixteen's, none of which had the attachments that Dan's sported as if that somehow showed

20

that he'd levelled up. He fought a brief internal battle as he always did before going out, wondering if they were rolling either a little too heavy for a simple supply run, or far too light. Getting a grip of his inner fears he assured himself it was the former, so, overstaffed and over-armed they got underway.

THE ROAD

Leah took her hands off the reins to rub them together and tuck them under her armpits. Her fingers were chilled to the bone despite the gloves she wore because, like Dan, she wore thin gloves so she could still use her weapons if she needed to.

"Oi! Hands on the bloody wheel!" Dan said.

Leah, treating him to a withering glance of such condescension that Sera would've awarded the full ten points, intentionally steered her horse left and right to weave along the road beside him.

"Yours has wireless controls? That's not fair!"

Leah laughed even though the Dad joke was a poor one.

"Knees, dumbass," she explained. "Just a little change in pressure here and there. If the horse trusts you it'll go with it. How do you think people fought from horseback for thousands of years before God created the Land Rover Defender?"

Dan eyed the back of his own mount's head, seeing both ears twitch back to point at him in case he was foolish enough to chance it.

"I wouldn't," Leah warned, annoying Dan by naturally 'being good at bloody horses' as he called it. "Like I said, the horse has to *trust* you, and that one is just waiting for you to fuck up so she can dump you in the snow."

Dan's eyes narrowed at the back of the mare's head, muttering darkly about steak as the animal refused to turn and meet his gaze, further proving that the plan to unseat him when the opportunity arose was true without reservation.

"Trading post in sight," Leah called out, more for Neil's benefit so he could take up the reins on his two placid beasts and halt the cart's progress.

Leah gave Dan a look, smiling as she nudged her heels back gently and let her horse break into an effortless canter. Dan grunted, gripped the reins tightly in anticipation of being thrown off, and raked back the heels of his own boots to force his reluctant mount to follow.

Ever since the trading post had been attacked by the pirates who idiotically visited their little adopted slice of the world, they took a more defensive stance when it came to their outposts as all of them were pitifully defended compared to Sanctuary's high, ancient walls.

Neil, keeping the majority of their group and all of their supplies well out of sight, deployed his few people in all-round defence to protect the wagon as the two mobile escorts moved independently towards the distant building. He'd stay there, watching, until the agreed signal was given to say all was well.

Dan looped right over the flat field, wishing that he'd moved first and stayed on the road where Leah had gone. Even without optics Dan could see the all-clear signal from the trading post ahead, as the bright cloth of the *Senyera*, the Catalan flag, was lowered on the tall pole and raised back up again to stand almost rigid in the stiff breeze.

Dan felt a pride at the sight, as much as he ever had for the Union Flag he'd gone to war under, and the sight of the red and yellow horizontal stripes blazoning from the blue point of a starred triangle set light to something fiercely patriotic inside of him.

The actual flag didn't matter as such, he believed, but if the feelings and pride were attached to a place and that place was home then how could sight of that flag flying *not* instil some raw emotion in a person?

Relaxing at the sign that all was well – not that they expected otherwise – Dan steered his reluctant ride back towards the road where Leah had stopped, standing tall in her stirrups to wave the wagon up. He pulled up beside her, swearing unkindly at his animal for not wanting to do what he tried to make it do.

"Don't yank on the reins like that!" Leah chided him.

She'd learned to ride a horse at the same time he had, only she'd taken tuition well, whereas he'd wondered why his motorbike refused to budge and insisted on stopping to shit everywhere.

"*Ease* the reins, like you're making a suggestion to her instead of screaming in her face."

"I didn't scream in her face," Dan argued, stopping talking as Leah waved her hand at him in annoyance for taking her words literally.

"When you yank the reins hard it hurts her, so naturally she wants to fight back and *that's* why she doesn't trust you."

"So why do I get this one and not another one?" he demanded. "I dunno, maybe one that fucking *works* properly?"

"The others would throw you off or run away," Leah told him. "Because you're a brute with them. She seems to be able to tolerate you so just…just *try* to be nice."

"I *am* trying to be nice, but this waste of decent meat won't do as it's told!"

He felt ashamed of himself as soon as he'd said it, and even more so when Leah dropped the subject and looked away as she always did when he went too far or said something that offended her.

He was kind to animals, but his frustration at horses or, he was forced to admit privately, his frustration at *himself* for not understanding horses made him act badly and he knew it.

He leaned forwards, bunching the reins in his left hand, and patted the side of the mare's neck to earn a nervous sidestep from the animal and a suspicious glance back at him.

Neil caught up with them then, having recalled his small force of militia and urged his own obedient horses along the road.

"*Roland's* on the ball I see," he declared, lavishly investing the name with too much accented flair, evidently pleased to be doing something worthwhile and enjoying a little freedom even if it was still cold.

Roland, the old Frenchman who preferred the majority of his time to be spent in watchful solitude, had reopened the trading post only a week before in anticipation of the spring bringing travellers past his position. He had nothing to trade, not yet at least, but Neil allowed the warm greetings to play out before he had his young apprentice offload a fully stocked crate of various liquids in corked bottles, no doubt to ward off the last of the cold Roland might feel before the warm weather came.

Roland insisted on making everyone a cup of broth already warming in a metal pot suspended over the fire. The trading post was well provisioned with last year's cut and split logs of ash and oak, and enough preserved food to keep the man happy and healthy.

"You will be going to the farms, yes?" Roland asked them, looking only at Leah as he always did.

He'd held a soft spot for the girl, the young *woman* now, since she was a filthy teenager arriving at the head of a ragged band of exhausted and injured travellers so long ago.

"Maybe on the way back," Dan answered before Leah could speak. "We're on a bit of a tight timeframe for the first run."

Roland nodded sagely, knowing that he would get his opportunity to visit Sanctuary and catch up with those he hadn't seen for months soon enough when the relief shift took over for the next season.

He usually alternated winters at the outpost. The young woman he'd known in his *before* life and had adopted as a kind of surrogate family member had given birth at the end of summer, and he wanted to be there to help over the cold months.

Dan tipped the cup high and slurped the last remnants before holding it down for Ash to complete the cleaning process and leave the inside of the cup visibly clean.

"*Merci*, Roland," he said. "*Nous devrions aller.*"

"*Oui, oui, bonne chance*," Roland said, not betraying any opinion at how badly Dan butchered his native language as he collected the empty cups. He said his goodbyes and waved them off before restoring the mothballed regional centre of commerce to its usual standards of cleanliness.

Approaching his horse again, after first walking Ash away and making him sit and stay so forcefully that even Nemesis obeyed with a confused look at Leah, Dan backpedalled while keeping a wary eye on his dog, and tried to radiate happiness at being on horseback.

He drew level with his horse and began the awkward process of trying to hook the toe of his boot into the stirrup and hop on the spot until he built up sufficient momentum to launch himself upwards into the saddle.

"Wrong side!" Leah warned him too late.

He went for the mount as the mare bolted forward a few steps, sending him sprawling with a yell before he found himself in a cold

26

puddle in the roadway, lying on his back and looking up at the cloud-filled sky where he sucked in a long breath and let the world know what was on his mind.

"Fuck!"

Ash, concerned as any good wingman should be, trotted over to lick at his face with reassurance and amusement in equal parts written all over his chops.

"Why don't you ride on here for a while," Neil called out from the front of their wagon. "Let the horse walk or someone else ca—"

"No!" Dan barked, hauling his wet, armoured body to his feet. "What's the saying about falling off the horse?"

"Err," Leah answered, finger raised and mouth open, about to say something she and Neil would definitely find funny but Dan likely wouldn't.

She didn't finish her sentence, instead she watched as Dan caught up with the mare and leaned close to mutter a few low words of warning to her before leaning away fast like a professional boxer when the horse tossed her head dangerously close to his skull.

Repeating the process as before, only from the left side this time, Dan hauled himself up into the saddle and managed not to sit on the rifle's suppressor as he did so.

Turning awkwardly, still putting too much force into the tug of the reins but trying to be gentler and more suggestive, he shot a look of triumph at Neil and Leah as the mare undermined him again and began walking with purpose back in the direction of Sanctuary.

SPRING

The seasons changed quickly, much as the transition from day to night and back again did, being far closer to the equator. For those more accustomed to living the better part of a thousand miles further north, the change was still alien to them even after all the years they'd been there.

For the start of spring, even though the temperature had broken and all but the highest distant peaks of the Pyrenees were devoid of snow, the wind and light rain still made it feel distinctly wintery.

Dan, after another hour and a half in the saddle, declared privately that he'd made his point and allowed one of the militia members to ride the mare while he rested his aching joints on the bench seat beside Neil.

"Giving the unemployed a rest, eh?" Neil asked him as a bump in the road made him wince in a way another man could understand on a very personal level.

"What? Oh…yeah. Not made for blokes, are they?"

"Saddles or horses?" Neil asked playfully, prompting Dan to ignore him and change the subject.

He dug into the leg pocket of his combats and retrieved a tin filled with pre-rolled cigarettes.

"What's got you so chirpy, anyway?" Dan asked, cupping his hand to shield the wind as he used the tiny flamethrower he carried to light the smoke clamped between his lips.

"I need a *reason* to be happy? Can't I just be pleased to be enjoying the beautiful landscape?" Neil answered grandly, sweeping a hand theatrically over the green ravine they plodded uphill through.

Given the lavish response, Dan knew his oldest friend was most definitely up to something, while Neil, sensing the quizzical look being aimed at him, raised his eyebrows high and spoke in a sweet voice dripping with sarcastic innocence.

"What? Can't a man just be happy to be alive? Why are you looking at me like that?"

"Because you're up to something," Dan stated in flat accusation. "And the fact that I don't know what means one of a few things…"

"Haha!" Neil snorted. "I like this game. Go on then…"

"Either you've been told by someone else to keep it a secret from me, which means Leah or Marie because I don't know anyone else you're scared of…"

"Nope."

"…or it means that you think it's so funny you don't want to spoil your own punchline…"

"Ha! Nope!"

"…or you aren't certain it's going to work and you don't want to look like a dick if it doesn't."

"*Steeeee-rike a-thuureee,*" Neil crowed loudly, too loudly for the time of day, startling birds from a nearby tree with his over-the-top nature.

"I give in then," Dan said. "What's got you so happy?"

"I farted and it hasn't hit you yet," Neil answered with such forthright belief that Dan didn't doubt it for a second.

Dan shuffled further to the side of the wagon's bench earning a grumble from Ash who had his personal space encroached upon, and leaned away to smoke in relative comfort.

Leah, body low and weapon hanging down on its sling, drew the suppressed pistol and waited. Dan, stacking up behind her carrying the same weapon tapped her twice on the right shoulder with his left hand before stepping out away from the wall and drawing up with right foot to stamp out hard against the wood where it met the lock.

The wood splintered, betraying some levels of decay through mis-use, and Dan rolled aside to press his body against the opposite side of the doorway against the rough, uneven stone.

"Seek!" Leah hissed.

"Find it!" Dan echoed, as both dogs rocketed through the open door to check over the building. Both had been trained to the same standards exactly, and although a lot of it was off-book it followed at least the concepts, if not the true manual for police firearm support dogs from the world before.

No barks came from inside to indicate a person seeking cover, and no screams or snarls or sounds of crunching bone reached them to indicate anyone dumb enough to take on the two land sharks.

A low whistle brought the dogs back outside, both being told how good they were, before Dan gave Leah a nod.

She drew a small torch running on batteries which were stock-piled in plentiful supply back in Sanctuary. The size of the torch was disproportionate to the blinding brightness of the beam that lit up the room so much it was almost possible to see the future.

Dan followed, his own light less powerful for many reasons, cov-ering the angles she wasn't pointing her weapon at as the two pairs – human and canine – moved through the cottage before doing that most reassuring and masculine of things such a situation dictated.

"Clear," Leah announced, earning the same call from Dan in an-other room upstairs after they'd split off.

"Plenty of space for everyone," Neil announced loudly as he strode in downstairs.

The building clearance had been training, or at least ninety-nine percent training, but in the same way that it never hurt to run a whetstone over the edge of a blade, missing an opportunity to refresh room clearance skills after a winter spent inside gaining weight like a bear was unforgiveable.

They ate and enjoyed a glass of Neil's pale lager which had been perfected over the last few years. Neil preferred a darker, bitter beer to the light and refreshing one he'd brought, but Dan enjoyed goading him and likened them to meat-based protein shakes too often for Neil to endure any perceived insult to his alcoholic offspring.

"Plus," Neil claimed, "the darker beers didn't travel well, which leaves more for me!"

The weight he'd lost the previous year after catching a British Army bayonet in the guts was starting to creep back, which only made him seem more...*Neil*.

Even though they were still well inside what they considered to be home territory, they posted a sentry and rotated between themselves every two hours so the disruption to sleep was minimal. Leah was excused the duty by unanimous vote as she'd been out of the game on maternity leave, but she claimed to have the casting vote and refused any special treatment.

Still, Dan arranged the sequence of who was on duty and engineered it so he took a four-hour shift and Leah slept through, with him waking a militia member to take over so he could grab another couple of hours before the day began.

Breakfast, inexplicably, was what woke Dan. Neil had used a camping stove and a gas bottle, another dwindling resource, but the oil and skillet he'd found in the kitchen served to fry a dozen sausages which were placed inside chunks of bread torn open.

"Any ketchup?" Leah asked as she made noises and fanned her mouth after biting into a sausage she'd already been warned was too hot.

It was a long-standing joke, one that was barely even a joke any longer but more of an expected ritual like so many small quirks their lives held.

Marie would tell someone to text her a reminder, or suggest Googling something.

Mitch would ask about satellite comms and aerial reconnaissance.

Dan would go on and on and on about driving, or tell someone to "pop it in an email", or if he was really trying to be funny and someone asked him a question he'd hold up a finger and say, "Hey, Siri..." then ask it out loud.

Neil referenced the internet and movies constantly to a generation who'd never heard of any of it, and when people looked confused he'd tell them he'd "burn them a copy" as if they understood him.

So many staples of their lives had been reliant on technology that was now effectively a paperweight that people paid hundreds for back when it was new, and so many terms were like another language to the younger generation. The odd juxtaposition of the older members of their group saying words they hadn't heard of, held a fascinating amusement to them.

Selfies, social media, online shopping and takeaway food. Audiobooks, streaming TV services, virtual assistants. Zoom calls, contactless payment, cookies and spam – very confusing to some – Ubers, dating apps, podcasts, livestreams, viral trends...

All of these things that never existed when the majority of survivors were growing up were extinct now, and yet they still clung to their memory like their grandparents did to tales of ration books and air raid sirens in the 1940s.

Dan, being the magnanimous and kind leader he was, tossed the end of his sandwich at Ash who opened his mouth to accept the sacrificial offering. He chomped once before swallowing the morsel and looking up expectantly for more. Such was the intensity of the dog's gaze that Neil picked up on it and admonished his friend.

"Did he even give you any sausage in that? The big meanie, here you go, boy…"

Ash glanced back at Dan to convey with a fleeting look that he'd wished Neil was his real dad, before stepping up to receive his own sandwich which poked out of alternating sides of his mouth until it disappeared to leave the dog expectantly sniffing at the floor in case any meaty goodness had dropped out during the chomping phase.

"Time to go," Dan announced.

With a groan of effort he stood and leaned over until he found the right angle to cause his back to issue a popping noise and release whatever knot of age and mistreatment was caught in his lower back.

They set off before the sun penetrated the steep-sided valley in another cold spring morning until midday came and they were treated to a warming wash of sunlight.

"Definitely spring," Neil announced to Dan who rode alongside the wagon with Leah out ahead of them.

The horse had reluctantly accepted the burden of carrying him, and he had to admit that treating it with more kindness was starting to work.

"You'll be complaining you're too hot soon," Dan said

"True," Neil admitted, "but it's better to moan about hot weather than cold, right?"

THROUGH OR OVER?

That night they repeated the process of tucking in for the dark hours, making Dan consider the good sense in opening established rest stops along the route between Andorra and Sanctuary to promote more travel between the two places. He tucked that idea away at the back of his mind in the file where all of his orphaned ideas sat gathering dust and considered the moment. It hadn't been a consideration until the previous year when they still had enough fuel to run larger trucks between their satellite settlements, but now with the future of travel involving horses, he told himself it couldn't be put off for another year.

He'd been forced to remove his vest during the last stop and take off the windcheater he wore underneath, leaving him with the pale skin of his arms on show until their journey wound higher up into the mountains nearing their destination.

Now, with the increase in altitude, he had to reverse that clothing decision as the temperature dropped noticeably even though the bright sun still shone down on them.

The roads were familiar here, mostly because he'd first seen them through eyes attuned to the threat of ambush after he went in search of the man who'd tried to kill Leah. He rode shotgun at the head of an armed party then, not in the saddle and riding on an animal he was sure would enjoy watching him choke on something.

The mountain roads swung left and right as the contours of the rocky high ground were followed, all the while avoiding the worst of the crumbled sections of road and the many rockslides that weren't severe enough to warrant clearing yet, which led him down the path of figuring out the logistics to send a protected party so far from home to keep the roadways open and moving.

"Is this on our patch or Andorra's?" Neil asked, seeing the same thing Dan had or simply reading his mind.

"It's theirs," Leah answered before Dan could. "That last bend marked the border."

"Do me a favour and remember where the rock falls are?" Dan asked Leah, delegating the responsibility to her to inform the Andorran leadership of their responsibilities under their long-established trade agreement.

Up that high, with snow on mountain tops what felt like only yards away which could be reached out to and touched, the landscape was either rocky and barren or plush and green, as though to make the point that life depended so wholly on where the water flowed.

By the time the last left-hand bend was rounded and the old, abandoned customs office came into sight the sun was beginning to descend on their third day since leaving home.

The road led them to the scene of a brutal fight a few years earlier that had forged their strong bond with the survivors in Andorra. The scorch marks of the fires caused by Mitch's forty-millimetre grenades still decorated the frontage of the abandoned hotel and brought back memories so vivid Dan could smell them in his mind.

At the junction of roads leading two ways, Dan turned to Leah and asked her preference.

"I'd rather go over," she said.

Dan didn't blame her one bit. Of all of them in the party, three had spent a terrifying and uncomfortably extended amount of time in the pitch-black darkness of the long tunnel leading through the mountain to reach the safe interior of Andorra inside its bowl of natural protection. But unlike Dan and Neil, Leah had first been ambushed in that tunnel and had escaped only through the taking of lives in an intense and brutal fight for survival.

"Good plan," Dan agreed as he twisted in the saddle to speak to Neil behind them. "You go through and let them know we're taking the scenic route?" he asked.

Neil nodded and added a casual salute.

"Go now and you'll catch the sunshine," he answered. "I'll make sure they've got hot food and cold beers ready!"

Leah urged her horse onwards with ease, making Dan mimic her natural authority over her ride by clicking his tongue. To his delight, and annoyance, the mare walked on with the slightest of touches to its flanks with his heels and he started to believe that the relationship between man and horse was very different to the nature of man and dog.

He was in charge of Ash. Ash worked for him. The horse demanded to be treated as an equal and took every opportunity to remind Dan that he was there only by the animal's good will, and also that it could easily mess him up if it chose to. The partnership approach was beginning to dawn on him as the horse bobbed its head with the effort of attacking the sudden incline of the mountain road going over the ridge the tunnel was cut through.

"More slack on the reins," Leah advised him kindly. "Let her have her head a little more."

"Let her have her..." Dan muttered, mirroring the words as if repetition would help him make of them. "What the bloody hell are you on about?"

"Would you find it easier to climb a slope if someone was holding your head still?" she asked.

Dan looked down, letting the reins pull through his fingers and surprising himself by not being instantly thrown from the saddle as the horse sensed freedom.

"Huh," he commented, annoyed and impressed at the advice.

"And lean forward a bit," Leah added. "It makes it easier for her if you centre your weight over her shoulders."

Dan complied, not sensing anything different or easier about it but then he reminded himself that he wasn't a horse.

"Get on," he hissed at Ash who loped alongside him with his butt slanted out to one side as if in power saving mode, and he wanted the dog tired because he wouldn't be getting much exercise during the following day of endless talking and meetings.

Ash responded, loping away faster as Leah sent his daughter after him. The road settled out on a bend and began to climb again before a long, uphill stretch took them to the highest point looking down on the distant exit to the tunnel Neil would still be coaxing his wagon through. Dan paused at that highest point, fumbling for a cigarette and very cautiously watching his mount for signs of wanting to throw him off a cliff as he tentatively clicked the lighter.

"Stunning," Leah said almost breathlessly. "Absolutely stunning."

"Why thank you," Dan purred demurely in a passable Sean Connery voice, earning a scoff of laughter as their horses shied away from one another and Dan snatched up the reins fearfully.

"It really is the top of the world, isn't it?" She looked out over the snow-covered caps and the burning orange of the western horizon preparing to accept the sun at the end of its shift.

"Not quite," he told her, pausing to take a pull on the cigarette and blow a stream of pensive smoke into the breeze. "But it's definitely the top of *our* world. Come on, I don't want to finish this trip in the dark."

They went, making quicker progress on the downward slopes that twisted back on themselves another dozen times until the roads met at the tunnel where a guard station sat. It had once been a toll booth for drivers paying for the maintenance of the path cut through the mountain, but now served to keep the sentries sheltered from the weather.

Neil, true to his word, had been and gone, riding ahead to the main town to announce their arrival. A familiar figure, rifle slung tightly over his back, stepped forwards with his arms held out wide and wearing a broad smile.

"It has been too long, my friends," Rafi greeted them warmly.

Leah swung her right leg up over her horse's neck as she simultaneously slipped her left boot from the stirrup to slide effortlessly to the ground. Taking two long paces toward him she threw her arms around his neck to lock him into a hug that would've hurt a smaller man.

"Rafi! *¿Como estàs amigo?*"

Dan, moving with infinitely more care, gently dismounted and paused as the blood flowed back into parts of his body he felt instantly sorry for. Standing upright he clamped his hand around Rafi's and squeezed, feeling the tension mirrored as the two men did their own, more private version of showing affection.

Rafi had grown into an impressive man over the last few years, after having been captured and tortured on the first, ill-fated mission to the mountain country that was now their ally. He had stayed there, training Andorra's own militia as part of the exchange program that forged a stronger alliance through mixing their people. It was mainly those with knowledge and an affinity for the sea who returned to Sanctuary, but Andorra had recruited more than enough of the town's people to make up for it.

"I think everything is good at home?" Rafi asked, his Spanish accented English far better than it had been when they had first met. "And my brother? He is well?"

"Mateo's fine," Dan answered.

"He told me he take you back to England. I should write to him more, only I am a very busy Rafi this days."

"I can imagine," Dan said, his eyes caught by a glint of sunlight on metal behind the old toll booth.

Rafi saw it and gave a lavish gesture of welcome.

"I have come to bring you the last of the ways in style," he said.

Dan stepped closer, almost forgetting that he held the reins of the horse that reluctantly followed him out of nothing but sheer stubbornness. He smiled, having his suspicion confirmed by the presence of the electric car he'd seen before when they'd first visited the country.

"My men will walk your horses back to our stables and see that they are looked after," Rafi assured them, gesturing towards the car. "*Por favor?*"

Dan smiled, unclipping his carbine so he could sit comfortably in the front passenger seat, after slipping off the straps of the small day sack he wore on his back and placing it in the front cargo section where a conventional engine would be.

Leah, relegated to the back seat with both dogs, made no objection as Dan leaned back before messing with the large control panel on the dash to activate the massage function of his seat.

The people of Andorra, just as he remembered, still knew how to live well.

HAPPY BIRTHDAY

The hospitality was as warm as ever, with the exception of their first visit so long ago, and the food was as plentiful as the drink.

Neil was acting oddly, which in itself was normal but he was acting oddly even for Neil. He was smiling too much and whispering in ears as though Dan wouldn't notice, so when he found himself cornered he feigned innocence.

"What are you up to?" Dan demanded menacingly.

"Nothing," Neil answered with all the credibility of a designer handbag sold from the back of a car.

"You're up to *something*," Dan said, subtly switching tactic from asking him to telling him. Neil cracked, unable to keep the smile from creeping over his face.

"Usually," he admitted roguishly, "but you'll have to ask *her* if you want to know."

Dan allowed himself to be fooled and followed the line of Neil's glance to see Leah sitting with Rafi. She talked animatedly, laughing and smiling, and when Dan turned back to Neil he found his quarry had escaped during the distraction. Following the lead through frustration he advanced on Leah and interrupted her conversation.

"What's Neil up to?"

Leah's expression locked into a stony gaze, and she turned to him, her face morphing into a smile of pure sarcasm.

"Hi, Leah. Are you okay? Oh, I'm sorry, I see you're talking to Rafi, so I'll wait an—"

"Yeah, yeah, sorry. Hi Leah, hi Rafi. Leah? What's Neil up to?"

"No idea," Leah answered.

"No bullshit?" Dan demanded, speaking as if invoking some ancient clause she was sworn to abide by.

"No bullshit. Dan, why are you stressing out? Neil is *always* up to something!"

Dan gave a grunt and walked off, turning back to see Leah smiling broadly at something Rafi had said to entertain her. The two had always been close, but Dan understood how a shared traumatic experience can do that to people. More often, though, he knew it forced them apart as it served to be too painful of a reminder.

These two had journeyed to Andorra together, and only one of them made it home. But far from pushing them apart it had driven them to form a close bond that not even Leah's husband, the young man who had helped them rescue Rafi, would be concerned about.

Unable to let it go he spun on his heel to wheel back to Leah, confusing Ash with the unexpected rerouting.

"Seriously," Dan insisted, "he had his naughty schoolboy face on and everything."

Leah blinked at him twice, glitching like she was processing the elevated risk level by hearing that fact.

"Oh God," Leah groaned as she stood and finished her wine with a gulp before scanning the room for any sign of the man. "Come on, let's see what the bugger's planning."

Neil, for all of his ebullience and girth, was remarkably adept at slipping unseen through a small crowd, but for two people who knew him very well, he was unable to remain hidden forever.

"*There he is!* Ten o'clock and moving," Dan said after spotting him.

The humour of Neil's behaviour was soon diminished when Dan's naturally suspicious nature began inventing all manner of betrayals, each less likely than the last, until he was forced to shake his head to clear it of the stupidity.

Dan caught Leah's eye after they'd broken free of the busy room in the town's heart, not too dissimilar to the great halls of the ancestors, throwing out quick hand signals to send her left when he went right.

Ahead, Neil was making progress, moving fast in a straight line away from the building towards a darker part of the town.

Dan considered sending Ash after him, but scrapped that thought almost immediately, knowing that Ash wouldn't remain impartial when it came to that particular subject being tracked because the slightest morsel of food from Neil would distract him easily.

Neil had clearly planned ahead there, waiting for the day he could prove that Ash's loyalty could be bought.

Dan ducked right, aiming to cut his friend off as the road looped around, but when he emerged from two tall stone buildings Neil was nowhere in sight. Leah, rounding the corner at a slow jog, held her hands out to her sides indicating that she had no idea where he'd gone.

"Well!" Neil's voice rang out in the darkness startling them both. "Seeing as how you don't trust me, you might as well see what it is!"

They turned, looking up at the open window of a small industrial unit which, going by the faded signs above the large shutter door, was once a commercial garage of some kind. Dan walked over, saw the person-sized door cut into the shutter had been left ajar, and stepped inside as the sound of strip lighting buzzing into life filled the cavernous space.

With a clicking, humming sound the garage blinked into light to reveal not one but two monstrous trucks. Dan, unable to fully suppress that little boy inside him that would stop and stare open-mouthed at any impressive machine, allowed the dawning expression of glee transform his features so that the vertical scar over one eye disappeared along with the resting malice.

"Neil…" he said quietly, his voice amplified by the empty space echoing, "what have you done…?"

"Not me, I'm afraid," Neil admitted. "Not directly anyway. Call it something of a correspondence project."

"Correspondence?" Dan asked, confused as he stepped forward to run the palm of his hand along the nearest sweeping piece of tough plastic over a wheel arch.

That wheel arch rose to the height of his chest, which made the scale of the trucks underappreciated until judged side by side with something people knew the size of instinctively.

These trucks could fit Dan's old Discovery in the back and still have room for supplies.

"How?" he asked, turning to Neil in the hope that he understood the question.

"You've been moaning for five years about the fuel running out," Neil answered gleefully. "You think I'd let that go and do nothing about it? Biodiesel, my friend. *Biodiesel.*"

"Yeah, but…*how*? You said there wasn't enough oil! You sa—"

"Remember when we came here last year?" Neil interrupted. "Late in summer when all those fields had this…waist-high yellow stuff growing in them?"

"Rapeseed," Dan muttered, still walking around the dark blue truck and marvelling at the sheer size of it. "You've made *vegetable oil?*"

Neil hid his laugh at Dan's ignorance and explained anyway, although in a simplistic enough style that he wouldn't sound offensive.

"Again, not me. I didn't harvest it all! It's been planned for a while now," he explained. "They've built up the crops enough to start making their own oil year on year. They use it, filter and wash it, process it with chemicals and then…well…do you *really* want the science lesson?"

Dan said nothing, only shook his head distractedly and reached up to the driver's side door to pull the handle and open the cab. The inside was so new it still had a clear plastic sheet laid over the seat.

"Not sure it matters that much to him right now," Leah said.

"Well, end result is that there's enough *bio-jûs* to run these puppies for a few thousand miles a year at least, and more when the production of oil increases and the reach is extended. More reliable transportation leads to more resources leads to more reliable transportation. You know how it goes," Neil said, finishing with a self-depreciating shrug.

Dan did, in that sense at least. Victor, the resident academic in Sanctuary who stayed shut away in his tower like an unfortunate-looking, bespectacled princess awaiting rescue had once asked him if he knew how the weapons he used were made.

Obviously he didn't, but he knew how they worked and could instruct others in their use. He saw this in much the same way.

"Don't you have to…like, change engine parts or something? Modify them to burn the chip fat or whatever?"

Neil laughed again, although not unkindly.

"Totally drain the fuel system, fit brand-new filters, draw down then restart the pressurised fuel system. Easy as running a normal diesel tank dry," Neil explained as if the dark arts of vehicular engineering were so simple.

"But…do they work properly?" Dan asked, allowing the characteristic pessimism to infect his elation. "I mean, are they underpowered as a result?"

"No." Neil chuckled. "From what my guys here said they've got more grunt than they can handle."

Dan believed it. A vivid and unbidden memory returned to him then, of him and Steve using the might of a similar truck to literally tear a hardened steel door out of a reinforced concrete wall. That effort had destroyed the vehicle they'd found back then, but it was neglected and asked to do the impossible from a cold start.

"Did I ever tell you me and Steve found a Unimog like this once?" Dan asked them as both Neil and Leah had walked to the open driver's door to watch with happy pride like parents seeing their child moved to tears by a gift.

"You did," Neil told him. "But this isn't one of the old ones, this is *brand spanking new,* my son. And it's a civilian model, not military, so it actually recognises that humans need to be comfortable."

Dan scoffed a dark laugh at that, muttering the words, "military grade," unkindly.

"You know what I *don't* get?" he asked, earning shakes of Neil's and Leah's heads.

"I don't get how, you, the biggest gossip in the town, could *possibly* keep a secret this long!"

Neil beamed proudly, choosing to intentionally misinterpret Dan's abuse as praise.

"So," Leah said. "That one's yours; twin cab and a flatbed back. The other one has a covered load space but only three seats, so it's more for haulage with a light escort. Extended range fuel tanks on both, fitted for obvious reasons."

"Yeah, you just need to flick the switch over to change tanks when the fuel warning light comes on, saves you sucking anything up to clog the filters," Neil finished.

Dan stopped, furrowing his brow and turning to face Leah like a tank's main gun rotating to aim at her amused grin.

"Hold the fucking phone," he grumbled, "*you knew* about this?"

She shrugged, reminding him of the innocent girl the two proud men had met a decade earlier.

"Happy early birthday!" she said simply, reminding Dan that he'd completely forgotten the personal relevance of springtime.

BOOMING TRADE

Dan, annoyed that he was the only person not to know, soon discovered that the secret had been closely guarded by the few people involved and, unsurprisingly, at the heart of this deception was their own lead scientist.

The terminology was bizarre in that he only knew one scientist, but Emma's request to move to Andorra for the last winter was easily explained by any number of reasons not barring the desperate need to see a different four walls.

He didn't know that she'd been working with a few others who possessed engineering, agricultural and chemical knowledge to recreate a machine to process and filter the vegetable oil into fuel. He also didn't understand how it happened, or why the same stuff used to deep fry a battered sausage could run a truck, but he'd grown accustomed to compartmentalising things that were beyond his grasp.

"And you're confident you can convert the boats to run on this stuff too?" Dan asked, lifting a plastic tub of the thick, golden fluid and eyeing it sceptically.

"Most," Neil assured him. "The bigger trawlers anyway. The smaller ones aren't so important and most of the sail-equipped ones have already got used to doing without…And obviously the last Defender can be switched over too."

Dan grunted noncommittally in that annoying way he did, wandering back over to the big machine that churned rhythmically. He'd been halfway through the explanation he wasn't following when he'd interrupted Emma, asking her how she'd moved from viruses and genetics to chemistry.

"It's middle-school level science, Dan," she'd chided him gently.

"I didn't pay much attention in school," Dan admitted in response. "Probably why I ended up getting shot at and hit in the head for a living."

The plan was simple enough: some of the winter's worth of processed biodiesel would be taken back to Sanctuary where Neil and his minions would go about draining the diesel engines chosen for a second chance at life, before cleaning their filters and Frankensteining them back into animation.

The processed vegetable oil sat in clearly marked plastic barrels so as not to become confused with the same-coloured oil mixed with the additives that made it burn under compression. That was for use in Sanctuary's kitchens until it could be brought back to Andorra for processing into engine fuel.

Dan marvelled at the ingenuity of it all, loving how it seemed so cyclical that their waste products could be recycled to keep them mobile for years to come, and the source of their cooking oil and fuel quite literally grew out of the ground. It enthused him, filled him with excitement and hope, and he couldn't wait to get behind the wheel after finally accepting that it was a chapter of his life he had to turn the page on.

Two of their militia, those rotating back to serve in Sanctuary after a winter in the mountains, volunteered to take the slow route back with the horses and wagon and Neil's understudy. They didn't waste the opportunity to bring back a full bed of traded supplies which left Dan, Leah and Neil to take their newest toys back and arrive home far ahead of schedule.

Their new trucks, both capable of carrying tonnes of equipment without affecting their ability to move, were loaded and strapped down tight with all manner of things either produced or processed in Andorra over the winter.

It was a fleeting visit, as they too often were, and the evening's festivities had led into a subdued breakfast where more serious matters were discussed.

"I have a gift for you, my friend," a rich female voice purred behind Dan.

He turned to see the leader of the small country, a strong and politically minded woman who oddly insisted on using all of her given names when she introduced herself.

Carla Sofia Rovira was lean, tanned, and attractive in many ways. If strong women were a type then she definitely fit that bill, but Dan found that her personality lacked the humour he enjoyed. She smiled politely when he made jokes but never retorted with one of her own.

Dan turned, smiling at Carla and accepting a large pouch of what he knew would be a dense block of dried and cured tobacco.

"You know me so well, organ grinder," he answered, sharing the jest in their first meeting so many years earlier.

He still had a tiny amount of the last block he'd brought back when the first snows of the previous winter fell on their outward journey to the inland community, so the arrival of a fresh batch was more than welcome. What he didn't tell her was that he'd already bartered with one of the Andorran locals for double that amount which was already stashed safely in his pack.

"I always know what to give you for a gift," she said. "It is either this or the new socks, is that how you English say?"

"Always needed socks," Dan answered wistfully, slipping the heavy brick of tobacco into his pack and fastening it again. "Not the kind of thing you think to go out and buy for yourself, you know?"

Carla smiled, either not understanding his tone or mistaking his response for entirely serious and changing the subject.

"You will be back soon?" she asked.

"Maybe not me, but someone will be. There's a bunch of your people coming back for summer, the seasonal workers, and there's the fresh fish to come soon."

Carla nodded, giving him the impression he'd somehow given her the wrong answer.

"This is a good thing, the new fuel for the cars, yes?"

"Bloody right it is," Dan answered happily.

He was like a man with a reprieve on the day of his execution in some ways, as taking away the freedom of driving the open roads in an empty country was a loss he felt all too keenly.

"There is…there is a thing I must tell you," Carla added in a lower tone as though concerned her words would be overheard.

As if to solidify his concerns Dan saw how she glanced nervously over both shoulders after speaking so he nodded knowingly, producing his tin of rolled cigarettes and heading for the door. Carla took the hint and followed him, producing a thin cigar from her own jacket pocket as he produced his lighter and offered to light her cigar first.

"Twelve nights ago," Carla said quietly, pausing to puff on the cigar and bring it up to temperature, "we have a visit from people we do not know."

"Friendly?" Dan asked, lighting and inhaling thoughtfully.

"They seemed to be this way, yes."

51

"But you're not convinced?" he asked her, seeing the answer clear as day on her features.

She shook her head after a brief hesitation.

"Tell me about them."

She did, listing off all of the information he wanted to know in search of signs that they were dealing with a potentially hostile or organised invasion force, but not one single thing she said gave him any kind of concrete evidence to go on. Nothing twisted his gut, made his skin prickle or go cold, and as much as he wanted to think otherwise he had to admit that the visitors, whoever they were, might have been just as they appeared.

"And where did they go?"

"Go?" she answered. "Some of them have stayed here with us! They wish to work on our land in return for acceptance into our country."

"Some?" She nodded.

"Eight of them left a week ago to search for a place to live near to the sea."

"And do they know about the vehicles?" Dan asked. "About the fuel or the electric cars you have?"

She shook her head which made him feel marginally reassured. Obviously, those who stayed would be aware of them by now, as Andorra's hydroelectric power supply was their biggest asset and some of that power was used to charge the small fleet of electric cars they'd recovered over the years. They made transportation around the tiny country far simpler, but for any kind of meaningful distance journey they would be useless. It had been tested once, but even their longest-range vehicle didn't possess the battery power to safely manage the hundred or so miles each way, tackling diversions and the steep inclines to get back to Andorra. Some people suggested only doing it in the hottest part of summer, where apparently the batteries would perform better, but Dan suspected that Andorra wanted to keep its precious fleet quite literally in-house.

Having to avoid all of the hazards on the roads between there and Sanctuary risked destroying them or at least doing serious damage, so they didn't venture outside of Andorra for those reasons and Dan respected that decision.

"They'll know soon enough," Dan admitted out loud, "if they hung around this area anyway. Did they say east or west?"

"They did not say either," Carla admitted. "But they left through the only road and went down the mountains which will make them go to the east and south."

Dan pulled a face and mused that piece of information, knowing logically that way in and out of Andorra led travellers to naturally follow the gorge in the direction of Sanctuary and the protected bay leading to the plentiful Mediterranean.

Dan smiled, putting on the mask to alleviate her concerns while simultaneously planning the advice he had for Rafi after they left.

"I'll let you know if they pay us a visit," he told her just as a shout from nearby grabbed their attention.

Dan watched a man run across the road, looking both left and right before he did so like muscle memory was so deeply ingrained it defied logic. He listened to an exchange in rapid fire Spanish, or Spanish edged with different words and pronunciations, much as natives of Newcastle spoke English in their own particular manner, barely managing to decipher five percent of the words used.

The man had brought Carla a message on a tiny scrap of paper that caused her to look deeply concerned.

"It is from Sanctuary," she said after dismissing the man and holding out the scrap of paper out to Dan.

He took it, recognising the words were written in English, but before he could read the message Carla summarised it for him.

"A message by the pigeons. They say people have come."

RETURN LEG

The urgency of their journey home took away a lot of the fun from being back behind the wheel after so long deprived of the pleasure. The Unimog, tough and reassuringly solid with more grunt than should be possible in a truck of that size, ate up the road like it was as hungry and eager as the driver was for progress.

The message, after the highlights had caused panic, went on to explain that a group of unarmed travellers paid them a visit, evidently searching for a new place to live. Given the nature of their long-range communications system the message was brief, and any further interrogation was likely just as quick as getting behind the wheel and driving home to find out for himself.

The two new trucks were already loaded so their cargo was secured and checked before the five people and their two dogs climbed aboard to head home.

Leah and Dan, along with the four-legged duo, took the front truck with the back seat where the dogs bounced around excitedly and didn't stop until the darkness of the long tunnel quieted them.

Neil, driving the other capable and oversized pickup, kept a distance Dan would describe as tactical. Their load was primarily fuel, or at least the first stage oil to be used for cooking before it could be returned to Andorra and processed because, apparently, that made the fuel more viable. They carried some other cargo but these were mostly luxury items such as tobacco and home brewed alcohol.

While they operated without a recognised form of currency, the value of trade was generally agreed and goods were exchanged for their counterpart worth. The politics of the past were long dead, and most surprisingly the concept of a co-operative society involved a heavy dose of socialism to ensure that those who had little never went without and were afforded every opportunity to have more. Capitalism was dead, because anyone attempting to control all of a vital market would find themselves the subject of unwanted attention.

After all, what good was it owning all the fish if that's all you'd ever have?

"Enjoying yourself?" Leah asked innocently.

Dan turned to look at her, having forgotten that she was even there for a few miles when the sweeping bends of the mountain roads took up all of his concentration.

"What? No. Yes...shut up."

Leah smiled at him, watching how he moved his whole body as he swung the nose of the truck out wide to lean on the brakes, stabbed at the throttle to force the automatic gearbox down two cogs, then reapplied the power to keep the driving wheels glued to the road's surface through the bend.

For such a large vehicle, especially one so heavily laden, his driving was a masterclass in smoothness and control. As a result of that control, as though a by-product of technique, Dan was leaving Neil behind.

"We're losing him," Leah said with an exaggerated lean to take in the massive side mirror.

"What?" Dan said, not because he didn't understand but because his concentration had rendered him deaf to what she'd said. Leah sighed loudly and shook her head.

"I knew the dementia would set in one day, old man," she lamented sadly, turning to face him and speaking louder as though he was ancient and almost devoid of all senses. "We...are...losing...Ne-il...You...were...go-ing...too...fast..."

Dan slowed on the downhill straight to allow the following vehicle to catch up, and also to consider the best response to the insult.

"Little shit," he grumbled, having tried and failed to conjure a witty retort. Leah let out a bark of laughter as soon as she knew she'd scored a hit.

"Hey, reality check, Granddad! The message didn't say anything bad, it just said new people turned up. You're making it into a big deal when it probably isn't!"

Dan said nothing for a long while and Leah stubbornly refused to break the silence after she'd said her piece. That silence lasted over a mile of spirited driving before Dan was the one who broke it.

"Want to play I-spy?" he asked jovially, as if genuinely changing the subject and letting the argument go.

"Sure," Leah answered, sitting up in her seat in readiness for entertainment that would focus her mind.

"I spy," Dan said, "with my little eye...something beginning with...*P*!"

"Pole."

"Nope."

"Pavement?"

Dan shook his head.

"Inside or outside?" she asked, wanting to narrow down the field because she hated losing at anything even more than Dan did.

"Inside."

Her eyes roved over every unfamiliar section of the truck cab's spacious and, she had to admit, pretty comfortable interior. "Plastic?"

"Uh-uh," Dan answered, with another shake of his head and a smirk beginning to form on the side of his face not bearing the long scar.

"Player?" Leah asked, pointing at the slot where a CD could go.

"No."

"I give up!" Leah snapped, annoyed at him instantly.

"*Pedestrian*," he said, a smirk growing to crack his entire face in half with smugness that his elaborate joke setup had been so successful. "Now shut the fuck up and stop calling me Granddad."

They made it back just as night was falling, forcing them to use their headlights against all operational sense from a lifetime ago.

Having passed the trading post at speed Dan yelled a brief apology out of the window at Roland, who was standing on the raised porch of the building with a shotgun held resolutely in his hands. His expression, illuminated by the headlights, told Dan that the man was prepared to use the weapon if these unexpected newcomers meant to cause trouble.

Dan bawled his badly accented apology out of the open window as both trucks rolled through without stopping.

"*Désolé! C'est moi!*"

The gates of Sanctuary came into sight, shut tight and guarded by armed silhouettes. Dan stopped short, still inside rifle range but far enough away that nobody would panic enough to activate the last remaining mine they had buried under rubble near the town's approach.

Leaving the engine running and the lights on he stepped out, arms half raised to show empty hands, and called for Ash to come to his side as the dog was likely more recognisable than he was, but the combination of them together was the key to re-entry.

French was shouted from the tops of the walls ahead and the gates began to open in response, and Dan tried to hide his annoyance that no further checks were made. Just because it was him didn't mean he wasn't under duress or anything. He planned a quiet word with whoever was in charge of the gate when he got inside, vaguely aware that he might be overreacting because he wanted to be let in fast, only to be annoyed that he was.

Both trucks rolled in, stopping side by side in the inner courtyard while barrels pointed in their direction from the walls.

"*C'est toi, ma amour?*" Lucien's voice rang out, echoing off the cold stone to amplify his words in volume and strength.

"*Ouais,*" Leah called back. "*C'est moi!*"

Lucien stepped out of the shadows, one hand sweeping through his wavy hair, rifle lowering and walking without concern to greet his wife and seemed to ignore the presence of his father-in-law. Dan was not having that. Not at all.

"You just let two unexpected vehicles drive straight into town? You might've ID'd me, but wh—"

"I apologise, Dan," Lucien said, unafraid of his anger and proving he was man enough to handle Leah's confidence. "But Victor tells me our pigeons can fly at almost one 'undred kilometres an 'our. Andorra warned us of your early return."

Dan deflated, abandoning all thoughts of chewing him out in front of everyone.

"The newcomers?" he demanded to change the subject. "Where are they?"

WARMTH OF HEARTH AND HALL

Dan strode through the town. He didn't run, didn't rush, didn't hurry in panic or fear but he *did* move with such determined purpose, such cold resolve, such a manifestation of inevitability that the people who saw him coming scattered out of his path.

Of all his failings when it came to speaking other languages, it seemed that his intent communicated itself clear as a lighthouse beacon warning people to stay the hell away from his rocks.

The doors to the main hall banged hard when he slammed the heels of both hands into them, forcing them inwards and announcing his presence with enough noise and aggression that everyone went silent and turned to stare at him, framing himself in the doorway armed and armoured wearing an expression that would frighten children and adults alike.

The scene he took in, not that he had any idea what he was expecting, was a warm and peaceful one. Faces he didn't recognise, none of them appearing to be unwell or exhausted by travel, watched him with a mixture of emotions including fear, surprise and amusement.

"You're back early," Marie said loudly, swinging her legs out from a bench and walking towards him wearing a smile so obviously false it did nothing to alleviate his concerns.

She reached up on tiptoes and kissed him on the cheek, whispering a succinct report as she did. "We disarmed them at the gate but I'm not convinced about their story," she said fast, withdrawing so quickly that the kiss looked genuine and fleeting.

Dan smiled at her, hoping to convey his thanks and respect for her razor-sharp intellect and instincts. He walked with her back to the tables where the small group of outsiders were enjoying the literal fruits of their labours. Salt fish, fresh bread, olives, pickled vegetables and some fresh salads were arrayed on plates running down the centre of the long table. He stood at the head of that table and unclipped his main weapon from the sling attached to his vest.

He turned, pointed to a spot near the fire and waited for Ash to move there, watchful and reluctant but obedient.

"Hello everyone," he said loudly, earning mumbled responses and smiles. He laid the H&K rifle on the wooden surface, sending the resonating thud down the table before standing back and loudly tearing open the Velcro to lift one shoulder of his vest and slide his body out of it. If anyone thought him removing the body armour was designed to make him appear less intimidating, they would be wrong. Dan had spent much of the winter months training with Mitch, and the result was that his thick chest and rounded shoulders seemed somehow more intimidating than when he appeared dressed for combat.

The vest was dumped heavily on top of the carbine, leaving him wearing the crumpled, black windproof that couldn't hide his large frame. Disarmed and vulnerable without the vest, anyone with a keen eye would be able to recognise that he was still dangerous should he choose to be.

He was a far cry from his peak physical form of over a decade ago, but the years of living as they had had left him muscled and lean. His strength was *real* strength, and his reflection was just a side effect of his lifestyle and intent.

His eyes roamed those of the outsiders, and in that flickering moment he thought he saw at least a glimmer in three of those pairs of eyes; a glimmer of calculation, figuring if they could take him or not.

"Where have you come from?" Dan asked, still smiling and reaching out for a chunk of bread to tear a corner off and dip it in a dish of olive oil before speaking loudly through a mouthful.

"And where are you heading?"

He chewed, making the silence he created more obvious and uncomfortable so they were forced to fill it. Instead of putting the next piece of bread in his mouth he tossed it without looking, having zeroed his target beforehand, to send the morsel through the air where the sound of massive dog chops snapping shut over the edible projectile punctuated the sounds in the room.

It was theatrical bullshit, Dan knew, but theatre counted for a lot when it came to the subtle art of psychological combat.

"We've been living past Perpignan," a man said, his accent a meld of English and French that made it impossible for Dan to say for certain which was his native tongue. "And we're heading west."

Dan carried on chewing slowly even though he'd reached the point when he could've swallowed the mouthful. His hands were busy selecting another piece of bread and dipping it to soak up the rich oil.

"We've moved every year," the man went on nervously, filling that void of sound so deliberately left with more information to be assessed and deciphered. "Picked up some people along the way, left others…"

Dan's eyebrows went up a little.

"And what are you hoping to find here?" he asked. "We have plenty of jobs that need doing, but we're always looking at starting new projects, and those require a little extra work."

He put the next piece of bread in his mouth and chewed slowly, eyes fixed first on the man who'd spoken before shifting his gaze to the next stranger, subliminally telling their guests they'd have to take their turn talking.

Dan noticed the glances, nervous and surreptitious, aimed towards the foot of the table where an older man with what Dan guessed was a prematurely greyed beard sat with his head bowed to Polly's. The two muttered in whispers so as not to disturb the main conversation but he could tell from her body language and the look on her face that she was entirely under his spell.

"That's something we'd be interested in," Mister Talkative said enthusiastically, effectively volunteering himself for unknown tasks before remembering himself. "Uh, depending on what they are, obviously…"

"Any of you engineers?" Dan asked after swallowing the chewed bread and beginning the process of dipping some more. "Skilled with boats? Agriculture?"

None of them answered so Dan went on.

"Any of you have any rare skills…? Know any old remedies or recipes…? Can you *fight*?" Still, blank expressions avoided his gaze. "Know any decent jokes?"

As if invoking the comedy fairy the door burst open again, only this time, instead of it being an angry Dan it was a hungry Neil. Bustling towards the table, his expression eager and hopeful, Neil threw himself into an empty seat and began reaching out with both hands in different directions like the buffet equivalent of a prodigal maestro orchestrating a full symphony.

Dan stepped around the seated diners, running a hand over Marie's shoulders as he moved until he reached over to pick up a jug, which he was forced to refer to as a flagon, of Neil's famous beer. He poured two cups and put one down wordlessly in front of Neil's spot before turning his attention back to the unelected spokesperson of the visiting group.

He smiled, disarming the man while simultaneously figuring out if he was going to toss him off the walls or just into the sea. He couldn't say why, but something about the group in general just made his balls itch.

"So what's your story?" he asked, still smiling.

Talkative Man seemed to forget his nervousness and launched into a tale that smacked so hard as being a careful recital that Dan smelled bullshit the second he began speaking.

"Oh, you know, it was hard for the first few years," he said sadly. "Getting over losing so many people and starting over...we banded together, moved from place to place and lived off the land..."

He trailed off, looking at the others from his group and unwittingly indicating five more people Dan had to be wary of. Four of them returned the look with bland, emotionless stares that tried just that little bit too hard to give nothing away, but the last ignored him entirely and muttered to Polly in French. The talker went on, leaving Dan enough opportunity to time his interruption like a marksman.

"We decided to move west this summer, an—"

"Where did you split off?"

"I'm sorry?"

"Your group," Dan asked, taking a gulp of the beer and fighting the urge to let out a noise of satisfaction. "Where did you split off to go to Andorra?"

Mister Talkative's mouth clapped shut so hard it made a popping noise, followed so fast by a babbled attempt to explain that Dan thought he'd suddenly developed a stutter. He said nothing, just watched as the man's attempts to dig himself out of the hole only served to fill more dirt in on top of him.

"It wasn't…we didn't…" He looked desperately at the others, ending with a pleading look at the man doing his best to stay out of the conversation.

"Take your time," Dan said calmly, smiling wolfishly and finishing his beer before putting the cup down firmly to clack the wood.

He walked very deliberately back to his equipment and rested his hands on top of it without picking up a weapon.

The man stared at him, panic rising in his flushed cheeks until the sound of a chair scraping on the stone floor broke the spell.

"There were more of us," the man who had ignored his presence until then said from his standing position.

His accent was so odd and yet so familiar, being the deeper version of Polly's. Dan knew two things instantly; the first was that this man was a French-Canadian, probably what Polly called *Quebecoise*, and the second was that he didn't like him.

"Some wished to go north, some to go south and others west. We chose this way." He looked down at Polly and smiled like a smitten teenager. "And I am eternally grateful that we did."

Polly blushed deeply and Marie, if Dan knew his wife at all, was holding back a forced retching noise at the display.

"So," Dan asked, his right hand resting on the grip of the carbine, "planning on staying long before you resume your journey?"

"We are looking for somewhere to settle. Somewhere to lay down permanent roots after too many years spent living off scraps."

Dan let a silence hang for a few seconds before he spoke.

"You look like you're thriving to me," he said quietly.

It was the kind of quiet that, for those who knew him, dropped the temperature in a room by ten degrees. The man held his gaze and didn't flinch. Being the only two men standing in the room and being at opposite ends of a long table meant that the other diners were like the spectators at a slow tennis match and their attention was locked back on the outsider, waiting for him to either concede the point or send his response.

"And we are," he answered. "But this life grows tiresome for us now."

The eyes turned back to Dan, waiting for his response.

He looked at the man, standing tall and proud, and his experienced eyes saw something different to what the others might. They might see a man in his mid-forties, a shade taller than Dan but leaner even if their shoulders were matched in width but not size. Dan saw an upright man who knew how to carry himself and that third eye, that damn spidey-sense, told him that he would be a challenge to knock on his arse.

"So the six of you just want to live here, that right?"

The eyes switched again.

"Of course, we understand that you will be suspicious of us and our intentions," the man answered, scaling back his confrontational tone as deftly as Dan corrected aim for a gust of wind, "and I know you will want to be sure that we are not a threat to you and your people. This is why we have agreed to the terms offered."

He gestured to Marie at that, shifting the room's focus to her.

Dan didn't look away at first, like he was proving he wasn't so easily distracted, then broke eye contact to fix Marie with a look, seeing a calm and competent expression on her face which served to remind him that he'd married her not just for her good looks but for the fact that she was an astute, dangerously clever woman who was as tough as granite when she needed to be.

"They'll be staying in the guest quarters," she said quiet enough for only Dan and the few people around them to hear. "And they'll have a member of the militia with them all the time. Mitch insisted." Dan softened slightly, taking a long blink in thanks that others were just as capable, and often more so he knew, to keep their people safe when he wasn't there.

"You have to admit," he said to the newcomer, revealed as the true leader of the group, "your timing is pretty bloody suspicious."

The man spread his hands wide and smiled, cracking his rusty brown beard apart to show white teeth in stark contrast to the gaps where some were missing.

"Appearances aren't always what they seem," he said.

Ain't that the fucking truth, Dan thought, knowing in his heart he'd end up going toe to toe with the man soon enough.

HEADSHED'S MEETING

The small, covered circle at the end of the sea wall protecting Sanctuary's bay under the watchful gaze of a mounted heavy machine gun, became the meeting place for the senior members of the town's militia.

Dan, Mitch, Leah, her husband Lucien who formally managed the militia members, and Neil who had a finger in every pie the town had – both figuratively and, Dan guessed, literally – walked under the cover of the tiled roof to dismiss the duty guard.

"Take five," Dan said kindly, patting the young man on the back and handing him a wrapped bundle of something warm fresh from the kitchen ovens.

The man, Leah's age if he was a day, looked shocked to be surrounded by what amounted to the government and the senior military advisors who also doubled up as a special forces' detachment, hesitated long enough to invite a good-natured sweetener from Neil.

"Off you fuck, there's a good lad," he said jovially, ushering the man away up the sea wall away from the prehistoric dinosaur he was guarding.

The mounted fifty calibre machine gun, a Browning dating back to a time probably before any of them were born, was kept in obsessively good condition for more than a couple of reasons. One, sea air had a nasty habit of ruining weapons, and two, they only had two spare barrels to serve the two guns so their access to ridiculously destructive automatic fire had a finite timeframe on it.

They all hoped the guns would rust without ever being needed, but Dan and his top echelon considered weapons to be the same as condoms – better to have one and not need one than the other way around.

"Heads up," Mitch said, nodding upwards with his chin at a shape stepping deliberately and confidently along the sea wall with only one possible destination.

"Don't suppose anyone wants to say they haven't seen me?" Dan joked, recognising not only his wife, but the fact that her strut meant she was looking to bust some balls.

"You're joking, right? I'd trip you to get away from zombies, pal," Mitch said. "So there's zero fuck'n chance of me stepping inside *that* firing arc."

As it was, Marie was in a fighting mood only not, for once, with her husband. She walked past both dogs with an impunity that couldn't be explained by any logical means and straight into the centre of their group discussion.

"Thanks for the invite," she said, smiling in no way to disguise the obvious passive aggressiveness of her tone.

"We didn't think you'd want to be a part of this," Leah tried, earning a sharp look from her adoptive mother.

"I don't trust these fuckers," Marie shot back. "They rock up three days after you leave, travelling light, and give over some bullshit story about looking for a new home? No. I don't buy it."

"We're agreed on that part then," Dan answered before turning to Lucien. "You've got your people on them twenty-four-seven?"

"Four guard them at night and twelve in the day. Two are always in civilian clothes," Lucien answered, his own English far better than Dan's French would likely ever be.

"Good," Dan said. "And their gear? We've searched everything?"

"They've got bugger all on them," Mitch said darkly. "Almost as if the bastards have a cache dumped somewhere nearby…"

"But they had weapons?" Leah asked. She was unsure why anyone would walk around without the means to protect themselves from people and the wolves who roamed the mountain regions of southern France and Spain now that their freedom was restored.

Twice they'd been forced to lay up at night and use the moonlight scopes to reduce the numbers of wolves around Sanctuary, and that task was a permanent one in the area of the farms further inland.

"They did," Mitch answered. "All locked up in the gatehouse armoury. Crap mostly; shotguns and small hunting rifles."

"Any tactical gear? *Any* evidence to justify how we feel about them?" Dan asked.

"None," Mitch told him.

"So we have to be thorough," Dan said, looking around at his people. "We all think this doesn't add up, right? So we put in the due diligence. Marie?"

"I'll start with interviews," she said. "Nothing too strenuous to start, just the basics to see how their stories stack up."

"No challenges on inconsistencies," Dan warned, earning a look from Marie which served to remind him she used to put murderers away for a living.

He held up his hands to signify that the caveman would stay out of her professional business.

"Everyone else," Marie said, "eyes wide open, okay? If they're really up to no good we need to know why."

"I could drop a glass to see if Beardy catches it and says *sorry*?" Neil asked hopefully. "Find out if he's a secret ninja spy?"

Marie looked from Dan to Neil in the way a schoolteacher would eye the two kids she'd already separated and who were still managing to disrupt her class.

"Take a day off the movie references, will you?"

Dan's mouth shut before he said anything that might be construed as a movie reference, deciding to change the subject.

"Start with the ringleader," he suggested. "I doubt he'll give you much, but you might get a sense of what he's about. I'd do it but the guy's voice makes me want to self-harm…"

"Sounds like an overly happy American on a damn space hopper," Mitch grumbled. "Voice all *booncing* up and *doon* like that…"

"I wouldn't be so quick to write him off," Dan said seriously. "There's something about him I *really* don't like."

"Aboot," Neil corrected helpfully.

"I got that," Leah agreed, having joined the frosty meeting late to meet the six awkward visitors. "Like a hawk pretending to be a pigeon."

"Eloquently put," Dan told her. "*Exactly* like that. He's a damn fox in a chicken suit.

"The others think we're being totally over the top about this," Marie added. "Some are even whispering that it's about keeping hold of power…"

Dan made a disgusted noise at the stupidity of the suggestion, one easily thrown about by those who had never volunteered to take any kind of responsibility for themselves. The 'agents of change' were all the same in the entirety of his life experience; they called loudly for change but when asked to sacrifice anything to make that change happen, they suddenly lost their voices.

In truth none of the people around him ever wanted the power that came with leadership, but all of them were the kind of people who knew they had a responsibility to the others around them to do their best, and their best included running the town because there wasn't anyone better suited to keep them all safe.

"That's the real issue here, isn't it?" Leah asked, scanning faces for signs of agreement. "It's about the normal people and what they aren't seeing."

Murmurs of agreement rippled back to her as they all acknowledged the limitations to their leadership when they led by the consent of the people and not through force: they could be voted out and charismatic newcomers who had the ear of influential Sanctuary residents might just be able to take over without bloodshed.

"On that note...someone needs to have a word with Polly. She sat there like a lovestruck teenager."

"I'll ask Alita to speak to her. They get on well," Mitch said.

"Good, you get her to grab Polly and I'll get her new beau split off from the pack."

"Aye, good plan," Mitch said, eyes meeting Marie's. "Give me time to tell Alita what we need before you try and suss out the man."

Dan watched Marie for her agreement before thanking Mitch.

"Seeing as we can't just force them to leave," Lucien asked, "we must have proof that they are not good people, this is correct?"

"Yes," Maire answered. "Just because we don't like the look of them doesn't mean they don't have a right to live here and be a part of the town, only..."

"Only we don't like the look of them," Dan finished, "so we're going to find out why they're really here."

The plan of attack was agreed, the interviews arranged, and the security forces organised to keep watch on their visitors who, even as the heads of the town met to discuss getting rid of them, were busy ingratiating themselves with the people of Sanctuary.

Victor, their resident wizard locked in the tallest tower by self-isolating choice, wanted to speak to all of the newcomers as he always did, only when he learned that Marie was interviewing them first he sent word for Dan and Marie to attend his office.

Dan, annoyed by both the presumptuous nature of the summons and for having to climb a lot of unnecessary stairs, was red-faced and utterly devoid of patience by the time they arrived.

"I 'ear that you wish to assume my duties as official record keeper in this place?" he asked Marie without even observing the scant niceties one usually received on such a visit.

"You hear wrong," Marie answered flatly, returning the lack of manners by flopping into a chair uninvited and putting her feet up on the coffee table. "It's a security matter, nothing to do with your encyclopaedia."

Victor ignored her words and turned to fix Dan with a look.

"Security concerns are your area of business," he said. "So why is she doing this if not to replace me?"

"First off," Dan said, holding out a hand to tell Marie he had this before she went off like a fireworks display. It wasn't to protect her poor, offended womanly virtue but more to protect Victor from the consequences of his assumption.

"*She* is way overqualified to do this, and *she* is part of the security element here."

Dan's restrained anger bled through his words and Victor's face dropped as though he'd stepped on something in a minefield and heard a faint click.

"I...I forget," Victor said with much more respect in his tone.

He restored his round spectacles and flipped open a large, leather-bound book to run a finger down a list in search of something. "You were an officer of the police force, were you not?"

"Major investigations unit," Marie corrected him. "And I was a Detective Sergeant."

Victor stopped scrolling as the purpose of his reference was lost now, and turned to face them to ask a direct question.

"We have accepted people into our society 'ere before, so why are these people different?"

"*Because*," Dan explained in a tone bordering on insolent, "these people are *different*."

The climb and the summons had already annoyed him, so he missed out the part where he explained himself like a reasonable person.

"All of you people seem so happy and willing to accept just anyone into what we've built here."

"Like we did when you first arrived?" Victor asked.

The question was innocent enough, but it was meant as a hostile challenge.

"Like us?" Marie snapped before Dan could gather himself enough to answer. "We were accepted here before *this* existed. Before us, you were just a bunch of lucky survivors who would've lasted two, maybe three years. You think you'd have survived the pirates? The group who attacked Andorra? Wolves? No, Victor. What *we* have here exists partly because *we* are here."

"So, to follow your logic, the town of Sanctuary will be better for the inclusion of these people in the future, yes?"

Dan sighed, rubbing his eyebrows with forefinger and thumb as their point was so obviously missed. Victor sat back and tried to look smug, thinking he'd scored some major win with clever words.

"Look," Dan said, "we haven't traipsed our arses all the way up here to your OCD pad to fuck about. You think they're fine; we have concerns. Innocent until proven guilty, right?"

Marie's eyebrows went up to hear her husband being so democratic about safety matters but she said nothing, because she knew when he was appeasing someone.

"So we keep them under observation and conduct interviews until we're satisfied there isn't a risk. Does that suit you, Victor? Does that meet your standards?"

"And when there is no evidence to suggest that they are bad people, you must permit them to stay unmolested," Victor said with all the confidence of a man who believed he was at least partly responsible for making the rules there. "And you will 'old no... 'ow you say, no *éritage de colère*?"

Dan stared at Victor who wore the look he had when he was trying to appear intellectually superior. He switched gaze to Marie who translated for him.

"Legacy of rage. I think he means a vendetta but he's being intentionally smug," Marie said flatly, staring at Victor as she casually insulted him.

"If they check out, all's fine by me," Dan said, managing to keep a lid on his legacy of rage against the annoying man he used to think was odd and amusing.

"Although, until this time, we must insist that you do not restrict their freedoms," Victor went on.

Dan stared, his scarred cheek twitching almost imperceptibly under his right eye.

"Come again?" Dan enquired almost sweetly.

He spoke with that same tone many people had heard shortly before witnessing a transformation the older generation referred to as him 'hulking out'.

"You 'ave armed guards following them everywhere they go, do you not?"

"Yes, for obvi—"

"This practice must cease immediately," Victor said, producing a letter from his desk. "'ere is the petition signed by other members of the town's leadership."

Marie took the paper, written in French which was no surprise, but the surprise came in that it was unmistakably Polly's handwriting which made the statement.

"It says that the 'mistreatment' of visitors must cease immediately," Marie explained, knowing that her ability to read the language had surpassed Dan's long ago. "It says that we're infringing on the human rights of free people."

Dan groaned. He'd encountered more than enough of this during his visit to Steve the previous summer and felt foolish for bragging that his own people hadn't needed to establish a justice system.

"You said *other* members of the town's leadership," Dan said, picking up on something he'd heard but not registered yet. "Did you get a promotion nobody knows about?"

Victor's chest swelled and his lips tightened, but in the face of Dan's hungry smile he controlled himself.

"Ha! It says we are 'denying them their rights to liberty and respect for their private lives'," Marie finished, dropping the paper with barely disguised contempt.

"Article four and article eight," Dan grumbled.

"Five and eight, dear," Marie corrected gently, her eyes turning to fix Victor's. "Correct?"

The scholar nodded graciously, seeming glad and surprised that they understood.

"What about everyone else's right to life?" Dan shot back, prompting a sudden and unexpected anger from the man.

"*And their right to a fair trial? To no punishment without law?*" Victor snarled before getting himself back under control quickly. "I apologise…it is just…"

"It's just that other people want them to stay," Marie finished for him, having seen through the front the man was hiding behind and intuiting the truth as she always did.

Victor had long since been the companion of Polly, their town's former leader who stepped down almost as soon as Dan and his gang arrived. Now it seemed that with the arrival of the big, charismatic Canadian who seemed purpose-made for Polly, the reclusive Victor was no longer in favour. In his own way, he was dealing with the rejection by championing the cause of the usurper, and both Dan and Marie found that pathetic.

"So we just let anyone walk around here and do what they feel like, do we?" Dan asked after a pause to understand the unspoken words. "Regardless of whether they pose a threat to us or not."

"I rather think that they do not pose a threat to *everyone*, Dan," Victor said. "Per'aps only those in charge?"

EYES ON

"Withdraw the armed escort," Dan instructed Lucien, getting annoyed at his son-in-law when no answer came. "Did you hear me?"

"I did, it is only that..."

"Only what?" Dan growled, venting his anger at one of the few people he really shouldn't, and likely one of the very few people in their town who could drop him like a hot rock if caught unaware.

Leah's husband's reputation as a fearsome boxer didn't deter Dan because they weren't in a ring wearing gloves. His world existed *outside* of the rules.

"It is just that...we could still leave the others watching them, no?"

Dan deflated, having overreacted to the perceived disagreement when in fact the young man was very much on the same page as he was.

"Sorry, Lucien. Yes," Dan agreed. "I'll take responsibility if it blows up, but yes. Pick your people carefully though, okay?"

"Okay, I will, as you say, pull them off?"

Dan laughed despite the gravity of the situation, coughing to cover his amusement.

"Yes. You do that. You go pull them off now...but wash your hands after."

Lucien nodded his agreement with a confused look at Dan, having already chosen his people very carefully but not burdening Dan further with unnecessary 'I told you so's'. The insistence had been

Leah's after she'd learned of the pressure to relax the limitations on the newcomers, and she'd told her husband much the same thing about taking responsibility for any backlash.

Dan thanked him, trusting him to get the job done. If he was strong enough to handle Leah then Dan had absolute faith in his abilities, even if Dan could be a little intrusive in his supervision at times.

He wandered outside, leaning against the stone wall to look out over the interior of the town. Hands moving on autopilot he retrieved the pouch to work clumsy fingers over the process of sharing out the dry strands of tobacco along the length of the paper before coaxing the ensemble into a tube ready to lick, seal and light.

He fumbled with it, ending up with an attempt better than his usual efforts but still poor. He lit it, looking down the length of the smoke that was supposed to be cylindrical but looked like it was pregnant.

"You're still planning on quitting then?" a voice asked from behind him. He didn't turn, knowing that voice better than he did his own.

"Got a new brick from Carla," he told Marie, referring to the summer's supply of dried tobacco that would take him months to burn through.

"Ah," Marie purred, ducking under one arm and sliding her body around in front of his. "And how is *Senõrita Rovira?*" she asked, rolling her Rs theatrically.

She'd visited Andorra, had seen the way the woman eyed Dan up and recognised the jealousy in an instant.

The two women had avoided one another like two cats pretending the other didn't exist so that they weren't duty-bound to fight over territory.

"She's thriving," Dan said. "Runs a tight ship, that woman…"

"Sounds like you *admire* her," Marie asked playfully, only with a hint of warning in her voice that he wouldn't be wise to push the joke too far.

"I can appreciate a job well done," Dan admitted. "And I can't be rude to another town leader and refuse a gift now, can I?"

"And that was the only tobacco you got, was it? An unexpected gift? I suppose I should lecture you about the health risks, but you're still more likely to die doing something stupid…"

"I never do *anything* stupid," Dan argued weakly, knowing that almost everything in the last almost decade would prove his assertion to be total bullshit.

He pulled a face and gave a small shrug. "Okay, maybe you have a point…"

"I do and you know it," Marie told him, aiming a bite at the tip of his nose and just missing intentionally. "So what are you going to do?"

"Don't you mean *we*?"

"No, I mean *you*," she answered. "Because *we* don't have bad ideas that turn out to work by luck; *you* do."

"So you're trusting this situation to luck?" Dan asked, half joking and half concerned that Marie had been abducted by aliens and re-placed with a doppelganger.

"No, I'm trusting this situation to you, mostly."

"I know," Dan said in a voice deep with stress. "And that's what bothers me the most."

As it was a Thursday, and Dan was a creature of habit even if he didn't like to admit that fact, he wandered down to the docks and walked over the footbridge connecting the town from the scattering of buildings lining the southeastern edge of the town to visit old friends.

It was part public service, part guilt, and part something else he hadn't figured out yet that made him spend an hour each week with the quiet couple living out a peaceful retirement down by the water.

Lexi and Paul, aged so prematurely by their ordeals both physically and emotionally, kept a neat little garden that supplemented their food allocation. To further supplement that generous ration, Paul spent most afternoons sitting on the sea wall in all weathers with a pair of rods dangling the long drop into the Mediterranean below.

Dan found him there, sitting on a cushion with a thick coat keeping him warm even though the air temperature wasn't chilly. It was the stillness of inactivity that allowed the cold to seep in, Dan knew, but he lacked the patience for fishing. If he was going to hunt food he'd rather adopt an approach of direct action over lying in wait.

Dan put down the small crate he carried and sat beside him, groaning as his joints protested the need to get on the ground. Ash snaked in on Paul's other side to shoot out a lick at the man's face which yielded a slow response.

"Bloody dog," Paul slurred slowly, but not unkindly.

His speech had been that way for years now, like he was drunk, and Kate was certain it was a result of being beaten half to death just prior to his arrival at Sanctuary. She'd tried to treat him with mild blood thinners, but when none of her attempts succeeded she concluded that he'd suffered a bleed leaving him with symptoms similar to a stroke.

He turned to face Dan, smile spreading slowly and lopsidedly over his face as he greeted his friend.

"That some of Neil's new batch?" he asked hopefully.

Dan nodded his head to the small crate containing dark brown glass bottles.

"Last year's final apple harvest," Dan said with a shrug. "Neil reckons his cider's good for either drinking or a chemical peel. Up to you which…"

Paul laughed, placing his rod down securely and climbing awkwardly back to his feet. Dan fought the urge to help him, torn between pity and empowerment as he always was, and forced himself to wait awkwardly as Paul finally stood unsteadily just as Lexi walked from the small stone cottage they shared.

She, like Paul, walked stiffly with a stoop to her back making her seem twenty years older than she was.

"Our social worker's here, Paul," she said, smiling past the gaps in her teeth. Her eyes were heavy with bags and Dan guessed neither of them slept much. "Isn't it irresponsible to bring us old cripples alcohol?"

Dan smiled at her self-effacing joke. She was ten years younger than Dan, but if he went by the adage he liked to use about himself then her mileage put her beyond resale and into scrap territory.

"It's on prescription," Dan argued. "Doctor's orders."

He bent to pick up the crate before either of them tried and he felt awkward about being able bodied, even more so that he constantly complained about his aches and pains.

Could always be worse, he reminded himself privately. *Could always be much, much worse.*

"Have you decided what you're going to do about them yet?" Paul asked, lifting up one of the bottles and inspecting it before popping off the lid and earning an accusatory stare from Lexi.

"What? It's almost six."

"Not here it isn't," Lexi told him, making no effort to take the cider away from him which told Dan she was mostly joking.

He had to admit, if all he had to do all day was sit still and fish then he'd likely start drinking at breakfast. To make matters worse still, both Lexi and Paul had been fit, energetic people who would've been active well into later life if not for the torture they'd undergone at the hands of a man trying to undermine Dan's ability to defend the town.

That was where the guilt and responsibility came in, even though he tried not to let it show.

Dan took the bottle from Paul's awkward grip and poured two measures into cups, careful not to disturb the gritty sediment at the bottom of the bottle too much.

Taking a sip he made an appreciative noise as Paul's eyes closed and he breathed deeply to enjoy the satisfaction of the alcohol, knowing only too well how that satisfaction can become a crutch without a person ever even realising that particular slippery slope had been slid down.

He took a sip and Dan pretended not to notice when some of the drink escaped the slack side of his mouth to run down his stubbled chin.

Paul raised a sleeve to wipe it away and released a satisfied gasp.

"Like all young apples," he said slowly, putting so much care into not messing up the joke Dan had heard a dozen times before. "He dreamed of being *in-cider*."

Lexi scoffed at his crudeness but Paul made a grab for her backside before she could escape, issuing a shriek of protest that turned into a genuine giggle.

Dan smiled too, happy that they still found some happiness after what they'd been through.

"So," Lexi asked, lowering herself into a chair and sitting at an angle like a person who just got used to living in pain would. "You decided what you're doing about it yet?"

"I've tried to," Dan admitted, filling them in on the story so far and the resistance they'd met from the others over it.

"Do you want my advice?" Lexi asked Dan, guessing that was exactly what he'd come to see them for that day.

He nodded silently, inviting her to talk.

"You know, when the twins turned up and everybody thought the sun shone out of their arses, I got a feeling. Like a...like a *sense* that they were no good, you know?"

Dan did indeed know what she meant.

"Well I tried to make others see it, tried to force them to accept my point of view, so by the time it came down to it..." She hung her head sadly. "By the time I knew for certain it was too late. Rich was most likely dead by then, and the only choice we had was to run. All because I handled it wrong."

Paul shuffled in his seat, turning stiffly and placing a weak hand on top of hers to reassure her. Dan didn't doubt that he'd told her a thousand times it wasn't her fault, but from personal experience he knew that reassurance only went so far.

Lexi coped with her injuries, with her mental scars, because part of her believed she deserved the punishment and that broke Dan's heart every time she spoke of their past.

"If I'd...if I'd gone about it another way, been friendly to them and played the game a little better, then all of those people might still be okay. Might still be there living in peace."

"So I should make friends with them?" Dan asked, unsure what her advice really meant.

"Face value, Dan," she said, being the one to offer sage advice to him instead of it being the other way around. "Take them at *face value*. Give the impression of being their friend, but don't ever turn your back on them, you hear me?"

The intensity in her words spoke less of her own trauma and more of Dan's responsibility.

If he played the game wrong, Lexi and Paul were at risk just as much as he was, if not more.

INTERROGATION

Marie, unlike Dan, had an actual method to her approach. She was meticulous, clever and emotionless about it while all the time making the person she was talking to believe that she was on their side.

Dan, in contrast to this higher level of psychology, was something of a blunt instrument when it came to the extraction of information from an unwilling opponent.

He'd been better at it in the past, when it was an occasional requirement of his job to conduct interviews, but in recent years he'd found it more helpful and far more time efficient to simply half drown people who were reluctant to offer time-sensitive intelligence.

Ash was about as subtle as his owner was when it came to the task, and the combination of the two together made a fearsome duo when it came to interrogation.

In all of the cases when they'd done that, however, there had been a need to get the information out of their adversary fast. There also wasn't a large majority of what Dan still thought of as the civilian population against such ill-treatment of a person not yet convicted of any crime.

With those factors all considered, Marie politely but firmly informed Dan his assistance would not be required during the interviews.

"Why?" he asked, even though he knew the answer if he'd had the brains to stay quiet long enough to think about it. "I can help."

"It won't be helpful if you start jumping up and slapping people around when they're lying to me. I may as well not bother if they think that's on the cards."

"So what will you do when they lie to you?" Dan asked.

"Smile, write down their answer like I believe them, and move on," she told him.

Dan opened and closed his mouth knowing that, as usual, his wife was two steps ahead of him and everyone else.

He was in *her* territory now.

"You know they'll fall back on a cover story, right? Some agreed second layer of information that admits to some minor fault everyone will forgive them for. They'll be rehearsed an—"

"Six people witness an incident," she interrupted sharply, smiling to show she wasn't angry at him but speaking forcefully enough that he shut up and listened. "Six people all give their accounts. What do you get?"

"Six slightly different stories," Dan admitted, leaning back in the chair which must have appeared to be an invitation because his Ashodile shot up on his lap to force the air from his body. "Six different perspectives, six different biases," he went on, the words coming muffled from underneath his dog.

"Six different sets of values affecting their outlook. Six different amounts of varied life experience affecting their perception," Marie finished. "You know this. So what would you think if I got six identical stories?"

"I think *you'd* think it was total bullshit," Dan told her.

"And it would be, so when I find a crack in the armour I don't immediately try and force my fingers into it...I wait, I check the armour of the other five people, then I come back with a cutting torch and rip the whole fucking thing wide open."

"Which is when you'll get your cover story," Dan warned her.

"What was it you and Steve called it? The controlled release of information, right? So if anyone tortures you for intel you hold off as long as you can until what you know isn't relevant any longer, then you give it up to save your own skin, don't you?"

Dan nodded, unsure why he'd ever assumed she wasn't paying attention to anything psychological being discussed.

"So they'll have a backup story, and *that's* the one that will trip them up. If six people all tell the same lie, then the same six people all tell another lie after admitting that they were lying, how hard is it going to be to break that cycle?"

Dan shrugged. For him it wouldn't be hard at all, because he'd just single out the weakest link and dangle him or her over the sea wall while hyping Ash up to bite them until they talked.

Marie must've seen the look on his face when he opened his mouth to speak so she cut him off.

"Whatever you're about to suggest," she warned him. *"Please don't."*

~

Marie's first round of interviews lasted two days. She intentionally switched her pace between people, seeming to tick some off her list like she was late for something and simply going through the motions while others were treated to long, slow hours of repeating the information 'just so she could get it right in her head'.

If Dan was the armed robber, then Marie was the expert hustler playing the long game. She mixed her knowledge of psychology so effortlessly with her years of training and experience to somehow magically know exactly what would and wouldn't set a person off when she sat down opposite the table to them.

One woman, only one of two from the whole group of strangers, seemed so eager to help and pleased to have another woman to talk to that Marie threw her careful game plan out of the window entirely. She rushed the woman through her basic account of events so fast that she was left in a little shock when she was catapulted out of the door and told she was done with her.

Marie could've got so much more information out of her, but she wanted to have the opportunity when the woman wasn't totally prepared for it. If she wanted to talk then she could talk, but Marie wasn't going to sit and listen to a rehearsed speech from anyone who'd so obviously revised hard for their exam.

She took a day to consolidate her findings, checking up on the notes from all of her interviews and writing up a report if only to aid her personal understanding of the information better. Much to her disgust, as if she saw it as a personal failing, she found no cracks in any armour after that first round.

She tried again, using the term 'just to clarify' so many times she thought she'd mumble it in her sleep, and this time she took a varied approach to each person based on what she'd discovered about their personalities in round one.

Talkative Woman was treated to a ladies' coffee morning session, and instead of the formal interview setting she was bamboozled by Marie and two other women who had no idea they were part of the sting.

She talked, a lot, but only tiny snippets of what she said gave Marie anything to work with because the woman was obsessed with life before the fall and only wanted to chat inanely, over and over about things she missed.

"There's only two of them I think will crack," Marie told Dan, shuddering after taking a large gulp of something Neil had concocted in a makeshift distillery.

That shudder went all the way down her spine before she took another gulp, seeming to treat it more like cough medicine than enjoyment.

"The leader, even though everyone says he is, *isn't* the leader. It's Claude Beaulac. The Canadian guy with French parents."

"Lord Bollock," Dan said, tittering into the glass held up to his face and already on the fourth serving of what Marie seemed barely able to swallow down. "Sorry, *Lord Bolloque!*"

She ignored his immaturity, marvelling at how even at his age someone could say something that he'd immediately turn into a smutty joke like he was twelve years old.

"And the other one. The one who couldn't stop talking when you first walked into the dining hall? Hugo?"

Dan nodded, knowing precisely who she referred to as his face was the only one that came to mind when considering the dangling approach to interrogation.

"Yeah, he was okay sticking to the story but something tells me he'll fold like origami under the slightest bit of pressure."

"Didn't you pressure him?" Dan asked, coming dangerously close to sarcastic criticism.

"I meant *your* kind of pressure, dear," she answered sweetly. "The caveman kind."

OPSEC

Dan's suspicions, as strong as they were, could halt neither time nor tide. The weather turned rapidly, as everything did in that part of the world, and they switched from a form of bored, cold hibernation to one of such sudden activity that there weren't enough hours in the day to get everything done.

The longer days that came with the season were a blessing, because most people found themselves on their feet from dawn to dusk and beyond in many cases.

Fishing boats went out. The fleet of smaller, sail-powered craft initially until Neil and his minions could complete the mechanical work required to transition their two chosen big trawlers to run on their new, renewable fuel source. Being Neil he wanted to tackle both jobs at once, but saner heads prevailed and only one trawler was taken out of action at a time.

The other diesel boats were earmarked for stripping so that a store of parts meant the working boats remained serviceable for years to come, and some were even set aside to be converted into additional living space.

The boats that went out invariably brought back good hauls of fish, and when such a yield hit the docks a small army of men, women and children emerged from whatever task they were conducting to gut and dress the catch quickly with sharp knives and practiced hands.

As ever, the screaming army of seagulls descended for the fish guts as if they alone still had social media and the hashtag of free food suddenly trended among the local bird network.

"Fucking shite-hawks," Dan complained, looking up at the approaching mob.

They were an aggressive nuisance way back when he tried to eat an ice cream on the beach in St Ives, but here they were a menace and even a danger.

Until you saw one up close, you never really appreciated how big and mean a seagull was. When it was trying to literally snatch the fish from your hands with its devil beak, flapping its hell wings in your face and dropping globs of white acid from the other end, a person could rapidly learn to dislike them on principle.

Ash, eager for blood like all dogs are in their own way, and released to the chase by Dan's permission, set off at the mob who had been distracted with a handful of scattered fish heads, to scatter the troublesome seagulls like he was a bowling ball and they were the pins.

"Going for the spare?" Neil asked from beside him, picking up unintentionally on the bowling reference Dan was imagining in the way the two men often did.

Neil sometimes joked they had the twin thing where they could read each other's minds, and wouldn't hear any evidence to the contrary because he wanted it to be true.

"Anything new?" Dan asked, receiving the covert intelligence reports regarding their new friends.

"Not much," Neil said. "Two of them have gone to the farms, reckon they had knowledge or something but I'm not sure...Four are still here, including Mon-sewer Maple-*Sorrey*-Syrup...but nothing to indicate they're up to no good."

"But *are* they?" Dan asked. "*Are* they up to no good?"

"All signs point to it, bro," Neil quipped back in a surfer voice.

Dan didn't bother to attempt a guess at the overly obscure reference.

"Are we due a supply run this week?" he asked instead.

"Here to the orchards, back to here, up to the farms and onto Andorra," Neil answered. "Who's going on it?"

"Leah," Dan answered, having already discussed it with his daughter because he needed to stay behind.

He had that feeling, that sense of impending doom, that if both of them left the town they'd return to find a change of management and that they were no longer welcome there.

"Missing the chance for a long drive, mate," Neil told him, as if he didn't already know.

"Well aware of that," Dan answered. "She's going to speak to Nadine and the others at the farm about them, and if I know her, she's probably going to insist Roland gets an extra minder until things work themselves out."

Leah had been that way ever since she thought the kind old man who made the trading post his life's work had been killed by the pirates who came ashore, back when she first found out that she was pregnant. She had a soft spot for the old man, and it was obvious that feeling went both ways.

"Word from Andorra is that their new additions are model citizens," Neil went on, betraying the fact that he'd been utilising the pigeon postal service for covert intelligence reporting.

Dan pulled a face and shook his head, ready to launch into an explanation of how he'd be the one to get the blame for it when Victor inevitably found out and told Polly just so the woman would have the time of day for him again.

"My own personal runners," Neil argued, both hands held up to ward off the caveman wrath. "They report only to me and my sources in Andorra."

"Seriously? You're communicating in code? And who is this 'source'?"

"Do I look clever enough to use code?" Neil asked, eyebrows knitting together at the stupidity of the suggestion. "No, but pigeons come and go from certain spots, and these ones go from my workshop to...well, never you mind where. Opsec."

Dan turned a glare on his friend, pretending not to find the whole thing amusing.

"Opsec...?" Dan asked, keeping his face straight with massive effort.

"Yeah. In case you're taken, you can't reveal my source under enhanced interrogation. It's generally how these things go."

"This isn't *Game of Thrones*, Neil," Dan said. "And you're not the...eunuch one."

"Yeah," Neil snickered darkly. "Okay, *First Ranger*..."

"So we've got nothing then?" Dan asked, changing the subject as Neil seemed to be in even more of a hyperactive mood than usual.

"Square root of three-fifths of fuck all," Neil answered, using a saying so common to both of them that neither could recall which one had started saying it. "We could just lock them up anyway," he suggested helpfully. "Or one of them could have an *acc-i-dent*..."

"Internment without trial? Execution based on suspicion? Be honest, is your last name actually Stalin?"

"Subject change," Neil answered. "One of them was asking about helping on a fishing boat. Reckons he'd done some commercial fishing before."

"Which one?"

"Hugo," Neil told him, seeing a smile creep over Dan's face.

"Get him a spot on Mateo's boat right now," Dan said, turning away with purpose.

"Where are you off to in such a hurry?" Neil called out after him, smiling because he knew when his friend had just had an idea that was at best devious and at worst openly criminal.

"To speak to Mateo, *obviously!*

SPECIAL REQUEST

Mateo, tall and broad with knotted muscles rippling under his dark olive skin, looked every part the pirate every time Dan saw him. He was a skilled sailor and their resident expert on all matters nautical, but it wasn't for those skills that Dan wanted to ask for his help.

He was a peaceful man, which was as odd as it was reassuring given his size and strength, and he hated violence. Dan suspected this dislike of conflict was largely due to him recognising that, deep down, he possessed a natural gift for perpetrating it and probably enjoyed it so much it scared him.

His younger brother, Rafi, now captain of the Andorran militia, had been captured once years before. The prisoner Leah had taken when she'd escaped the trap designed to net both of them had been reluctant to offer up much in the way of information, that was until Mateo forced his way inside the room to run a slither of much-sharpened steel along an intimate part of the man's body.

When the blood – and there was *so much blood* for such a small wound – flowed freely from the man's perforated ball sack he'd sung like a canary.

Then he sang some more, remixed it, re-released it, collaborated to produce an EDM version and planned to dine out on it every Christmas for the rest of his life.

It was for this reason that Dan wanted Mateo to take their new 'friend' out to sea, far away from the prying eyes in town, to find out if the man wanted to get anything else off his chest.

Dan found them onboard the largest of their boats that dragged a long net in the sea behind it, and with him was another of the town's odd inhabitants.

Joshua Bucknor, more so than Dan and his crew, was an anomaly there. With no links to Spain or France, so with no reason to be in that area or even find himself there to settle down, he was doubly the outsider for being the only American in Sanctuary.

A native of Tennessee, he'd been part of a massive naval task force from multiple countries battling modern day piracy when the world ended. His experiences after life in the United States Navy, the way life and his captors had treated him, left him grateful for the security of his new existence in Sanctuary but, like many, he was ever watchful and suffered from the constant stress of hypervigilance.

"Alright boys?" Dan asked, pointing for Ash to sit on the docks while he threw an awkward leg over the side of the boat and wobbled aboard.

He produced his pouch and offered it to them, knowing that Joshua would politely decline and saw Mateo already banging the end of his pipe on the boat's rail to knock the residue of his last smoke out. He took a pinch with a nod of thanks and began packing the bulbous end as Dan rolled badly and talked well.

"Hypothetically speaking," he began in a tone that made it obvious to a five-year-old that there was nothing hypothetical whatsoever about what he was about to ask, "how would you two feel about helping me out with something?"

Mateo looked at Joshua, checking that the American mechanic was fully aware that a favour for Dan meant something dangerous and/or morally questionable, then turned back to Dan and smiled.

It was a sad smile, as if he was unhappy that Dan had asked him but knew why; his back was to a wall, and he was thinking outside the box because he was out of options.

That meant that Dan needed rules breaking that he couldn't break on his own.

"This have something to do with these new guys?" Joshua asked, peering suspiciously from behind his massive beard. "Hypothetically…"

"You wish for us to do something…*bad*, no?" Mateo asked.

Dan checked over both shoulders in the same way he would if he was about to tell a joke that would land him in an HR hearing years ago and leaned in to mutter his explanation.

The two men, both aliens to the place they now called home as much as Dan was, listened to the idea…And in that way that all people who knew they shouldn't be doing something did, offered suggestions to make the plan work more effectively.

That dusk, when the last of the boats came back to port and unloaded their final catches of the day, Dan found himself on the sea wall watching the vessel chug back into their protected waters. Bucknor was nowhere to be seen, likely below decks covered in oil as usual. Mateo was visible on the right side, or whatever side boat people called that, piloting the craft from the external controls he used when they were actively fishing.

He caught Dan's eye, giving a slow nod to silently report that their mission had been completed, and eased the hull into the cushioned side of the docks to unload.

Hugo, looking as pale as a full moon, hopped the rail on uncertain legs and walked so fast for safety that he couldn't have attracted more attention if he ran screaming with his hair on fire.

During a supper of cold meat, bread and olives, Mateo and Bucknor gave the quiet report to Dan and Marie.

Dan listened, encouraging more detail with questions while Marie stopped eating and stayed quiet. Dan knew it was because of the fishy smell radiating from the two men, something she still couldn't stomach even after the years they'd spent there, and not because of what they said.

"This Hugo dude," Bucknor said in evident amusement through a mouthful of cured ham and olives, "man, what a pussy…"

Dan smiled. The man didn't speak often but captivated an audience when he did. He was a mess, deep inside at least, and Dan knew he consumed enough alcohol each night to ruin the week of an average drinker but that was just how he functioned. Years spent as a captive, as a slave, left more than just a scar.

"How did you get him to talk?" Dan asked.

"Hell, soon as we killed the engine and asked him a question he started talking…couldn't shut the son of a bitch up, could we?"

"He wanted to say to us everything," Mateo agreed, also devouring the food after a day of hard work.

"Details," Dan said, giving in to his cruel inner child. "Give me details!"

"Well, we asked him up on deck, made out as though we were gonna show him how it all worked, you know?"

Dan nodded eagerly, prompting Bucknor to carry on.

"And he was all eager at first, started tellin' us all about how he'd done this and done that, but when we cornered him by the open rail he guessed something was up…"

"I tell him first of the sharks, and throw old bait to the water to show him," Mateo added.

Dan hid a smile, already loving the story and wished he'd been there. He knew he couldn't, that this part had to be done by someone else and far from prying eyes in the town, but that didn't stop him from wanting to enjoy the re-telling of the story.

"And?" Dan asked, totally immersed in the tale.

"And we said nothing," Bucknor told him with a shrug. "We just watched the water waiting for these imaginary sharks."

"But still he say nothing," Mateo added, picking up the baton.

"So *I* say to Mateo here, 'Hey, didn't a guy fall overboard last year?'"

"And I say to him that this is true, and that we never are to find the body…"

Dan fought the urge to giggle, imaging the two big men being very intimidating by their quiet presence.

"And he tried to back it up, you know? All casual like away from the rail…so I put a hand on his shoulder and, *hahaaa*, man…He just fuckin' *flipped*!"

"He is telling to us everything, how they went to another town before here, far to the north and east, and took over," Mateo finished.

Dan's humour evaporated at the words, extracting word for word every piece of intelligence he could gather.

His own appetite fled, much as Marie's had only for very different reasons, and he pushed his own plate across the table to them, standing and leading his wife outside to talk.

~

They decided to keep the confrontation small, to minimise the risk of grandstanding and using public opinion to stir the pot and lose the facts amid the emotions.

Marie, who Dan couldn't fail to notice had begun carrying a Glock on her right hip for the first time since pirates had threatened their home, engineered a chance meeting with the obvious leader of their new neighbours in a way that cut down on the chance of spectators.

She got straight to the point, telling him what she knew and asking for an explanation.

Beaulac smiled condescendingly, offering a willing account of what she'd heard. She told him that she knew what had happened in their last settlement, how they'd taken over, but he refuted the accusation of that takeover being in any way hostile.

"There was a place that we went to," he said confidently, "we found it being run by someone who didn't want to work like everyone else. He wanted…well I won't say exactly what he wanted but let's just say the people there didn't agree with his style, eh?"

"So you took over," Marie told him.

"Not exactly," Beaulac corrected her gently. "We only helped facilitate the town taking back control for the benefit of everyone."

Marie took a step closer to him. Being a head shorter she had little chance of physically intimidating him, and she was careful to keep her hands on her hips so she could use the weapon if her approach backfired.

"But this place isn't like that," she warned. "So there'll be no socialist revolution here, is that understood?"

Beaulac conceded, reassuring her that his people – and she was painfully aware of his choice of words – had no intentions of causing trouble.

That assurance, just as Marie was in danger of finding no evidence that allowed her to disbelieve it, was woken early the next morning by Dan throwing clothes on and lacing his boots fast. There'd been a knock at the door, a hurried conversation, then she was awake.

She sat up, seeing him snatch up a pistol and check the chamber through obsessive habit, asking him just what the hell was going on.

"A body's been found," Dan told her. "Get the kid and go to Leah's room with the baby."

SUSPICION

Dan's fears ran riot in his mind as he made his way fast through the castle to reach ground level and the commotion that surrounded the scene. Something inside him snapped as he forced his way through the forming crowd, annoyed that they were only up and active that early because there was gossip to be had.

Old Dan, tucked away at the back of his mind, was screaming about the loss of evidence by having so many people poking around the body, but new Dan reminded himself that forensic science was no longer a thing, at least not until they re-learned it as a species, so it made no difference in reality.

"Clear a path!" he yelled. "*Mouve*! *Dégaz…degah*— OUT THE FUCKIN' WAY!"

He scattered people aside, thrusting his way to the front all the while panicking that one of his own, or selfishly, one of his close friends had been the victim of something terrible. He knew it was linked to the outsiders. There was no other possible explanation in his mind.

Bursting through the ring of onlookers he saw a body and his first impressions punched holes through his thoughts.

*Male, adult…*he looked from the body lying face down, to the sky, calculating the drop from the ramparts above. He figured it must have been fatal three times over. Looking back to the body he knelt, knowing on some instinctive level that he didn't know the man well, and reached a hand into the twisted fold of his neck to touch cold skin with two fingers.

He withdrew the digits, knowing from all the other signs that there was no point in wasting time searching for a pulse. The skin was cold, pale, and the blood pooled around the body was thick and had seeped into the old stones.

"Let's get some space, people," Mitch's voice rang out so loud it was more parade ground than ever before.

He translated his words into French as others came to their senses and ushered the onlookers away.

Dan waited, watching the crowd disperse before attempting to move the body. He pulled on the left arm, feeling the beginnings of resistance as the muscles had stiffened, and wincing at the crunch of broken bones grating on each other.

He flinched away, shaking his fingers and making a juddering noise before trying again and ignoring the sickening noises to force the arm down beside the body and roll it over.

The face, having borne the brunt of the landing, was a mess. Pooled blood obscured whatever features remained, causing them to bloat a luring purple colour, and all semblance of facial shape had been obliterated by the impact with the unforgiving stone.

How many deaths had this wall seen? he thought, his mind taking off on a tangent to avoid the brutality of detail before him. *How many lives had ended here, and how many more will there be?*

His dark thoughts held his attention for a few seconds, blurring out the grotesque images his eyes saw but his mind shied away from. Dan ran hands over the rest of the body, shuddering again at the cold wetness of the man's pockets and knowing that a combination of bodily fluids would need washing off his hands at least half a dozen times before he began to feel clean again.

"It's him," Marie said from behind and above him. "It's Hugo."

Dan turned, looking up at her and seeing a dishevelled woman who had thrown on the nearest clothing to hand before following. He noted the tumble of messy hair, so uncommon for her to be seen in public without making even minimal effort, but he also noted the gun held low in her right hand as though even she, who saw no need to partake in any violence personally, was on edge every second.

"I know," Dan answered, the identity of the man suddenly so obvious to him.

"Mitch, keep everyone away from here," she said in a commanding tone before fixing her husband with a look. "With me," she ordered.

The steps, once dispatched at a dead run every day as training but now more of a struggle to even walk up without a break, led them out onto the ramparts. Marie glanced over the edge to the solid ground below inside the walls to check where the body had landed.

Taking three strides further along the wall she knelt and ran her fingertips carefully, gently over the surface of the stone and the gritty dust covering it in a fine layer.

"Any sign?" Dan asked, earning an annoyed shush from Marie who wasn't ready to assign brain power to answering him yet.

He waited, watching as she searched every inch of the area where the long drop would have started until rising back up off her feet.

"Nothing obvious," she said, annoyed at the situation.

"Find it," Dan said to Ash, who was hanging back instinctively until he was called up.

He loped forwards, nose to the ground before looking up at Dan as if to question what was needed from him.

"Seek!" he hissed, sending the dog searching along the wall in vain.

"It's no good," Marie said, showing that she knew more than most about scene investigation. "If the body's cold he won't find a scent now."

"I know," Dan admitted, "but it makes him feel better to do something, even if it's pointless."

Marie smiled to herself, knowing that her emotionally backwards husband was really talking about himself and not the dog.

"You never know," she said. "He might track right back to your friend Lord Bollock and point the paw…"

"*J'accuse*," Dan muttered half-heartedly, glancing back down at the body of Hugo and wondering just how terrifying it would've been for him on the way down.

~

With no evidence to the contrary, in spite of Dan deploying everyone he had to question each inhabitant of the town, Hugo's demise was ruled as an unfortunate event. Just a tragic accident that served as a reminder to everyone to watch their footing on the ramparts.

To label it a suicide was the obvious choice, because the alternative was to admit that a murderer roamed free inside Sanctuary and that was an uncomfortable thought.

Uncomfortable was the theme, given the conversation between Dan, Leah and Marie when he said that Marie was to travel to Andorra with their son and granddaughter for the summer until the situation resolved itself.

Marie's reaction, easily predicted by anyone who knew her, was to launch hell at them for undermining her and relegating her to a safe position where she couldn't get hurt.

Should I, 'not worry my pretty little head about it' while I'm there?" she demanded angrily.

"It's not that," Leah argued, having discussed the best plan of attack with Dan beforehand, "it's that I don't trust anyone else to keep my little Adalene safe."

So stung was Marie by the force of the words that she deflated and lost all impetus of her anger. She agreed, reluctantly, to take the children inland on the next supply shipment due in under a week but left the seed of suggestion in Dan's mind in case he was willing to handle matters on the same level as his adversary allegedly had.

"You could always take him with you somewhere," she suggested, speaking of the French Canadian. "See if *he* has an accident…"

"You know," Dan said thoughtfully. "You're the second person to suggest I do that. Is that what you all think of me?"

Leah and Marie exchanged a look, which let him know that was precisely what they thought of him.

"You haven't done it before?" Marie asked innocently.

"What was that guy's name again?" Leah asked in the same tone. "Parkes?"

Dan's mouth tightened and he sucked in a breath loudly through his nostrils. He wasn't ashamed of what he'd done in that case, and he'd do it again in a heartbeat, only the situation wasn't the same. He didn't run a small group, but instead he was relied upon by an entire town, an entire *region*, to do the right thing. He had to keep them safe with their consent to do what he did, and when he acted outside of that he was no different to Bronson. To Patrick. To the prick who'd sent people to attack his home, Richards and the two

Frenchmen he'd stacked up against, or to the cruel bastard who'd attacked Steve back in England and stuck a bayonet in Neil.

He was a sheepdog, to use the analogy Leah was so fond of, not a wolf.

The town was changing rapidly, preparing for full summer mode now that the initial springtime work had been completed, ready for the repeating cycle of growing and harvesting crops, and processing, pickling and salting everything to store for the next winter.

People left, moving out to the orchards and the farms as migrant workers had done for centuries, as those places couldn't sustain the mouths to feed over winter when those same mouths were much needed in summer.

Lucien, along with two members of the militia who knew how to hunt, went north in search of an aggressive pack of wolves seen encroaching on the borders of the farmland. Leah didn't want him to go, but she accepted that he must, just as he had accepted so many times that she did too.

They weren't the only couple saying a terse goodbye, but they were the parents saying farewell to their children and forcing their faces to be happy, like everything was okay.

Lucien timed his departure to escort a reluctant Marie and the children as far north as where the road split left to wind its way to the fertile lands that seemed to expand year on year, where the population had taken over a large village and done the hard work over winter to adapt the homes for an altogether older style of life.

Trees were felled, logs were split, ground was cleared and seeds planted.

Wine and beer were decanted into bottles, grain was broken out of storage and tools sharpened ready for the endless, backbreaking long days of work that each year brought with it along with the knowledge that the ensuing winter would be unforgiving if they relented in that effort.

The world still turned, and Dan still had a job to do, even if both hands were tied behind his back.

UNSUPERVISED

"I have to say," Kate told Dan carefully, "that I'm…*uncomfortable* with this idea."

"And I'm sorry to ask it of you," Dan said with genuine apology radiating from him. "But I – *we* – need to be thorough."

The request he'd made, that of examining the body of the visitor who everyone believed had died in a tragic accident, had already been done but Dan wanted to know more.

"I *have* been thorough," Kate argued, her professional pride wounded by the implication. "He had massive external injuries consistent with a major fall, and there was no other evidence. I can't run blood results for toxicology because that expertise is lost to us, so I'm not sure what else I can tell you."

"Maybe if you took another look, you coul—"

"No, Dan," Kate insisted. "Just…*no*. If you want to find evidence that's fine, but you need to look elsewhere. If you're asking me to drop my integrity and fabricate something then I'd be open to the idea if you could bring me anything I could use, but you can't, can you?"

Dan couldn't. He apologised for asking and for interrupting her, leaving the medical wing where their former paramedic spent her days treating the illnesses and injuries of the growing town and training others in basic emergency care whenever she had the time.

He was grateful at least that Sera wasn't there, because if Kate was angry with him then God only knew what Sera would make of his request. He wasn't even sure what he was asking for, as if Kate could somehow magically examine the ruined body again and find irrefutable evidence that Beaulac or his other cronies were involved in the murder of one of their own.

He walked through the main castle, dropping down to sea level via the stone staircases and smiling at those he passed. He saw some furtive glances sent his way, and more than one person avoiding his gaze if they were unable to get out of his path. Glancing down at the dog walking beside him he voiced his concerns loud enough that others could hear.

"Do we smell or something, boy?" he asked in a loud, sarcastic voice. "Everyone's looking at me like I've got a dick on my face."

Ash, unsurprisingly, said nothing but Dan felt as though the dog shared his confusion.

He stopped in at the large hall beside the kitchens in search of the hot tea he'd grown fond of recently, replacing his usual copious amounts of strong, black coffee with the stuff in the uncertain belief it might be good for him when in fact it was a necessity due to the expired stores of coffee.

When the women running the kitchen seemed reluctant to help him, and even more reluctant to engage in conversation, he abandoned the idea of a drink and lit a cigarette as he was walking out of the huge doors leading down to the dock.

Feeling oddly lonely and on edge after Marie had left, Dan stalked through the town in search of a man unlikely to disagree with his most outrageous schemes.

Neil, tinkering with an engine taken from something, looked up at his approach and wiped his hands on a towel to rid them of the oil residue. Glancing left and right suspiciously even though he knew he wasn't being eavesdropped on, he muttered low words to Dan.

"*Hoozhe cahh we takin*?" he asked in a passable Boston accent, still acting furtively.

Dan, disarmed by the man's intentional stupidity, relaxed a little.

"No judgment," Neil said, his voice back to normal and hands held up as if apologising for some imaginary slight he'd caused. "I don't need to know details. Just know that I'm in."

"Nobody today," Dan admitted. "Although it's only lunchtime so no promises. No, I wanted you to get word to your secret squirrel in Andorra."

"Secret *squirrELS*, Daniel. Plural. And anyway…IF – hypothetically – IF I *had* such contacts," Neil answered with false suspicion in his words. "What would I say to them?"

"Tell Rafi," Dan said, completely ignoring Neil's terrible attempt at denial. "That Marie is coming with the kids and that I want him to make sure she's safe, okay? I want him to keep a close eye on the new people there, just in case."

Neil's face was aghast at his words and he stammered a response. "Ah! *Pfft*, who…err…who said anything about Rafi?"

"Oh come on, mate," Dan said. "I was born at night, not *last* fucking night."

Neil gave in, his face as much as admitting that his primary secret contact was indeed Rafi, and promised to send the message straight away.

He led the way inside his 'humble' shack, which when Dan's eyes had adjusted to the lack of daylight seemed oddly reminiscent of Doc Brown's place in the first *Back to the Future*.

He half expected some kind of process to set the toaster going and feed the dog but it seemed, to his dismay, that the massive collection of partly disassembled gadgets wasn't intrinsically linked after all.

He led the way out back, earning an excited cooing and fluttering of wings as his small army of carrier pigeons responded to the arrival of the man who fed them.

Snatching up a handful of maggots, not that Dan wanted to know how he got them, Neil scattered the tasty morsels inside the handmade cages which were wooden frames covered in taught wire mesh, and reached inside to select one.

"Paper's behind you," he instructed Dan. "Ben here will see to it that word reaches him."

Dan began to write but stopped, fixing Neil with a confused look. "Ben?"

Neil beamed a grin, letting Dan know he'd fallen for Neil's setup like a fish taking a hook.

"Ben Aflap," he said, gesturing to the selected pigeon. "There's Jeremy Runner behind him next to Nick Caged."

Dan groaned and lowered his head but Neil had been fully activated, stepping towards the cages and pointing at another.

"This cage is called Flight Club. There's Bird Pitt and Eggward Norton – the big one's obviously Beakloaf but, you know..." Neil hunched closer and whispered behind his hand. "We don't talk about it..."

Dan shook his head, flatly refusing to play along.

"Seriously...that's the first *and* second rule of Flight Club..."

Dan still refused to join in despite the smile that wanted to creep over his face.

"And while Sam here doesn't do errands, he's still entertaining."

Dan squinted into the gloom at a larger cage with the door pinned open, and a solitary bird perched in regal comfort with one malformed wing hanging lower than the other. To his surprise it wasn't a pigeon but a large crow.

"Neil…I can't believe I'm going to ask this, bu—"

"Sam Jackson. I thought he was a crow but he's actually a raven. One of the kids found him a couple months back after he flew into a wall, so I fixed him up and now he lives here because he can't fly."

Neil stayed stubbornly silent, clearly waiting for something, so Dan groaned inwardly before he opened his mouth to ask about the name.

"*Motherfucker! Snack!*"

Dan's eyes went wide and blinked twice as his brain struggled to process what his ears gave him to work with. When his mouth fell open again to ask one of a dozen questions he had, the bird repeated the abusive demand and a chuckling Neil obeyed, bringing the bird a morsel for it to cackle in a low, menacing tone of amusement.

Dan, now understanding the name, didn't ask and returned to writing his message.

Finally handing over a tiny scrap of paper he watched as Neil rolled it up and slid into the tube attached to the chosen courier.

Neil went to the window and helped Ben Aflap take off before telling Dan to write another which was similarly dispatched, this time carried by Nick Caged.

As the second bird flapped into the sky with the two men watching from below Dan asked the obvious question. "Wouldn't it have made more sense to send Jeremy Runner with him?"

"What are you on about?" Neil shot back, confusion all over his features.

"Seriously? *Hoozhe cahh we takin'?* Ben Afleck and…"

He trailed off, seeing Neil's face start to crease with amusement at having finally played his oldest friend.

"Dick," Dan muttered meaning it, only without malice.

"Think she'll be okay there?" Neil asked after the second bird was long gone from sight, swinging northwest from Neil's chosen spot on the eastern edge of town.

"I bloody hope so," Dan answered. "Safer than here at any rate."

"Not what I meant," Neil chuckled. "I meant *Carrrla Sofia Rrrro-virrrra*…You think she'll be safe from Marie?"

Dan sighed, annoyed at people blowing things so far out of proportion when he knew there was nothing to feed the flames.

"She'll be fine," he told Neil with a tone of finality to the discussion. "Now tell me what else your little network of spiders has reported."

The argument over Hugo's burial came that evening, starting with a loud conversation within Dan's earshot that resulted in Neil stopping eating long enough to give his friend a warning look.

"We should have a service on the cliffs," a woman said in French.

She spoke slowly enough that the English speakers among them could understand, making a point to repeat it again.

"That would be very kind of you," Claude Beaulac answered, "it would mean a lot to us to know that Hugo will rest among friends."

"Yeah! Friends who toss him off a fucking wall," Dan grumbled, again loud enough to be overheard.

The room went silent. There were close to fifty people in there for the evening meal and the tension was palpable.

"*Reeeeally* need to work on your stage whisper," Neil groaned quietly.

He knew Dan well enough to know that things were about to get messy, so he pushed his half-eaten meal away for the sound of wood scraping on stone to punctuate the atmosphere.

"What did you say?" the big French-Canadian demanded coldly.

Dan slowly turned to look up at him, intentionally not rising from his seat for many reasons.

"I said, 'friends who toss him off a fucking wall'," Dan said. "*Les amis que jètent lui du mur.*"

He saw a few faces turned his way contort in pain as he butchered their language, but he didn't have time to figure out which parts he'd got wrong. He had other priorities. Priorities who had stood up and walked closer to him, hands balled into fists and eyes squeezing tears onto his cheeks.

"Oh!" Dan laughed, lifting his hands to offer light applause. "Out*STAND*ing acting skills. Bravo."

"*Our friend died here!*" Beaulac spat. "In a town that *you* supposedly keep safe, and now you make jokes and accusations about it?"

"No jokes," Dan said, deadly serious now. "Just straight-up accusations."

Beaulac still towered over Dan, who refused to rise and meet his threatening posture. Far from making him look afraid, it was a power play that told everyone Dan wasn't intimidated by Beaulac, and it forced Beaulac into escalating or backing down.

"Stand up," Claude demanded.

Dan smiled, picked up his cup to drink and spoke quietly, "Make me."

Dan expected a lot of possible things to happen then. He expected to be called out loudly. He expected to be berated in rapid-fire French so he couldn't understand it. He expected the man to

116

storm off, to be insulted by the people who looked up to him so recently.

What he didn't expect was to have the chair he sat on kicked out from underneath him so hard that two of the legs broke to sprawl him backwards onto the cold stones.

He rolled with it, rocking back onto his haunches and rising up with both hands ready.

When he stood, he stood as a different person. Gone was the man enjoying days spent among family and friends, and in his place was that person hidden by the veneer they all thought they knew.

When Dan rose to his feet he wasn't the man the people of Sanctuary knew. He was the man who burned a barn full of people alive. He was an uncaged monster.

"Oh crap," Neil said, wriggling himself free of the chair to try and end the conflict that was about to get bloody.

He didn't get the chance, because the big French-Canadian launched into an attack that drove Dan back three full paces to avoid the combination of punches thrown at his head and body.

Beaulac's last attack was a lunging straight right cross that set Dan up to receive a liver shot capable of sending him to another dimension. His thoughts moved faster than nerve impulses, and in a split-second his brain registered that the man he faced could box, and could do it well.

But Dan was no boxer. Dan fought to win by any means necessary, not to engage in a fair contest for judges to decide the winner.

Instead of reacting to the cross with a block to open the door for the body shot and invite a brutal left hook to his liver, Dan slipped under the jab and moved. He stepped left, moving closer to his opponent to kill any power a connecting shot might deliver if the man was fast.

He wasn't fast enough. Dan felt the fist graze his ribs as he ducked his body low and grabbed Beaulac around the waist, lifting him and turning him off balance to throw him backwards into a table.

"*You piece of shit,*" Beaulac spat at him, his breathing rapid and chin quivering with the adrenaline and emotion of the fight.

Dan said nothing, not wasting an ounce of concentration on dialogue when he had a job to do, and that job was dismantling the man in front of him piece by piece for everyone to watch.

Beaulac advanced on him again, shoulders bobbing, but he came more cautiously this time. Just as Dan had assessed his opponent had some degree of skill; in turn Beaulac had learned Dan was agile, fast and most dangerously, *smart.*

Dan's display of skill made him cautious, advancing slower and using his footwork to back Dan into the corner where he couldn't slip away so easily.

All around them men and women shouted and screamed for them to stop, for them to take it outside, while others yelled, baying for blood while they cheered on their preferred champion.

The jab tested Dan again, the stance of the experienced boxer at odds with Dan's casual manner. Neither man knew the full capabilities of the other so neither wanted to close the gap fast, so they danced around one another like rival dogs posturing over territory.

Dan lectured others that nine in every ten fights ended up on the ground, and that was the last place they wanted to be if their opponent knew what they were doing there.

Dan did, but he didn't know if the man in front of him did too. He'd seen evidence of boxing skill, but he wasn't keen to take him down and grapple if his larger opponent had skills in that department because he didn't feel like having his clothes folded while he still wore them.

The jab shot out again and Dan switched his head to the right, snapping out a savage low kick into Beaulac's leading leg to connect heavily with the calf muscle. He stepped back in time to avoid the wild swing of Beaulac's right fist that, while not accurately aimed, was brutally fast and powerful.

Dan watched as he righted his stance and made to approach again, this time switching to the offensive and throwing out a boot connecting with the bigger man's chest and forcing him back a pace.

Anyone who'd truly seen him fight knew he could've tripled the power behind that kick to launch the man clean off his feet, or followed it up with any number of savage attacks, but Dan was still testing the man to see what other skills he'd been hiding.

The French-Canadian was heavy footed, advancing in short steps keeping his bulk centred underneath him to stay on balance while all around them the crowd still screamed and yelled their protests and encouragement.

Dan probed again, stepping left and back to his right to see how the man responded, but when he stepped back Claude shot out a savage side kick forcing Dan to block it with his hands and take the force of the kick to throw him to the side off balance. Unlike Dan, Beaulac elected to follow that kick up with a bull-rush that Dan managed to slip away from in time, ducking to avoid two more potential knockout blows as he retreated to give himself space.

He felt reassured that he was right not to assume he possessed superior skills, because the patience and pressure had already forced Beaulac to reveal he could employ his feet with the same brutal efficiency as his hands, but Dan felt confident he had the man beaten on speed.

Dan took his turn then, aiming a telegraphed kick at Claude's left thigh. As soon as he saw the reaction, as soon as the leg began to lift and move back, Dan threw his body weight forwards to aim the kick at the opposite leg to make solid contact on the inside of the thigh, the toe of his boot burying deep into tensed muscle.

Beaulac hopped backwards, evidently feeling the sting of the kick, but Dan didn't let him rest for long. He risked coming in close to deliver two sharp punches to the ribs before launching himself back out of reach of the answering swing.

Still people screamed and shouted in mixed languages but Dan listened to none of them; his focus was on beating and exposing the man who clearly wanted his crown.

Claude lost his temper then, roaring a challenge and picking up a chair to swing it and send the projectile screaming through the air at head height. Dan ducked it, barely, and looked up in time to receive the rush and the ensuing tackle that thumped hard into his chest.

Dan wasted no time, letting the man drive him back and wrapping his right arm around Claude's neck and under his jaw. He let himself be driven backwards more, picking his moment and lifting both feet off the ground to hook his legs around his attacker's waist before dropping his entire body weight onto the arm wrapping the neck tightly in a guillotine hold.

They hit the ground together, Claude grunting and trying to power his way out of the hold by reaching his right hand up in an attempt to get at Dan's face, but Dan dug in tight and leaned his head back, adding more pressure to the arm restricting the supply of blood and air.

People screamed for him to stop, for the fight to end or for someone to do something. Dan heard none of them, simply sucked in a deep breath and bore down with everything he had to tense all the muscles he could summon and squeeze the breath out of the bastard.

Beaulac's hand fluttered at Dan's elbow, his fingertips tapping weakly at the limb choking off his oxygen supply but Dan ignored it.

This was no octagon. There was no referee and no rules to abide by; the bastard had started this and Dan damn well was going to end it.

"Stop!" Neil yelled, thumping Dan's shoulder hard to try and bring him out of the rage he'd flown into.

He lifted Beaulac's right hand in front of Dan's face then dropped it to show that the man was limp and unconscious. As that realisation hit Dan he released the hold, not wanting to kill the man just yet, allowing him to flop free and slump on the stone floor.

Dan turned to face Neil, just in time to see a solid wooden chair swinging at his head.

ON THE ROAD

Lucien, confidently riding his horse alongside the slow-moving trucks that still seemed so alien in their good fortune, chatted amiably to his adoptive mother-in-law through the open window, periodically brushing his hair back out of his eyes where it fell in lazy waves.

She held her granddaughter, Lucien's child, on her lap as they talked in mixed French and English over the chugging sound of the engine.

"You think they'll be okay?" she asked conversationally. "At home, I mean?"

"They will be okay," Lucien reassured her. "With those two nothing can stand in their way, no?"

Marie let out a dark chuckle, more for the wellbeing of anyone who tried to get between Dan and Leah and anything they believed in. He was a stubborn bastard. Emotionally backwards and blinded by his feelings half the time but he was so resolute, so loyal and committed to his people that everyone who had ever threatened them had lost.

Leah, as much as she rolled her eyes about that aspect of their girl's personality, was every part as strong and stubborn as Dan but with more of the subtle intuition Marie possessed.

Her own skill at reading people was part natural ability and part careful study of the human condition, whereas Leah's was an odd hybrid of ability mixed with necessity having been forced to abandon her youth and mature into a world where gauging the true nature of strangers quickly meant the difference – quite literally – between life and death.

"We will have to leave each other soon," Lucien told her, changing the subject as the road climbed away to their right up ahead.

He would be taking the left fork in the road to drop down through a winding valley that led eventually to the inland farms and his destination.

"I'll look after her," Marie said, stroking the head of the chunky baby who had fallen asleep in her arms. "Don't worry."

Lucien smiled, conveying his feelings that he had no doubts for the safety of his only child in the loving hands of family. Steering his horse closer and calming the nervous animal at being so close to moving machinery, he leaned over out of the saddle to kiss the fingertips of his right hand and touch them gently to the wispy curls on top of Adalene's head.

"Je t'aime, ma petite," he said tenderly, gently tugging the reins to move his horse further away and allow the truck the room to speed up.

With their escort standing aside, the Unimog picked up speed and went up a gear. The noise of the engine grew louder with the increased speed. One gesture from a man of the militia, more loyal to Lucien than he was to Dan or Leah, implied a solemn promise of solidarity to keep his family safe. Lucien returned the gesture, holding his clenched fist to his chest, and watched until they drove out of sight before turning his horse to face west.

It took them until nightfall to arrive at the farms, but the pace had remained sedate so as not to stress the two horses pulling the laden cart unnecessarily. That cart – filled with salted fish and other goods produced in Sanctuary over the winter – would be exchanged for fresh fruit and vegetables from the first harvests.

After this first convoy the shipments would go both ways every week, with carts moving in either direction, crossing over in the middle. This would continue over summer, with the roads seeing constant traffic between settlements as each traded the excesses of their produce for the things grown or made elsewhere. It was regional commerce at its most simplistic, and it worked well.

It was a basic version of trade mixed with a pure form of socialism which, when uncontested by capitalistic ways of life and uninfected by the greed of human nature, worked far better than anyone could have predicted.

Lucien, the nominal leader of the biggest militia in their region, organised those roads to be patrolled regularly and for any strangers to be politely challenged as to their intentions.

It wasn't common to see people from anywhere else, not after the first few years anyway, because he imagined that other survivors, like them, had banded together in places where natural resources were as important as natural defences.

After the years since they'd formed their town into what it was today and built on the alliances between the few settlements within easy reach of their home, it was unlikely that they'd meet many others unless some tragedy had befallen them where they lived.

The reception at the farm was warm as always, and when Lucien took the large, padded rifle case from the back of the wagon he was met with a low cheer of gratitude as, ever since the inaugural battle for Sanctuary, their saviour from the roaming wolf packs had been sadly absent.

Nadine, the tall woman with short dark hair beginning to grey at the roots who had led the settlement since its inception, spoke in a low voice to Lucien as they walked towards the houses set aside for the visitors.

"We have had three attacks on animals in the last week," she told him in French. "And a close call only last night."

"Close call?" Lucien asked, not feeling enthusiastic about her tone.

"A child went outside in the night…they were here, inside the village, and only luck prevented a tragedy."

Lucien's heart rate had sped up during the telling of the story, and his rapid questions about securing the place with fences were answered effectively. They had been doing everything they could to deter the attacks, but the population of predators had grown so much at the end of the last summer that by spring the nearby packs were driven to encroaching on their territory to survive.

Lucien understood. He felt no joy in killing anything, animal or human, but each time he'd taken a life was for a good reason. For a just cause and for the good of the majority. Simply moving out of the area where the wolves lived was not an option, because even if they did then the same problem would occur the following year when that territory was no longer large enough to sustain the growing numbers.

Unchecked by man or any other predator, the wolves had bred and were seeking to re-establish themselves at the very top of the food chain.

As he emerged from his thoughts, he saw something in Nadine's face that made him press for more.

"What is it you are not saying, Nadine?" he asked with narrowed eyes.

Nadine visibly squirmed, uncomfortable with something, before relenting and blurting out the words she feared might make her sound crazy. "The kid says it wasn't a wolf. She says it was a monster."

Lucien insisted he speak with the girl, not understanding why Nadine said it would be pointless until he met her and her grandfather. Both were Spanish, neither spoke French or English and Lucien doubted either knew much of the world even before the end. The girl had been born at the farm to an absent father and a mother since passed, leaving her in the care of her grandfather and neighbours until she grew old enough to be helpful. Her education wasn't prioritised, but that was a personal opinion Lucien made sure to keep to himself.

He smiled, got down to the girl's eye level like he thought he should, and told her his name in slow, simple Spanish before he asked her what she saw.

"*¡Un demonio! ¡El diablo!*"

She visibly shook as she spoke, her eyes glazed and staring at a point just past his shoulder and another thousand miles away. Lucien gave up and spoke to the grandfather who turned out to be just as superstitious and even less descriptive. He crossed himself obsessively as he spoke, offering Lucien the least helpful information he'd received.

"*No és cap llop…és un home llop. Un dimoni.*"

A werewolf? A demon? He shook his head and caught himself, freezing the unintentional gesture and preventing his eyes from rolling. He thanked them and stood, ushering Nadine out of the simple dwelling to breathe fresh evening air again.

"If it is okay," he said, ignoring everything he'd just heard about the predator plaguing the farms, "I will begin tonight."

"Do you not need to rest?"

"I will sleep tomorrow in the day," he assured her, "but if it is okay with you I need to eat something first."

He turned and rattled off a series of orders to the three people he'd brought with him – one militia and two others with hunting experience – telling them they would be working the night shift with him.

They decided on two positions, one facing north where the flatter plains provided far-reaching views and another facing west, watching the approach to the livestock pens. Lucien, torn between his skills at distance shooting and his need to put himself at the front of any action, elected to cover the livestock pens.

"Drink plenty of coffee, my friends," he told them with a glance at his watch. "It will be a long night."

~

Adalene woke during their drive through the long, dark tunnel and cried loudly. Marie, already uncomfortable after hours spent keeping a baby happy and her own son entertained, shifted position to soothe the girl and show her the way they were going. She crooned reassurances in English, promising her that the light would return just around the bend and gasped theatrically as the exit of the tunnel showed ahead, tickling the girl to elicit a dirty chuckle of amusement.

"Are we here?" Benjamin asked, sitting up in the seat behind her with renewed interest in the world outside after all views had been extinguished by their passage through the mountain.

"Yes," Marie told him. "We are here."

"I want to meet Rafi," he said, clinging on to the last words his sister had left him with, making him promise to be good for Uncle Rafi and to make sure he didn't get up to any trouble. "Is Rafi here?"

"We shall see," Marie promised him, using the same words her own mother had when she was younger to acknowledge her words but give very little in return.

There was no reception committee waiting, but then she didn't expect one as there was no scheduled convoy expected, but that didn't mean they didn't know she was coming.

If she knew Dan at all, and she knew his mind better than he knew his own most days, then word would already have spread as to why she was coming there with the children.

Her husband would've made sure that advanced warning reached Andorra ahead of his precious cargo, and to that end Marie was certain that Neil would be involved somehow.

Sure enough, as they rolled to a stop by what had once been the toll booth, a very tired Rafi emerged into the evening air and stretched his back. Marie greeted him warmly, wearing a smile that let him know that *she* knew why he was there personally so he didn't have to go into it.

"You are just in time," he told her, looking at his watch. "The evening meal is not yet on the tables."

"I need to get this one down to sleep soon," Marie said, hefting the baby up as she blew another signature raspberry and clapped her dribble-covered hands together loudly. "I'll have to get something later."

Rafi accepted her words with a small bow of his head and stepped back to rattle off instructions in Spanish so fast that it sounded like a single, long word instead of a sentence. Their driver, an older man from Sanctuary who was allied with Neil and the various pies he had a finger in, drove them down the slope into town where Marie was helped out of the truck and shown into a guest house. She set Ben up with pencils and paper to occupy him while Adalene was given milk and changed into bedclothes.

The guest house, an odd custom that all of their settlements adopted, was kitted out for every eventuality and came complete with a cot for the baby. As she was settling the girl and laying her down to sleep, she heard voices from downstairs so hurried down to find out who had visited them.

Walking into the front room she saw a woman crouching down beside her son chatting away. As Marie walked in the woman stood and addressed her formally.

"Marie, it is good to have you here."

"Thank you, Ms. Roviro," Marie said with an edge of cold formality in her voice.

She contemplated switching to French to tell Ben to tidy up his things but she knew that the leader of Andorra was fluent in all three languages, so she stayed with English for dominance.

"Tidy up now," she told him, following up her words with a look of gentle warning when he immediately pulled a face ready to argue.

He saw the look, turned back to his things and began to put them away.

"I heard of your arrival," Carla said. "And as you have not come for the meal I had it brought to you. You must be tired after travelling, no?"

"We managed just fine, thank you," Marie said, turning to take in the generous portions of food sitting on the table and softening slightly. "That was very kind of you."

"It is fine," Carla said. "It is my pleasure."

She smiled, not making any move towards the door to leave which set Marie on edge. She was tired, but she was damned if she was going to show weakness to a rival who, she knew for a fact, had made more than one attempt to entice her husband to move to her town permanently with no mention of bringing his family.

"And your new arrivals?" Marie asked, uncovering the food and selecting items to feed her son. "How are they?"

"They are…" Carla waved her hands looking for the right terminology. "Fine. They are *too much* fine, if you understand?"

"They seem perfect, like they belong here and couldn't be more helpful?"

"Exactly this," Carla answered, pausing to gesture at a vacant seat and raise her eyebrows.

Marie nodded graciously, allowing the woman to sit. It was a small exchange of manners, like two territorial cats mutually ignoring one another so they weren't forced to puff up their fur and deal with confrontation.

"These people," she said, leaning over to help herself to a meatball from a tray and bite a piece off. "These people, they are too happy to be here, like it is acting…"

"You're suspicious of them?" Marie asked, trying out one of the meatballs for herself and chewing slowly to leave the woman more time to speak.

"I am, as are many others, but when I speak of this the people of Andorra do not see what I am seeing. They think it is just I who is unhappy about them."

Marie still chewed, nodding and forcing Carla to fill the silence.

"They are thinking that I do not like it that other people from the outside are, how is it said? *Agradar?*"

"Popular?" Marie asked. "People *like* them?"

"*Si*. Pop-u-lar. They are liked by many people and this, to them, is making it okay that we know nothing of where they have come from."

"We had the same issue," Marie admitted, reaching forward for more food. "Only there are – *were* – six of them in Sanctuary."

"One has left? Where did they go?"

"Off the wall," Marie said, miming a one-way dive and clapping her moving hand onto her thigh.

Carla's eyes went wide. "Did someone do this to them?"

"We think so," Marie told her. "Only people don't believe our suspicions…"

"Because these people…they are…pop-u-lar," Carla stated.

"They are," Marie said. "And people think it's just Dan who's unhappy about it."

ANOTHER TALLY MARK

Dan's eyes opened. He blinked his world into focus showing him a ceiling, and let out a noise through his nose that was somewhere between a grunt and a groan.

His jaw felt like it was wired shut and his head exploded with a searing pain that threatened instant nausea before another, more worrying sensation reached his consciousness.

"I can't move my legs," he mumbled.

Kate appeared over him, shining a tiny pen light into his eyes as she had done so many times before.

"*I can't move my legs!*" he repeated, desperation creeping into his voice as the fear rose up in his chest.

"Oi," Kate hissed. "*Get down!*"

Her words were answered by a whining, grumbling complaint that was more annoyed than threatening, and unmistakably came from Ash who knew better than to growl at her but still wouldn't budge.

"*Down!*" snapped another voice from his right, blocked from view by Kate's body.

Ash responded to Leah's voice, removing the eighty pounds of fuzz and meat from Dan's lower limbs and causing instant pain when the blood was permitted to return.

"Fucking...goon," Dan moaned, cursing Ash for scaring him like that.

"Him?" Kate said, almost shrieking with angry indignation. "What did I tell you? One more concussion and I'm retiring you. If you were a professional boxer then nobody in their right mind would let you step foot in a ring."

"Good job I'm not a boxer then," Dan murmured, waving her attentions away and sitting up with evident difficulty.

His movement was restricted by a padded contraption around his neck forcing his spine into a neutral position.

"What the fuck is this shit?"

"Let me fill you in on what happened, shall I?" Kate said angrily. "*Yet again*, you decided to catch a solid object with your *bloody skull*."

"Standard," Leah interjected, finding her interruption ignored by both of them.

"And forgive *me* if I didn't want you paralysed *and* concussed. You're dumb enough already without tempting fate for another TBI."

"Sorry," Dan said weakly, reaching up to fumble for the Velcro straps to remove the neck brace. "I'm fine, just a headache."

"You're *not* fine," Kate warned him. "You got knocked out again, and I have *literally* no idea how you aren't dead most days. You realise skulls aren't designed for the kind of use you think they are, right? You need to wear a helmet everywhere you go…" Kate moved away, hands rising up and slapping down onto her legs as if giving up on him.

"That's *exactly* what skulls are designed for. I'm fine," Dan insisted, sitting up awkwardly and twisting his upper body to see Leah.

When he saw her face he was most definitely *not* fine.

"What the fuck happened?" he snarled.

Leah smiled, in spite of the swelling to her left eye and the bruise already forming on the shiny skin.

"Let me *sseeee*," she told him, sounding far better than she looked.

"You gobbed off about Claude Bollock killing his own guy…"

She ticked off one finger on her hand.

"He came at you, you went at it like a pair of apes, then you choked the living shit out of him…"

She ticked off more digits.

"Then someone else took you out with a chair—"

"Bastard," Dan muttered.

"—so I took *him* out," she completed the raised fingers of one hand and started over.

"Then two more people tried to get involved so I had to put them down, th—"

"So it started a mass brawl and I slept though it?"

"Pretty much," Leah said, dropping her hands as though losing track of events. "That's basically it. Yeah. Neil said it was like, and I quote, '*somefing out of a bloody western!*'"

Dan groaned again, acknowledging a sulking Ash and allowing him back up on the hospital bed to assault him with licks he felt too weak to fend off.

"Still," Leah said with a chuckle. "Nice takedown on the big guy."

"*Pffft!*" Dan pushed Ash away and made him keep his distance with a raised finger.

"He ran headfirst into it," Dan said, recalling with satisfaction how he'd choked the Canadian into a non-consensual nap.

"He knew what he was doing though," Leah said in a warning tone. "A couple of times he could've switched your lights off if he'd been lucky or you'd been any slower."

"I don't swing and hope like him," Dan grumbled back, his bravado as weak as his legs which he swung off the bed. "I aim and fucking *fire*."

He looked up at Leah's face, wincing at the movement of his head and neck before anger took over his features at the sight of the damage someone had done to her.

"Who hit you?" he asked.

"Forget about it."

"Who. Hit. You?"

"It doesn't matter, okay?" Leah insisted. "It was a cheap shot I should've seen coming so it's my own fault."

"Oh good, you're awake," a flustered Neil said from the doorway.

He stomped in, his face red from either the fight or the exertion of his oldest enemy: stairs. "It's bloody hell-up down there."

"What happened?" Dan asked in a murmur behind clenched teeth, leaning back to rest his head carefully and close his eyes.

"Which bit?" Neil asked.

"How about everything after I got banjo'd with a bloody chair?"

"Oh, right, well it went off like a grenade after that. Militia and other people kicked off, on both sides, an—"

"On both sides of what?"

"The fight," Neil answered.

"So our own people were fighting *for* these fuckers?"

"Kind of," Neil went on quickly. "But then it got *really* carried away and some weapons got drawn."

"That's when I stepped in," Leah said. "Really need to rethink shutting the dogs away at mealtimes."

"Stepped in how?" Dan asked, opening one eye to peer at her.

She shrugged. "Someone pulled a weapon…so I took it off him."

135

The simplistic explanation told Dan there was far more to it than that but now wasn't the time to press.

"One of ours or theirs?" he asked.

Leah glanced in Neil's direction.

"One of ours. French guy who now finds himself *ex*-militia. He's apparently been getting pretty vocal about a change in management," Neil explained.

"Well, not anymore," Leah added.

"Meaning?" Dan demanded.

"Meaning he's having a little nap now, and likely won't be up for much in the way of public speaking for a few days...probably won't be having children either, but that's a different conversation," Neil said.

Dan peered harder at Leah again and weakly mimed a fist bump towards her.

"Dick shot?" he asked.

"Knee to the plums. Pretty sure I heard one crunch."

"*Noice*...What's happening now?" he asked, turning back to Neil and not enjoying the answering silence.

"Neil?" Dan said, drawing out the man's name almost threateningly.

"People are having kittens about what went down," Neil finally answered. "Some are calling to disband the militia, or at least your part of it, and leave Lucien in place as the leader..."

"But?" Dan prompted. "There's definitely a 'but' there."

"But others are saying he's too close to you two...most people agree that there should be, like, a *civilian* leadership instead though."

"Mission accomplished, Lord Bollock," Dan groaned. "Mission fucking accomplished."

He stood. Slowly and in stages with rest periods in between but he got back to his feet and fought the urge to sway in the imaginary breeze.

"Let's go and see how bad the shitstorm is," he mumbled, taking unsteady steps towards the door.

Passing Kate he tried to ignore her picking up a piece of chalk and adding a mark on the board next to the words 'Dan's serious head injuries.'

~

He couldn't raise his voice to speak loudly. He couldn't turn his neck to sweep all of the faces there and he couldn't stand the noise in the room.

Beaulac's people, huddled in one corner surrounded by far more support than Dan was comfortable with, made representations for compensation or punishment.

Those supporting Dan wanted Beaulac's group expelled from Sanctuary for disturbing the peace.

Of all the time spent there, all the time he was looked up to as a leader and enforcer of that peace, they had never needed to lay down the law.

"Where's old Mrs Beachball when you need her?" Dan said to Neil, earning a chuckle at the memory of the leader of the separatist's front in Steve's town back in England.

"This is funny to you?" a woman yelled in good English.

Dan focussed on her, recognising the woman as the wife of one of their more capable fishermen and a working-class leader for many in the town. In days gone by Dan thought the woman would've made a formidable union representative.

"No," Neil said. "We were talking about something else."

"You think a fight is a funny thing, is this right? You think it is your joke?"

She was wound up, animated, and getting louder with each word she spoke.

"I'm sure Dan is as upset about his part in this as everyone else is," cut a loud, confident voice over the noise.

Dan turned his stiff neck to regard the new speaker, recognising Polly's voice but not being prepared for the expression on her face.

She'd always been scatter-brained, happy, and forever looking for the good in people but now he saw a different side to her. He saw a cold, calculating anger behind her eyes and he knew he'd misjudged the situation, no matter how satisfying it had been to lay hands on the man.

"Don't look," Neil warned under his breath. "Tall guy by the fireplace. Left side, hanging back."

Dan deliberately turned to look somewhere else and took a snapshot of the man being pointed out.

"What about him?" Dan asked, studying the image in his head of a tall, fit man maybe fifteen years his junior.

"That's the one that hit Leah. Full-on sucker punch. They call him Bastin, but I don't know if that's his name or what…"

"Mist*aaake*," Dan murmured, covering his anger behind a weak attempt at humour.

If he didn't do it himself, then he was fairly certain that Lucien would want to discuss the matter with the man when he returned, and that wasn't even counting what Leah would do to him.

Probably sneak into his bed and Jane Wick the bastard with a pencil, Dan thought, shocking himself that his little girl was no doubt capable of doing just that.

"Save him for Leah," Dan muttered under the sound of someone yelling in impassioned French and pointing at them, no doubt extolling the evil of the tyrannical dictator.

"She's not bothered about it," Neil answered. "Not that I believe her but, hey ho."

He shrugged as if the concept of violent revenge was a normal topic to discuss while being berated publicly.

"Hold the bloody phone," Neil said, suddenly taking interest in what was being said.

Dan focussed his full attention on it, wishing they'd slow down so he could get more than half of the words. "Fuckers are calling for us to be disbanded."

"Disbanded?"

"Broken up. Split up...something about too much power..."

"And how do you expect the town to defend itself?" Dan asked loudly, repeating his words in primary school level French but giving up and letting people mutter the translations for others.

"How do you expect to fight off another band of pirates from the sea? Another invasion by a hostile force, eh? Tell me that?"

He fixed the skulking members of Beaulac's group with an obvious and very deliberate stare when he said that. Most likely because he'd pointed directly at them when he said the words "hostile force".

Dan went on, taking centre stage and speaking slow enough that the translators among them could keep up.

"I never thought you people – *my* people – would be like this. The world was filled with your kind before; those who think they don't need anyone to enforce the rules and laws that keep them safe. People who think they should be allowed to do whatever they want just because."

He paused, waiting for the murmurs to die down as his words reached everyone.

"You want us gone? You want to live your best life here undefended? Crack the fuck on, I'll take some time off and see how quickly some of you morons run crying when someone takes your lunch money."

"Mate," Neil said quietly, trying to get him back under control.

But Dan was gone. He'd been pushed too far.

"Who's going to make sure all of the trade routes stay open? That they're safe? That there aren't, *quite literally*, wolves at the walls?"

"Dan," Polly said in her most diplomatic of voices. "You're overreacting. Calm down and we'll talk about thi—"

"Calm down?" He wheeled on her, pain washing over his eyes and threatening his balance. "*Calm down*? How am I overreacting? These fuckers show up, their stories don't check out, the one person who was about to tell us what was really going on suddenly decides to" – he threw up two exaggerated air quotes and changed his voice to match the level eleven sarcasm – "*hAvE aN AcCiDeNt*, and you gullible bloody idiots *lap it all up*."

"Dan," Polly said again, a little more steel in her voice this time.

"And *then* one of them attacks me in my own damn house, gets educated for it, and now *I'm* the problem? Fuck this," he said, wheeling on Polly to demonstrate just how far past sensible he'd been driven.

"Fuck this and *fuck you*. Some fresh meat turns up and you just roll over ready to believe everything he says? *Wake up*, Polly. Wake up and remember why *you* asked me to take charge here. Wake up and think how many times you'd have been turned out of here or worse."

He glared at Polly for a long time, seeing a veiled but savage hostility reflected for how badly he'd embarrassed her in front of everyone. Finally coming down from the dizzy rage he'd worked himself up into he turned and stepped through the crowd, parting people with his hands and leaning on them for support as his head swam painfully. Neil followed him and Leah emerged from the shadows at the back of the hall to fall in beside them.

"I think we need to get away for a few days," Leah said.

"What? I've just argued to keep us here!" Dan snapped back. "Why would I just fuck off now?"

"Well for one I don't think you won over many hearts and minds with your speech back there…I mean, come on…" Leah pulled a grumpy face and puffed her chest up before doing her "Dan" voice. "*Fuck this and fuck you! Grrrr! Me Caveman Dan!*"

She dropped the impression and shook her head at him, finally relenting because she understood how badly he'd been triggered by what just happened.

He'd been betrayed by people he'd almost died trying to defend.

The injustice of it, the ingratitude, all of that felt like the cruellest sting of rejection to Dan and that was why he blew up. He may not have recognised that about himself but Leah certainly saw it for what it was.

"But no," she said gently. "We need to get away for a few days because they won't know what they've got until they don't have it anymore."

"So we run away?" Dan asked tiredly, drained by his injury and emotional exhaustion.

"No, we conduct a tactical withdrawal and observe," Leah told him, making him wonder when she'd become the adult in their dynamic.

HUNTERS

Movement showed in the shadows to his left. Careful not to twitch the barrel and expose his position, Lucien – his hair tied up in a comical bun – put his eye slowly back to the scope and crept the optic that way until a pinprick of reflected moonlight froze him.

He let out his breath carefully, blowing the air into the black shirt rolled up in front of his face to catch the condensation and prevent the puffs of hot breath from showing where they were. Nudging off the safety catch with infinitesimally small movements he took a bead on the shape creeping towards the massive chicken pens which had, at long last, gone silent in the night.

He watched, expecting more eyes to appear as the pack drew closer, but when none did, he paid closer attention to the shape of his target.

It moved in a way he didn't expect, creeping low to the ground, eyes staying fixed and not bouncing with canine movement. Lucien sensed it wasn't a wolf before that, ever since the old man's superstitious warning, but the movement of those eyes confirmed it.

He racked his brain for wildlife knowledge of the world, unable to recall any natural predators in the area other than the wolves and the occasional bear, but they never roamed this high. At least they never had before. He dismissed that idea because the shape he saw slinking low and silent through the darkness was no bear.

It didn't move like any bear he'd ever seen, and it was silent as death. In his mind there was no doubt that it had to be a big cat, though he had no idea how one could have found itself in the wilds of a country it wasn't native to.

He took up the pressure on the trigger, fighting an internal battle between not wanting to kill a majestic wild animal and needing the people of the farms to thrive safe from the threat of this creature.

He'd long since come to terms with having to kill wolves – especially as his side of the bed was often occupied by their own wolf in the form of Nemesis – but he accepted that, just as nature was hard, he had to be too.

He breathed in and out again once, holding it to settle his oxygenated body lying prone in the chill night air, and put the crosshairs on the chest of the wild cat heading for the egg production factory.

A sharp crack far off to his right echoed over the whole valley and made him jump. He almost snap-fired the shot but held off, which was smart because his target had vanished in a heartbeat. He flicked the safety back on and hoped that the shot from the other side of the valley had been worth the disturbance and had resulted in a kill.

He relaxed, knowing his position would be devoid of life until whatever predators lurking there felt safe enough to emerge back into the open.

Safe enough…or desperate enough, Lucien soon realised, as shadows began to stir again. Three sets of eyes reflected the ambient light telling Lucian the cat had moved on and the wolves were now pressing close. Lowering his eye to the scope again, he took aim and made sure of his first shot.

~

Morning, thanks to the clear night sky devoid of heavy cloud cover, brought with it just the slightest hint of a frost. It was more of an ice-cold dew, but for someone who had travelled all day and lain awake all night on the ground it was uncomfortable to put it mildly.

Lucien made his way down from the high ground that had been his bed and workstation for the night, shivering as he walked his tired, cold muscles through the long grass to retrieve the three carcasses he'd transformed during the night.

They were all younger pack members, maybe two or three years old, and it broke his heart to have to do it but he reasoned that it was part of the ecological process so both the wolves and his own species could keep on thriving without conflicting to the point where one of them was either driven off or killed off.

What he thought he couldn't do, which struck him as odd because he'd never once owned a cat as a pet before, was kill the big cat which had made a terrifying appearance only once during the night.

In his mind he reviewed his glimpse of the shadowed shape, mentally comparing it to the pictures he'd seen of the massive, magnificent cats with their pointed tufts of ears, only more solid – what Leah would lovingly call *chonky* – and appeared more than capable of carrying off any domesticated animal or even a person.

The other hunters of his militia had scored two similar kills but claimed a third was hit and driven off wounded which stung Lucien. As much as he regretted killing the wolves, he regretted causing suffering much more, and knowing that a wounded animal had fled to die in pain turned his stomach sour.

"That's not all," one of his men told him in French. "We saw more than wolves prowling in the dark."

"The cat?" Lucien asked, wondering how many of the secretive creatures prowled the night.

"No, two small bears."

"Bears?" Lucien blurted out. "*Here?*"

144

"They are in the mountains," he was informed confidently, rendering his guesswork in the night invalid. "So it only makes sense that they come down now that there are less of us in their way."

"This gets better," Lucien said, directing his men to leave the dead wolves in one place.

He knew that the people of the farm wouldn't allow the death of their natural enemies be wasteful, and the valuable furs would be harvested along with fresh meat for their hardy pigs to gorge themselves on.

Making his report to the leaders of the settlement he gratefully accepted a sandwich of fresh, crusty bread and runny eggs before removing his gear and boots to crash face first into the bed he'd been given to sleep solidly until his stomach woke him for the midday meal.

~

Miles away to his southeast, Lucien's young wife strapped two heavy backpacks together and lashed them over the back of a donkey who wore an expression of bored disappointment. It was tethered via a long rope to her own horse's saddle allowing her and her unwilling companion to travel lighter, with only their escape gear and their weapons on them.

"*Stay*, you bastard…" Dan snarled through gritted teeth, warning Ash off making a run at the mare's hind legs as soon as he tried to climb into the saddle.

Horse and dog eyed one another warily, waiting for the games to commence just as soon as Dan concentrated on nailing the mount like it was their personal starter pistol.

Dan hopped twice, grunting with his left boot in the stirrup before throwing his right leg up and over the horse's back.

The second he did that, the second he was committed to the effort and at most risk of personal injury, Ash rocketed low for the mare's rear left leg and snarled as his teeth snapped nowhere near the dangerous hooves which were already poised to make a strike at the dog.

The mare turned, lining up the kick should Ash be stupid enough to commit as Dan had, which spun him hard enough to make him cry out and almost spill from the saddle.

"Fuck! *Off.*" he snapped at the dog, turning his attention to the mare who had turned to eyeball him unkindly. "And you can shove it up your arse too, glue factory."

The horse let out a noise from its nose that sounded to Dan as if he was being told exactly where he could go and what he could do when he got there.

Regaining his composure, he turned to Leah to see her leaning over her own horse's neck with her arms crossed looking for all the world as relaxed as a charismatic cowboy in a seventies western.

"Yes?" he asked haughtily. "Can I help you?"

"You could help yourself," she chided him, "by not effing and jeffing at your ride for starters."

Dan grumbled a response under his breath, partly because he had nothing clever lined up as a comeback and partly because his jaw was hurting so much it hurt to talk.

It also hurt to stand up, walk, breathe and generally be alive but it was hardly as though Dan was a stranger to fetching injuries. Only this one felt worse. He was sure he'd fractured something in his face and knew that a few weeks of headaches and bad temper would follow until it started to go away.

146

"You're sure about this?" Neil asked for the tenth time in the space of thirty minutes as he handed up a flask to Dan.

He slipped it inside a pouch before Leah saw it and answered stiffly.

"We won't be far away," Dan promised, each word hurting his jaw. "And you'll let us know about anything we need to come straight back for, right?"

"I will," Neil answered.

He'd opted out of the arguments that raged among Sanctuary's more concerned citizens, claiming that he just wanted to potter about and do his own thing without getting involved in politics. For most people who knew the overweight amateur comedian and took him at face value that truth was evident, but for those who had known him longer, had seen him early on when the humour was a way to disguise how close he'd come to opting out, they saw a far deeper and more resilient side to him.

They knew Neil was a dangerously capable man hiding behind his social clown costume.

Luckily for Team Dan, those people wouldn't do or say anything to jeopardise Neil's remaining in Sanctuary while Dan took a voluntary leave of absence to, as Polly had claimed, 'let things settle down'.

He'd announced, and by announced he'd intentionally mentioned his plans in earshot of people who were known for spreading gossip faster than wildfire, that he was going to use the good weather to thin out the predators around the orchards.

Now two people, two dogs, a donkey and two horses waited impatiently as the gates of Sanctuary creaked open allowing them to leave, and Dan didn't cast a single look back.

"You're sure?" Leah asked, doubting her own plan now that it was happening.

"Neil and Mitch have got it," he told her, knowing that many more besides would be watching the new favourites suspiciously.

His words sounded relaxed, sounded confident, but inside he was screaming.

THE ORCHARDS

Dan and Leah were greeted warmly, as they always were. The people of the Orchards were peaceful although not very defensively minded, and wanted to live out their lives at one with the countryside.

Over the years the outbuildings had been repaired and retrofitted to act as a kind of dormitory for the seasonal workers required to help with the main harvests, much as the farms had, and as these workers had already arrived in early spring to begin work none of them knew about the issues back in Sanctuary.

Dan put on a brave face, in spite of the beard he'd started growing at exactly the same time Marie had left for Andorra covering the worst of the bruising. His right eye still showed a half halo of purple fading into orange, but he brushed off any questions about it with a smile and humour.

That first night, when they sat among the people who had dedicated their lives to tending fruit trees and farming, Dan couldn't prevent the muttered swearing brought on by the pain in his jaw.

"Are you okay?" a woman asked him in good but accented English.

"Fine," Dan lied. "Just a bit of toothache is all."

Toothache wasn't something to play down given the years they had spent without dentists, as none seemed to have survived and found their way to that part of the world.

They'd all seen people driven to near insanity by the pain of a wisdom tooth bursting through inflamed gums, or by a cavity that rotted a tooth from the inside and caused an abscess to grow and distort the look of a person's face.

More than once Kate and Sera had been called upon to take drastic measures and extract a tooth, but the patient in every case suffered terrible pain as a result of amateur dentistry and Dan was clearly becoming concerned that he would be the same.

"You should try mint leaves," she told him knowingly. "It will soothe your pain."

He thanked her graciously, or as graciously as he could with the throbbing pain in the back of his mouth, and promised to walk in the herb garden after the meal to pick some.

"Like you know what mint looks like?" Leah muttered to him.

"I don't need to," Dan answered. "It'll be the green one that smells like mint, dumbass."

Leah paused her chewing for a moment as she considered the stupidity of her joke before continuing and ignoring the interaction.

"So tell me…" a man Dan knew from Sanctuary asked loudly. "What do you make of the new people?" Dan looked up, his face giving nothing away as his mind calculated how he would know about them.

Reaching the conclusion that he'd been one of the last to arrive at the Orchards, Dan settled on a truthful response.

"Not much, actually," he said, taking a small, tentative bite and chewing awkwardly on one side of his mouth. "I don't believe their backstory and I don't know what their intentions are."

The conversation all down the long, wooden dining table hushed without fully stopping, as over half of them listened intently. Word had clearly spread here about it, and no doubt gossip and opinion based on little or no fact had distorted the tale.

"What is not to believe?" the man asked in polite challenge.

Dan rested down his cutlery, his appetite fleeing after the pain in his tooth flared again, and gave the man his full attention while speaking loud enough for everyone to hear.

"If four of you moved to somewhere else, and you were asked about your experiences," he said slowly, "then all four of you would have a different story. There would be differences because different people see things in different ways. Now, if four of you all auditioned for a role in a film, and you all learned the lines, then the only difference would be if someone made a mistake, you see?"

"I am afraid I do not," the man said with a frown. "Are you saying to us that these people are…actors?"

"Not very good ones," Dan agreed with a nod. "And the one who got his lines wrong…fell off the wall and died."

Muted gasps ran along the table at the news, but Dan smiled and waved it away.

"Accidents happen," he said dismissively. "I'm sure it'll all work out in the end. Now, tell me about any wolf sightings this last week?"

~

They slept in the seasonal accommodation after refusing the offer of rooms in the collection of farmhouses and barns there. Dan was polite about it, but adamant that he expected no preferential treatment, that he was just a worker like everyone else, and that he was there to perform a task just as the others from Sanctuary were.

They patrolled the perimeter of the Orchards in the day, taking shots at the large rabbits unafraid of humans through a lack of experience. Dan and Leah soon rectified that by bagging two pairs each, only Dan's second kill was appropriated by Ash who saw his opportunity for fresh produce and took it with no regrets.

Feeling sorry for her own dog, Leah secured another for Nemesis and the two rested on a fallen tree trunk as their sidekicks crunched and slurped at their fresh snacks. Dan ignored the sounds but Leah, oddly, was squeamish about it. Even more so when Dan took out a sharp folding knife and began dressing the rabbits right there beside her.

"What's the plan then?" she asked him after standing and walking a few paces away.

"Go back, hand these over, grab some food and rest. We'll go back out tonight and see what we can see."

"I meant the real plan, but okay," she answered.

"The *real* plan?" Dan said in amusement. "Oh, Neil has that in hand."

He refused to say more on it, which was as uncommon as it was annoying to her, but she'd learned a great many things since her life was changed by the two men she saw stealing Land Rovers a decade earlier, and oddly patience was one of them.

Not that either man possessed the quality, but being around them had forced her to learn it without mentorship.

Dan finished his task and wiped the folding blade clean on the fur of one victim before restoring it to a pouch on his vest. Ash, having finished his own snack, quickly sidled closer to Nemesis who was taking her time. She responded to his casual interest with bared teeth, a snarl that sounded like sailcloth tearing in a storm, and a big paw resting over the half a rabbit she was enjoying. Her sire just as casually steered away as if he wasn't intending on going near her in the first place and she was just overreacting.

None of them believed it, especially when Ash made straight for the pile of inedible parts Dan had left in the grass. He redirected his dog away from the guts, getting the big German Shepherd to clean his bloody fingers with his tongue. Leah pulled a face at that but relaxed when he fished in another pouch and came out with a packet he tore open to use an antibacterial wipe to clean himself properly.

"Come on," he said with a groan as he stood, making what he referred to as the unintentional noises related to age, mileage and damage. "Let's head back for a snooze before the sun goes down."

~

The night shift was spent in silence for the most part, as part of their daytime reconnaissance had been to scope out the best spot to spend the dark hours after establishing the best observation posts in the area where wolf activity had been noticed.

Both lay in position on their insulated mats, separated by twenty metres and some foliage, and both had their dogs by their sides for warmth and early warning of any approaching animal which could be illuminated by the bright lights mounted on their weapons.

As much as he hated doing it, Dan had a rope secured around Ash's neck to stop him running off into the dark and picking a fight with a pack of dogs all his size and bigger. Nemesis possessed a different temperament in that regard, but Ash had often considered picking fights with animals much larger than him to be an opportunity he couldn't resist.

As he lay there throughout the night his mind was assailed by the what ifs; by the possible outcomes to a situation with or without certain actions and options open to him.

He ran those scenarios over and over, each time making a different choice and allowing logic and experience to guide his imagination to the likely outcome.

Had he been at home, had he been in bed with Marie, he wouldn't have been able to sleep that night anyway, just as he never could when experiencing that elevated level of stress. His mind raced and none of it was made any easier by the fact that his whole face throbbed in waves.

He knew he'd been damaged by the bastard who swung the chair at him; the same bastard who'd dropped Leah with a cheap shot. He was more pissed off about the latter if he was honest with himself, but he couldn't escape the raging pain in his tooth as a direct result of it.

He toyed with it, wiggling the molar back and forth as if messing with it would make it any better, and even though it hurt he felt better for keeping some kind of pressure on it. He tapped his fingernail on it, checking for the tell-tale stab of pain indicating that an abscess was forming, but he found none as though that fact was any kind of reassurance when he was in unending pain.

That worrying about everything, even though Ash dozed pressed up against him for most of the night, took him through to the grey predawn without incident.

He groaned as he stood, joints cracking like small arms fire in the distance, and called out to Leah that their night was done.

"Come on, kid," he said, leaning back in search of the dull pop hiding in his lower back. "I need food and sleep."

WHILE THE CAT IS AWAY

Neil kept to his usual schedule, busying himself inside the walls fixing things and overseeing projects. He and Mitch intentionally avoided one another so as not to give anyone the impression they were colluding with one another in Dan and Leah's absence.

They were, but they didn't want anyone to know.

Neil's network of runners and apprentices, the people of all ages who loitered around him hoping for some snippet of knowledge from the growing tomb of Neil's life hacks he bragged about often, were key to his appearance of going about his business as usual.

The younger members of his growing cult, the wily children who got by on speed and stealth and had dreams of being like Dan or Leah when they grew up, were indispensable in running the messages between the two men. Messages for Mitch, unless urgent, found their way to him via Alita, his Spanish wife and mother of his little girl, in case anyone watched him during his duties.

Those duties were still carried out as though nothing had changed. He still set the guard rotations and checked the positions each day. When asked outright about the current political situation, he dialled up the ancestry and made comments about his people being well acquainted to rulers born far beyond his land.

The cryptic response left a few doubting his loyalty, but the absence of anything resembling an insurrection took the focus away from him. Similarly, far from avoiding his duties in protest, he was careful not to appear over eager in his role with the militia and alert anyone watching for his malicious compliance.

Neil never usually busied himself inside the main residence in the town. It was something of an underwhelming way to describe a grandiose, medieval castle but after years of habitation it had taken on far more of the comforts of a 21st century home than the bare-walled, exposed stonework that had been restored as a tourist attraction.

Late that morning, however, he had business in there as word had reached him of a faulty toaster in the kitchens.

Being a man who fully understood the importance of morning carbohydrates, and fully appreciating a thick slab of bread perfectly scorched on both sides crying out for a slice of fresh butter, a rarity which he paid a heavy price in trade for, Neil prioritised the task over all others.

Dropping his tool bag on the wooden worktop with a loud clank, he looked around smiling as he gained the attention of everyone working in the kitchen.

"Bonjour, Monsieur Neil," a boy of maybe eight said to him formally.

Neil recognised him as one of the earliest post-event offspring who usually ran around with Dan and Marie's son, and returned his greeting with the same formality.

"I heard there's a poorly toaster in here," Neil said, bending down with both hands resting on his knees.

He lowered his voice, talking conspiratorially to the boy. "And I heard it might be…" He looked left and right in case any eavesdroppers loitered. "*Sabotage!*"

He gasped, slapping a hand to his mouth which the boy mirrored, eyes wide at the heinous thought. Neil straightened, checking around him again to be sure they still spoke safely before giving his instructions.

"I'll need you to keep watch for me while I work," he said seriously. "And I'll need two croissants and a cup of tea every thirty minutes."

The boy nodded and turned on the spot to repeat the orders in French like he ran the entire show, and Neil half expected a chorus of 'yes chef' to answer him.

Smiling, he unplugged the large conveyor machine and spun it around to start loosening the screws keeping the greasy stainless steel panel in place at the back. He was sure it would be a fuse, or a loose wire to the power supply, but it always served him well to take something apart and make it look like a far more complex job than it was.

Dan always joked that if Neil said a job would take an hour he was factoring in forty-five minutes of making himself look indispensable, which Neil couldn't argue with as it was often the truth.

Usually with such repairs as the ailing toaster, he located the source of the fault early on, but spent time disassembling the majority of the machine to clean each part and lay it out on a once white cloth like he was stripping a weapon.

That tactic had backfired more than once, usually when he became distracted by performing one of his stories, and when it came to the reassembly going wrong, he declared the task impossible and often said a few words over the device with his head bowed.

His first task was removing weeks of accumulated crumbs from the lower section and he pulled the small brush from his kit to do that. By the time he was ready to attack the next part his tea and fresh pastry treat arrived, along with a generous helping of a plum jam.

Neil thanked the boy and chatted companionably to him while he ate, seeing the amused smirks of the others working in the kitchen at their interaction.

"So," Neil said in a lull in the natural conversation. "What do you know then?"

Speaking in rudimentary French came easy to him up to a level of vocabulary he struggled with, and an eight-year-old was a good match for his language skills.

The boy, possibly in mimicry of his own actions, looked over both shoulders before he leaned in and spoke quietly.

"There is a meeting happening upstairs," he said. "The new people are deciding what to do…I heard them say they will be given guns and they are to join the militia."

Neil smiled at him, took another gulp of his tea and snatched up the croissant before walking out of the kitchen.

"Need another tool," he said loudly on his way out. "This is a tricky one!"

~

"Wake up, old man," Leah said. Her words were accompanied by a mild shove to his shoulder but no unkindness, more that the friendly mockery of his biggest insecurities amused her.

"Whu?" Dan snorted, one eye opening while the other stayed firmly shut.

He looked right, staring at the wall directly beside his bed, then turned back to the left where Ash was poised ready to slap him in the face with a perfectly timed lick.

"*Fuggoff, dog,*" he grumbled groggily but without malice. "*Wossappenin*?"

The last gurgle of attempted English was aimed at Leah who, much to his disgust as he peered his one open eye at his watch and calculated the three hours of sleep he'd had, looked fresh as the proverbial daisy.

Dan struggled up and turned to his left, planting his feet on the cold floor and resting his face in his hands. He stayed there for a moment, just breathing and letting the world put itself back in order. If he'd slept for another hour he'd feel better, or at least not so bad, or if he'd been woken up just after falling asleep then he would be so...so...

"Discombobulated much?" she asked him.

He grunted in response, wishing he was her age again and could survive for three days on a half hour power snooze.

Scratch that, he thought, *I wish I was her age but with my experience...*

"Ready for words yet?" Leah enquired sweetly.

Dan nodded, missing the irony of not being able to make words in answer to the question.

"Message from Sanctuary," she said, holding out a scrap of paper to him.

Dan squinted at it, widening and narrowing his eyes as if working a telescopic sight into focus, then testing the range from his eyes with the hand holding the message like he played an imaginary trombone before Leah grew annoyed at the delay and huffed.

"Armed strangers sighted northeast of *CC*. Camping two miles away," she said, reading it herself.

"CC?" Dan asked, earning another huff of displeasure from Leah who had grown bored with the delay.

"*Comptoir commercial,*" she told him. "The trading post?"

"Ugh," Dan answered, giving the grunt the inflection that encompassed acknowledgement and apology.

"No approach made. Provide instruction."

Dan raised his eyes to meet hers, seeing that she had finished reading and looked to him for answers.

"From Roland?" he asked her.

She nodded, her mouth forming a tight line of concern. Dan knew her soft spot for the old man, and if pressed he'd admit to a fondness for him too. A fondness and a hint of jealousy of being left alone for long periods of time without anyone bothering him and only really working for half the year.

"He sent that home and they sent it here?" he asked, trying to work out the logic. "It didn't come from Neil?"

"No," she said. "It came from Victor and the original note was attached."

"And what did Victor say?"

Leah smiled at the question and handed over the second scrap of paper.

It was written in English with no grammatical inconsistencies that Dan could make out.

With Lucien gone I do not know who else to tell, the words read. *If I ask Mitch to investigate, I do not know what will come of everyone's return.*

"What does he mean by that?" Leah asked impatiently, not waiting for Dan to finish the note before she asked.

He read it again, searching for the meaning behind the words and applying all possible undertones to the way the man spoke, the way he thought, and the way he viewed Dan.

"It means he thinks there's a takeover happening," Dan said. "And like every idealistic thinker in the history of the world, he wants his tame stormtrooper to come and save him…make your bloody mind up!"

"What?" Leah asked, unsure who he was talking about.

"Victor! Not two weeks ago he was giving it Billy Big Bollocks about me breaching their human rights, and now he's scared he thinks the devil he knows will save him?"

He stood fast, exciting Ash in to turning a circle on the spot like he was celebrating with a single doughnut, and fixed Leah with a stern look.

"So what do we do?' she asked.

"We ride," he said.

"We ride or die," Leah answered, chest puffed up and face set aggressively.

Dan stopped and turned a quizzical look on her.

"Yeah, I'm sorry," she said, shaking her head, "I don't even know where that came from. Forget I said it."

"Okaaaay," Dan answered, keeping his eyebrows bunched up above his nose as he walked out of the room keeping an eye on her.

POLICY CHANGE

Neil walked back to his own place as though he genuinely needed another tool. He was careful not to rush too much, nor to seem too relaxed, and he walked every step of the way assuming he was being watched to avoid any mistakes.

He hated every second of it. Hated feeling unsafe in his own town where the impenetrable defences were supposed to keep all the evil in the world out instead of locking it up inside with them.

He was convinced, on his own merit and not simply because Dan felt the same way, that the newcomers were either some kind of advanced reconnaissance force of infiltrators or else they were engaged in a specific kind of psychological warfare with the intention of taking control over Sanctuary and all of her domain.

Their home was like the old English burghs: regional strongholds with a force of dedicated warriors where the vulnerable settlements around them could run for safety when the Vikings decided to raid. Only he was concerned that the Vikings had sent their people ahead of the main fleet to start dismantling the defences from within.

Stepping inside his house, which merged into his adjoined workshop in that he ate at the tool benches and disassembled engines in the kitchen, he walked directly to the rear yard where he hoped one of his apprentices would be tending the few pigeons he housed there.

He found one, a young girl leaving via the rear gates to the stone walled yard and called out softly to her in French. She hurried back to him and listened intently to his instructions before promising not to fail him and scurrying away into the narrow alleyways between the buildings on that side of the docks where no wide wagon or vehicle could go.

He rummaged around in his tools; all left in such disarray that he knew the vague location of each item requiring minimal searching. Selecting a clamp that he could use but didn't actually need, he made his unconcerned way back to the kitchens.

Mitch was on the sea wall showing a member of the militia how to prepare the belt of massive bullets for the big fifty-calibre in the unlikely event they should need it. As Neil's messenger approached someone she knew nearby, careful to observe the rules Neil gave that she shouldn't be seen talking to him directly, she found herself unable to speak for how fast she'd run.

The young man, Alex, told the young girl to take a breath and slow down before listening carefully and not interrupting with questions. Telling her to wait where she was, Alex walked casually up to Mitch and spoke in a low tone, saying he needed to talk to him.

Mitch turned to argue at the interruption but stopped when he saw the grave expression on the young man's face.

"Don't bloody touch anything," he told the militia member under instruction before walking away out of public sight with Alex.

The girl talked fast – faster than Mitch could interpret – and when she began tugging urgently on Mitch's sleeve he had to crouch down and calm her.

"My French is as bad as my English," the Scot complained, seeing the confusion on the girl's face.

"She says the new people are being given guns," Alex explained in good English. "She says Neil has heard this."

Mitch stood, face set rigid with indignation that anyone thought they could just help themselves to his armoury, and thought of a way to reward the young message runner for her work. His hand rested on a small folding knife he'd found when clearing out some old kit and handed it to her.

"Don't hurt yourself with it," he warned, glancing up at his militia man for a translation to be certain.

The girl promised she would be careful, opening the small blade as her eyes filled with pride.

Mitch walked away stiffly, seeming to fight the urge to break into a jog, heading for the bridge over the docks where he stalked directly past the central keep towards the gate and the armoury secured nearby.

Arriving there to find a small gathering of people crowding by the door, he enquired in a loud, polite manner what they were doing there. "Who gave you wee shites permission to look at ma fucking armoury, eh?"

His voice silenced them, turning every head to face him before he spoke again.

"Oh, don't all answer at once," he said, anger filling every word. "Who said you could open that door?"

"We did," a voice said from the far side of the group of outsiders.

Polly stepped forwards, chin raised in the manner of someone caught out doing what she feared others might think was wrong but that she believed in.

"With everyone gone, we need more defenders. A group of strangers has been seen nearby and we need to defend ourselves."

"For starters," Mitch said, "everyone *isn't* gone. I'm still here, and I can have twenty militia members on the wall inside of ten minutes. The guard is still there, the fort is still manned and last I checked the gates were closed."

"We have doubts…" Polly began, glancing up at the tall man with a yellowing bruise on his cheek. He seemed to nod his permission or encouragement to her. "We have doubts that everyone has the best interests of Sanctuary at heart."

"As do I," Mitch shot back, unable to hide his anger and not making any secret of the malevolent look he levelled at Beaulac. "But that door stays closed until I'm ordered to open it."

"I'm ordering you to open it," she said, some of the conviction fleeing her voice as she spoke.

"All due respect, Polly," Mitch said flatly, "last I checked you handed over control to Dan and Marie. Neither of which are here, so delegation of such matters falls to the militia."

"So you're in charge now?" another of the group asked him in English.

Mitch slowly turned his gaze on the tall man, much in the same way a tank's main gun would rotate to point at something it wanted to convert into burning rubble.

"Of this room and what's inside it, aye, laddie. I am."

The quiet challenge in his tone was evident, but the leader of the little group bent down to mutter in Polly's ear.

"You work for the people, do you not?" she asked, switching tactic to appeal to his sense of moral propriety.

"I do what I do on behalf of everyone here," Mitch answered. "But that doesn't mean I take stupid orders from stupid people who want to do stupid things."

"You follow orders of your commander," Beaulac told him. "This...*Dan*, the man who wants everyone to do his bidding."

"First up, ya maple-munching bampot, he's no' my *commander*. He's my *friend*. I have faith in his intentions."

"Meaning you don't have faith in mine?" Polly asked, seizing the opportunity to press on his conscience again.

"Right now, Polly," Mitch said sadly. "No. I do not. Now if you want to try and break this door down to take what's inside I'll be forced to do something we'll all no doubt regret, so if it's all the same to you can you kindly fuck off?"

"Fine," Polly snapped. "We'll hold an election and see what happens. Would you go against the will of everyone and keep the guns all for yourself? Will you try and stop us?"

"Polly," he told her gently, "you make that kind of mistake and I'll be the first out the door with my family and you'll no see us again."

"That would be a shame," the tall man who'd sucker-punched Leah said with a smirk aimed at Mitch.

Mitch wanted to tell him that he'd had harder shits than the kid, but he was too old, too wise to argue with idiots who would drag him down to their level and win through experience.

"We all get what's coming to us eventually," Mitch told him, treating him to a cold look filled with promise as he stepped through them to put his back to the armoury door. "Remember that."

~

True to her word, Polly called a meeting of the townspeople that afternoon. She asked for those at sea fishing to be spoken for by family and friends, and laid out the problems they faced as a society.

Speaking to them in impassioned French she said how they had become a town ruled by military will, but people who were not held accountable to the people for their actions.

"Dan saved my daughter's life," a man yelled from the crowd.

"And my sister," another voice shouted. "When the men came from the sea."

"He saved all of us from the people who attacked this place," a woman called out, only to be yelled down by a shrill voice directly behind her.

"From the people he brought here chasing *him*," she shrieked. "Since then we have lived in fear of attack!"

"Since then we have lived *free* from the danger of attack, do you not see this?" a man known to be close to Neil spoke up. "Our lives are better now; I say things stay as they are."

"And who decides who stays here?" Polly asked. "Are the militia responsible for immigration now? Who are they to say who stays and who leaves?"

Murmurs rippled through the crowd, but nobody offered any refuting statement to that point. Public opinion, while not turning away from Dan's leadership, couldn't fully support his denial of citizenship to the outsiders.

Not without proof.

Neil, loitering at the back of the room with one of his followers beside him translating the words he couldn't make out, ducked out before the meeting was concluded.

Making his way to his home, he shook a handful of coals onto the cooking range in his small kitchen and opened up the vents to heat the pan of water he placed there and, for the first time in forever, he slid over the bolt on the door of his home.

Retrieving the Glock from the holster inside his waistband where it had spent to afternoon digging into his muffin top, he rested it on the worktop beside him and picked up a piece of paper to scribble the first of his notes.

The first, attached to the bird taken from the cage marked 'Orchards' was a brief summons for Dan and Leah to "get their arses back, ASAFP".

The second, destined for the farm, advised Lucien to wrap up his hunting tasks and head home.

The third, one which he copied out word for word to send two birds in the direction of Andorra, advised Marie that her presence was sorely needed back in Sanctuary "to prevent a misguided uprising".

Sending that last message into the sky attached to the feet of a pair of his fastest pigeons, named Usain and Stirling, he watched them disappear into the sky and hoped he was doing enough.

Behind him the raven with the deformed wing flapped both wings to adjust itself, and uttered a single croaking word to express his opinion on the matter.

"*Motherfucker.*"

Neil couldn't have put it better himself.

THE RETURN

"Straight in?" Leah asked.

"Straight in," Dan answered. "Get the report, head out and find out what's what."

"And if there isn't any new intel?"

"Then we work off the last known location and go from there," he told her. "But I want at least two more able bodies on that trading post until we get some answers."

"Have you considered," Leah asked carefully as she urged her horse into a comfortable canter beside Dan's awkward and painful looking attempt at a gear change. "That this might be coincidental?"

"I have," he answered stiffly as his inability to flow with his mount made it sound as if the breath was being driven from his body. "And I'd bet my left nut it isn't."

"Not the right one?" she asked.

"What?"

"Never mind. Why aren't we going straight to the trading post?"

"Because we need to make sure of what's happening back home first," he told her, not elaborating on the subject.

Dan urged his mare on with a growl and a jab of his heels which Leah matched with an encouraging click of her tongue. Beside them both, effortlessly covering the terrain, their dogs kept pace.

Had the news not already reached them, had they been at the Orchards none the wiser about the report regarding the sighting of strangers, then Neil's message would have found them by nightfall. That message wouldn't have given them anything else to go on, other than to increase the urgency of their already fast pace.

"Gates are closed," Leah reported as soon as they turned left to descend the long, sloping roadway to their town built at sea level.

Her own eyesight was far superior to his now that his age dictated a waning in physical skills, but even from that distance he could see the dark wood of the heavy gates barring their access through the perimeter wall.

"Good," he said.

"Unless they're closed to *us*," Leah prompted, not entirely sure her adoptive father fully understood what she meant.

He said nothing, merely treated her to a strained grunt that didn't really convey anything other than his obvious testicular and dental discomfort.

They rode up on the gates, seeing a silhouetted form appear above the parapet and turn to shout something down. The right gate swung inwards before they had to slow their approach and admitted them without challenge, which made both father and daughter breathe a private sigh of relief.

Mitch was waiting for them, and the look on his face took that relief away in an instant.

"Bad idea, everyone buggering off at the same time," he told them after doing the double shoulder check like he was about to crack a joke he really shouldn't.

"The New People's Communist Party of Sanctuary has been active, and they're after a formal change in leadership."

"And?" Dan asked, climbing down from the horse and cupping his groin without caring who saw him.

"And they don't have that kind of support," Mitch answered. "But that's not to say everyone's on your side…"

"Meaning?" Leah asked, sounding every art the younger, feminine echo of the man beside her.

"Meaning public opinion isn't entirely behind your policy on immigration."

"They think the new people should stay," Dan said. "And that I don't get to play judge and jury."

"Along those lines, only not as harsh," Mitch told him. "I tell you what though…the minute they start giving the bastards my rifles, me and mine'll be on the next wagon to Andorra for good."

Dan looked at him for a second, trying to gauge if he was serious and not liking the obvious answer that he was.

"It won't come to that," Dan promised. "Is the selection process for the militia still the same?"

Mitch nodded.

"Then they have to pass basic assessments to get in," Leah finished Dan's thought for him. "And *we* still decide that."

"Anyway," Dan said to change the subject. "What's the latest?"

"No updates since Roland's message yesterday," Mitch said.

"No contact at all?" Leah asked, concerned for the old man at the trading post.

"He sent an all-clear first thing," Mitch admitted, "only he sent it via the private line to Neil so it isn't common knowledge if you catch my drift."

Dan did, but given the worrying events to have taken place in their very short absence he didn't want to leave their town without him and Leah right then.

"I'll go for a look-see," he said.

He turned to Leah to stop any protests forming and gave her orders.

"You stay here, watch what's going on closely and keep this damned gate open to me, understood?"

She nodded.

"I need Neil to get a message to Marie about what happening here," he went on, taking items out of his pack and switching the heavier rifle from Leah's saddle to his own, cursing the horse for spinning on the spot to see what he was doing near its back end.

Leah took hold of the mare's bridle and soothed the animal which, much to Dan's disgust, settled for her.

"Neil has that in hand," Mitch said, turning to Leah. "And he's sent word for Lucien to come back."

She thanked him with a nod and led her horse away before turning back to Dan.

"Wait, you're going right now?"

"Yep," he told her, snapping his fingers at Ash and pointing him away from the animal in the hope of preventing their usual dance putting him in danger.

He hooked his toe into the stirrup again, hauling himself up into the saddle before his dog launched at the horse's back legs.

The horse shied away, snorting, and the dog snarled. Both settled down when Dan added his own growl to the noise.

"Don't push too hard," Leah said, her voice edged with concern.

"I'll be fine," Dan assured her dismissively.

"I meant the horse," Leah corrected him. "Don't push her too hard. If she runs off you'll be walking back."

Dan grunted in answer, wincing in discomfort as he tried to simultaneously turn the horse and readjust his position in the saddle.

"Low profile," he warned her. "And keep Nem handy from now on."

She nodded, giving his thigh a pat as though she would the horse's back end and watched as he trotted awkwardly back through the gate and up the gentle slope leading to the road north.

"Fuckin' one man band marches again," Mitch grumbled, offering a rare negative opinion about Dan.

SHADOWS AND TEETH

The nights had grown colder since spring's early promises. Cold enough that breath fogged in the dark and frost glistened faintly on rooftops before dawn.

Each evening Lucien waited until the last smear of colour bled from the sky, lying prone in the dark with rifle in hand and over-looking the livestock pens with every sense wired tight. He waited without comfort, without a word, his heart hammering beneath the stillness for three nights of nothing but wind, rustling leaves, and the distant, maddening screech of owls.

On the fourth night, it came too close.

Someone had stepped out to relieve themselves after dark, just feet from their door. A sound had frozen them mid-step, and the muted thump of something hitting earth made them dive back inside and slam the door shut as claws raked deep lines into the thick wood.

Guttural yowling and rolling growls of frustration provided the soundtrack to this horror show, but by the time he and his militia members had responded, the feline attacker had melted away into the night.

Nadine brought him back to the scene to see the marks in the door the next morning, carved through seasoned timber as fingernails through wet clay.

Lucien traced the grooves with a thumb, his lips tight. The depth, the shape, the spread of the claw marks all indicated a massive predator was now actively hunting humans.

"It could carry off a grown man," he muttered, mostly to himself.

"*Pardon?*" Nadine asked, thinking he had spoken to her and not himself.

Lucien dropped his hand away from the claw marks and turned to face her.

"This has to end," he said abruptly. "I need you to make sure that nobody leaves their home after dusk. Not for water, not for a piss, not for anything. Everyone inside. Lights off and curtains drawn. You understand?"

She did, but when Lucien's fear and frustration made him angrily demand a verbal response she gave one.

"I understand. Nobody is to leave their homes after dark."

Lucien nodded, relaxing slightly as he descended from the mountain of apprehension he'd climbed, but Nadine only looked worried as if there was something else she didn't know how to say.

"There is more, no?"

"There is," she said solemnly. "During the night we lost one of our best milk goats—"

She held up both hands to ward off his building interruption.

"They were all locked away, just like you said, only…"

Lucien knew it then, and with realisation came shame and the evaporation of his anger. "Only it was taken when I left my position to chase the cat."

Nadine nodded, not implying any kind of blame but that didn't stop the responsibility he felt. He shuffled off to get a few hours' sleep, unable to rid the notion that this cat was smarter than he was, and had intentionally caused a scene elsewhere to lure him away from the livestock.

The next night, it came again.

Lucien waited, stiff with fatigue, hidden in the darkness on the roof of their bakery. He hadn't slept or eaten enough and his muscles ached from dehydration caused by staying still all throughout each night. His eyes stung with tiredness as he subtly shifted his body weight by tensing the muscles in his legs in sequence to squeeze the blood back towards his heart, trying not to breathe too loudly. Nothing.

Then, from the far side of town came a faint, deep growl.

Something about it told Lucien it wasn't simply the vocalisation of an animal warning, but the low, confident sound of a predator stalking.

He hesitated, thinking that the animal might just be smart enough to lure him away, wondering if he should hold his ground or hunt the hunter.

The sound came again, more of a supersized purr than a growl, and Lucien bolted. He sprinted between buildings following his instinct of the direction the noise hadn't come from but was *going* to be. He heard it again, more intense now, before the growl became a snarl.

The snarl turned to a yowl and then a scream: human, and filled with unbridled terror.

Lucien skidded around the corner, rifle snapping up. One of his hunters staggered backwards, clutching a torn and gushing right arm with his left while the hand of that wounded arm fumbled desperately for his sidearm. The animal – a full-grown damn *leopard* – was advancing, low and fast, muscles bunching beneath its rosetted hide as it gathered speed and displayed huge teeth in preparation of the kill.

Lucien fired.

The beast twisted mid-leap, struck clean through the chest. It crashed into the dirt and slid to a twitching halt, freezing everything as if the impact had knocked the air from the world for a moment. The size of the beast stunned Lucien as he watched the body make a few final twitches. The raw power in its limbs, the menace in its dying growl fascinated and terrified him.

The wounded man groaned snapping Lucien back into the real world. He ran over and crouched beside him, adding pressure from his own hands to staunch the flow as blood ran between his fingers.

"You will be okay, just hold still," he said in French as he tore open a pouch in search of a dressing.

He turned his head away and sucked in a breath to fill his lungs. Bellowing for help, that they could come out, he yelled that he had an injured man.

"Did you see that thing?!" that man gasped. "What is it?"

"Just an animal," Lucien said, his voice low and confident to reassure the man, but inside he felt just as incredulous.

Boots came running, questions were shouted before gasps and screams showed their reaction to the thing that had been hunting them and their livestock.

Lucien ignored the questions about the leopard, not even wanting to acknowledge it was there, instead he barked orders that the man was to be carried somewhere clean to deal with the wounds now that he'd managed to stop the worst of the bleeding.

They worked through the night. The injured man was stabilised and sedated, Lucien himself cutting the torn clothing away as the blood flowed again. He irrigated the wounds – savage, diagonal slashes that tore the skin and muscle beneath rather than slicing it. Something in the back of his mind warned him of infection from the scratches of predators, and whether that was right or not he took no chances.

The man screamed as salt water was poured over the slashes, and again when Lucien ordered a second flushing before using tweezers to remove scraps of bloody clothing that stubbornly refused to be washed away.

He was pushed aside when he tried to thread the needle and stitch the ragged lines of torn flesh closed, as his hands suddenly began to shake so much he wasted too much time.

"It is the adrenaline," Nadine explained. "Let someone else do this."

Lucien's first reaction was to argue back, to say that he was calm and in control, but he was too tired. He was physically and mentally exhausted through nights of cold watchfulness and days of little sleep. He was away from home, away from his wife and baby, cold, tired and…and *terrified*.

He had been utterly terrified coming so close to a leopard – an apex predator with no right to be living wild in their part of the world – and the fear of what could've been threatened to sap the power from his legs.

~

Dawn broke pale and slow. The corpse of the leopard was dragged through the street, and even the bravest among them turned pale.

Lucien sat on the steps of the bakery with a mug of strong tea in his hands, steam coiling up into the cold. His shoulders sagged and dark rings circled his eyes as his breath came in shallow heaves of his chest.

Nadine approached him, her steps light, before she held out a folded note without speaking. When he reached for it, Nadine flinched at the dried blood coating his hands.

Lucien read the note, recognising Neil's handwriting and poor grammar, then he nodded once.

"I have to go."

"You cannot go," she said quietly. "There are still wolves. *Bears.* You are running on empty."

Lucien stood and tossed the remaining tea onto the ground beside him.

"Someone has to stay, I agree, but I must answer this," he said, holding the note up.

"But…your man? He cannot travel. He has lost too much blood and there is the risk of infection. He must stay until he is better."

"I agree, and my other militiaman will stay also, but I…"

"You already said, you must go."

Nadine sounded annoyed, disappointed even, but Lucien could no more ignore the summons from Neil than he could've left had the leopard not been killed.

"I…I didn't thank you. For last night," Nadine said hesitantly.

"Thank me?" Lucien scoffed, some hint of dark amusement souring his reaction. "I don't want thanks for what I did. For what I *had* to do, no…that animal should never have been here in the first place. How did it find itself in southern France? Do you know?"

Nadine didn't know, but her guess was the same as Lucien's. The same as any logical person could deduce. It had escaped, either from a zoo or some other tourist attraction, and had found itself unmatched by any other predator native to the countryside it ruled over.

"But why here?" he asked. "Why now?"

"Some people think it is old…do such creatures not seek weaker prey when they get old?"

Lucien accepted the theory with a tilt of his head, but it didn't matter to him anyway. It had been there, through whatever twisted version of events that led to their paths crossing, and he had killed it because he had no other choice. *C'est la vie.*

He left the orders. His other, uninjured man was to remain and set traps around the southern perimeter then keep watch at night until the wolves had lost enough of their pack to be driven off for good. Still nobody was to leave town at night, and if something moved in the dark, they didn't chase it.

He worried that this was only a temporary fix, that when the bountiful summer drew to a close the predators would be back with desperation driving their need for food, and his mind began running training scenarios and recruitment to increase their numbers sufficiently for a larger permanent presence there.

Lucien mounted his horse, bones aching already, and set off without fanfare. Some people cheered him like a conquering hero, but Lucien felt wretched for what he'd had to do and his failings leading up to it.

The road back towards Sanctuary was rougher than he remembered, as each twist and turn made his body ache more and each inch the sun climbed in the sky made the growing daylight hurt his eyes. Every gust of wind stirred up phantom sounds, and he had to check himself more than once to stop from raising his rifle at shadows.

Mid-morning brought the distant murmur of an engine that startled him out of his half-asleep plodding. Lucien blinked at the road behind him to be sure he wasn't imagining the sound, then he climbed down with great difficulty and tugged his mount off the track to crouch low, cradling his weapon.

A truck came into view, slowing as it spotted the lone rider taking scant cover behind a large rock, creeping to a stop beside him before the window rolled down to fill the air between him and the truck with an electric hum.

"Lucien?" Marie said.

He exhaled, lowering the rifle as he stood stiffly and walked his horse closer.

"You look well," he croaked.

Marie leaned further out, eyes narrowing. "And you look like shit. No offense."

Lucien managed a thin smile. "You English always think that saying 'no offense' means I am not permitted to be offended...but anyway, I am not. I *feel* like shit, *maman*, but you should've seen the leopard."

THE ROAD HOME

Andorra, earlier that day

The pigeon came in low over the valley, flitting through early sunlight that painted the Andorran peaks in gold. It circled once before landing with a flutter and a coo on the windowsill of the upstairs hallway.

Rafi had the message unwrapped and halfway to Marie within a minute.

She recognised Neil's handwriting at a glance, heart plummeting before she'd even read the words. This was always going to happen, she thought. She'd known it in her bones, long before any message arrived.

Outside, Adalene giggled in her pen, holding a leaf like it was treasure. Ben kicked a football back and forth across the short grass, occasionally bouncing it off the fence to make his niece squeal with delight.

Marie held the note loosely as she watched them, torn between dread and the dull comfort of the scene, reading it over and over in the hope that it would cease to be real until a knock on the open doorway drew her from the spiral.

Marie turned to see the door opening and stiffened at the sight of Carla Rovira.

"Can I help you?"

"Your man from home sent a message," Carla said, offering a neutral smile.

Marie blinked. "How did you—?"

Carla laughed lightly, diffusing the cold air between them. "Rafi has lived here for a long time now, and he does not hide his secrets well."

Marie's posture eased, her expression flickering with fatigue. "Then I suppose you know it isn't good news."

"I think I do," Carla said gently. "But I do not know what kind or *how* bad. Will you tell me, Marie?"

Marie hesitated for a second before she handed over the crumpled letter. Carla read quickly, her brow tightening.

"You have to go."

Marie nodded, her voice tired but resolved. "I know."

"But you cannot take them, yes?" Carla asked, her eyes fixed on the children.

Marie didn't answer.

"Marie," Carla said, her tone firmer, "you know I am right in this, yes?"

The silence stretched before Marie exhaled sharply through her nose.

"Polly's under the spell of the bastard who leads them," she muttered. "A man who calls himself Beaulac. If he gets control of Sanctuary…"

Carla's mouth twitched with distaste. "Then you definitely cannot take the children, so I will keep them here, with your permission."

Marie turned, surprised. "*You're* offering to take them?"

Carla blinked. "Of course I am. Why do you say it like this?"

"I…didn't think you…"

"You didn't think I liked children because I do not have any of my own? I know many things, Marie, but above everything I know how to keep children safe," Carla said, a smile creeping up her face before she added more. "And besides, I have two women who live with me and have babies of their own. They will help."

Marie looked out at Adalene and Ben again.

"What about the newcomers...are they safe?" Marie asked, speaking of the danger these strangers might represent.

"They are being watched, every night and every day. Rafi watches them like a hawk. Others too. At the first sign of trouble, they will disappear for the good of the whole country...I have made mistakes before, thinking that every rule from the old world must be followed, and I will not make this mistake again. You have my word, Marie, at the first sign of trouble these strangers will be dealt with."

Marie nodded, still not meeting her eye.

"I want you to tell Leah also that they will be safe. Like I just said, you have my word. I will die before I let harm come to them."

"But...why? It's not like we ever got along...why would you do this for me?"

"For you? No. We are not friends, but there is no reason for this. We are both busy women – leaders – and friends are not the most important things to us all of the time...we are not friends, but I would like us to be. I do this for them" – Carla held out a hand towards the children who played, oblivious to their fate being decided only feet away – "and so you, your husband and Leah can deal with this problem. We are not much of fighters here, you know this, so we need your people to do this. For all of us."

Marie was stunned by the speech, by Carla Sofia Rovira herself deigning to show emotion and compassion in place of her usual steely exterior, and she saw so much depth to the woman in that moment that she knew everything she'd just heard was the unfiltered truth.

The farewell was quietly painful in its softness. Marie knelt by Ben and held his shoulders, trying to sound like their parting was only going to be brief and resist the urge to hold onto her son like it might be the last time she saw him.

"You must do exactly as you're told. No wandering. No sneaking off, *compris?*"

Ben nodded solemnly. "*Oui, maman.* I'll protect Adalene with my *life.*"

Marie pulled him into a hug and pressed a long kiss to his temple. "You're a good big brother uncle, Ben," she said warmly, teasing him with the blurred distinction in his relationship to his baby niece.

She lifted her grandchild to raise her high and make her giggle, bringing her back down to kiss her chubby cheek noisily before passing Adalene into Carla's arms, whispering something only the baby could hear.

She was careful not to look back, not to give either child a glimpse of her pain as she walked away.

By the time she climbed into the truck her face was hard again, but the tracks of her tears hadn't fully dried.

The driver, one of Lucien's militia – middle-aged, solid and fiercely loyal to her son-in-law – watched her quietly. As they pulled out of the compound, he asked only one question:

"You are sure about leaving the baby?"

"I am."

Marie didn't look at him when she answered, and he didn't offer another word on the matter.

They drove in silence, the road winding away from green peaks and narrow bridges. Hours passed. When the truck finally crested a ridge and rattled down into a familiar valley, Marie blinked against the light.

Ahead, far in the distance, a rider slumped in the saddle of a tired-looking horse.

Before she could give her driver instructions the rider slid awkwardly from the horse and crouched behind a boulder for cover.

The driver slowed, lifting a pistol onto his lap as Marie had, until realisation dawned on them both.

"Lucien?" she asked after opening the window.

He limped more than walked his horse towards her, looking like he'd been on the road all night and day.

"You look well," he said, sounding just as exhausted as he looked.

"And you look like shit. No offense," she told him honestly, inviting an explanation for why he was out there alone and looking like he did.

"You English always think that saying 'no offense' means I am not permitted to be offended...but anyway, I am not. I *feel* like shit, *maman*, but you should've seen the leopard."

"Leopard?!" Marie stared at him, brows raised. "Like...*an actual leopard*?!"

Lucien nodded, his cheeks filled with water and swilling like it was mouthwash before he spat the road dust into the grass.

"Big male. Big enough to carry off an adult. The bastard tried to drag someone from their house two nights ago and clawed the door to hell trying to get in."

"Christ," Marie muttered.

"I am not sure he was involved…" Lucien retorted drily, proving that he wasn't exhausted beyond sarcasm. "It was old, at least that is what some people believe, so it makes sense that it would seek easy prey, no?"

"Well, yes, but…Lucien, I didn't think there was anything out here except wolves and the odd bear?"

Lucien drank again, shaking his head and swallowing before he answered. "That is right. It is what I believed also, so how is it you say? Your guess is as good as mine?"

Marie smiled, as she always did when the young Frenchman used an English idiom courtesy of Leah's influence on him. "Probably escaped from a zoo or something," she guessed, earning a confirmation from Lucien.

"That is what we thought also."

"And you went out every night hunting a *leopard?* You were lucky it didn't get *you!*"

"I was lucky, yes, but one of the others was not. It came back last night and attacked my man, only I shot it before it could finish him."

Marie put a hand on his arm, having already noted the flakes of dried blood in the small creases of his hands and waiting for him to tell her instead of pushing.

"You did what you had to do, and I'm glad you're safe," she said quietly, offering him the reassurance she felt he needed.

Lucien smiled and perked up, sucking in a breath before digging into a pocket and holding out Neil's message to her.

"Then I got this, and I knew I had to leave right away."

"You should've said no," Marie told him, opening the curled piece of paper to read it.

"And when have I ever done that?" Lucien snorted.

187

They stood for a moment in the stillness, listening to the quiet creak of the cooling engine as Marie read Lucien's message twice before pulling the folded scrap of the same paper from her jacket and handed it over.

"Mine's from Neil too."

He read quickly, exhaling through his nose. "So, it has begun?"

She nodded, noting that Lucien's summons held much less information and far less urgency than her own. "We need to get moving. You two swap and he can ride your horse back. I'll drive; you sleep."

Lucien didn't argue. His eyes flicked to the driver still at the wheel, staring straight ahead and pretending not to listen until Lucien spoke to him in low, rapid French. He thanked the man, apologised for imposing on him, and smiled when the man said it was an honour to be of service.

Marie climbed out and took the wheel while the militia man dismounted and climbed into Lucien's saddle. The horse didn't look pleased, but it didn't have much choice.

As the truck turned and started the descent toward Sanctuary, Lucien leaned his head back and let his eyes close.

Marie drove in silence, jaw tight, knuckles white on the wheel. They were heading into the storm.

TOOTH AND NAIL

"Easy, boy," Dan murmured softly as the dog fidgeted beside him. He knew Ash wasn't ill-disciplined enough to be moving out of boredom, not when they were both in work mode anyway, but more that the dog was feeling the same unease that he was and needed to communicate that to his master.

"I know," Dan reassured him, slowly stretching out his left hand to soothe his best friend. "I know."

The toothache was still there. Not sharp, not deep, but just enough to make its presence known. It was a dull throb that radiated up his jaw and behind his eye like old guilt, constant and wearying. He didn't know if it was a real infection or just one more physical echo of the stress bearing down on him, but it pulsed in time with the thoughts circling his skull like vultures.

He'd been watching them for close to an hour.

The group hadn't seen him, crouched above the rockfall on the low ridge that overlooked their temporary camp and tucked into the side of a thorny bush to break up the shape of his silhouette should any keen-eyed watcher decide to scan the skyline.

Yet they posted no sentries, just sat a loose collection of relaxed bodies and quiet conversation as they lounged around their camp.

They seemed unconcerned, but Dan's worry was exactly what they were waiting for.

A couple of them sat cross-legged with mess tins in hand. One had unfurled a map, dog-eared and creased, tracing lines with his finger as if working out future movements. Another cleaned a rifle like he was in no hurry but expected to need the weapon soon. These men weren't lost, weren't scavengers. They were preparing.

Fifteen of them, all armed but lacking even the most basic military sense. They acted like they weren't an invading force behind enemy lines and that bothered Dan. Their collectively relaxed demeanour made him doubt his instincts, even though they were screaming at him and blaring warning klaxons in his mind.

Dan's tongue prodded the broken molar again, feeling the sharp edge rubbing against its fractured twin. He winced.

How the hell did I let this happen? he thought, backing out of the bush to slink downhill away from the camp, heading for where he'd tethered his unwilling ride.

He felt uneasy about the presence of the strangers, but he was just as concerned about trying to silently remount the horse while Ash attempted his usual pantomime fight scene.

He rode in silence, boots loose in the stirrups, reins slack in his hand as the reluctant horse trudged along the chalky rutted track back to Sanctuary. Ash padded ahead with that rangy, low-slung gait, tail flicking and tongue lolling.

He was in a rush to get back, but Leah's warning not to push the mare who barely tolerated him bounced around his thoughts like an old school screensaver. He could tell she was tired, and instead of being angry with her and trying to force the pace up as he would push an engine, he allowed his own tiredness to dictate a safer choice, and the mare seemed to thank him for it by walking along and doing her best.

The warm breeze did nothing to ease the dryness in Dan's mouth or the tightening knot in his chest caused not by their slow progress home but by the fact that he didn't like what he'd seen out there.

Early summer had turned the hills dry and whispering. The grass had only just begun to lose its spring-green flush and dust kicked up from the roadway clung to his boots and coated the sweat-damp collar of his shirt. Above, the sun filtered through a haze that wasn't quite cloud, leaving the sky a dull milk-glass colour.

His thoughts returned to the group, to the odd stillness of them. The way they looked like men waiting for some kind of signal.

That's what this is, he thought. *They're waiting for a signal.*

Which meant whoever led them in had already set the plan in motion. It meant the enemy wasn't out *there* anymore, they were *inside*. Inside his home and among his people.

He couldn't prove any of this as much as he could logically explain the train of thought that led him to that conclusion, but somehow, he just *knew* that the troublesome newcomers spreading dissent among his people were all part of the same confusing shit storm he felt was about to make landfall.

He could smell it in the air the same way he could tell if it was going to rain, and still he couldn't put his finger on a single thing that would make anyone else believe him.

He slid from the saddle a hundred yards from the gates and walked the rest of the way after seeing open gates, preferring the quiet crunch of his boots to the rhythmic ache in his jaw. Ash trotted through the gates and stopped near the shadows just inside as Leah stepped out into the light with Nemesis in tow.

"Alright?" she asked.

Dan nodded once. "We need to talk."

Leah turned and spoke in low French to a teenager who ran forward to take the horse's bridle. Dan took his small pack and the rifle from the saddle holster before thanking the boy.

Only when he was ten paces away did Dan call out to him.

"She did well," he said, unsure if that was what a person said about a horse. "Give her some...some extra hay or something."

The kid nodded, accepting Dan's orders with a stoicism equal to being ordered to defend the gates to his last breath holding nothing but a spoon.

He turned to see Leah smiling at him. "What?"

His tone was snappy through exhaustion and embarrassment, but Leah knew him too well to be put off by that.

"Give her..." she said in a grand whisper, as if quoting Keates. "Some extra hay...*or something...*"

"Oh fuck off."

Leah smiled wider and jerked her head for Dan to follow, holding out a hand to take the big rifle from him. He let her, telling himself she could do with the exercise because the truth he understood about him feeling his age wasn't one he had the time to acknowledge right then.

They passed through the outer buildings, all quietly busy as they were at that time of the day. She led him not to the main fort, but towards the docks, winding their way between the small, stone-built dwellings and through a web of tight alleyways until she reached a wooden door in one wall. Leah opened the door and Dan stepped into the candle-lit interior where his friends were already gathered.

Marie, Neil, Mitch and Leah. His "old guard", and when he had that thought it stabbed him in the heart how many of his original, most trusted people were no longer in the game. Some had been left behind in England, some more had fallen along the way in one form or another, so as much as it warmed his heart to see the people he trusted with his life it also weighed it down with a heaviness no medicine could reverse.

Lucien was the only addition to the gathering who hadn't earned his place in the fiery crucible of traversing half the continent from north to south, but he had more than earned his spot among them. Plus, he was family now.

Neil poured from his unhealthily healthy supply of calvados and slid a dented cup across the table. Dan took it and swilled the liquor in his mouth, letting it sit on the bad tooth before swallowing. It burned like fire and felt earned.

"Are you okay?" Lucien asked, nodding at the grimace.

"Toothache."

Marie studied Dan for a moment but didn't press. He swallowed the drink and gave a theatrical grunt implying it was strong before he bent to kiss her on the cheek.

"Where are the kids?" he asked as he pulled a chair out from the table and began tearing open Velcro to release his vest's grip on flesh.

When Marie didn't answer immediately, Dan raised his head until he met her eyes. He looked from Marie to Leah, then to Lucien and back to Marie as neither his adopted daughter nor her husband would look at him

"Marie…where are the kids?" he asked again, carefully enunciating every word like he did when someone was about to regret something.

"They're in Andorra. With Carla Sofia Rovira," Marie said, not rolling the Rs in her usual sarcastic manner.

Dan didn't react at first, just blinked. "*Carla?*"

"Rafi's with them," Marie added. "Watching every move. Carla's not charmed by strangers, and she knows how to keep them at arm's length."

Dan sighed, not out of frustration but more to cover the time it took him to process what he'd just heard.

"Alright. If you trust her, I trust you," he said.

Lucien and Leah exchanged a brief look, and Dan recognised their interaction as one of them being proved wrong by the other.

"Really? You...you're okay with it?" Marie asked, evidently not being the only one around the table with an opinion on how Dan would react to the news.

"Yes. Carla's never given any of us a reason to distrust her," Dan said, sitting down and ticking off his points on the fingers of a raised hand. "She's only got a few of the bastards there to watch and enough dedicated people to make sure they won't be taking a run at replacing her, Rafi's there and I guarantee he'll bite the fucking face off *anyone* who tries to go near either of the kids, plus they're safer there right now than they are here. So yeah. I'm okay with it."

Neil leaned forward, bottle subtly tipping a little more of the strong apple spirit into Dan's cup. "So...what did you find?" he asked, clearly attempting to get their secret meeting back on track.

Dan exhaled slowly. "Fifteen, all male from what I can make out but you never know...all armed, and they're just...waiting. Like they're waiting for something specific. Or like they know more people are coming. They're complacent bit not disorganised – not a single sentry on duty like they don't expect to find trouble – but I'd bet my left nut they're not just passing through."

"What about the right one?" Neil asked before Leah could.

She let out the breath she'd sucked in to deliver the same line for Dan to ignore, sagging with disappointment because she'd been beaten to it.

"I argued with Polly," Marie said. "It got…*heated.* I don't think that's fixable right now."

She frowned, eyes fixed on nothing as she stared back into recent memory. "Yeah, I don't think it's fixable in any reality if I'm honest…"

"That bad?" Leah asked.

Marie pulled a "*girl, you don't know the half of it*" face and nodded.

Dan picked up his drink and lifted it to his mouth before he spoke. "Focus on what we can—" He winced and withdrew the cup, screwing his eyes shut for a moment. When he resumed his thought his voice shook a little.

"We can't afford to ignore this. If they're here to open the gates, to let something worse in…"

"Tooth?" Marie asked, but Dan waved her question away.

"Point is I'm ninety percent sure they're here for…what's the word?"

He looked at Neil and snapped his fingers as he thought.

"Nefarious?" Neil offered.

Dan's snapping turned into a pointed finger. "They're here for nefarious reasons," he finished.

"So why didn't you just shoot the bastards?"

All eyes turned to the speaker. Mitch looked unfazed by the shocked attention and shrugged his shoulders.

"Just statin' facts," he said unapologetically. "I'm guessin' the man had the high ground from his OP, and I'm guessin' he could've easily slotted every last one o'the bastards, am I wrong?"

The eyes collectively turned back to Dan.

"You're not wrong, but…"

"But you don't know for sure they're not just innocent travellers taking a break," Marie said. "And despite some people's beliefs, you're not a cold-blooded murderer."

Dan pulled a face that Marie chose to put down to toothache, but a brief silence lasted a fraction of a second too long to be ignored.

"Not without damn good reason," Dan admitted quietly, thinking of Joe's body hanging from a lamppost so many years ago and what he did in the aftermath.

He'd assured himself it was justice. That it was self-preservation. That he did what he did to protect other people. That by doing something so terrible he was ensuring their safety, but he knew the truth went deeper than that. He'd killed indiscriminately, and he'd done it not with a bullet or a blade but with fire. He'd locked people inside a burning building to live out their final minutes or seconds in abject horror, had heard them crying out to be saved, crying out for a bullet, crying out to curse him.

"Neil, haven't our little spies learned anything that could help?" Marie asked, clutching for a constructive shift in the tone.

Neil shook his head and lowered his own cup gently to the wooden tabletop. "Nope. Their lips are sealed tighter than a nun's chuff. They don't let a damn thing slip, which makes it all the more suspicious if you ask me. I mean, what group of people never discuss shared experiences?"

"The absence of proof doesn't constitute it though, does it?" Marie asked rhetorically. "Under other circumstances I'd be more than happy to seek some preventative justice here, but the truth is we *are* still outsiders and we could easily be turned out on our arses if we play this wrong. We need proof, or we need them to slip up in a way that they lose support. This isn't going to be tried in front of a judge. *We're* the ones on trial by public opinion."

"Which is why I'm going back out to watch and listen," Dan said finally, sitting up straighter as he climbed out of the mental black hole he'd re-entered during their chat.

"You're not bloody well going alone!" Leah said firmly.

"No," Mitch cut in. "He's not. I'm going with him."

Dan gave him a look, then nodded. "You're sure?" he asked, knowing Alita disliked him going far from home.

"I'm sure," Mitch replied. "It's time I got in the fight. Can't keep this place safe if some other bugger decides to invite the wolves into the damn henhouse."

Lucien didn't speak. Leah just rested a hand on Nemesis' flank. Marie crossed her arms but said nothing more as Dan stared at the cracks of light showing around the edges of the shuttered window. The light was fading outside, and Dan's mind conjured the long shadows that would already be stretching over the town.

"We'll go tonight," Mitch said confidently. "Quiet and fast. Find out what they're waiting for…and put a stop to it before it arrives."

"We go now," Dan insisted.

"Are you touched in the head, man?" Mitch shot back. "It's bad enough you went off like a one-man-band in daylight as it is, but now you wanna go *back*? When was the last time you slept?"

Dan opened his mouth to answer before he realised he didn't actually know.

"That's what I thought. No, we go at night and we do it properly. I'm talking NVGs and proper tactics, not cowboy shite."

"*Cowboy* shite?" Dan asked in a challenging tone borne of tiredness and toothache.

"Aye! You rode off into the sun on a bloody horse!"

Mitch's smile at the working simile was infectious, and Dan found himself mirroring the smile and shaking his head before the throbbing in his jaw reminded him it still existed.

"Alright," Mitch said, sliding back his chair and slapping both hands on his thighs before pointing a finger at Dan. "You get something to eat and get your head down. I'll see you at dusk."

Dan slid his cup towards Neil without looking, leaving it there even as the man poured a measure he deemed sufficient. Neil sighed, reserving only a small amount of judgement, then topped up the cup over halfway.

"You should see Sera," Lucien told Dan, speaking for the first time.

When everyone but him showed amusement in varying ways, Lucien looked confused until Leah explained.

"Trust me, *chéri*, Sera's the *last* person Dan wants going near a bad tooth with a pair of pliers," she chuckled.

At the mention of the words, Sera, tooth and pliers Dan visibly winced again.

"Or you could drink that and let me deal with it," Neil offered kindly, as if ripping out a tooth without anaesthetic was just the kind of minor favour mates did for one another. Like lending Dan a hedge trimmer from his shed.

"Or I could drink this," Dan said, taking a gulp and screwing his eyes shut again as the painful tooth was doused with a different kind of anaesthetic, "and you lot can all piss off!"

INTERROGATION

The moonlight barely reached the forest floor, fractured by tangled branches overhead. Dan lay on his stomach in the undergrowth, Ash beside him as still as stone, while Mitch crouched nearby, peering through the same knot of brambles Dan had chosen earlier that day.

Dan felt like death, as not only had the alcohol not dulled the pain as much as he'd hoped, but it had plagued him with uncomfortable sleep that was somewhere between consciousness and comatose but aware. When he finally gave up and hauled himself out of bed to wash and dress in fresh clothes, his nagging stomach complained that he'd not only neglected its needs but actively tried to poison it with apple flavoured disinfectant.

Marie had intuited his problem, as she usually did, and had gone down to the kitchens to personally make up a batch of soup he didn't need to chew.

He gulped down the soup in massive spoonfuls before asking if there was more, smiling as Marie produced two flasks of the same batch.

As the sun slipped deeper over the high hills to their left, Mitch and Dan rode slowly out of the gates with Ash loping loyally beside them.

"Would ya just *look* at 'em!" Mitch whispered. "All clustered like bloody cattle and no a bloody braincell among the bunch."

Dan agreed, watching the newcomers sitting close together around the embers of a low fire. Their gear was too clean and their confidence too easy. They weren't soldiers pretending to be settlers, but Dan knew in his bones they weren't innocent or harmless.

"You see my point? No sentries, no awareness, nothing…"

"We could take them," Mitch said. "Right now. End it before it starts."

Dan didn't answer. His tongue probed the fractured molar in his mouth, the pain a persistent companion these last few days, and no matter how hard he tried he couldn't leave it alone. He winced as the broken edge caught the inside of his cheek, the pain he triggered acting like smelling salts to sharpen his senses.

"They're just waiting," Mitch added. "For orders."

Dan's brow furrowed, but still he didn't respond.

"I say we flat-pack every one'o the bastards and be done wi'it," Mitch added, but still Dan didn't answer. "Did you hear what I said?"

"I heard you," Dan growled low. "But that's not how we do things!"

Mitch went quiet for a long time and Dan knew it was not because the man was cowed by his anger, but more that he was controlling his own.

"We wait," Dan said softly. "And we watch."

"For what? For one to stand up and give a bloody TED talk on how they plan to take our home?"

That was when one of the group stood and wandered away from the fire, a roll of tissue in hand and a sense of urgency to his gait.

"We wait for that," Dan said. "Come on."

They moved fast and silent, like wolves, until they found the man finishing up his task and tightening his belt. He checked behind him, kicking a paltry scuff of dirt and leaves over his deposit, then turned to freeze with a rifle barrel pressed under his chin.

"You've got two options," Dan said, voice low and cold. "Talk, or die."

The man's eyes were wide, and to Dan's massive surprise he spoke with a soft, English accent that reminded him of the home counties. He held the rifle in place with his right hand while his left patted at all the places a person hid a weapon, finding an old semi-automatic tucked in the back of his belt. Dan tossed it on the ground and shoved the man back a pace with the rifle barrel.

"Please...I didn't want *this*. I didn't ask to be part of this!" he blubbered, hands up in the dull moonlight.

"Then tell us what *this* is," Mitch snarled, emerging from the shadows to make the man flinch.

He tried to back away from Mitch who made no show of stopping, twisting the skin of his neck against the suppressor of Dan's rifle, but a low, ripping snarl from his other side completed the trifecta and froze him to the spot.

Dan forced himself to hide a smile. He hadn't planned or rehearsed this with Mitch, and Ash wasn't capable of learning any lines but the whole thing had fallen into place so perfectly, so frighteningly for the man, that half the work towards gaining a confession was already done.

The man sobbed, his shoulders shaking, and an acrid smell rising from his trousers despite having just been.

"You better start talking, laddie," Mitch said in a kind, fatherly way as he put a hand on the man's unresisting shoulder and forced him to sit with his back to a tree trunk. "And you better start soon, 'cause our dog's no been fed for a day..."

Dan, hearing Mitch's unplanned prompt, lowered his head in Ash's direction and hissed the command to watch him.

Ash shot forward and snapped his big teeth only inches from the terrified man's face making him stifle a sob.

"C-c-olonel Bowlack. He told us to come here. T-t-to blend in and wait. W-w-we're waiting for the signal to take control of some bloody town! It's strategic! There'll be no fighting if we do it right."

Dan stiffened. "Colonel *who*?"

"*Bow-Lack*. He's a real officer. From before, I mean. H-h-he has orders. We were told to wait, that's all I know, *I swear*."

"Orders from who?" Mitch pressed.

"From Carcassonne!"

"That's a *where*, not a *who*. Try harder."

"I don't *knowww!*" the man pleaded, almost crying as he dragged the word out. "He never said, just that we're part of something bigger."

He looked genuinely scared now, shaking and blubbering.

Dan exchanged a glance with Mitch.

Then the man's eyes flicked downward – towards the pistol in the dirt – and his hand moved.

Ash moved faster.

The dog hit him in the side, teeth clamping hard on his arm. The man began to shriek as Mitch raised his rifle to deliver one clean shot that stopped the screaming instantly.

"Leave it," Dan said. He recalled Ash, who hadn't let go of his target, on the assumption that a rifle round through his brain and both sides of his skull meant he was no longer a threat.

Mitch bent to rummage in the dead man's pockets, making a disgusted noise as his fingers discovered a wet patch, before he stood empty handed.

Dan turned to Mitch and sucked in a sharp breath, holding it as though he hadn't quite decided on the right words to use.

"What does *Bowlack* sound like to you, mate?" he asked in a conversational tone at great odds with their situation.

"It sounds exactly like you bloody think it sounds," Mitch retorted angrily. "So *now*...and I'm asking very politely mind you, *now* can we go back and flat-pack every one'o the bastards and be done wi'it?"

Dan hefted his rifle with purpose and locked eyes with Mitch. "Yes we can."

They turned to retrace their victim's steps, secure in their assertion that they were ambushing an enemy force and not merely murdering innocent travellers.

They didn't speak again until they rode through Sanctuary's gate in the grey light of the following dawn.

SCORCHED EARTH

Leah and Marie waited on the walls at sunrise, both of them with their hands tucked under their armpits to save their hands from a chilly morning breeze.

"You think she's okay?" Leah asked, referring to her baby daughter in faraway Andorra.

Not far by old world standards, but it might as well have been a thousand miles in their current situation.

"You know they are," Marie answered, adding her own son and Leah's younger brother to the conversation without any hostility intended. "You read the message too."

Leah had. Rafi had been sending two pigeons per day back to Neil – morning and night – and each message had been reassuringly boring about life in the mountains.

"You want to tell me about your fight with Polly?" Leah asked, changing the subject.

Marie stiffened and breathed in loudly through her nose, holding the breath like she was considering how best to answer.

The previous morning Marie had walked through the main fort when she heard her name called. The clipped, urgent tone was unmistakably Polly's voice, and the way Marie was feeling right then she wasn't of a mind to back down from a fight. She stopped just short of the room they sometimes used for meetings, exhaled hard through her nose, and stepped inside.

Polly was already pacing, arms folded tight across her chest like she was holding herself in.

"We need to talk," Polly snapped. "*Now.*"

"Alright," Marie said evenly, closing the door behind her. "Go on."

"You need to back off," Polly blurted. "You, Dan *and* Leah."

Marie raised an eyebrow. When she spoke she heard the polite sarcasm ringing a challenge. "Back off from *what* exactly, Polly?" she asked, as if she didn't already know.

"From *everything*," Polly snapped, voice rising. "This place, the decisions affecting my people...every time someone speaks out, you shut them down. Dan doesn't even have to *do* anything anymore. He just looks at you and you do it for him."

"Is that really what you think?" Marie asked, allowing her tone to match Polly's. "You *asked* him to step in. You practically *begged* him to take over the way I recall!"

"*That was before!*" Polly yelled. "Before we got turned into some...some *dictatorship* in the name of safety. Before everything had to go through one of *you* to be agreed. Before we started pretending like anyone who questions *the great and all-powerful Dan* isn't worth listening to!"

Marie's jaw tightened, but she held her ground. "Polly, where's this coming from?"

Polly scoffed. "You know *exactly* where it's coming from, you just don't like it. You don't like that someone's actually listening to *me* now. That someone treats *me* like I matter."

"You mean Beaulac." Marie said the name like an accusation.

Polly didn't answer, but the heat in her cheeks said enough.

Marie folded her arms. "So that's what this is. You're smitten with the first man who shows you attention and suddenly we're the enemy?"

"*Excuse me?*"

"Which part didn't you understand?" Marie asked affably.

Polly's eyes flashed. "*Smitten?!* Don't you *dare* reduce it to that. Claude treats people like equals. He doesn't act like...like a *king.*"

"He's manipulating you, Polly," Marie said, letting a little more edge creep into her voice. "And you're so desperate to feel important you can't even see it. He's saying what you want to hear, and you're eating it up like you've never been fed the truth before."

"You think I'm stupid?"

"I think you're blinded," Marie shot back. "And maybe you need to ask yourself *why.* Maybe it's his voice. That accent? Maybe it reminds you of home. Of your father maybe?"

Marie knew it was a low-blow, and that she'd gone against her own ethical code by using basic psychoanalysis as a weapon against someone, but Polly was lost, and the things she were saying were dangerous.

Polly flinched like she'd been slapped, then stepped forward fast, eyes wide and furious. "*You don't get to talk about him!*"

Marie didn't back down; she doubled down and laughed. "No? You want the truth? You've been cosying up to someone dangerous because it makes you feel safe, and you're turning on the people who actually *are.* You think we're the problem? That we want to be *worshipped?* Jesus fucking Christ, Polly...you handed over leadership because you said you weren't fit for it, and now you're calling us tyrants?"

"You *are!*" Polly screamed. "You've taken over everything, and anyone who doesn't agree just disappears!"

Marie stared at her, the words ringing in her ears. "That's not true and you know it."

"Isn't it?" Polly spat. "*You* want control, *Dan* wants control, *Leah* wants control and you'll burn this whole place down to keep it."

Marie shook her head slowly, angry at how disillusioned the woman she called a friend had become. "You're wrong, Polly. About all of it…and right now you're too stupid to see it."

She turned and left, swallowing the shaking in her chest, slamming the door harder than she meant to behind her.

A second later, something heavy smashed against the wall inside.

~

"So…yeah…pretty scorched Earth on both sides of the fence," she told Leah, sounding almost ashamed of herself now that the emotions had settled.

"Sounds to me like she deserved a slap," Leah offered, making Marie crack a sad smile.

"And there's your father talking…"

Leah didn't shoot anything back as Marie expected, and when she looked at the young woman beside her to check she hadn't actually offended her she saw her squinted gaze locked onto the road leading up and away from their home.

Marie looked too, making out two darker shapes in the early morning gloom. Just as she held her breath waiting for confirmation of her husband's safe return, a smaller shape on four fast legs ran ahead of the two men on horseback to make both women relax.

Dan and Mitch trotted their horses through the gates and slid from their saddles, one man looking stiff and unhappy while the other seemed fresh. Marie and Leah exited the stone staircase in time for Dan to order the tired militia guards to close the gates and bar them.

Marie looked at Dan and recognised the storm brewing behind those blue eyes. It was a look she'd seen before, and she felt her chest tighten because it never ended well for everyone when she saw it.

Mitch unstrapped a large satchel from where he'd lashed it behind his saddle, heaving the strap over his shoulder and looking to Dan for orders.

"Gather everyone," Dan said, his eyes fixed on Marie's.

"What happened?"

Dan glitched, not mentally prepared to explain it now when he was still rehearsing the grand reveal in his head, so he reached inside his vest and pulled out a folded piece of paper to hand it to her.

Leah crowded her, looking over her shoulder as the words written in French were mentally translated. While both could speak the language passably, reading colloquial French was something that took time to process.

"That *bastard*," Marie breathed eventually.

"My sentiments exactly," Dan growled.

~

The large satchel of confiscated weapons thumped onto the ground in front of the people of Sanctuary, before a folded piece of paper followed it.

Dan raised his voice. "These were carried by *your* friends," he said, left index finger levelled at Beaulac's face across the large hall. "Orders, signed by *Colonel* Claude Fucking Bollock, to make camp nearby and wait for a signal to take control of this town."

Gasps, murmurs, shouts. Beaulac stood at the back of the crowd, arms folded, a half-smile curling his lips.

Dan glared at him, incensed by his casual insolence. "Anything to say, you piece of shit?"

Beaulac stepped forward, smile widening, to shrug so effortlessly Dan felt the fingers of his right hand twitch as though he'd inadvertently sent the signals from his brain to draw a weapon and shoot him in the face.

"Only that you're too late," Beaulac said.

Polly broke from the crowd that issued a collective gasp, her face pale and her pleading eyes wet with fresh tears.

"Tell me this isn't true," she hissed, turning on Dan and raising her voice. "You're lying. Tell everyone you're lying! You forged that!"

Dan followed the direction of her pointed finger to the piece of paper and back to Beaulac, not wanting to take his eyes off the man and cursing his tiredness for allowing the momentary distraction.

Beaulac looked at Polly and softened his expression before cupping her cheek with surprising tenderness. "*None* of it was real," he whispered. "But it *can* be. Help us remove the...*obstacles*. There needs to be no bloodshed over a result that's inevitable."

She slapped his hand away. "*Va te faire foutre.*"

French speakers flinched, and even Dan didn't need a translation for that one. He let out a huff of laughter at the savagery of Polly – sweet, timid, mildly spoken and kind Polly – telling a man almost twice her size to go fuck himself.

Beaulac's expression hardened. "You're all making a mistake," he growled ominously.

"*Actually,*" Dan said, drawing the word out like some basement-dwelling online moderator weighing close to twenty stone criticising weightlifting techniques on the internet. "The mistake was yours by coming here in the first place."

"Ha! You want another round, Mister Big Shot? Still fancy yourself king of the fuckin' hill?"

Dan smiled. He gave himself a rapid, honest assessment – he was exhausted from barely getting any sleep in the last week, and the pressure throbbing deep in his lower jaw told him he wasn't at full physical ability even if he was rested.

What he did have were his rifle and pistol, he had armed backup, and he had two hungry land sharks on standby. He wasn't a man to back down from that kind of goading no matter what.

Dan stepped forward, but Marie cut between them.

"That's what I thought!" Beaulac laughed mockingly. "Go hide behind your woman, *Dan*."

Dan moved to step around Marie and plant the muzzle of his rifle in Beaulac's throat, but his adversary's smile vanished. Beaulac lunged, grabbing a young woman from the crowd who screamed as he pulled a small pistol and buried the muzzle in her side.

"Here's what's going to happen," Beaulac roared over the uproar breaking out all around them. "We're walking out of here, and you're not doing a damn thing about it!"

Dan's hands twitched and the rifle was up in his shoulder in a second, red dot resting on Beaulac's forehead, but the invader's people had acted fast. As one they made a dive for the captured weapons, snatching them up to form a loose perimeter around their leader.

"Mitch?" Dan asked, not needing to explain what he wanted to know.

"I wouldn't," the Scotsman said, his own rifle trained on Beaulac.

Dammit! Dan thought, not blaming Mitch but cursing himself for not unloading the captured weapons or insisting they were emptied.

Shouts, screams, the barking of dogs all merged in the cacophony with loud orders in English and French to drop the weapons.

The big man with the shitty grin called Bastin – the one who'd taken Dan out with a chair and cracked his tooth before sucker punching Leah in the face – proved he wasn't anywhere near as dumb as he looked by snapping back the charging handle on the rifle he held, ejecting a live round to be sure the chamber carried a lethal payload.

He aimed the rifle at Dan and smiled, but the smile wavered when he was forced to blink and break eye contact for the laser pointer dancing across his eyeballs.

Searching for the source of his annoyance he looked up to where Lucien rested a large rifle over the railing of the upper level. He never usually used the visible dot, finding it more useful to indicate something than to use it as a targeting aid, but the psychological warfare aspect to it impressed Dan.

"*Dan? Oui ou non?*" Lucien called out.

Dan's mind flashed fast, and oddly his first thought was gratitude for Lucien using the most basic French possible so he didn't have to think. It registered just as fast as English would have, but Dan didn't answer immediately.

His mind spun with angles and educated guesswork, coming to the only conclusion he could.

"No," he said, loudly and clearly while not taking his eyes off the smiling bastard Beaulac.

The calculations had been him trying to figure out if he could somehow get all of his people to fire, somehow coordinate their aim to be on a single enemy skull each, but he knew it wouldn't work. Best-case scenario was that the young woman would die, and die horribly from a small calibre pistol bullet through her guts from the side.

Worst case scenario involved all of their rounds over-penetrating – a near certainty given their close proximity – and the collateral damage turning their dining hall into a charnel house.

Marie intuited it too, even though her hands were wrapped around the grip of a Glock that didn't shake one bit.

"Let them go," she said, her words carrying the full weight of her natural authority.

Beaulac smiled, tempting Dan to say to hell with collateral damage just to see the bastard dead, but he was still a clear mile away from that critical level of containment loss.

Beaulac didn't move, like he was waiting for Dan to shoot him or give the order himself just to add humiliation to the grievous wounds he'd inflicted on Sanctuary and her people.

A young man, yelling and sobbing with incoherent fear and rage, fought with two people holding him back as he screamed the name of the young woman over and over.

Dan saw it, saw the pain of love threatened by unnatural mortality, and his resolve returned in full strength.

"No. Get the fuck out. All of you," Dan said in a hard, flat tone.

REGRET

Beaulac smiled graciously, even offered a sarcastic bow of his head, as their huddle of people shuffled toward the door.

People still shouted on both sides of the battle, with guns shoved in faces and threats snarled as those deemed too close were pushed away.

Dan followed, weapon always trained on Beaulac's head in case any opportunity arose to drop him like a hot rock.

The slow, shuffling procession covered the short distance to the main gates amid more shouting, more promises of retribution, and more laughter from the invaders as their fraught nerves drove them to act with suicidal arrogance.

"Nobody fire!" Dan warned, still following with Ash pressed to his leg and the rifle tucked hard into his shoulder.

"Open the gate," Beaulac snapped. "We walk, *or she dies.*"

He underlined his point by forcing the muzzle of the pistol hard onto the girl's side, making her cry out in fear and pain as the front of her blue dress turned dark.

Marie's voice cut through the noise when she called to the militia guarding the locked gate. "*Ouvrez-la!* Open it! Let them go!"

The two guards jumped to comply, lifting away the heavy locking beam before pushing the doors wide open and standing back hesitantly, gripping their rifles with no idea just what in the hell was going on.

Dan's jaw clenched when they reached the threshold. "He won't let her go."

Beaulac, either miraculously able to hear him through the din or just intuiting his logic, confirmed it with a nod. "She goes free when I'm out of range."

Dan followed them through the gate and stopped, flipping over the scope on his rifle to magnify the image. He tried not to focus on the girl who had given up screaming and fighting to break free of Beaulac's iron grip. She meekly shuffled along, walking backwards with uncoordinated steps as if she'd decided to remain a human shield forever.

Dan still watched through the scope, ignoring the noise all around him, until Beaulac stopped near the crest of the hill and filled his lungs to shout back, carefully pronouncing each word to be sure the message carried clearly back to the gates.

"This is not your home. Le Maréchal is coming…and you – *outsider* – will learn what it means to be unwelcome in France."

Dan kept the crosshairs steady on Beaulac's skull. His finger held tension in the trigger but he didn't fire, although it took every last shred of restraint and self-control to keep that final ounce of pressure out of that hooked finger.

Minutes passed. Then, over the rise, the girl appeared sprinting and sobbing as she fell, got up, fell again to repeat the process halfway back to her home before the man so torn up by her capture met her halfway and scooped her up.

She collapsed into her lover's arms, but as Dan flicked on the safety of his rifle and lowered it, he found himself the subject of close scrutiny from an older man. Dan recognised him, knew now that he recognised the girl as his daughter, and through red-rimmed, tear-stained eyes the old man looked right through him, not in blame, but in demand.

A demand for vengeance.

"Dan, I'm really fuckin' sorry, man. That was mah fault, I should—"

"No mate. It was as much mine as yours," Dan said, meaning every word.

"I wish you'd shot the bastard," Marie said out of unhelpful frustration beside him.

"Me too," Dan said.

The sound of hooves and Leah snapping at people to move in French, utilising some of the more colourful phrases Dan had memorised to speed up her progress.

She stopped beside Dan and held out the reins of a horse that eyed him suspiciously.

"No, kid," Dan said.

Even without looking he could tell she was pulling a face at him, but he knew she was still young enough and not yet wise enough to choose good sense over action.

Just like he'd been.

Mitch saved him the trouble of explaining.

"Those bastards'll have ambushes waitin' at every bend from here to Timbuk-bloody-tu. You'll sooner catch a bullet than you'll catch them."

Before she could open her mouth, an echoing report of a single gunshot rolled over them.

Lucien's legs burned as much as his lungs screamed for mercy. The large rifle was not a weapon built for running with, and especially not in the tight confines of the stone stairs carved into the mountain itself.

He tried to think for the first few hundred steps, tried to calculate how long it would take for someone to walk out of the gates and away from their town, but he got only as far as the gates in his imagination before his body protested at being pushed too hard.

Exploding into the fresh air he gasped, stumbling into the sunlight to suck in clean oxygen and startle the two people standing bored sentry in their high fort.

Lucien ignored their startled questions, running past them the second he caught his breath to where the walls overlooked the last part of the approach road with a commanding view.

He saw them, already disappearing out of sight, and tried to force his shaking hands to be still as he rested the barrel on the ancient stones and tried to locate his targets in the scope.

His vision was blurry and his entire body trembled as his chest heaved huge gulps of air into his body. Every part of him shook from exhaustion, but he had only seconds to make a difference.

"Shut up! Why are you laughing?" Beaulac snapped in French at two of his people who found something amusing.

To him there was nothing amusing at all, and for minutes – long, terrifying minutes – he'd expected Dan to execute him no matter the consequences. He controlled his fear, releasing it as anger on his people who acted like children, and yelled at them to run faster and laugh less.

He wanted to be long gone from this valley before they decided to come hunting, decided to loose their dogs on them and chase them through the rolling countryside.

He fully expected to hear the thunder of hoofbeats in the distance, to hear the snarling of dogs, but when no pursuit came he began to hope he would survive.

Eager to reinforce his leadership over the gathering of idiots he'd chosen for the task, Colonel Claude Beaulac turned on the two who began laughing again, pinning the big Bastin to the spot with an angry growl and a pointed finger. The man went still, dropped the grin, and waited to take his abuse like a man.

"I *told you* to stop *laughi—*"

Beaulac blinked, unable to comprehend the warm, fine mist covering his face. He blinked harder to clear the pink haze from his vision, spitting to rid his tongue of a metallic taste, but when he tried to restart his speech he realised Bastin was no longer there.

His body was, at least it was on the ground leaking an impossible volume of blood onto the dusty roadway from a ruined neck that trailed scraps of shattered skull.

Bastin's right leg twitched like he was still trying to move, to outrun a bullet, when reality dawned on Beaulac and he yelled at his people to run.

AFTERMATH

Dan stood on the ramparts above the gates to Sanctuary, brooding silently as Leah stood by ten paces away. She knew he liked to stand on the ancient defences while he thought, and she knew he didn't like being crowded so she waited.

Ash sensed the building thunder in his friend also, and responded by lying down with his chin resting on his front paws while his eyes tracked every tense step of Dan's restless boots.

Nemesis was the only living thing on those walls not to be in a kind of wary standby mode waiting for Dan to get his mental ducks in a row and decide what to do next.

He stopped and dug into the leg pocket of his trousers to retrieve the tin of rolled cigarettes, cursing as he opened it and found none ready to light.

He switched the tin for the pouch of tobacco – a thing of leather so old it was as supple as skin – and with hands trembling through adrenaline and anger he did exactly what Leah expected him to and made a mess of his first attempt.

"Fuckin'…*shit!*" Dan snarled, hurling the torn paper and lump of tobacco over the wall to scatter in the breeze.

Leah said nothing, simply pushed herself off the wall and held out a beckoning hand.

"I *can* do it, you know?" he snapped, his face sagging as soon as the words had left his mouth.

His shoulders followed the collapse of tension in his face, and with a muttered apology he handed the pouch over to Leah who began to roll with delicate, dextrous fingers.

She wasn't upset, wasn't offended, because she knew the man better than just about anyone. Almost as well as Marie, although her two adoptive parents shared a different dynamic. Dan allowed himself to be vulnerable with Marie, whereas with Leah he always tried to shield her from the adult responsibility even though she was in her early twenties now.

She finished her task and handed it over, keeping the pouch and asking for the tin in return for the rolled cigarette. Dan complied, lighting the smoke and resuming his pacing as Leah began resupplying his tin.

"You can stop going over it in your head now," Leah said after another minute of watching him suck angrily on the smoke and pace up and down.

"Easier said than done," he grumbled.

Leah hid a small smile, knowing that was him admitting that he was, in fact, kicking himself for the things he could've and should've done differently.

"It's done now. Think about what comes next instead what could've gone differently."

Dan stopped and looked at Leah, his face registering mild shock at remembering that she was an adult now and possessed more than enough life experience to offer many such pearls of wisdom.

Before he could summon a response, his eyes flickered to movement from the stone stairs. Leah's head snapped around to acquire a target lock, only she relaxed when her young husband walked into view with the long rifle slung over one shoulder.

"Where did you go?" Dan asked him

Lucien walked closer, his cheeks flushed pink. He was still out of breath when he arrived beside them to rest the rifle against the stone wall and sink down so sit with his back resting beside it.

Sweat clung to his temples, and the front of his shirt was soaked through, half stuck to his chest. He was breathing hard, but he smiled like he was charged up, still riding the aftershock of violence.

Dan's eyes narrowed in Lucien's direction, arms folded and body angled like a man expecting bad news.

"I took the stairs," Lucien said simply, not waiting to be asked. "I guessed they might not let Camille go, so I went to the fort."

Dan didn't move, but his face twitched as he worked out how far his son-in-law had run and how many steps that run involved.

"And?" Leah asked.

Lucien smiled. "I made it just in time...It seems that *Bastin*" – he spat the word with undisguised hatred – "lost 'is 'ead."

"Wait, *what?*" Leah's voice cut the air. Sharp. Disbelieving.

Lucien gave a one-shouldered shrug, the corner of his mouth twitching with something too dry to be amusement.

"I 'ad, how you say...*du bœuf*...with 'im, too, no?"

Dan stared at the young man, jaw clenched as everything began falling into place.

Leah folded her arms more tightly, fingers digging into her sleeves with an expression dark as thunderclouds. "*I* wanted to kill him," she snapped.

"Yeah. Me too," Dan grumbled.

"What is the thing you say? Right place, right time?"

Dan turned to stare up at the fort, recalling the painful memories of climbing the stone staircase under immense pressure while already exhausted. He looked back at Lucien and wondered if he'd have been able to match his speed twenty-plus years ago carrying a rifle, then being able to make the shot at the top.

"That was you? The gunshot?" he asked, having already convinced himself that one of Beaulac's people had fired into the air to signal some group he hadn't known about.

Lucien closed his eyes and nodded smugly, making Dan look back up at the fort in case the climb in his memory had suddenly become any easier. When it didn't, he looked back to Lucien.

"Fuck me…nice work!"

Lucien placed his right hand flat on his chest and bowed his head to graciously accept the praise.

Leah knelt down beside him, face still like thunder, and stared closely into his eyes.

"I told you *I* wanted to kill him," she said, before bending to kiss her husband fiercely. "But I'm proud of you," she said, leaning back and letting him breathe again.

Neil appeared then, moving with a stiff, hurried pace in their direction along the ramparts. His face was pale, the lines around his eyes set hard, and everything about his appearance spelled trouble.

"Where the fuck've you been?" Dan demanded. "You missed everything!"

Neil looked at each of them in turn, then lowered his voice. "Sorry…news from Andorra."

Dan's expression darkened to something nearing murderous as he read the note Neil thrust out towards him.

"Got a pigeon," Neil explained pointlessly.

Dan's eyes roved over the words but Leah's stare bored holes into Neil's soul and made him summarise out loud.

"They caught the strangers plotting to take the kids. Rafi found weapons in their stuff too."

221

Leah's posture changed to alert and dangerous.

"And?" Dan's voice was low, the words on the note forgotten in favour of Neil's explanation.

Neil's mouth worked for a second before he spoke. "Carla made the call. They're gone. Rafi handled it."

Leah said nothing. Dan just nodded once, slowly.

"Good."

Word reached both Carla and Rafi at the same time from the spy network deployed to keep tabs on everything the strangers said or did. The two met randomly in a hallway as they went in search of one another, and while Carla was clearly annoyed that Rafi had been informed either before or at the same time she had, she let it go on account of there being much bigger problems to deal with.

"They said it, word for word," Rafi told her in Spanish. "After Marie left the kids behind it must have been obvious something was going on, and I think this is their plan to gain leverage."

"I agree," Carla answered in her their native tongue. "But I swore I'd protect those kids with my life."

"I did too," Rafi responded darkly.

"They are safe?" Carla asked as the two of them walked fast.

"I have three men with them now, and the two women with babies are there too."

Carla opened her mouth to ask if Rafi trusted those three men, but she knew him well enough that he wouldn't have left them there if his trust wasn't absolute.

They turned a corner and went outside, crossing the street to a small hotel where the three strangers had been given a large room to share.

"Do we need more people?" Carla asked, but Rafi shook his head and handed her one of the two pistols he carried.

She took it confidently, checked the chamber for the glint of brass just as she'd been taught, and nodded to him.

Rafi didn't knock, he simply barged in to prompt a scream from the woman, a strangled cry from a man lying flat on his back, while the third man jumped up and began shouting in French.

"*Putain, qu-est-ce t—*"

Rafi grabbed him by his jacket and planted a vicious headbutt into the bridge of his nose.

There was a wet crunch, a louder scream from the woman, then Rafi turned his attention on the man who'd been sleeping when the door nearly came off its hinges.

Carla silenced the woman by levelling the pistol confidently at her face, but Rafi's anger was up and he didn't seem to be in the mood to accept a surrender.

The man on the bed scrambled away to the floor on uncoordinated limbs, begging "*Non! Non!*" as Rafi lifted one corner of the single bed and tipped it on top of him. Grabbing a boot he dragged the man out, betraying a terrifying strength fuelled by rage.

Rafi hit him in the face to stop him pleading for mercy, then again twice more until he gave up trying to defend himself and lay still save for a heaving chest and blood gurgling from his mouth.

Switching off the rage as fast as it had risen, he turned to see Carla holding the woman at gunpoint with her hands held meekly up in defeat.

Rafi nodded, reached into his vest and flipped both half-conscious men over onto their front where he yanked plastic zip ties hard around their wrists. He checked Carla had the third one under control before he started tossing the room.

He didn't search like a racoon on meth, just tossing things everywhere like they used to do on television shows, but instead he went straight to the best hiding places. Not the obvious ones, but the places a smart person would hide something.

Thirty seconds later he came back with two pistols and a small flare gun – the kind found on small boats for emergency use – and unloaded them onto the only unoccupied bed still the right way up.

"You have three seconds to begin speaking, or I shoot you in your left foot," Carla told the woman in French.

She spoke in a tone that Rafi very much believed, as did the terrified woman who began spilling every detail of the plan they'd concocted.

Ten minutes later, with only one further threat of violence being required, both Andorrans were left angrier than when they'd started.

The strangers had seen Marie leave, had known some urgent message arrived probably by pigeon, and deduced that their plan to take Sanctuary was reaching critical mass. Unsure what to do, the three of them decided to kidnap the children and steal a vehicle, join up with their own side, and use them as leverage to secure ownership of the town.

"W-hat are you going to do with me?" the trembling woman asked.

"What are going to *do* with you?" Carla shot back, eyeing Rafi for any indication of his feelings.

"I say we just shoot them now," Rafi said, responding to a grunt of fear from the man with the flattened nose by kicking him hard in the gut.

"No," Carla said, gun still levelled at the woman and eyes still narrowed. "They have to go."

The woman looked relieved and began to thank Carla, but the heavy barrel of the pistol slashed quickly to smash her in the side of the head.

The truck wound up the narrow road toward the ridge, tyres crunching through loose stone, the silence inside colder than the wind outside. The prisoners – all three of them bound at the wrists – hunched low in the back under the watchful, malevolent gaze of Rafi.

Only one of them met his eyes, although the eyes streamed from the ruined nose and burned with indignation. The other two were silent bar the occasional sob from the woman, and the frightened mutterings of the man who'd woken to a fury that had left him battered and afraid.

That man began to pray, and Rafi only smiled when he heard the pleas to God to save them.

"Will you at least give us food and water?" Broken Nose asked sullenly, his voice muted and nasal.

Rafi said nothing, just smiled with a jaw set like granite.

Carla stopped the truck at the edge of their territory, looking down over the mountain road weaving southeast. The peaks rose around them like jagged teeth, the wind whipping her coat and tugging at her short hair as she climbed out and opened the tailgate.

"Out," she snapped, her eyes hard.

They filed out slowly, awkwardly. Bound hands and trembling legs trying to portray vulnerable innocence.

Carla didn't look at them at first. She just stared beyond them, down the mountain and all the way into her memories. Without a word she turned them roughly around and used a small knife to cut their restraints. They rubbed at sore wrists, made pained sounds, and turned to give them stares of mixed anger and fear.

Carla pointed the knife out with her left hand without taking her eyes off them. "France is that way. *Go.*"

Behind her Rafi was resolute and unmoving like a statue.

Hesitantly the three strangers began to edge away toward the road when Carla spoke again.

This time she sounded wistful, almost nostalgic. "You know…I once let a dangerous man go on this very road, just as I am letting you go now."

All of them turned and met her eyes as if spellbound by her words. "That was a mistake, and I promised I would never make that mistake again."

Rafi drew a pistol.

The crack of three gunshots was whipped away by the wind, echoing off the stone like an afterthought.

Carla stood for a moment, staring at the three bodies before she turned back to the cab. "Send a pigeon," she told Rafi. "They need to know what has happened."

The ramparts above Sanctuary's gate hadn't changed in the years since Dan first stood watch there. The same view. The same wind.

Leah sat cross-legged on the stone, flanked by both dogs, casually rolling cigarettes into Dan's battered old tin while he paced.

"I don't like not knowing," Dan muttered.

"You never did."

"This *Maréchal*...whoever he is. He's not just some regional thug. He's organised. Dangerous. He didn't send Beaulac here to win. He sent him to see if we were worth bothering with."

Leah handed him a cigarette. "And now he knows."

Dan lit it, took a long drag and stared off at the horizon. "Big players wear crowns. Or they think they do."

Leah raised an eyebrow.

Dan exhaled slowly. "Time we reminded the world how to cut off the fucking head."

I SPY

No official war council was called, but that's what their meeting became nonetheless.

In the high-ceilinged room that at one time had been a library, six of them gathered around a heavy, old table littered with maps, ink stains, and the ghosts of history stretching back as far as the seventh century.

Sanctuary had been a stronghold through hundreds of years under the Counts of Roussillon, the Knights Templar and the Kings of Majorca; had been besieged and surrendered; had existed through Revolution and continent-wide war. The very room they occupied had seen the Spanish take possession from the French, only to see that ownership reversed after a siege.

The town may have become a protected tourist attraction before their arrival, but centuries of tension had bled into the walls just as it did now. In more recent history it had been of minor importance but couldn't remain unaffected. Many of the residents had marched north in the early part of the previous century, and the memorial standing in the town paid respects to the names who did so and didn't return.

Some years later, when the war to end all wars had merely been a premonition of further bloodshed, Sanctuary had been a conduit for people fleeing persecution, for those smuggled to safety by the resistance, and had been a hub of partisan activity. It had been bombed by German forces to deny the allies use of the port, had been occupied and garrisoned by Nazis, used as a place where both the brave and the unlucky were imprisoned and interrogated, before events further north forced their retreat.

It had not always been a place of conflict, however. Many of the historical information boards had been left where they stood, and they had been pleasantly surprised to know Picasso had visited there, as had many other famous artists seeking inspiration, just as Dan sought some spark of inspiration himself.

He leaned over a folded map that had been annotated so many times the paper looked like patchwork. Lines had been drawn and drawn again, areas shaded with hatch-marked lines and routes laid out. Dan stared at it until the lines blurred and his brain couldn't make out what his eyes tried to show it.

Leah stood behind him with her arms folded tight, not for warmth but to keep from fidgeting out of frustration. Marie perched on the edge of a chair, legs crossed and one foot twitching restlessly while Mitch, fresh back from a perimeter check, smelled of sweat as he hunched over with a pencil tucked behind one ear.

Lucien stood to one side, hands on both hips and lips drawn tight as he thought, making him look older than was. Neil, as ever, had the look of a man trying to keep a dozen plates spinning while someone kept handing him more crockery.

"Sanctuary's fine," Dan said, more to himself than anyone else. "Thick walls, high ground, and enough firepower to handle anything barring a main battle tank. If we—"

"Oh, we can handle one," Mitch interrupted with a dangerous smirk on his face. "Just not *two*."

Leah's expression didn't shift, but she gave a small grunt of agreement.

Dan saw the look on Mitch's face and didn't doubt the blood-thirsty truth behind his smile. He hadn't seen him so fired up for action since pirates came calling and his family's safety was threatened.

"If we're attacked here," Dan went on, "it'll be a fucking siege, and we're the ones with the food, water and ammunition."

"Plus we've got boats and enough people to land a strong force further down the coast to properly fuck up their supply lines," Mitch added. "Not to mention the fort...I don't see any siege lasting long when it starts raining seven-six-two around the clock, eh?"

"Exactly," Dan agreed. "So it doesn't make sense for them to come at us directly, plus their *indirect* approach didn't work, so..."

"The farm and the orchards?" Mitch said, tapping the map. "If the bastards know about *them*..."

"That's the question," Neil said. "*Do* they know?"

"You think that being here for weeks didn't teach them anything?" Leah asked rhetorically. "You think people didn't talk to them? That they didn't see wagons and trucks coming and going?"

"We can't take that chance, can we?" Marie asked, voice quiet but steady. "We have to assume they know about both places, and it tracks logically that they'll use that as a way to gain control in the area. A lost summer's crop would affect everyone; not just us here, but Andorra and every other place within miles. *Everyone*. Next winter will be lean without those preserves, and the livestock can't be replaced without a few years of breeding."

"*Lean* doesn't cut it," Neil said solemnly. "Try catastrophic. We'll be on starvation rations eating nothing but fish...And a few years? It'll take us close to a *decade* to replace that kind of loss. It'll put people in danger having to travel and catch replacements too, and while we've got people off in trucks or boats looking for wild sheep and pigs they aren't fishing or farming or defending…losing the farm would cripple the whole region. No two ways about it."

Dan stood straight and exhaled through his nose, running both hands back through his hair until they caught on the rough collar of his jacket. He paced to the fire and stared into it.

"Okay…so we have to assume they're aware of both places, and we have to assume the fuckers know where to find them," Dan said, turning back. "Andorra can look after themselves. They've got numbers, weapons and the terrain to funnel attackers. I say we let them handle their own defence."

Leah raised an eyebrow and glanced at Marie. When the older woman said nothing she turned to look at her husband who spoke up before she did.

"I don't need to remind you that we 'ave…a *stake* in 'ow well Andorra can defend 'erself."

"The facts are not lost on me, Lucien," Dan answered with a cold formality. "But if it makes everyone feel better…Neil? Can you check in with Rafi and see if they need any hardware or advice on how to fortify? I'd recommend a stronger guard on the mountain road, sentries on high ground with line of sight on the approach road and blocking the tunnel with something nasty."

Neil nodded, understanding his task and no doubt having a few ideas for the "something nasty" element.

"The farm and the orchards we *can't* afford to lose," Dan continued. "We post twelve militia between the two and I want twice-daily check-ins by pigeon. Any sign of movement, we roll out a QRF in trucks: hard and fast."

"What is this…*QRF?*" Lucien asked.

"Quick reaction force," Mitch told him. "A bunch of our people on standby ready to rock around the clock."

"Ah, *une force d'intervention rapide. D'accord.* And 'ow do we do this?"

Lucien frowned in thought for a few seconds. When he spoke his tone wasn't defeatist, but pragmatic.

"So...I lose twelve people to guard the outposts, and the same again for this QRF? 'ow do I keep enough people on the walls?"

"It's called overtime," Dan answered, sounding short on patience for explaining things he felt were obvious. "You extend duty hours, cancel days off, you tell anyone who complains to suck it the fuck up and you make it work."

The two most important men in Leah's life stared at each other for a beat too long to be comfortable before she broke the silence.

"Old guard room by the gates would work for a QRF base," she said, trying to refocus their attention on the task and not the fact that they were getting on each other's nerves. "Put some cots in there. Off-duty can sleep in shifts with their gear ready to roll so we rotate a squad there permanently."

"It's full of storage crap," Neil muttered.

Dan looked at him, tone flat. "Then have people move it."

Neil didn't argue. He just nodded again, lips tight.

He wasn't enjoying the return of the old Dan – the one who didn't tolerate having to ask for anything twice – but his greater concern was that if this iteration of the man was needed again, it meant the quiet, peaceful days were over.

Marie broke the tense silence this time. "What about Polly?" she asked. "She might know something. Beaulac was...*fond* of her. He may have let something slip."

"You think she's in any way willing to help after what went down?" Dan asked uncertainly.

232

"I'll go speak to her," Marie offered. "Last I checked she hadn't left her room in two days."

Polly's room was dim. The curtains were drawn, leaving a sickly grey light to slant in around the edges. Plates of untouched food sat gathering dust on a bedside table and the air inside was stale with the scent of sweat and shame. It felt close and oppressive inside, like a sealed tomb.

Polly didn't look up when Marie knocked and stepped in, merely let out a tired complaint that she just wanted to be left alone.

"Polly?" Marie said, peering into the gloom.

Polly shifted position to sit on the edge of the bed, knees drawn up, fingers clenched white into the bedsheet. Her hair was tangled, her skin pale, and Marie could sense the conflicting emotions radiating off her.

Marie said nothing at first, simply crossed the room with quiet, confident steps and sat beside Polly. She showed no reaction to stepping over the bones of a broken chair, and acted as though the smell of the room and the woman she sat close to weren't anything to repulse her.

"We need your help," Marie said gently. "We need to know more about those people and where they came from, so if there's something you remember…anything at all…"

Polly didn't move for a long time. Then her lips parted and she exhaled like she'd been holding it in since the moment her dreams had turned into smoke.

"I thought he loved me," she said, voice breaking in the middle. "I thought…I don't know *what* I thought."

She spat the words angrily, but the anger was directed all at herself. The weight of the blame she carried was immense, and instead of owning the responsibility she'd been crushed under the weight of guilt.

"I said terrible things to you. To Dan. To Leah...now...now I can't even look at myself."

Marie's eyes involuntarily moved to the mirror, intuiting some meaning from Polly's words, until her eyes rested on a crack in the ruined glass.

Marie understood the act of attacking one's own reflection from a textbook perspective, and she applied the concepts to Polly's situation easily.

Self-loathing. Self-rejection. A rage-fuelled dissociation between the person staring back and who they thought they were. It also spoke of a symbolic punishment and Marie felt the disgrace radiate from the other woman again for the shame of breaking something irreplaceable.

"You were hurt," Marie said softly. "We've all made mistakes, but you know it isn't luck that makes us strong enough to survive them."

Polly turned her head, eyes wide. "*Mistakes*? Marie, I didn't make mistakes, I ruined *everything*!"

"You didn't," Marie told her gently.

She judged the time right to employ physical touch as a way to extend an offer of reassurance. Of acceptance back into her life.

"They're gone, and there isn't any damage done here that can't be mended in time...but there is a greater threat out there. We know that now. When Beau— when they left, they said a name. They said something about Le Maréchal..."

Polly shook her head slowly, knees still drawn to her chest and hugged close, eyes fixed on nothing among the detritus on her floor.

"Wait…I do remember something. He said a name to one of the others. Not a person but a place. Carcassonne. I asked him what it meant but he brushed it off, acted like he hadn't spoken. At the time I…"

Marie nodded slowly. "Carcassonne?"

"Yes…I think so."

"How did he say it? In what context?" Marie asked.

"I think…I think he said something like, 'they will be pleased in Carcassonne…' that's all. Sorry."

Marie patted her shoulder and stood, leaving the hand resting on her until the last minute to reinforce the acceptance it had demonstrated.

"I'll ask someone to bring you food and water. And some warm water for washing, if you want?"

Polly gave the barest nod, but her hand reached for Marie's as she moved away.

"Thank you," Polly whispered. "And I'm sorry. I'm so…so very sorry. For everything. For everything I did, I—"

Marie stepped back and wrapped her arms around the woman, holding her breath so she didn't risk reacting to the smell of her unwashed body.

"You don't need to apologise to me. You aren't the first person to be lied to and you won't be the last…You're our Polly, and we can't forget that over one mistake."

~

Dan paced the ramparts, the wind pulling at his coat and tangling his hair. It was where he went to think, to breathe, to be angry where no one could see. Leah sat cross-legged on the stone nearby, a dog on either side of her, rolling him cigarettes without being asked.

"Carcassonne? I've never bloody heard of it," Dan said eventually.

"Apparently it's a city," Leah replied. "Old. And with a wall."

Dan ignored her apparent knowledge because his mind had skipped ahead. "You think this *Maréchal* character is there?" he asked.

"I think that's a logical conclusion."

"Where is it? How far away?" Dan asked.

"Victor say's it's about a hundred and fifty kilometres northeast. Reckons about five days on a horse…went on about average walking speed and some other bollocks, so I'd say probably four days' hard ride, a week or more being careful, or a day by vehicle."

Dan made no comment on the source of Leah's intel, being too busy thinking to let out even a scoff at Victor's involvement. She looked up to see the face he pulled when he was working something out, and decided to ground him with the tried and tested tactic of annoying him.

"One-point-six to one," she said. "Making it a little und—"

"About ninety-five miles," Dan finished.

He reached down and took one of Leah's constructions from the tin in front of her, lighting it to look out over the ramparts staring north again.

"Yep. Not too far if we use the new trucks, but not exactly *incognito*."

"Incognito," Dan echoed, like he was impressed with her word choice. "And no. It's not…hey, what's the French for incognito?"

"Errr…I think it's still incognito. Lucien says if you understand Latin you can pretty much figure out most European languages."

"Yeah? If he's so smart how come he can't figure out how to cut his hair?"

Leah tutted but smiled, knowing she was getting some part of the old Dan back. The one who wasn't accused of being a bully because he was frightened and stressed, and his words came out wrong.

"Seriously. If he goes to prison with hair like that he's going to be *very* popular!"

Leah went quiet at the mention of the word prison. In many ways an old prison – even if it was a grand old mansion – had been her family home. It had been where she'd grown up because her memories from before she stumbled into Dan and Neil were locked away tightly in a box she kept under the stairs in her mind, hoping never to find it and open it up again.

That prison had been where she'd decided what she was going to do with her life. It had been where she'd felt safe, happy even, and it had been the first place she ever shot and killed anyone.

"He's very fond of his hair," she said, falling back on a safe subject so that box didn't remind her where she'd hidden it.

"Most ladies with nice hair are," Dan breathed wistfully. "Come on, give me those and get your arse to bed."

He held out a hand and waited while Leah finished rolling her current project and gave him back his pouch and tin.

"Don't stay up all night," she warned him after accepting a hand to haul her to her feet.

Dan didn't answer so she added some authority to her tone. "I mean it. You're on until midnight, then you join the QRF downstairs where you'd better get some sleep."

"Yes master," Dan answered with his best Renfield lisp, aiming for sarcasm and only achieving pain as he sucked in cold evening air to aggravate his broken tooth.

"You need to get that thing pulled out," Leah said firmly.

"I need someone coming at me with a pair of pliers as much as I need to get sent down for a five stretch with Lucien's hair and baby-smooth skin!"

The next morning Polly found her way to the meeting room. She was cleaned up, hair damp from a recent wash, shoulders straighter. She didn't knock. She walked in and laid a finger on the map.

"Here. Carcassonne. That's where he's going."

Dan's expression was unreadable. "You want to go there, don't you?"

"I need to do something that matters," Polly said unflinchingly. "I need to make this right."

Dan looked like he might refuse outright. His plan had been correctly predicted in that he absolutely wanted to send someone to Carcassonne on reconnaissance, but Polly's motivations were what caused him concern.

"You're not ready," he said flatly.

Lucien stepped forward, his voice calm. "I think it is a good idea, but she should not be going alone."

He raked a hand through his long hair to cover his trepidation about what he was about to suggest. "Someone who can blend in and pretend to be something that they are not."

Leah scoffed, reaching up to tuck an errant strand of hair behind his ear. "You're talking about yourself? You're too easily recognised."

Lucien didn't smile. "Then I'll cut my 'air."

The laughter stopped.

Dan looked at him, at Polly, then out the window toward the ocean.

"Let me think on it."

THE COMFORT OF GLORY

Carcassonne had been reborn. Not as a relic of mediaeval grandeur but as the pulsing heart of a new order.

The ancient city's streets were swept clean of broken glass, burnt-out vehicles, and the refuse of old wars just as the previous inhabitants had been swept clean or swept up into their revolutionary mentality.

Every stone in the double layers of wall stood in quiet obedience, not merely mocking the lawlessness that existed beyond them but daring it to come.

Daring it to try and infect the town with its anarchy.

Everything within the perimeter moved with calculated purpose. The air held the metallic tang of industry and not decay. Citizens marched, not because they had to, but because they were told it was right and they believed. Weapons of various type and size leaned in tidy rows against sandbag walls where crates of ammunition were counted, logged and stacked.

Banners bearing the revolutionary insignia of Le Maréchal hung over the gates and rippled from ramparts to flutter faded red stitched with black on the early summer breeze.

The symbol itself was stark: a laurel wreath encircling a single downward-pointing sword, blade flanked by twin sheaves of wheat and the tip resting atop a closed book. It was emblematic of discipline, sustenance, and doctrine with the sword sitting above it all.

The city no longer looked like it was preparing for war. It was the future.

In the centre of it all, poised like a conductor before an obedient orchestra, stood Le Maréchal. He dressed with the stark authority of a man who rejected excess but demanded precision: a plain, dark blue military jacket, immaculately tailored, devoid of insignia save for a single silver aiguillette that looped at one shoulder. Every stitch spoke of quiet power, and he wore it with the pride and precision one would wear the gaudy uniform of a general or an emperor.

His posture was faultless – chin lifted imperceptibly as he addressed his people from the makeshift stage set beneath the mediaeval arches. Light filtered through high windows and cast pale, angular shapes across the stone floor, bathing him in an almost ecclesiastical aura.

"Citizens," he began, his deep voice crisp and cool, each syllable sharpened like a blade. "We are not merely *surviving*. We are *rebuilding. Refining.*"

He let the words settle, his gaze travelling over them like a tutor assessing pupils before an examination. Some held tools while others bore rifles but all stood attentive, caught in his gravity as though mesmerised by a demigod come to save them and show them the way.

"We do not merely *ask* the world to yield to us, but instead we show it *'ow*...and 'ow do we show the rest of the world what is expected? Through *order*. Through *will*. Through *fire*."

Another pause. His eyes moved slowly across the crowd, not with emotion, but calculation.

"Voltaire once said, 'Those 'ho can make you believe absurdities can make you commit atrocities', but he also warned that, 'It is

241

dangerous to be right in matters on which the established authorities are wrong.'"

Le Maréchal paused, waiting for his wisdom to be absorbed through osmosis, as if the very air could infect his followers with enlightenment.

"'e also wrote, 'We must cultivate our garden.' A man a'ead of his time, no?"

Le Maréchal chuckled and dropped his head to shake it once, listening for his crowd to follow and send a ripple of muted laughter back to him. He didn't know if it was ignorance or disbelief that made the laugh less intense than he had anticipated when memorising the words he now orated. He suspected that most of his followers lacked the depth of intelligence to comprehend the irony.

"Voltaire knew the danger of letting the world fall to ruin while waiting for perfection. We are done waiting…but I say, *let them try*! Let them *see* what order looks like. Let them understand that chaos was the indulgence of the weak. *We* are not weak. *We* are *necessary*."

His hands never gestured wildly. Only one subtle movement at a time, delivered with the precision of a surgeon. There was no teleprompter, no visible notes. He did not smile because he did not need to. His voice was the scalpel and his words the incision. Timing his biggest gesture yet he lifted his right hand, fist clenched, high into the air.

"And we will be victorious!"

When he left the stage it was to the thunderous noise of agreement and support. He smiled to himself because he knew that was the sound of loyalty and belief.

The citizens returned to their duties like gears resetting in a clock, and when Le Maréchal looked back he found himself smiling. A genuine smile, now one of tactic or impersonation, not a disguise worn by people to hide their intent, but a genuine smile brought on by the sight of three boys only a few summers away from conscription mimicking his gesture of power with their little fists held aloft.

~

In the upper chambers of a once-noble house, now stripped of its character and turned into a hub of administration, Le Maréchal sat alone.

His study was pristine; every item placed with intent. He read from a leather-bound folio with eyes that didn't blink often while a silver tray rested beside him, the remnants of a perfectly portioned meal left largely untouched. Two hardboiled eggs and the end of a loaf. Every morning, without fail, the same cold request for the same breakfast that was rarely consumed in full.

A servant appeared soundlessly to remove the tray but Le Maréchal did not look at him, merely detected the young man hovering for permission or instructions before waving a hand over the tray as if lazily dislodging an opportunistic fly.

The servant stepped in to take the tray while Le Maréchal offered no word of thanks. The servant bowed and retreated like vapour, entirely ignored by his master.

Only when the door shut behind him did the silence break. One of Le Maréchal's personal guards stepped forward from the shadows by the doorframe and stomped lightly to attention as his body attempted a throat-clearing noise without sounding presumptuous.

"Colonel Beaulac has returned, sir."

Le Maréchal turned another page in the folio, appearing to have not heard the words until he'd finished reading the final line of a report, then gently closed it to lay it atop a stack.

"Wait," he said simply.

The guard retreated to his spot without another word.

Le Maréchal rose, moved to the ornate but unostentatious mirror beside the fireplace, and studied his reflection for a long time. He straightened his collar, smoothed the front of his jacket, turned left and right before he gave a single, approving nod to his reflection.

His expression did not change, but there was a subtle flicker of pride in his eyes as he regarded the symmetry of his appearance, and only then did he exit the study.

His footsteps echoed on the ancient flagstones as he walked slowly and deliberately, hands clasped behind his back like a man browsing the artefacts in a museum, admiring relics no one else but him could ever begin to comprehend. The light followed him, angling in from high windows to paint clean lines on the floor as his shadow marched with perfect synchronicity behind.

When he arrived at the mess hall, the atmosphere shifted. Five ragged figures, mud-streaked, dust-covered, sunburnt and half-starved, sat around a table devouring hot food like they'd been denied it for days.

Colonel Beaulac saw him first and sprang to his feet, smacking the table and barking at his people to do the same. Chairs scraped hurriedly as half-chewed bites were swallowed with difficulty.

"Maréchal, I—"

"*Qui loquitur, perit,* Colonel," came the crisp interruption, underlined by a hand raised casually to prevent another word being spoken aloud.

Beaulac snapped his mouth shut, not understanding the Latin quoted at him as a demonstration of superior intellect, but because he'd interpreted the meaning clearly enough by being interrupted.

Le Maréchal didn't even glance at the others around the table. His eyes stayed forward, gaze unyielding. He turned and walked away without giving any orders, but it was clear to Beaulac he was expected to follow.

So he followed, boots slapping hurriedly on the flagstones to catch up. He looked like something the road had chewed and spat back out: hollow eyes, cracked lips, coat clinging to skin where sweat had dried into salt. His breathing was quick and irregular, as though his body didn't trust the calm.

They stopped at a set of grand double doors at the end of a corridor where Le Maréchal's two silent guards stepped forward in perfect unison to pull them open. He stepped inside and moved toward the tall window that overlooked the central square, while Beaulac hovered three paces inside the room where the sun sliced across the floor in neat diagonals, permitted entry as heavy curtains had been drawn back just enough.

Le Maréchal's silhouette stood sharp and motionless against the light.

He did not speak at first, leaving Beaulac uncomfortably aware of how loudly he breathed.

"Come," Le Maréchal said, without turning.

Beaulac approached with a slight limp, the wear of the journey still etched into every step. He squinted against the power of the light blasting painfully into his eyes, lifting a hand to shield him from the worst of it before he'd crossed the room and stopped beside Le Maréchal to wait.

"What do you see?" Le Maréchal asked.

Beaulac blinked, brain frantically spinning for the right answer but struggling to provide any words through dehydration and exhaustion.

"Strength," he answered cautiously. "I see power...I-in the walls. In the banners...In the people."

Le Maréchal nodded slowly, his gaze unmoving.

"Power, yes, this is true and cannot be denied, but look again. Look closer and tell me what you see."

Beaulac's mouth opened and closed but still the correct response eluded him.

Le Maréchal sighed faintly, as though burdened by the necessity of explanation.

"Do you see the flag?" he asked, speaking slowly as though explaining something to a young, unruly child.

Beaulac stared, uncertain what answer was expected. When none came, Le Maréchal told him what he was looking for.

"The laurel," he said, his voice quiet. "Victory, but not glory. As Voltaire wrote, 'The comfort of glory is the torch of fools.' It must be earned, again and again. The sword? Authority, but not violence. A reminder that force exists, but should not need to be used. The wheat, Colonel, the wheat is life. Without it, none of this matters. And the book..."

He trailed off for effect, then turned his head slightly to look up at the French-Canadian he knew he needed but enjoyed intimidating.

"The book is doctrine, Colonel. Law. Memory. Without it, the rest is nothing but savagery. *We*...are not savages."

He let the silence hang for a moment longer before turning fully to face Beaulac, dropping the veil of magic that held the bigger man rooted in place.

"Now," he said. "Tell me everything."

THE PASSAGE OF LIFE

The chamber was tall and narrow, lit not by the sun but by oil lamps set into iron sconces along the stone walls. Their flames hissed and danced in the gloom, casting long shadows over the old, rectangular table where Le Maréchal's top advisors sat. Each man wore the sharp expression of someone rehearsing what *not* to say, and all eyes turned as the door creaked open.

Colonel Claude Beaulac stepped inside, instantly sensing the thick tension of competition in the room. Each man there, himself included, vied endlessly for position and favour with Le Maréchal, and Beaulac had long since come to terms that this was precisely what the intelligent man wanted. He wished he'd been permitted the time to change, to wash the road off his body and attend his own trial wearing the finery of a senior man, but Le Maréchal had insisted the news he had should be shared and discussed immediately.

Beaulac's skin was burnt and peeling, a stark contrast to the immaculate presentation of the men around him. Dust clung to his coat and boots, and his eyes were hollowed by sleepless nights and days of hunger. He walked with the heavy, unhurried steps of a man who'd travelled far too long without good news.

The silence thickened as he reached the table, broken only when Le Maréchal gave the faintest nod.

"I am glad to see you return, Colonel. What news do you bring?" asked the man seated nearest the head of the table.

He was a hawkish, sharp-jawed officer named Renaud, whose ambitions far outweighed his tactical insight. His dark eyes glittered with anticipation, eager for the colonel's failure.

Beaulac suppressed the urge to sneer at the false manners coming from a man who had appointed himself the rank of commandant.

Beaulac remained upright, holding Renaud's gaze a second longer than was comfortable for the small man.

"We reached Andorra," Beaulac said. "Left three people there and moved to the place they call Sanctuary."

"We know this, *mon Colonel*. If I may, per'aps it would be better if you began at the end, no? Per'aps you could explain why you returned with only an 'andful of your forces?"

"Because we were discovered, driven out, and I watched my best man get the top of 'is 'ead blown off in front of my eyes."

A ripple of noise travelled through the room as questions overlapped and accusations lay half a breath away.

"Enough."

Le Maréchal's voice was quiet, almost bored, but the silence that followed struck like thunder.

He didn't look at Beaulac yet, instead he flicked a glance to Renaud that lingered just long enough to make the man flinch before he returned to skimming the report in front of him with apparent disinterest.

"For the benefit of those 'ere 'ho do not already know, please tell the 'hole story, Colonel."

Beaulac swallowed.

"We made contact, but when we arrived the military leaders were not there. The place is run by a…a man, an Englishman, and what I think is his daughter. They both have big dogs that are trained like military or police, and the man's wife is the one running the civilian side of everything…As for the town itself, their defences are formidable and we believe they have maybe two heavy machine guns, but there is also an armoury I could not look inside. Rumours are that they have rockets and explosives, and one person told us of how they used military mines to destroy an attack many years ago…since then they have been attacked by pirates from the sea and, if the stories are to be believed, just two of them boarded the boat and killed every one of them."

Silence followed his thorough, condensed run-down of Sanctuary's leadership.

"And what of the people, *mon colonel*?" Renaud asked far too politely to be genuinely respectful. "Are they many? What resources do they 'ave?"

"The people are united, although we managed to find a crack to press on and divide them for a time. They send out fishing boats daily but have preserved stockpiles of many things. They have a civilian force, a militia as they call it, and they are well trained but some of them there – like this Englishman and another who claims to be Scottish, as well as the girl – they appear to be *highly* trained."

"A *girl*, Beaulac?" Renaud scoffed, intending to undermine his bravery and authority so publicly. "Sure you are not afraid of *one little girl*?"

Beaulac fixed the small man with a deathly stare and spoke coldly.

"This *girl*, Renaud, moves with a confidence I cannot explain to someone who does not possess it themselves. She has killed men with her bare hands, of that I am sure, and I fear she is capable of more than that."

"And the defences, Claude," Le Maréchal said gently, bringing the discussion back to the topic in hand. "Tell them of the defences."

"The land around them is not just defensible, it is prepared. They've planted food, built infrastructure, and while the rumours about landmines are only rumours, I believe them to be true."

"You say the man in charge is an *Englishman*? What of our French brothers and sisters? Have they abandoned their duty to the Republic?" interjected Major Courbin.

He was a tall, ungainly but heavy-set man with a quick temper and a reputation for excessive punishment. The fleshy-faced, jowly man wore a ceremonial sabre at all times, as though it might elevate his opinions.

Beaulac turned, but didn't raise his voice. "They survived, they built, and they consolidated. They did not always follow this Englishman, but they follow him now because…"

Beaulac trailed off, about to say that they followed Dan because he was the strongest, but he doubted that to be true.

"Because I believe he is willing to do whatever it takes to ensure his people's safety. The people there chose to act. They did not wait to be rescued."

Courbin's fat cheeks flushed pink with indignation at the veiled accusation of cowardice levelled at him. Nobody who knew the true facts of Courbin's "rescue" had uttered them aloud since a very public punishment of a man accused of spreading sedition had resulted in his death.

"A *convenient* excuse for treason," Courbin muttered.

"Everything is treason with you, Major," complained another calmer, deeper voice.

Capitaine Armand, bearded and broad-shouldered, leaned forward with his fingers laced. He was a decade younger than any other man at the table and always fought against the urge to prove himself and therefore prove the incorrect theory that he was hot-headed and inexperienced.

"The colonel brought back intelligence," Armand said flatly. "Please, let him speak it."

"And your reinforcements?" another man snorted.

Beaulac looked directly at a man named Duval, an old rival who'd once served under Beaulac many years earlier before politics reversed their fortunes. His uniform was pressed so sharply it might have stood without him inside it, and Beaulac often wondered if that was the closest the man would ever come to possessing a spine.

As much as he postured and manoeuvred, Beaulac couldn't doubt the man's skill at inserting himself into positions of power.

"Dead. Or captured, but probably dead."

"And those you left behind in Andorra?" Duval asked acidly.

Beaulac looked him directly in the eye. "I would have to assume the same."

The room went uncomfortably still again. Several of the men exchanged glances, sensing opportunity. Sensing weakness and misstep to be exploited for their personal advantage.

At last, Le Maréchal looked up. "Tell me of their food supplies."

Beaulac broke eye contact and shifted in his seat, grateful for the excuse to break the tension.

"They have orchards and farmland. Enough to feed many more people than are in the town, and I know this because they trade between there and Andorra, and also a few smaller places but I cannot be sure. I believe I can locate these places."

"Excuse me, *Beaulac*, does that mean you didn't even find out *where* these places were?" Courbin demanded, sensing his first opportunity to strike back after Beaulac's barely disguised insult.

General Moreau, the eldest at the table – a relic of several regimes past with a baritone like a cracked bell – cleared his throat.

"Then we must besiege them! *Starve them out*! As was done when we retook it from the Spanish!"

Beaulac's mouth curled. "My apologies, *mon general*, but I am not...*experienced* enough to recall the 1700s? Are you the last man alive who remembers it?"

The old man bristled, drawing a breath for a retort that would likely shake the room as the man's explosive anger was legendary, but Le Maréchal's chair creaked and that was all it took to collapse the air within the room.

He raised a hand, just a small, simple gesture, and the insult faded before it could catch flame.

"They will not be besieged," Beaulac said, shaking his head. "Not successfully. The hills are high and their snipers see everything. Any camp in range will be a slaughterhouse by dusk."

"That is assuming they have ammunition and soldiers with the right experience," Duval interjected.

"I can personally attest to their skill, and I have no reason to doubt their ammunition reserves," Beaulac said angrily, barely keeping a lid on his desire to explain in detail how Bastin's head came apart in front of his eyes.

"So what do *you* propose, Colonel?" came a clipped voice near the back.

All eyes shifted to lock onto an aide too young to be so cynical. Second lieutenant Bellier visibly quailed under the scrutiny, and his ink-stained hands quivered.

"You are here, *boy*, to record the facts and not speak," General Moreau growled.

Beaulac answered the question anyway, directing his response to Le Maréchal. "We take the farms, cut the road, and let them starve. We let them know we control the passage of life."

A long pause followed before Le Maréchal stood. He folded his hands neatly together behind his back and began walking slowly, moving only one foot at a time as he spoke.

"Gentlemen, do any of you know what Boneparte did at the Battle of Ulm in eighteen-oh-five?"

They all knew well enough that the question was rhetorical, so none offered an answer even if they knew.

"The Austrians, in their...*infinite* arrogance...marched confidently into Bavaria, presuming to hold the line like a dam against the tide. They brought with them the baggage of old-world warfare, displayed linear thinking, suffered their honourable delays, and enjoyed the fantasy of reinforcements arriving like cavalry in a stage play. They did not account for the emperor's genius...He did not meet them, he *outmarched* them. Circled behind them like a surgeon drawing the first incision in what he described as his manoevre sur les derrières. Their lines of supply were cut, their roads denied, their messengers intercepted.

"Their great army, over thirty thousand men, had been reduced to a garrison surrounded by wolves in a single day."

Le Maréchal stopped and spun almost theatrically on his heel, having timed his movement to place himself directly behind Beaulac's chair so all eyes on the room faced their way.

"At Ulm, the Austrians surrendered without glory. Thirty thousand men – *thirty. THOUSAND* – devoured not by musketry or artillery but by isolation and *inevitability*."

He leaned on the back of Beaulac's chair and clenched a small fist tight to reinforce his point. He held that fist like he gripped the very ability for anyone to speak in his hand, then he let it go and spoke with less intensity as though bored of the story.

"Such is the fate of those who mistake presence for power. The emperor taught them that war is not won by standing one's ground, but by denying the enemy theirs."

He moved again, walking faster to retake his seat and arrange his jacket before he spoke once more.

"He wrote to Josephine after this, not to boast but to simply state what lesser men would inscribe in marble: *I have made a new strategy,* he said, *completely different from that of others. I have surrounded the enemy army without a battle…*Ahhh…such elegance. Such…*precision.* The efficient annihilation of *presumption.* That is art, my fellow citizens. That is *pow*er!"

The silence still hung thickly in the air as Le Maréchal sat back with a satisfied smile and sipped from a glass of red wine, assessing his warped reflection in the glass.

"Victory is not glory," he said softly. "It is *comfort.* Glory is what fools die chasing, while comfort is what kings die hoarding."

He turned, eyes falling on Beaulac with cold appreciation.

"Your strategy is good, Colonel. You will show us where the food grows."

Beaulac nodded while Le Maréchal held another pause. When he spoke again he moved faster, smiled, and raised the pitch of his voice to infect them all with his confidence.

"And then, gentlemen, we will show them what hunger truly is."

That evening, in a quieter part of the citadel, a pair of mismatched chairs sat before a dwindling fire in captain Armand's quarters. A bottle of brandy rested between two tired men, their glasses already half-drained.

Beaulac slouched deeper into his chair, the lamplight softening the gaunt lines of his face. His coat hung open, collar undone, revealing the fading bruises where a man as skilled and filled with resolve as he was had left his mark.

Armand leaned forward, elbows on knees. "You spoke well, Claude. You held your ground."

"They'd piss on my boots if I turned my back," Beaulac grunted, his tongue loosened by the brandy and his mood darkened by exhaustion and defeat.

"They'd piss on their *own* boots if they thought Le Maréchal would enjoy it."

Beaulac chuckled, then winced. "This *Dan*...he is dangerous...Clever and calm. The sort of man who waits until you've spent your last bullet before he raises his own."

Armand studied him, seeing the faraway look in Beaulac's eyes he read as something bordering fear. "And yet you told them only enough to convince, not to warn," he observed drily.

"I will not give them a hero to rally against," Beaulac said angrily, leaning forward to refill his glass. "But make no mistake...that man...he is not just *surviving* like so many we have seen. He is...he is..."

"Winning?" Armand asked.

Beaulac's sullen growl affirmed his guess.

"And this bruises your pride!" Armand said with a light chuckle, able to take such liberties with a senior officer because the two men enjoyed one another's company.

Beaulac didn't answer. He swirled the glass, watching amber shadows rise and fall.

When Armand next spoke, his voice had lowered to a warning tone. "Do not let this blind you, Claude. You are not just fighting a town; you are fighting what it *represents*. 'e is just one man, but 'is strength comes from the people who support 'im, no? So believe that 'e is just one man, because pride makes poor armour and vengeance clouds judgement."

"You sound like a priest," Beaulac said with a dark chuckle escaping his curled upper lip.

"No," Armand answered affably, lifting his glass. "I just sound like a man 'oo prefers to outlive his enemies."

Beaulac watched him sip the brandy, assessing the ambitious, cautious younger man as if he detected many more things unspoken behind his words.

"You are not talking about your enemies out *there*, are you, Alexis?"

Armand smiled again and inclined his head to half acknowledge the accusation, speaking softly as though worried he'd be overheard.

"Tell me truthfully, Claude…what do you *really* think of our Maréchal?"

Beaulac eyed Armand sceptically for a long while, weighing up the risks of honesty before deciding he trusted the man enough. "I think 'e's a very clever, very knowledgeable tactician who studied many battles in great detail…"

"*But…*" Armand prompted, steering Beaulac toward the truth both of them knew but neither had yet said aloud.

"But 'e's no fighter," Beaulac admitted quietly into his drink.

"No, 'e was a teacher, you know? An 'istory professor. The man is all words and no *spine*. I truly believe if the man ever 'ad to do any of 'is own dirty work, 'e would piss in 'is pants."

"Is that what you believe, Alexis?" Beaulac asked, but the smile on his face radiated amused agreement.

"I…believe in a unified France," Armand finally admitted in a louder, more confident tone. "I may not agree with the means in which it is achieved, and it is no secret between us that I do not believe in the leadership always, but—"

"*Alexis!*" Beaulac said, hushing him with a waved hand. "Some-one might overhear an—"

"I choose my company and my surroundings very carefully, Claude, I ask you to please trust me in this…but what I said is still true. There will be a time…long after all this…when the people will not *want* to be lectured by an old schoolteacher with an undying love for Boneparte and we won't 'ave to learn Latin and listen to the ram-blings of Voltaire."

"I cannot disagree with that, but I still urge you to observe cau-tion."

"Caution and discretion are the very bedrocks of my personality," Armand assured him with comical formality. "But I do know one thing…men 'oo like to make speeches and idolise tyrants usually tend not to die of old age, and nor do those who follow them."

"*I* would like to die of old age," Beaulac groaned as he shifted position in his seat. "In my own bed, with a full belly and a pair of smooth, warm thighs wrapped around me."

"I wish for that too, my friend. Just make sure you are like me, and don't get yourself killed chasing someone else's dream."

They drank in silence after that, each watching the flames dance and flicker, both knowing that the next fire they light might not be for warmth.

GATHERING STORM

The cart creaked under the weight of its burden as it trundled across the courtyard, wheels lurching in rhythm with every uneven flagstone as each bounce sent a judder through the frame. The groan of wood and the clink of iron fittings turned heads that would normally stay buried in tasks, but nobody spoke. They just watched the cart roll closer as Neil led the big, placid horse pulling it.

The noise wasn't overly loud, but it carried. That morning even the smallest sounds seemed amplified to Dan, who had woken after a terrible attempt at sleep with a higher sensitivity to noise and a lower tolerance threshold for just about everything. He recognised that as a sign of elevated stress in himself, and tried his best not to snap at people for just existing, but the throbbing pain and swelling in his lower jaw was making life almost unbearable.

The horse seemed old to Dan, but he reminded himself he knew little of horses. Her gait seemed stiff with age, as though she would much prefer to be resting than pulling a cart laden with crates and sacks of produce to sell the ruse.

She didn't need coaxing or pulling along by Neil who held the reins loosely like he was walking a well-trained, and very large dog at heel. She followed the path like it was routine – like she trusted Neil to be leading her somewhere fun – with her ears twitching at the occasional footstep or cough, but otherwise unmoved by the tension that hung in the morning air.

Polly stood beside Dan, one gloved hand touching the cart rail as it creaked to a stop in front of them. Her coat was done all the way up, high collar pressed tight to her throat despite the rising heat of the sun. She didn't fidget or pace, didn't speak, she simply stood like a fixed point with an unreadable expression on her face.

There was no softness to that expression, no air of vacancy, but there was no steel either. Just stillness. Her hair was tied back in a tight knot that pulled at her temples, and she looked like she was bracing herself for something to go wrong.

Dan recognised the expression along with her body language, seeing her internally doubt herself. Doubt her resolve and bravery, her abilities, but most of all he felt her fear of the unknown. He knew Polly had barely left the immediate surroundings of Sanctuary in all the time he'd been there, having only visited Andorra twice, and he felt her fear of the big, bad world beyond her comfortable geofence.

Leah lingered a few feet away, doing her best impression of nonchalance. She fussed with a pack that had already been secured twice, running the straps through her hands like she expected them to fray. Her mouth was tight, her eyes flicking back and forth between Polly and the horse without ever landing for long. Her movements were methodical and too precise to Dan's watchful eyes. The kind of thing people do when they don't know what else to say so they try to be busy.

Neil stood by the horse's shoulder, his hand moving gently across the mare's neck in small circles. The gesture seemed to be borne more of habit than comfort, and his voice stayed low as he spoke.

"She's one of my best girls is Clémence," he said lovingly, like it was the only introduction needed. "She's not the fastest, but she's steady and reliable and that's what you need. Give her a good brush at night, she likes that, and don't skimp on the oats or she'll sulk."

Polly gave a small smile. It didn't last long, but it was real. "Got it. Don't be shy with her supper."

The rest of the courtyard was still. Half a dozen people worked nearby, close enough to listen but not close enough to be seen watching. Crates were lifted, tools passed between hands and buckets refilled, but none of it carried the sound of normal work. It was quiet, deliberate work that felt somehow staged. Everyone knew what was happening, and no one wanted to interrupt.

Dan retreated a few paces up on the stone steps, arms folded, weight set heavy on one heel where Ash found an uncomfortable-looking spot to lay down. His eyes tracked everything while his body remained still, just as Dan did: The cart. The people. Polly. The horse.

It wasn't command but something more personal. He'd stopped pretending it was a routine send-off hours ago, and the lines at the corners of his mouth hadn't shifted.

He hadn't spoken yet, partly because he didn't have anything useful or helpful to say and partly because the painful swelling in his jaw made speaking a chore to be understood.

He didn't speak but he did *feel*. He felt guilty mostly. Polly didn't owe them anything, and he'd only relented in letting her go – in letting an untrained civilian conduct a covert mission among the enemy – because she'd been so adamant to play a part in making it right and he hadn't come up with a good enough reason to say no.

The sound of boots on stone shifted his attention. He twisted his upper body to see Lucien walking out from the side building with long, measured steps. The muted conversation in the courtyard stalled and even the mare flicked her ear toward him.

He was nearly unrecognisable.

Suddenly aware of the attention he'd drawn, Lucien rubbed a hand self-consciously over his head.

The hair was gone, shorn down to the bone like a summer sheep stripped of its dignity and its winter fleece, his scalp pale from years in shade. It changed the shape of his whole head, made him look younger and more angular. There were small nicks above his left ear where the blade had caught. He hadn't asked for help with it. Of course he hadn't.

Without the usual curtain of hair, the bones of his face stood out more sharply. Cheekbones, jawline, the slight asymmetry of his brow...all of it had changed to make him appear somehow thinner. Physically reduced, like his charm and presence had been stripped away with the thick, wavy hair.

Neil leaned in slightly toward Dan. "Bloody hell. He's gone *Full Metal Jacket!*"

Dan didn't respond, disappointing Neil who as ever wanted some form of praise for his movie referencing powers. Dan caught Lucien's gaze and held it for a second before the young man looked away, but the flicker in his eyes had said enough.

The change wasn't merely practical, it *meant* something. It was a transformation in more ways than just a physical disguise.

Lucien came to a stop a few paces from the cart, standing straight with his arms relaxed at his sides. He looked at the ground as he spoke. "Is this better?"

The words were aimed at Leah, but his eyes took a moment to rise as though he feared a bad response from his young wife.

When they finally lifted they landed just short of hers, like he wasn't quite ready to meet them fully.

She blinked, thrown by his changed appearance.

"Oh dear God!" she said, her right hand lifting involuntarily to cover her mouth. "You you look...*different.*"

He nodded once, the movement short and shallow.

Dan stepped down from the stone and approached, boots grinding faintly on the old stone. He stopped a pace in front of them, looking first at Polly, then at Lucien, then back again. His mouth worked before any sound came.

"Last chance," he said, the words thick in his mouth making him sound like his jaw was wired together. "Either of you want to back out, now's the time."

Polly shook her head, the motion calm and resolute. Lucien shook his head but didn't speak either, his eyes still fixed on Leah as she fussed with the same straps on the pack that required no adjustment.

Dan held the silence for a second. "This is recon *only*," he said. "In, observe, get out. You—" He broke off, closing his eyes and suppressing an involuntary shudder at the pain in his jaw. "You smell trouble, you turn around. No hesitation, understood?"

Lucien gave a single nod.

"Where's your rifle?" Leah asked, realising her husband wasn't carrying his usual long-range weapon.

"I 'ave a Glock with five magazines, and an 'unting rifle with a scope. It is bolt-action, but it works. I will be fine."

Lucien gave a depreciative shrug and Dan grunted a noise of approval.

"No vest, no HK-four-seventeen...You look like a civilian. That's good. You'll blend in."

"I will not need a vest, because I 'ave no intentions to get shot at."

"Just you make sure you don't," Leah added.

Polly met Dan's gaze. "We'll bring back what you need, I promise," she said in a soft voice that carried none of the convictions of her word.

Dan opened his mouth to call the whole thing off on the spot. Polly's words, her inexperience prompting her to make a promise she couldn't guarantee to keep, screamed in his mind that she wasn't cut out for the task. The pain flared again, stopping him from speaking which he took as a sign that the words needed to stay in his head.

Instead, he nodded his thanks to her.

"You know your route?" Neil asked, addressing both Lucien and Polly. "Avoid the main roads, and release your first pigeon when the town's in sight, unless you get in trouble then you send a few back – don't worry about attaching any message – and we'll be up your arse in no time."

"I would rather you stay away from my ass, Neil," Lucien said, the boyish smirk lifting one side of his mouth but the overall effect much changed due to his new haircut.

"Well, don't get in trouble and I won't have to. Besides, you look like the kind of man who doesn't even have to common courtesy to give someone a reach-around…"

Neil grinned, looking from person to person for a reaction before he remembered he only made the movie reference to Dan, and Dan didn't much seem like a man inclined to humour right then.

"Oh…*never mind*…" Neil said, and clapped the side of the cart.

"You're stocked with early summer goods," he said. "Strawberries, new spuds, spring onions, rhubarb and a few sticks of garlic, because we all know how much the froggies like their garlic!"

"As much as you *rosbifs* like their tasteless food, yes," Lucien retorted, playing the same cards he usually did when Neil jokingly insulted his entire country.

"A couple wheels of decent goat cheese and some smoked trout," Neil went on, ignoring the comeback. "That's your story. You're traders out of a village north of Béziers, you heard new people moved into Carcassonne, and you've been on the road a week."

Polly gave a second, quieter, "Got it."

"Repeat it back to me," Neil insisted.

"We are traders from near Béziers, we 'eard new people came to Carcassonne, we 'ave things from our farm to sell and it took us almost a week to get there."

"What things are you selling?" Neil snapped, speaking fast to put Lucien under pressure. "What have you got, eh? What do you grow?"

"Leave my son alone," Polly said firmly, her accent more French than French-Canadian now, and her voice thicker and harsher. "'e does not farm, 'e 'unts and keeps the wolves away. You 'ave questions, you ask me."

"Niiiice! *Yes,* I *like* it!" Neil answered excitedly. "Way to get into character…what're your names?"

"I am Paulette, and my son is called Lucas."

"*Smort…*Keep it close enough to your real names that any slip-ups aren't obvious," Neil said admiringly.

Lucien cast a warm, proud glance at Leah who smiled back, betraying where the spy craft tips had originated.

"Well, alright, let's not drag this out," Neil announced, clapping his hands together and rubbing them before apologising to Clémence for startling her.

Lucien turned to Leah and swept her up in a fiercely intense embrace, making the young woman giggle and kiss him back as the two muttered loving words to one another in both languages. They ended their embrace by holding tightly onto one another, eyes closed, as their lips barely moved to whisper promises to each other.

Polly climbed up into the cart first without hesitation. Lucien followed, lifting himself into place with practised ease. The reins were already looped and resting on the edge of the seat, waiting for him to pick them up, but he twisted to adjust the barrel of his hunting rifle to make it more accessible should he need it.

Dan opened his mouth to show he was pleased with that forethought and awareness, but nothing came out except a foul smell so he closed it again.

"We'll be careful," Polly said. She didn't raise her voice. It didn't need to carry.

Dan gave a slow nod.

The cart creaked forward, the wheels groaning as they rolled toward the southern gate with Lucien clicking his tongue and muttering encouraging words to their horse. The sound echoed across the courtyard, against the stones and back into the silence left behind.

No one followed. No one called after them.

"You're *absolutely sure* we shouldn't ride out with them? Even as far as the trading post?" Leah asked

Dan shook his head; his eyes were still fixed on the tail of the cart as it vanished from view.

Leah moved to his side and let out a slow breath through her nose. "I'm not sure I'll get used to that when he's back," she said wistfully. "He really did have pretty hair."

Dan's voice was quiet, almost resigned, but he managed to say a couple of words past the pain. "Yeah. Shame."

~

The cart rattled along the broken road, its wheels jostling through ruts and ridges worn deep by time, water and life. Dust clung to the hooves of the placid mare powering their progress and coated the cart's undercarriage in a pale, brittle film. Every few minutes, the rattle of the wheels would shift to a harsh clunk as one dropped into a deeper groove, jarring the frame and nudging Polly's grip tighter on the handrail.

They drove mostly in silence, with the road north offering little reason to speak.

Lucien sat beside her, his hands resting on his thighs where they held the reins loosely, binoculars hanging against his chest. He occasionally scanned the treelines, eyes shifting from left to right and back again as though the rhythm had become instinct.

Polly didn't know if his alertness was standard for people like him when outside the walls of their ancient, fortified home or whether his senses were heightened by their task.

Their *mission*, she mentally corrected herself, feeling the weight of expectation and responsibility to fulfil the promises she now wished she hadn't made.

Lucien frowned in a passive manner, and Polly didn't know if that was simply a by-product of his concentration or unhappiness. Unhappiness at what she didn't know, but she automatically assumed it was because he held a greater weight of responsibility on his young shoulders by effectively being out there alone and with a "civilian" to protect.

She tried to ignore that nagging doubt in her mind but it ate away at her, gnawing on her already exposed nerves until she had to say something else it would start to fester inside her.

"What are you frowning about?" Her voice was flat, but not cold. Just tired.

"Nothing," Lucien responded in the same flat, emotionless tone, but neither did he stop frowning.

"We're going to be on the road together, *alone*, for a long time…if there's something you need to get off your chest, now is probably a good time to say it."

Polly spoke more harshly than she intended, but it was out there now and couldn't be pulled back. She considered justifying her tone, fought the instinct to apologise for it, but decided to stay firm and appear strong even if that was the last thing she felt.

Lucien stayed silent and brooding for long enough that Polly felt the anger building up behind her teeth, urged on by her own fears and stress, but he broke that tension by letting out an exasperated huff of air and sagging.

"My 'ead is cold. I am…not used to being bald."

Polly responded with an involuntary chuckle that she stifled quickly, but when Lucien turned a hurt, almost childlike look of appeal on her it came again only much stronger.

"What is that funny?" he demanded sounding hurt.

Polly couldn't speak as a fresh wave of debilitating laughter overtook her, doubling her over and expelling the stress she'd been fermenting since before they left home. When she finally regained her composure she placed a gloved hand on Lucien's right arm and patted him reassuringly.

"I'm sorry, it isn't funny, it's just…I was expecting you to say you weren't happy about me coming along. Like maybe you wished you had someone who could fight instead. Someone more…*brave* than me."

Lucien's hurt look turned to one of sad apology as his head began shaking before his mouth opened to speak. "Polly, why do you think this? I am sorry if I 'ave made you believe this. I think what you are doing is braver than any fighter can be."

She stopped smiling, sensing the undeniable intensity of his belief. "Oh?" was all she managed to say.

"Yes. Our people 'ave been trained to fight, and that is what is expected of them, no? You are not expected to put yourself... 'ow does Leah say it? In 'arm's way? So no, what you are doing is *very* brave and I only 'ope I can live up to it."

Polly began to understand, only instead of feeling reassured she felt humbled by his admiration and the burden of success weighed even more heavily on her soul. She patted his arm again and stared out at the passing countryside so he didn't see her silent tears.

The land around them was beautiful in that quiet, careless way only post-collapse terrain could be. Wildflowers grew in thick patches between crumbling verges and small birds flitted from low branches, more curious than fearful. The occasional ruin of a farmhouse or derelict vehicle passed without comment.

Some had burned, others had simply given up and accepted their slow decay without putting up much of a fight.

Polly's eyes stayed on the horizon. She didn't look at him unless she had to.

Lucien's hands were steady on the reins, his jaw set tight as he periodically scanned the ground ahead with the binoculars.

Polly wanted to ask questions, wanted to know what it was about a certain patch of ground that made his nerves tingle in case that was a likely spot where an ambush would be sited. She wanted to ask so she could understand, so she could be more helpful than simply sitting there being chauffeured to their destination, but she wasn't ready for conversation.

They reached the trading post quicker than she anticipated, imagining it to be some faraway destination because her world had shrunk to something that could be easily contained within the walls of Sanctuary, and Roland accepted their unwillingness to discuss their destination with grace. He gave them a cup of tea, spoke about the weather, and while Lucien was eager to keep going and make more distance before nightfall Polly felt sorry for the old man who seemed to enjoy the company. He clearly wasn't finding much conversation from the militia member stationed there, sitting atop the roof with a rifle beneath the fluttering flag of their region, but Polly finished her tea and made their apologies.

Roland accepted their exit gracefully, offering last words to Lucien as they left which gave him no joy despite his smile.

"You look after that young wife and baby of yours," Roland told him.

DANGEROUS PLACEBO

Sanctuary had changed in their absence. Not visibly, not in any way an outsider would see, but it was there, threaded through the stillness like a taut wire.

The early morning light had a brittle quality, too bright and clean, as if the day hadn't quite made its mind up yet. The town was already busy with movement, but it felt like everyone was operating one gear higher than normal.

Boots moved faster, sentries' eyes darted more often, but no one shouted.

No one laughed, like the atmospheric tension had infected everyone.

Dan walked the perimeter with no urgency or purpose aside from simple visibility.

His presence was a steadying, reassuring factor, just as it always had been for him, Leah and Mitch. They were mascots, talismans of strength, like the force multipliers they were.

He nodded at sentries, adjusted a line of logs near a brazier on the north wall, and stacked a crate that didn't need moving. He was being seen to be busy for no other purpose than to *be* there. The quiet, constant ritual of someone trying to keep the place running by being seen to keep it running.

The pigeon coop had evolved to sprawl out of Neil's workshop like it had grown there. Ducking inside Dan blinked for his eyes to adjust to the gloomy interior, seeing Mitch sat at a table beside the cages, sleeves rolled up, scribbling entries in a ledger that was stained with feed dust and pigeon shit. Leah stood with one boot rested against the wall for stability, and when Ash slunk inside past Dan's legs Nemesis rose to all fours to greet him.

As the dogs sniffed and postured Dan lowered himself onto a bench, groaning with the effort and adjusting his slung rifle for comfort.

"That's just come in," Mitch said as he handed Dan a scrap of paper. "Making good progress."

Dan nodded, reading the note in Polly's handwriting updating them of their first successful overnight camp.

"They're holding up to the pace," Mitch added. "Not rushing it…but the mountains'll slow them down a touch I suspect."

Dan nodded, handing back the note before catching Leah's eye and raising his brow to ask for her news. "I caught two sentries asleep last night," she said.

"Anyone hurt?" he asked, clearly struggling to speak because of the painful swelling on the left side of his lower jaw.

Leah glanced at Mitch but the Scotsman didn't look up.

"No, nothing happened," she said. "But they were out cold. I didn't shout, just swapped them over."

"They all working twelves?" Dan asked, the words thick in his mouth that couldn't be opened fully.

"Some of them longer," Mitch interjected. "With our people out at the orchards and the farms, we're stretched. They're doing their best; they're just wrung out."

Dan sighed through his nose audibly, and his shoulders settled slightly lower.

"You don't need to get involved. I've handled it," Leah said.

271

"I'm not angry," Dan said, eyes closed against the obvious pain. "I'm just tired of having to worry about everything, all the time."

There was a pause, awkward and full, which Leah broke by holding up a scrap of paper and waving it. "Latest from Andorra."

Dan's brow lifted.

"Ben's apparently decided he's a ninja," she said flatly.

Dan tried to smile and grimaced.

"This time he's apparently serious. He made a zip line between two trees, then tried to use a stick as a grappling hook and nearly took out a goat."

Dan gave a low, amused grunt.

"What about Adalene?" Mitch asked.

"She's...become a *biter.*"

Dan turned to her properly now, eyes wide with amusement.

"Yep. Clamped onto someone's finger like a bloody crocodile and wouldn't let go until they bribed her with cheese."

That did make him laugh, a proper exhale through the nose with a shake of the head that turned into a sharp intake of breath before he screwed his eyes shut.

Leah and Mitch shared a look then, both of them on the same page.

"Christ...She's yours, all right," Dan finally managed to say.

Leah let the silence sit for a second. "I miss them."

Dan's face shifted, just a flicker behind the eyes but it was there. The kind of change most people wouldn't catch, but Leah saw it. "Yeah," he muttered through the pain. "Me too."

Another silence hung in the air until Leah pushed herself off the wall and cleared her throat.

"Listen, Dan, you need—"

Dan lifted a hand to stop her, shaking his head gently.

"I'm serious," Leah insisted. "You're fucked up. You're not combat-effective!"

Dan stood abruptly, ruining the effect by having to steady himself against the table until the wave of dizziness and nausea dissipated.

"I'm fine," he growled through clenched teeth.

He clicked his fingers once for Ash's attention, and walked out of the workshop looking more unsteady than Leah or Mitch liked.

"We can't let people see him walking around like that," Leah said after the sound of Dan's boots had faded to nothing.

"Aye, we're on the same page there. Bad for morale seeing your general staggering about with a golf ball in his cheek."

"We need to d—"

"Was that Dan I saw?" Neil asked loudly, bustling into the room holding a disorganised armful of tools and papers that he dropped on the desk.

"It was, and Leah was just saying that we need to do something about him," Mitch said, throwing Leah under the future bus marked "this was your idea".

"He's taking antibiotics," Neil admitted, apparently betraying a confidence by sharing that information. "But I reckon they're a good five-plus years past effective by now."

"So he's taking a placebo that might even do him *more* damage, and just hoping it'll go away?" Leah asked, becoming more animated now.

"Pretty much," Neil said. "But you know Dan as well as we do. You really think he's going to volunteer himself for sick leave at a time like this?"

The three of them went quiet, each deep in their own thoughts before Leah was the one yet again to break the stillness.

"Fuck this. I'm going to see what Kate and Sera say."

STILLNESS AND STONE

Lucien and Polly stopped only when necessary, making camp just off the road as night began to fall and the temperature dropped.

Polly watered and brushed Clémence while Lucian gathered firewood, and the horse was tied to a tree with a bag of oats and a bucket of water from a nearby stream. They ate a modest meal in silence before they went away individually to take care of personal business, then tucked themselves up in their bedrolls to close their eyes.

The next day passed by much the same as the first, the only notable difference to the mood coming when they deviated from their most travelled roads to strike further north and not split left to take them closer to the farms and the road winding up the mountains to Andorra. They stopped a few times, each time at a water source where Clémence was led to drink, but their steady progress was maintained to maximise the available daylight.

Lucien seemed colder, more brooding on that second morning, but Polly felt more confident to ask what was bothering him now that she felt reassured that it wasn't her presence causing the unhappy look on his face.

"The road will get much 'arder from 'ere," Lucien admitted. "There are many steep sections and it will get cold."

They broke camp just after first light and followed the road as it bent gently north, hugging the curves of the river like a cautious friend keeping its distance. Forest pressed close in places, thick with pine and beech that had taken full advantage of the absence of humanity to reclaim the concrete scars it bore. The scent of sap was sharp in the morning air and in places the trees had encroached so much that Clémence snorted nervously, but with soothing noises to reassure her she pulled them through those dark places to pick up the pace when daylight shone more brightly on the other side.

"Enfin, on voit le bout du tunnel," Polly intoned almost majestically.

Lucien huffed with dry amusement, explaining himself before she had to ask.

"Leah says something like this too. She says about 'the light at the end of the tunnel' …but every time she does this I see 'er eyes fade into memory."

Lucien's sadness for Leah's trauma was heartfelt, and while Polly knew of the story when the young woman was ambushed in the long, dark tunnel leading into Andorra, she knew that she couldn't compare any experience of her own to how that must have made her feel.

They rode on in silence, feeling like they were on the verge of crossing into another realm after the rocky hills and olive groves of the more mediterranean landscape they called home.

It was quieter there. Snatches of birdsong came and went with the wind, leaving just the soft creak of leather and the occasional breath from their horse, like she was an engine and a change of gear expelled exhaust gases from her nostrils.

The terrain dipped and rose like a slow, tired heartbeat. The road didn't climb too steeply yet, but the constant, steady incline would be enough to wear down the legs of man and beast alike.

Patches of scree spilled from the rock faces on one side, while the other dropped away in sudden views of the Aude River below, black in shadow and silver where the sun touched it, winding endlessly between the folded green and grey of the hills.

That night they made camp on a flat stretch of scrubby earth just outside the village of Lapradelle. It lay nestled in the looming shadow of the high forest and the black silhouette of Puilaurens Castle, perched above like an old scar that never quite healed. The castle's broken towers caught the last of the light, backlit in burnt orange, their jagged teeth outlined against the dusk.

The road had curved up from the gorge and released them into a wider basin, sheltered on all sides by steep woodland ridges. It was noticeably colder there; the kind of cold that crept up sleeves and under collars once the sun dipped behind the ridge, carried on a damp breeze, smelling faintly of pine needles and old stone.

Their breath misted as they unpacked, and Clémence huffed to send twin jets of visible breath while she waited impatiently to be released from her traces.

Lucien checked the area and gathered what wood he could find that wasn't too damp while Polly brushed and fed the placid horse, feeling a gratitude and affinity for how hardworking and uncomplaining she was.

Lucien dug a shallow trench for their fire, protecting it from the bitter wind that sliced through their chosen spot, and adding a windbreak by stacking some of the produce crates to form a low wall.

They huddled beside their meagre fire and ate, too tired and cold to talk, but what neither of them wanted to admit was that the place felt wrong. Something about the howling wind and the brooding, broken castle staring down on them gave their chosen spot an air of superstition, but it wasn't superstition that kept them quiet, it was exhaustion and instinct.

The following morning Lucien watched their daily progress report vanish into the sky. He stayed there, staring up, always looking a little longer than he needed to as though he didn't trust that the message would reach anyone.

The air felt even thinner that morning than it had before, and colder too, as if the very ground had forgotten how to hold warmth. They left Lapradelle without breakfast, opting to eat on the move while behind them, the ruins of Puilaurens Castle faded into the treeline like a bad memory that had finally turned its back.

The road traced the river once more, curling through deep forest where whole mountain sections had been cut straight out of the rock.

Once Polly leaned over to check how perilous the drop was, and since that one glance she kept her eyes resolutely on the road after steering Clémence a little closer to the rock face.

They passed Axat before midday and found nothing there but shuttered windows and the faint smell of woodsmoke that sent Lucien into a state of heightened alertness which didn't pass even after they'd cleared the town by over a mile.

They continued onward, with each rise in the land offered more of the same in the form of trees, rocks, and silence.

That night they made camp on a flat stretch of scrubby earth just outside the village of Lapradelle. It lay nestled in the looming shadow of the high forest and the black silhouette of Puilaurens Castle, perched above like an old scar that never quite healed. The castle's broken towers caught the last of the light, backlit in burnt orange, their jagged teeth outlined against the dusk.

The road had curved up from the gorge and released them into a wider basin, sheltered on all sides by steep woodland ridges. It was noticeably colder there; the kind of cold that crept up sleeves and under collars once the sun dipped behind the ridge, carried on a damp breeze, smelling faintly of pine needles and old stone.

Their breath misted as they unpacked, and Clémence huffed to send twin jets of visible breath while she waited impatiently to be released from her traces.

Lucien checked the area and gathered what wood he could find that wasn't too damp while Polly brushed and fed the placid horse, feeling a gratitude and affinity for how hardworking and uncomplaining she was.

Lucien dug a shallow trench for their fire, protecting it from the bitter wind that sliced through their chosen spot, and adding a windbreak by stacking some of the produce crates to form a low wall.

They huddled beside their meagre fire and ate, too tired and cold to talk, but what neither of them wanted to admit was that the place felt wrong. Something about the howling wind and the brooding, broken castle staring down on them gave their chosen spot an air of superstition, but it wasn't superstition that kept them quiet, it was exhaustion and instinct.

The following morning Lucien watched their daily progress report vanish into the sky. He stayed there, staring up, always looking a little longer than he needed to as though he didn't trust that the message would reach anyone.

The air felt even thinner that morning than it had before, and colder too, as if the very ground had forgotten how to hold warmth. They left Lapradelle without breakfast, opting to eat on the move while behind them, the ruins of Puilaurens Castle faded into the treeline like a bad memory that had finally turned its back.

The road traced the river once more, curling through deep forest where whole mountain sections had been cut straight out of the rock.

Once Polly leaned over to check how perilous the drop was, and since that one glance she kept her eyes resolutely on the road after steering Clémence a little closer to the rock face.

Saint-Martin-Lys came and went without incident, where they stopped briefly to allow Clémence opportunity to drink after her exertions.

The ridgelines began to roll softer, leaving behind the jagged peaks for the forest that broke apart into scrubland that had once been toiled by farmers. Rows of vines still clung to the slope, though clearly no living hand had touched them in years.

Crumbling stone walls marked out what had once been private land, and homesteads that had once been enviable stood derelict and forgotten.

They passed Axat before midday and found nothing there but shuttered windows and the faint smell of woodsmoke that sent Lucien into a state of heightened alertness which didn't pass even after they'd cleared the town by over a mile.

They continued onward, with each rise in the land offered more of the same in the form of trees, rocks, and silence.

By mid-morning, they passed a ridge that gave a sudden, sweeping view of Quillan below, tucked in the crook of a natural valley, its roofs dark and lichen-flecked like old playing pieces on a forgotten board. From that distance it looked peaceful, almost timeless, as though it had waited there undisturbed for something.

The descent was slow, with switchbacks stealing their momentum as the horse's hooves clacked and skidded against the rough surface of the road. As they approached the first buildings, Lucien asked Polly if she was comfortable driving.

She took no offence, recognising that it took skill and patience to allow the horse to pull their heavy load up the inclines and control it down the other side without letting it run away with them. She agreed, sliding along the bench to take the reins while Lucien pulled his unfamiliar rifle free and sat with it ready.

They passed abandoned hamlets on the outskirts, stone skeletons with ivy skins and doorways that yawned like tired mouths. Life had drained from these places long ago, but they still watched the road like stone sentries.

Quillan itself rose from the river, the buildings huddled tightly together as if afraid of the surrounding cliffs. The old town walls were half-collapsed in places, but sections still stood defiantly, patched with moss and bramble. They passed beneath an arch that had once held a gate, and the echo of hooves on stone gave the place a hollow, reverent hush.

There was no traffic, no traders, no footfall. No sign of life in years, in fact, but the absence of evidence only seemed to make Lucien more hyper-aware.

There was no sound save for the distant bubbling of the river and the wind threading through shuttered windows. The occasional creak of a sign swinging on one rusted hinge reached them, mesmerising Polly who feared it might finally give up and fall to the ground as if they were disturbing some ancient tomb.

A weather-beaten statue of Saint Roch stood in the central square, and Lucien smiled as he pointed to the dog at his feet, but the smile faded when he saw some long-dead soul had daubed a crude 'V' across the statue's chest in black paint.

Whether that stood for victory or vendetta, it was impossible to tell without further context.

They did not linger.

They rode ahead, Lucien scanning every rooftop and alley with the quiet, purposeful paranoia that years of danger had carved into him while Polly drove gently, just as alert as Lucien. She noted the way Quillan leaned into the land, as though even the town knew it represented a brief pause between the rise of the foothills and the true climb to come.

Leaving the ghost town behind, Lucien relaxed only a little.

North of Quillan, the road began to shift character seeming less worn and more treacherous. It tightened, forced closer to the contours of the hills, winding like a stitched scar through the flesh of the mountains and all the while the air sharpened with each section they climbed making Polly grateful for the gloves she wore.

Ahead of them lay high valleys and tight passes. Stone bridges with no railings, and a winding tunnel carved through dark rock that sweated cold drops from its ceilings. Lucien had to dismount, pulling a blanket from the back of the cart and gently shushing Clémence before draping it over her head. Polly watched, reins held slack in her hands, as Lucien spoke softly to the horse while leading it through until daylight showed at the far end finally.

Lifting the blanket off he fussed the horse, dodging a tossing head as if she was proud of herself for being so brave. Lucien restored the blanket to the cart and climbed back aboard while behind them Quillan sank quietly into the distance, swallowed once more by the arms of the land.

"Enfin, on voit le bout du tunnel," he told Polly, who clicked her tongue and urged them onwards. "The light at the end of the tunnel…"

When they made camp the second night, Lucien stared at the sky for a long time before deciding on something.

"We send a pigeon first thing in the morning," he told her, evidently having decided there was insufficient daylight for a bird to make it safely back to Neil's workshop.

The horse was brushed, watered and fed. They ate a small meal and fell effortlessly into the same routine as the previous night, but Polly woke before the dawn to find Lucien already sitting atop the wagon looking out at the break in the trees towards the road they followed inland.

Polly got up and stretched her lower back into renewed life, rolled up her bedding and strapped it tight before lifting it into the bed of the cart behind the driver's bench. She reached into a leather satchel and pulled out a scrap of paper to begin writing, but the pen stopped short of making contact.

"What am I telling them?" she asked, looking up at Lucien's back.

"That we camped just north of the town of Quillan."

Polly wrote the note and tied it to the pigeon's leg with practised fingers before she let it fly.

By late afternoon they reached a shallow hill with a flat crest. On the far side of it the valley widened, and the rooftops of Limoux came into view. They were huddled tight against the river, half-sunken in low mist, seeing chimney smoke curl upwards in slow spirals.

They didn't speak, instead they made camp well before the edge of town as strangers arriving anywhere after dark had a way of not being welcome.

They left the scrub of Limoux behind beneath a bruised dawn, the air still cool from the night but promising to warm up quickly. A light breeze drifted down from the hills, carrying with it the earthy scent of dry grass and distant smoke. The vines that crept along the

283

road were wild now, unpruned and clutching, their twisted arms reaching like they raced for some unknown finish line.

The cart creaked into motion with a protesting groan, its wheels finding the path through a land that seemed to exhale dust with every turn. The horse plodded forward, her head low and tail flicking with growing irritation as flies began to appear with the growing heat of the day.

Lucien kept his eyes on the horizon while Polly turned her gaze from place to place, as if memorising the shape of each ruin they passed.

Fields slipped by in a hush. Between dry stone walls and sun-bleached fences, the skeletons of once-ordered farmland stretched out wide, draped in the soft green of weeds and nature's slow reclamation while on the other side of the road evidence of human activity lay obvious to anyone with eyes.

An old scarecrow leaned sideways in one of the fields guarding a field of knee-high maize, its arms outstretched like it had been crucified for laziness. Beyond that tended orchards and vineyards stretched in neat rows. Lucien tapped Polly's arm lightly to get her attention, pointing out movement in those fields as a few people stopped to stare at their progress. No sound carried over the distance, but the body language visible in Lucien's binoculars showed an alarm being raised before two men armed with rifles came running onto view.

Lucien made no move to reach for his own rifle but he kept a careful watch on them until far beyond the range of even his own weapon.

Pieusse came and went, showing buildings sagging under the weight of time and neglect with chimneys cracked and empty. Somewhere behind one of the shuttered windows a dog barked twice, then stopped. No doors opened, no eyes met theirs, and it seemed even the birds gave them wary space.

Further on, Pomas held a little more life. A single column of smoke rose from a chimney, climbing a perfectly vertical path in the still air.

They carried on, too exhausted from travel and too intent on their goal to encourage interaction, until the road began to level out. Hills that had once cradled their route drew back, and the landscape broadened into flat, dry stretches peppered with stubborn weeds and the ghosts of past harvests. The river kept to their right, sluggish and dull, its banks overgrown and drowsy under the sun.

Then Carcassonne appeared.

Not with a grand reveal like Sanctuary did when a traveller descended to sea level and met the imposing walls, but Carcassonne rose. It grew into view, unmistakable and immovable, breaking the skyline with towers and battlements that looked as though they had been carved from the bones of giants. Its outer walls followed the ridge in sharp, defensive angles, dark stone warmed only slightly by the morning light as if the seemingly impenetrable fortress somehow made an effort to appear less imposing.

From that distance, it looked utterly indomitable. It looked alive.

Neither of them spoke as they drew nearer, but Lucien's keen, sniper's eyes saw movement. He detected figures on the high walls, shapes behind arrow slits, smoke drifting upwards from deep within.

Lucien slowed Clémence without a word. Polly adjusted the strap of her bag, her fingers twitching once as if remembering something she didn't want to before she recognised the fidgeting as an obvious betrayal of nervousness. She forced herself to sit still and wait.

"My name is Lucas," Lucien said in a soft, low voice. "You are my mother, Paulette. We are traders from Béziers, we 'ave smoked trout, goat's cheese, strawberries, potatoes, spring onions, rhubarb and garlic. We came 'ere to trade, and we've been travelling for a week."

"I know," Polly said, allowing fear to make her response sound like dismissive frustration.

"Tell me then," Lucien insisted.

"I am Paulette, you are my son, Lucas. We drove for a week from Béziers with fresh produce to trade because we 'eard there were new people living in Carcassonne."

Lucien nodded, pleased with the recital and how natural it sounded. Then he frowned, having entirely failed to consider what came after that cover story.

"What are we trading for?" he asked.

Polly thought on it for a moment before she spoke.

"Bullets for your rifle? Medical supplies?"

Lucien nodded, impressed with her subtlety.

"Good...this will show us if they 'ave a lot of ammunition...if they are an army, they won't want to give up bullets or bandages that they need, yes?"

Polly nodded, still thinking.

"We should also try to trade for more livestock, like a breeding goat or pig?"

Lucien took his turn to nod before glancing back at their laden cart, assessing if they had enough to trade for more.

"Bullets, bandages and livestock...I think this is good."

The road widened for the final stretch. On either side, wild grass and dry hedges framed their approach, and the path itself had worn flat from a thousand years of carts and boots and hoofbeats.

The gates stood open but guarded. Four men watched from the archway, all of them armed with modern weaponry that Lucien noted while trying not to stare at. One guard lifted a hand instructing them to stop while another turned to speak to someone deeper within.

The cart came to a halt a few dozen yards from the gate, dust swirling briefly around the wheels before settling. Clémence snorted and shifted before Polly hushed her soothingly.

"We'll get you a drink soon, don't worry, girl."

"What is your business 'ere?" a guard demanded, although not too impolitely.

Polly opened her mouth to speak, the tension beneath her skin vibrating with a low hum as she prepared herself to reveal their entire story.

"Trade," Lucien grunted, silencing her before she landed them both in trouble.

She looked at him, seeing her "son" hunched over on the bench and adopting a persona so unlike his usual proud, upright bearing. His mouth hung open and to the left slightly, and he eyed the guards with suspicion as if he expected to be struck at any moment.

Polly saw it all in that moment, and arguably too late, she understood the role she needed to play.

Slapping him with the back of her right hand she was glad to see him flinch away. Two guards began walking down the sides of their cart, flanking them as they peered at the crates and sacks in the bed.

"What 'ave I told you about respect, boy?" she growled, before turning a smile on the guard who spoke.

Following up with what was clearly an attempt at a sweet voice, all trace of Polly's Canadian heritage was erased.

"My son still needs to learn better manners," she said by way of a circuitous apology. "We 'ave goods to trade, and after a week of sitting on this damned cart, I need a drink!"

The guard smiled, evidently empathising with her need despite it being only the middle of the day. Polly recognised that connection instantly and doubled down on it through instinct alone. Reaching behind her she made a show of looking over both shoulders before pulling a green bottle free and cradling it in her lap.

"Two years old," she said suggestively. "Made from our own apples…"

The guard hesitated for exactly one second before he did his own subtle check for watchers in the vicinity. He smiled and walked around to Polly's side of the cart before muttering a question at his men.

"Anything?"

"No, just food," came the response.

The guard smiled, accepted the bottle from Polly, then stepped back and slid it into his clothing.

"The market is straight a'ead of you when you get inside, and the stables are to the left of it. Don't let the bastards rip you off for parking that thing."

Polly thanked him, adding a wicked wink about the secret they shared before clicking her tongue and flicking the reins to get Clémence moving again.

"Wait!" the lead guard snapped, sending a jolt of electric adrenaline through both of their bodies.

Polly hauled back gently on the reins to bring Clémence to a halt much to her disgust, and her angry snort coinciding with the toss of her head made that plain.

"You will need one of these," the guard said, pulling a folded piece of paper from a pocket and smoothing it out before offering it to Polly. "Or else the prévôt will shit kittens!"

Polly smiled, accepted the paper and handed it to Lucien before she urged Clémence forward again.

"And welcome to Carcassonne," the lead guard said as the wheels started to roll. "'ome of Le Maréchal."

TRADER'S LANE

Polly kept her shoulders hunched and her posture relaxed, scanning the square without turning her head. The cart beneath her creaked faintly as Lucien shifted beside her, hands loose in his lap, but eyes flicking in quiet rhythm. He took everything in, not with open stares but with the cautious precision of a fox that had outlived too many traps.

Every angle, every armed guard, every gesture was absorbed and catalogued.

The stalls were lined up in rows too perfect to be natural. Identical frames, identical white canvas stretched so tightly that any gust of wind would snap back like a slap. Beneath them, crates were stacked with jars and paper-wrapped bundles. Not a single item seemed out of place so even the clutter looked planned.

The smell hit Lucien first. Dried herbs, but muted beneath something harsher, like bleach. Not the fresh kind, not the chemical tang of a swimming pool in a half-forgotten previous life, but the cloying, old sting in his nose that never quite left. Under it all, the dusty scent of seasoned wood and metal left too long in sun. A chemical tang rode the air like a warning: sterile, clipped, too clean for any real market.

The people *moved* wrong to her eyes. Not hurried, but not slow either. They seemed purposeful, restrained, never bumping or brushing past each other. There was no laughter, no children darting between legs, no haggling or loud voices competing for attention.

There were just transactions. Simple, precise and somehow appearing pre-approved.

It felt like a village carved out by bureaucracy. Like they were extras on a movie set but nobody remembered to shout "cut" so they carried on until told otherwise.

They brought the cart to a halt between two unoccupied stalls, the wheels crunching over gravel that had been raked into obedient lines. Polly hopped down first, her boots landing without a scrape. She adjusted her shawl, not out of modesty but habit, and turned as the sound of footsteps approached.

The man wore a crisp, grey tunic. It didn't appear to be any kind of military issue garment, but close enough to suggest he'd earned the right to wear something like it; like he wore the coat as a status symbol they didn't yet understand. He wasn't bulky, but solid. An ex-soldier maybe, or someone who trained like one. A pistol sat snug at his hip, not as any kind of flex or power symbol, just a tool worn for practicalities as and when they might arise.

The clipboard in his hand said more about him than either the coat or the gun, and when he held it up ready to scribble some annotation he stared with eyes that didn't blink much.

"Names," he demanded, eyes flicking between Polly and Lucien with a mechanical sharpness.

"Paulette," Polly lied smoothly, her accent leaning further into something regional, something forgettable as she nodded toward Lucien. "My son is Lucas."

"Trade licence?"

A hand was held out, as if such a possession was commonplace and expected of them.

Lucien retrieved the paper from his pocket and passed it over. The man glanced at the trading licence before tutting and shaking his head.

"There is a problem?" Polly asked, not having to add much extra juice to her fear and confusion to be believable.

"The fools at the gate did not add your names, so I will 'ave to do it for you now…Your name again?"

It took Lucien a moment to realise the man had spoken to him first, and his delay in responding only added weight to their cover story.

"Tell 'im your name, *stupid*!" Polly snarled at Lucien, who caught on fast and cast his eyes down.

"L-Lucas, *monsieur*."

"That is better," Polly groused. "The boy forgets 'is manners."

The *prévôt*, who seemed to enjoy the grandiose title as if being some senior administrator was a great honour, grunted in amusement at Lucien's discomfort. Polly gave her own false name, adding the town they came from when asked.

"I 'ave not 'ad the pleasure of anyone visiting from your settlement…this is far away, no? Why come all this way to trade?"

"I need bullets," Lucas said, adding a dull heaviness to his voice and attracting the unwelcome gaze of the head bean counter and his pretend mother.

"*Monsieur*," he added, as if remembering his manners before his ear was cuffed.

"It is true, we 'ave a *wolf* problem, and even though my son is the best shot we 'ave, 'e still misses. A lot."

"Tell me, *madame*, do you 'ave many people in your town?"

"Almost one 'undred and twenty, and many of them are children...they can work when they 'it five or six, but until then they are just mouths to feed."

Polly played her part of the uncaring matriarch so well that Lucien only had to remain looking at the ground and fidgeting nervously to fulfil his own role.

"I see," the administrator said blandly, clipping an orange chitty to the front of their newly annotated license but not handing it over. "But why come this far? Why do you not trade at Limoux?"

There was a moment of silence when Polly just stared at the man. It stretched on a beat too long for Lucien, but just as he was about to say something Polly let out a scoff of laughter.

"Those peasants? Why would we trade for goods inferior to our own? No, we 'ave enough food, but we don't 'ave other things. Things we 'ope to find 'ere...so tell *me* monsieur, 'ow does this all work?"

The administrator smiled knowingly and handed her the approved trade licence.

"Each item you sell is recorded, and value is assigned by the quartermaster's office based on the demand of *Les Réunis*. You will receive requisition vouchers as payment, and these are valid within our walls only. Nothing is to leave unless cleared by my office, do you understand?"

"Excuse me, ahh, *Les Réunis*?" Polly enquired, doing her best to sound confused.

The *prévôt* puffed his chest up pompously and seemed to stand three inches taller. His face registered a stoic pride.

"Yes. We believe in the reunification of France. Le Maréchal 'as united many of our people under 'is one flag, and together we will restore France to 'er true glory."

Polly smiled, mirroring his enthusiasm, but she failed to sell it because the man frowned and lowered his voice. "You wish for this too, no?"

"Of course we do! This is what we 'ave been waiting for!" Polly agreed, overdoing the enthusiasm and making Lucien shift uncomfortably.

The *prévôt* saw the movement in his peripheral vision and turned his frown on Lucien.

"And you?" he demanded.

Lucien shrugged and looked down at his boots.

"I don't know about any of this stuff," he admitted tragically. "But if your *Maréchal* makes life easier, I am 'appy."

The man's hands tightened on the clipboard for a terrifying second, but Lucien's smart play to act believably disinterested in revolution and politics rang true. The *prévôt* relaxed and smiled patronisingly at him.

"Le Maréchal will make life easier and better for all of France, boy."

He turned back to Polly and pointed at the trade licence she still gripped tightly.

"You understand our rules?"

Polly met his gaze with a brief, flat nod. "Yes."

"*Bon.* If you wish to leave before the day you must obtain permission from my office" – he turned to point at a busy shop front on the far side of the square – "and return to the gate before dusk. Curfew is enforced, and the gates will not open during the night for anything. Any vouchers you 'ave must be spent before you leave, and your cargo will be inspected. *Bonne chance.*"

Just like that he moved on, his clipboard held up for inspection again before he'd taken three steps.

Polly exhaled loudly, releasing a hiss of tension through her nose.

"Friendly bunch," she said, her old accent creeping though but only spoken loud enough for Lucien to hear.

"You did well," he told her, speaking with the same conspiratorial tone and volume.

"Thank you. Now, let's get this crap unloaded and sold."

Lucien worked with familiar rhythm as he began to unload. The creak of wood and shuffle of wrapped goods gave the square some texture, and already their arrival and unloading were attracting a small crowd of grey-coated procurement people.

They moved together as they unloaded and stacked their ware, working fast but not rushed like people accustomed to long days and manual labour.

Moving too fast looked nervous, too slow looked lazy, and neither would help their anonymity stay intact.

Cheese wheels, wrapped trout that smelled more like salt then fish, jars of preserved peaches and cured meat sealed with wax. Polly laid them out in careful rows, trying to keep her hands from trembling while Lucien arranged crates into a low bench behind the table, then sat, letting his eyes skim the crowd again.

Lucien didn't fully understand the concept explained by the administrator, but Polly clearly had so he played his natural role as unskilled labour and sat back, waiting to be given a task while Polly did the talking. She tried to argue the price, tried to play the game according to the character she played, but the officials gave her stern looks and began to talk amongst themselves until the chief clipboard in charge was quietly summoned back.

"As you are new 'ere, *madame*, allow me to explain 'ow this works to you one more time. The value offered is the value offered, and there is no negotiation. France needs what you 'ave grown and France will pay you a fair price for your 'ard work."

Polly made the correct noises to appease the man and stopped trying to upsell the grabby hands pawing over the produce she had never personally grown or gathered, but she felt defensive of all the same.

Soon the produce was declared sold, and the goods began melting away in return for slips of paper bearing a crest the same as on the flags above the town gates.

Cheese, trout, a jar of dried apricots…all of it moved away one item at a time as the individual procurement busybodies fulfilled their quota of specific items. It was commerce with the pulse of a military drill.

Within an hour most of the stock was gone. Only a stubborn wheel of cheese and a few sealed jars remained, so Polly gave Lucien a nod for him to fetch their secret weapon from the cart and placed four bottles of Neil's distilled calvados into a crate on the table.

One man, grey-coated and bearing a clipboard, sidled closer. He didn't wear the uniform as the others did. In fact, his coat was shabby and dirty by comparison, and even the derisive way he held his clipboard spoke volumes about his belief in *Les Réunis*.

He checked over both shoulders with remarkable subtlety and stood close to Polly, appearing to inspect something in an empty crate while consulting his clipboard, but in fact he spoke to her in a hushed voice that was a world away from official.

"Are they your only two bottles?"

Polly smirked, played the game, and looked out at the square to perform a passable ventriloquist act sans puppet.

"They might not be, it depends on what you tell me they're worth like the rest of those greedy little pigs."

"No, no, you misunderstand me madame, *I* am asking *you* what they are worth."

"I thought that the brave men of the administration office dictated value among your...*cause*," Polly said, pushing the limits of her cover dangerously close.

"Ah, yes," the man said softly, still pretending to be looking at something else that didn't exist. "But I am not seeking to...*procure* these items for Le Maréchal and 'is...*over-inflated windbags* to drink while they congratulate themselves on '*liberating*' another town of innocent people."

Polly glanced at Lucien. Lucien reached a hand slowly under the bench of the cart where his Glock was hidden in a holster, but Polly shook her head.

"Why are you saying this to me?" she asked.

No accusation, just a polite enquiry in a tone that implied they could all still walk away like nothing had been said if he chose to retract his words and pretend they had never been uttered.

"Do you know 'ow I know you are not from Béziers?" he asked nonchalantly, still inspecting the empty crates.

When neither Polly nor Lucien responded the man continued like his question had been rhetorical.

"Because *I*...am from Béziers...and unless I am entirely wrong, nobody lives there these days."

Polly and Lucien exchanged glances again, and this time Lucien did move for the pistol.

"I assure you I mean you no 'arm," the man went on, unconcerned at the movement. "In fact, I rather suspect you and I are on the same side."

Lucien glitched, confused by the words and racking his memory for where he might have seen the man before, thinking him from Andorra or one of their outlying settlements.

"In fact," he went on. "I can even guess where you are truly from…it is either Andorra or the strong'old by the sea."

He glanced at Polly's face for a split-second before looking down. Evidently that snapshot had been enough to discern the truth, or at least steer his guess.

"So…you are from the place they call *Sanctuaire*. I must admit, I did not expe—"

"What do you want?" Lucien demanded in a menacingly soft voice.

"What do I want?" the man asked, turning a smile on him for the first time. "I want a drink, and I am off duty in 'alf an 'our. There is a place about a minute's walk away, called *Le Tonneau Citoyen*. It used to be a nice Irish pub where they 'ad live music almost every night, but that was many years ago now…meet me there in an hour."

With that he finished his mock inspection, bid them a formal farewell, and took his clipboard somewhere else.

THE CITIZEN'S BARREL

"Time for that drink," Polly said.

Lucien locked the cart with a pin through the wheel before they crossed the square and walked in the direction they'd been given, the Glock retrieved from its hiding place under the cart's bench and stowed inside his waistband.

Polly led, angling her path across the road towards the frontage of a pub that had clearly been repainted recently. The narrow entrance was marked with a faded beer stein above a sun-warped awning where the pub crouched under the stonework as if it had grown there, old and stubborn.

"*Try* to blend in," Lucien replied in a tone he intended to sound neutral, but instead came over as patronising.

Inside, the change in light was immediate. Dim. Dusty. The kind of darkness that made your eyes take a second breath. The air clung. Warm, stale, touched with old hops and polish. And something else, under it. Something faint and metallic, like a chemical residue from cleaning up an unpleasant mess.

The walls were cluttered with history. Photos gone brown with time, medals, framed posters for prize fights harking back to the days of moustached men adhering to the Queensbury rules.

Behind the bar a young woman with pale eyes and a braid accepted their vouchers without a word. She scanned them with those pale eyes, wearing the same disinterested look, then poured two tall beers that she slid across the bar.

Polly thanked her with a wide smile, no doubt either trying to infect the sullen young woman with some happiness or else ramping up her own to rub it in.

They found a table tucked in the back corner, facing the room at an angle. Lucien took the far seat with his back to the wall and his eyes on the crooked mirror that provided him sight of the door without ever turning. Polly sat opposite, her gaze drifting half-closed as she listened to the low buzz of conversation all around them, trying to tune out certain sounds to focus on words.

Two men sat nearby. Not officials or soldiers by the look of them, but they had rough hands and work-stiff shoulders. They seemed at ease in that place in a way few others were.

They talked with their bodies leaned in, feet stretched out, beers cradled loosely in big hands atop the small wooden table, looking like two men who'd had that conversation before.

"...I'm telling you, 'e is taking them *east*," one said. "I 'eard it straight from one of the guards on the gate."

His voice was low, but not hushed. As if no one would dare care about their conversation.

Polly tried desperately to make out the response but a figure drifted into their periphery, moving like someone with no need to be noticed.

Lucien locked onto him without staring open hostility, seeing a nondescript man wearing a plain, nondescript jacket; the sort that vanished into the backdrop of a dozen towns. He might have walked past them a hundred times that day and they'd never have registered him.

He lingered near their table for only a moment, as though he were checking for somewhere to sit, and more than long enough for both Lucien and Polly to grow nervous before he turned slightly, not quite facing them, and spoke in a low voice.

"May I join you?" he asked, his voice soft and unassuming.

Polly glanced up, ready to wave him away, but Lucien stilled. The voice wasn't loud, but it was familiar. Something in the rhythm, in the faint roughness beneath the calm, and his eyes tried to match the man with the voice.

Polly heard it too and looked again, properly this time. Without the grey uniform coat and the clipboard, the man was barely recognisable. Just another tired face in a tired town, almost invisible among a crowd.

Lucien gave the faintest nod and the man slid into the seat beside them with the relaxed ease of someone who had done this before. He didn't look at them, didn't speak again, just sat with his elbows resting on the scarred table, eyes half-lidded as though watching the same scene they were.

"They are confident," he said eventually, nodding slightly towards the men still talking two tables over. "They've been promised too much."

Polly shifted, not enough to draw attention, just enough to settle her weight.

"And you weren't?" she asked, her tone dry.

"I was promised *purpose*," he replied. "Not theatre."

There was a pause, filled by the distant scrape of a chair and the low hum of voices around them. Then he spoke again, just above the rim of his glass.

"Some of us still believe in France. We just think marching 'er backwards while waving a flag isn't the way forward. I am not sure if you know much of 'istory, but this 'as been done before."

301

Lucien's gaze flicked to the man's hands detecting no fidgeting or tension. He didn't seem afraid, just tired in a disappointed kind of way.

"What are they confident about?" Lucien asked quietly, but any answer he might've received was stifled by Polly's interruption.

"You're one of his?" Polly asked. "This *Maréchal*?"

"I'm one of many," the man told her quietly, wearing a thin smile. "But not all of us are true believers. Some of us are just waiting for someone to admit this isn't working."

His words hung for a moment. Not quite an invitation or a warning, but something that felt dangerously seditious nonetheless.

"If this next push fails," he said quietly, adjusting the cuff of his sleeve, "things will change. Whether 'e allows it or not."

He stood, finished his drink and gave them a look.

"I 'ope for your sake you make it 'ome safely, because this is not the place you want to be right now."

His head twitched with something close to a nod, then he turned and walked away without a backward glance before leaving the pub to melt away. To become just another nobody.

Polly's eyes tried to meet Lucien's but he was looking intently at the mirror's reflection showing the nearest table as his lip twitched.

"East? They 'aven't hit east in months! I thought they went to take over some shitty place with a port in the south?"

The two men spoke louder now, either through confidence from the beer or a false belief that their words were safe to utter in public.

"They *did*, but I 'eard this place 'as food stockpiled and no wall, so it will be an easier win."

Polly tilted her head a fraction, one hand resting lightly on her thigh as her heart hammered with adrenaline sparked by recognition.

"Why now?" the other man asked in a tone that implied he frowned over the question.

Lucien didn't move, just watched the mirror like a gargoyle.

"Because the 'arvest is starting," came the reply. "If they strike fast and pull out, they will cripple the supply lines and bring the food back 'ere."

Polly shifted, her elbow moving fractionally towards her belt. Lucien gave her a look that barely registered, offering the faintest shake of his head.

"We need to go," she muttered, her voice caught between breath and thought.

"We can't," Lucien replied, almost without sound. "Not yet. You 'eard the man's rules, we need to trade the vouchers and get permission to leave."

Her eyes locked with his, intensity burning through adrenaline-sparked tears. "They'll hit the farms. They'll kill *our* people."

"If we leave without spending the vouchers, it'll flag us," Lucien said patiently before draining the last of his beer. "Then we won't get out of the gate."

Polly's jaw clenched. "Then we spend them. Fast. Food, ammo, anything useful, and get on the road by nightfall."

Lucien nodded. "I'll find goats and ammunition. You get anything you can."

He stood and nodded again, accepting some of the vouchers from Polly before leaving the pub and walking with purpose that never reached an intensity that might draw attention.

Polly sat alone, hands shaking as they gripped the glass. She snatched it up and gulped the contents greedily, gasping and wiping her mouth before she walked too fast for the door and earned the attention of half the pub.

Lucien veered toward the livestock pens following his nose for the reek of animals. The scent was immediate. It was hot, sour, thick with piss and manure and the musk of animals penned close enough to sweat together among stale straw only made worse by the heat.

Pens lined in rows that sat annoyingly neat again. Numbered tags, traders stiff with suspicion as soldiers lingered, inspecting and not talking. Just watching with the attention of men rewarded for telling tales of misdeeds to their superiors.

Lucien found a pen with three goats and a man who looked older than the moon. With a flat cap, sun-bitten skin and hands the colour of tobacco stains, his eyes squinted at Lucien out of suspicion or habit.

"'ow many vouchers for the goats?" Lucien asked.

"Four each," the man said without a smile. "Six for the two bigger ones."

Lucien followed the crooked, pointed finger to see a pair of goats only slightly larger than the kids he was looking at.

"I'll take two small ones," he said confidently, pointing at two randomly after appearing to give the matter some serious thought. "That one…and *that* one."

The man sniffed. "You know your goats, boy."

Lucien felt relieved, but also annoyed because he'd just given the ancient man a reason to recall him. Running a nervous hand over his shorn scalp he realised not for the first time how much he played with his hair when he was nervous.

Lucien looked at his remaining vouchers and enquired if he could get another for just three, but the man shook his head slowly. "Three won't even get you a runt. They're worth five at least but these *parasites d'État* say they 'ave to control the prices."

The old man scowled at the back of the nearest grey-coated clip-board bearer and pulled a face.

"*Vive la revolution*," he muttered under his breath with dark sarcasm, but Lucien noted how cautious he was not to be overheard.

He held out the right vouchers for the man to take, watching him peer closely at them through myopic eyes before they shook to seal the deal, then whistled and waved over the bureaucrat he'd just privately insulted to record the transaction. It was recorded on the clipboard and both men had to make their mark.

Lucien had already made himself memorable to the old man, cursing himself for failing to follow Leah's advice on anonymity, so he decided he might as well limit his exposure to one person.

"*Pardon, L'ancien*," Lucien said, bordering on impoliteness with his informality. "Do you know anyone selling bullets?"

The old man eyed him with renewed suspicion, mouth twisted in thought for a long time before he spoke. "And why do you need bullets, boy? Are you a *fighter*?"

"Wolves," Lucien said, falling back on his character's low intelligence as camouflage. "I 'unt the wolves so they don't take our livestock."

The old man nodded sagely, still ruminating and taking enough time over his deliberations to make Lucien feel nervous enough to rub his head again.

"Go see Marcel over there," he said, pointing the same crooked finger he'd pointed at his goats. "'e 'as bullets, but 'e is a crooked bastard, so watch yourself."

Lucien thanked him, waiting impatiently as he groaned and bent to lash short loops of rope around the necks of the chosen goats and lift them out over the pen's rails with a strength no doubt carved by a long life of doing just that. The goats protested and bucked until

305

their hooves found the ground again, and Lucien tried to walk the unruly purchases back to his cart.

Manhandling both into the bed with difficulty, he tied them securely to the railing behind the driver's bench and spread a few of Clémence's precious oats to keep them occupied, moving the covered crate of pigeons beyond their reach.

Heading for the man called Marcel, Lucien prepared himself to be ripped off just to spend the last of their vouchers before they could begin trying to make their escape and carry the news of an attack.

He didn't make a show of looking around for Polly, but neither did he detect her anywhere in the market before he reached Marcel and began discussing the cost of ammunition. A clipboard bearer joined them almost immediately, stating a shortage of such items available to civilians as the need of the cause came first. Lucien listened, slack-jawed, just wanting the transaction over and done with.

He turned to scan the square as if bored by the long-winded explanation preventing him from being told the price when he saw the pigeon.

A dart of feathers across the pale sky, cutting sharp through the silence as it flapped noisily to gain altitude.

A shout rang out that stopped Lucien's blood cold in his veins.

"*Oiseau!*"

Men ran, uniformed soldiers and grey-coated administrators reacting to something he hadn't seen but knew to be wrong.

"*Tirez! TIREZ!*"

Lucien saw the guard's movement before he heard the shot. Before the thundering report of a shotgun that jetted flame from the end of the barrels.

Before the sky burst with feathers.

He saw two soldiers grab Polly, saw them dragging her away fast and brutal from the back of their cart. She screamed, resisted, cursed them foully before she accepted her fate and let herself be taken away, back straight, head high and eyes resolutely forward.

The guard who had fired the successful blast to atomise the pigeon at such short range beamed at his prowess and approached the carcass, lifting it by a foot to retrieve the note tied there while trying to avoid the blood and gore.

A small, thin man wearing a gaudy uniform coat marched his small feet petulantly across the square with a ramrod-straight back to demand the message. Small eyes set deep in his thin face scanned the paper before he turned a malevolent gaze on Polly, backhanding her hard across the cheek without warning.

Lucien reacted instantly, heart slamming his ribs like fists, but a firm hand gripped his right arm.

Turning a savage look on the person who had grabbed him Lucien reacted, bringing his left hand already balled into a fist up ready to connect with a jaw, but he froze as he found himself staring into the eyes of the man they'd met with in the pub.

"No. Come with me unless you want to be taken too," he growled low, tugging Lucien away from the stall.

He let himself be led, walking fast to keep up but twisting around for one final glimpse of Polly being led away.

ASPIRATIONS OF GREATNESS

Elías Roca Serra was just shy of his twentieth birthday when they sent him up to the ridge for his turn on watch. Wiry and sun-darkened, he had the look of someone carved from the hills themselves. Before he wore a uniform – or what passed for one in Sanctuary's militia – he had helped his uncle harvest olives on the dry terraces above Lleida with young hands blackened by oil and bark. He had known heat, thirst, and aching legs long before anyone gave him a rifle and told him to watch.

He'd been raised in a crumbling farmhouse with a roof that leaked each winter tucked into the hills outside Organyà, just south of the Andorran border in the Catalan foothills of Spain. His family had farmed the same tired patch of land for four generations, coaxing what they could from the arid soil in a life of small gains and hard losses.

Elías' father had died when he was five in a simple accident no one liked to talk about, so the boy had grown up in the company of uncles and cousins. He soon learned that the accident was more complicated than he'd been told at the time, and before long he came to understand the truth and stopped mourning his father entirely. Raised more by the rhythm of work than by any particular hand, Elías had never finished school.

Not properly, at least. There were books, briefly, but not the kind that kept his attention, and certainly not the kind that seemed to matter when there were trees to prune and nets to spread. He could fix an engine with fence wire, climb an almond tree barefoot, and butcher a rabbit with quick hands and a sharp knife, but if anyone asked him to solve equations or recite poetry he'd look at them like they spoke an alien language.

Then came the end of the world, and with it the end of the farm and the life he'd come to know. He didn't really recall much of what happened in the days that followed, but he knew he'd wandered. He'd wandered so long and so far that the arid farmland he knew as home was left far behind, and the distant, snow-capped mountains became larger than he ever dreamed they could be.

He was found, he was taken in by the people of Andorra, and ever since a girl not much older than he had arrived dressed as a warrior, a dog so large he thought it was a wolf by her side, and carrying weapons he'd only ever seen on a fuzzy TV screen, Elías had decided on the spot what he was going to be when he grew up.

By seventeen he was built lean, with ropey arms and a resolve so unbreakable it was almost a hindrance at times. He begged and pleaded with the people who'd taken him in to be allowed to join the ranks of the few fighters Andorra had, and when they said no he did what he felt he had to. Word of the pirate attacks at the coast had angered him, not for the audacity of the enemy's plan but at himself for not being there, so the day after he learned of this latest threat to the people of their region he packed his few belongings and left before the dawn. He walked all the way to Sanctuary and signed up for the militia not because he believed, but because he didn't see any other way his future could go.

His arrival caused a small stir, including the brooding head man sending word to Andorra to check Elías wasn't fleeing any kind of responsibility, but when they permitted him to try out he passed the tests with flying colours.

His marksmanship was good because he'd been shooting small game and birds with shotguns and rifles since the time his front baby teeth fell out. He was fit, lean, fast and strong because his entire existence had been that of long days of manual labour.

He achieved his goal of becoming a fighter, soaked up every lesson that was taught to him, and promptly found himself rotating an endless, monotonous cycle of guard rotations with zero action.

Now, finally with the prospect of real action close at hand, he sat behind a low wall of stacked stones and stared eastwards with the rough edge of the Pyrenees stretching up behind him like broken teeth.

Ahead of him the valley rolled in soft green and brown lines, wisps of overnight clouds still clinging to the folds like a blanket not quite thrown off, while the sky above was washed with early light, pale gold pushing back the grey.

Elías shifted his shoulders and let the weight of his rifle settle against his lap, finding himself daydreaming about the rumours he'd heard that had turned out to be true. About how Lucien, the militia commander he looked up to greatly despite being only five or so years Elías' senior, had hunted and killed a leopard not one mile away from where he now sat.

If he respected Lucien before then what he felt now came close to adoration, but he recognised that most of that idolisation came from the fact that Lucien had been the man to tame the wild young warrior girl who had changed his life simply by walking past him.

At times he wished he still had his grandfather's shotgun instead of the characterless military rifle he cradled now. The shotgun had been an old, battered thing, with barrels worn shiny and the wooden furniture polished by use and age. It had been used on rabbits, on various birds, on foxes and wild dogs and once, according to family legend, on a thief in the orchard.

Elías didn't doubt that, nor did he doubt that at one time in his life he'd walked close to where that thief had been buried in an unmarked grave.

He squinted down the slope, absently picking at a scab on the back of his hand and trying to count how many days he had been on rotation.

Quatre? No, cinc, he thought

That meant the day after tomorrow would be his birthday, at least that was what he reckoned from the day he believed it had been when they were sent to ride out to guard the farms, though up here that meant little.

There would be no *coca*, no sweet flatbread topped with delicious things. No birthday songs sung at him. Nobody pulling his ears once for each year he'd been alive and counting out the numbers to taunt him as they did it. No family coming together to sit down for a meal. No women yelling at the boys to wait, to wash their filthy hands, to stop fighting with each other and to cross themselves before they ate, muttering **"Beneïu, Senyor, els aliments que anem a prendre"** as **they asked their Lord to bless the food they were about to take.**

Elías let out a soft sigh and found himself longing for those days of working from sunrise to sunset until he fell into bed exhausted, because to him they were the only old days he knew so they were the good days he remembered.

All around him the world was still waking. Birds moved through the low trees, a goat bell clinked distantly as an annoyed bleat wove its way to his ears on the wind.

That wind stirred the scrub down the slope from his sentry position and carried up the scent of dust and something sweeter, blossom maybe, or thyme.

He saw them when they crested the far ridge, his keen, young eyes locking onto the movement like a predator in its prime.

Shapes in the half-light, not quite clear, but moving with a rhythm that caught his attention.

Not goats or dogs, certainly not livestock. The line shifted, reshaping itself with every step, but it had purpose. It moved deliberately.

Elías slid down behind the wall, breath caught sharp in his chest. Something deep inside him knew this was very, *very* bad news and yet his first potential sight of an enemy didn't turn his bowels to water or make him want to run. He felt the familiar feel of adrenaline flooding his system but it did so in a way he'd never experienced before. It was more intense, more visceral than ever, and as fearful as he was that he might want to flee his first ever fight he found a strength he always knew he possessed.

His hands gripped the rifle tighter, sweaty palms on modern polymer, but he stayed there, listening and watching, willing his heartbeat to quiet so he could hear better.

The murmur of movement became clearer, and even when his mind registered the flood of horsemen trotting into the valley from the far side, still he didn't falter out of fear. He only wished the rifle they gave him could shoot far enough and that he'd been trained well enough to shoot like Lucien or Leah and kill with accuracy over a great distance.

So he knew he would have to wait, have to let the enemy come to him so he could prove to himself and everyone else that this was his calling. This was what he was born to do.

Elías Roca Serra was about to prove his worth and begin his unspoken destiny to become a great military leader and maybe, possibly, be worthy of a woman like the one who had changed his entire world.

He watched as the horsemen turned their mounts into a patch of woodland and disappeared from view, but not before he'd hurriedly lifted a small set of binoculars to his eyes and counted as best he could.

Elías didn't know who they were, not yet, but he knew what he had to do. He had to fight them, but he had to warn everyone first.

He pushed himself to his feet and began to move low along the path, ducking behind rocks and trees being careful not to dislodge stones or snap twigs. All the while he kept his eyes on the far end of the valley and the woodland where this enemy – for they *had* to be the enemy – had disappeared.

When he reached the spot he was aiming for he stopped, pulled a scrap of paper from the weatherproof box, and gripped the pencil tight in his right hand while the sheer force of concentrated will pushed the tip of his tongue from one side of his mouth while he wrote.

Attaching that message to the leg of a pigeon he somehow sensed was the fastest among the half dozen still in that crate set high over the farmlands, he cradled it softly in both hands before whispering to it and launching it high into the air for an added speed bonus.

"*Vola rapid, amiga,*" he told the pigeon as it flapped away to streak south.

The snap of flapping wings snatched Mitch's attention from his spot near the main gate. His still-keen eyes located the tiny silhouette of a pigeon looping a lazy circle as it descended to a building halfway up the slope on the far side of the docks, and he began jogging toward Neil's workshop without a word.

Leah arrived just before he did, Nemesis sliding over the ground effortlessly beside her like a loyal shark, and her eyes portrayed the same concern he felt.

"Off schedule," Mitch muttered as he reached for the door.

Leah nodded but said nothing.

Inside, Neil was closing the door on a bird cage with one hand, holding a scrap of paper in the other. He glanced up when the door opened, nodded to both visitors as though he expected them to come, and flattened out the note on the table.

"Shit," he said flatly, prompting both Leah and Mitch to start speaking at once to demand more information than that.

Neil held up both hands and closed his eyes, to silence them, overwhelmed at the confusing cacophony.

"I'm not sure, but I think it's bad news. 'Men and horses' I can make out, and it's maybe an hour old, based on how fast he flies," Neil said with a jerk of his head back toward the cage where a pigeon was happily pecking at some corn. "At least that's what I can make out."

"How big a force?" Leah demanded.

"What's their capabilities?" Mitch said, speaking over her.

Neil screwed his eyes up again and flapped the note at them. Mitch took it and Leah crowded close to see the words.

Leah let out an exasperated noise as the note was scribbled in neither English nor French, and the handwriting was appalling. Mitch, being married to a Spanish woman, had a better chance but still he struggled to read the note.

Hombres y caballos vinieron del este. Escondíos en el valle.

Mitch frowned at it, filing the room with a palpable tension as he thought silently.

"Men and horses is right enough," he said. "And they came from the east…then something about the valley but I don't know what *'escondíos'* means…"

"Would Alita know?" Leah asked urgently.

"Aye, probably," Mitch said, already turning for the door.

They found Alita on the docks near her and Mitch's home. Their daughter played with a handful of seashells, squatting down with perfect form in that way very young children do, but on hearing running bootsteps she stood and moved to cling to her mother's skirt until she recognised her father and jumped up and down excitedly.

Mitch didn't mirror that excitement. Instead, he radiated an urgency, an anger that threatened to burst out unless he was able to direct it at something deserving.

He thrust the note at Alita who took it and swept her long hair away from her face.

"I can make out the first part, but—"

He stopped talking when her right hand shot up beneath her chin and the fingers flicked fast in his direction.

Leah recognised the gesture as one with multiple meanings, ranging from "Shush" to something far more aggressive, but in this context she took it just as Mitch did; a simple "shut up a second".

"Who is this from? Did they even go to school?" Alita asked, missing the urgency entirely.

"Doesn't matter," Mitch snapped back. "I got 'men and horses from the east' then something about the valley, but I don't know this word."

He leaned in and pointed a fingertip at the note.

"I think that they mean to say *esconDIDos*, but *esconDIos* means to be hiding."

"So there's still time maybe," Leah said with a low, urgent tone of voice that implied someone was going to get hurt.

"Aye!" Mitch agreed, snatching back the note and hurrying a kiss to his wife and daughter before turning to follow Leah at a dead run.

"Truck and QRF," he said, catching up to her.

"Yeah, but we need to tell Dan first!"

SUBSTITUTION

Dan was sitting on the ramparts of the north wall, his back pressed against sun-warmed stone, with a concerned Ash lying halfway across his lap letting out small whines of sympathy.

One eye was swollen nearly shut, the side of his face purple and puffed out like an overripe plum.

Mitch swore under his breath when he saw him, bending down to peer at the obviously bad infection distorting his friend's face.

When Mitch blocked out the sun and placed Dan's head in the shade, he murmured and flopped his head from side to side as if having a bad dream.

"How bloody long has he been like this?" Mitch demanded, turning his attention to the nearest militia guard on the wall.

Although clearly exhausted, the man seemed more concerned about being in trouble.

"I tell him he must see a doctor, but he said to me 'piss off'," came the hurt reply in Spanish-accented English.

"Yep, sounds like Dan," Leah said as she stooped to gain purchase under Dan's left armpit.

Mitch did the same on the other side, grumbling at Ash to move but the dog was resolute.

"Ash! *Back!*" Leah snapped, sending the dog reluctantly away for Mitch to help haul their leader to his feet.

"Satan's scabby ball sack, the man's on fuckin' fire!" Mitch exclaimed.

Leah felt it too. The sheer heat radiating from Dan was as uncomfortable as standing too close to a lit brazier during a night shift.

"That's not good," she agreed mildly, grunting with the effort of lifting Dan up.

He went with it, appearing about thirty percent conscious like he'd been fine drinking all night and suddenly crashed, but the muttering concerned her greatly.

With difficulty they walked him towards the steps but Leah's smaller, lighter frame couldn't hold her father upright.

"Sack this," Mitch growled, ducking down to let Dan flop over his back.

Settling the floppy weight of a full-grown man across his shoulders Mitch sucked in a deep breath ready for the effort. Standing, he issued a noise that was more steam engine than weightlifter, but Dan's form rose into the air and steadied.

Mitch took the stairs carefully, Leah snapping at both dogs not to get under his feet, and when they reached the bottom Neil was waiting for them.

"I've spun up the QRF. Someone's getting the truck ready," he reported before his brain registered what his eyes were seeing. "Errrr, what the fuck?"

"He's burning up with fever and the left side of his face looks like a basketball," Leah said. "We need to get him to medical."

"We'll handle it," Mitch said, hissing the words through the effort of carrying the deadweight. "You unlock the armoury and get me the crates numbered five and eight, got that? Five and eight. I want them in the truck ready."

Neil nodded, happy to be doing something useful instead of worrying about his oldest living friend.

"Five and eight, got it. I'll catch you up."

Kate appeared from the infirmary steps, eyes going wide at the sight of Mitch walking with short, rapid steps carrying Dan over his shoulders like a sack of grain.

"What's...?"

"He's got a bad fever," Leah barked with brutal efficiency. "Mumbling and not with it. The swelling's looking *really* bad too."

"Get him inside," Kate said, turning to hold the doors open.

Mitch followed, dropping Dan on his back on a bed while Sera shot up from behind a desk to join them. Her constant battles with Dan had been a staple of their group for a decade, but seeing that he was seriously unwell reset everything for Sera.

"I knew he wouldn't let anyone sort it," Sera complained. "Stubborn bloody fool!"

"Fever," Kate told her. "Bad, bordering on delirium."

"Could be bloody sepsis judging by that infection," Sera answered as she peered close to Dan's swollen cheek.

She forced his stubbled chin down to open his mouth and recoiled, coughing and gagging.

"Jesus Christ," she hissed. "Yep, that infection's rotten."

Mitch stepped back as the least qualified in the room when it came to medical matters, and while their former paramedic and former veterinarian began doing what he'd call "medic shit" Leah was stripping Dan of his rifle and vest.

The heat that expelled into the room when his vest was pulled open made her cheeks flush pink, and when she put her hand on his chest she felt his heart beating like the bassline of a dance track.

Kate felt it too, dropping her ear to his chest and listening for a few seconds before speaking to Sera.

"Shit. Sera? He's tachycardic."

Leah felt her world shrinking. Of all the things that had tried to kill Dan since she'd first met him, a bad tooth being the thing to finish him off was the cruellest irony imaginable.

Kate and Sera began the busy work of getting saline ready to forcefully pump into his veins as Neil jogged in behind them, red faced and sweating.

"QRF and three off duty volunteers are getting the truck ready now. They're all kitted out with lots of ammo and I've added a gympy and four belts," he said, speaking to Mitch.

"Good man. Mate, we need you here to run the defences. With her man off doing what he's doing and *him* all fucked up, I need me and Leah to handle the attack on the farms so you'll ha—"

Dan lurched off the bed, coming alive like something from a horror movie. He tried to walk away from the bed but his knees buckled before Leah caught him on reflex, barely able to hold his weight from wiping them both out on the floor.

Everyone spoke at once. Dan was told to calm down, to get back on the ned, to not worry because they could handle it, but there was something in his eyes…something very wrong.

He issued a grunt through his nose, his jaw locked tight by swelling and pain. His eyes darted all around, pupils wide with fear and confusion.

"Get the fuck back on that bed, Dan! You're not doing anyone any good like this!" Sera barked at him in her most commanding voice.

Dan gave the grunt again, more animal than human, then issued a single word through clenched teeth.

"*Farms!*"

He pawed at his chest, right hand postured by muscle memory to clutch the grip of his rifle where it usually hung, but his hands grasped at nothing. He took a handful of his sweat-soaked T-shirt and pulled at it, looking down with incomprehension at the missing rifle grip, then turned confused, terrified eyes back on everyone in the room.

The noise was overwhelming, with everyone trying to get him to lie down, with two dogs barking, Leah trying to push him back onto the bed. Dan's eyes were wild, glassy, darting between faces without recognition. His breathing came in harsh gasps. Ash was barking furiously now, tail rigid, snarling at everything and nothing.

Until something about it all tipped Dan's subconscious into fight or flight mode.

His right hand was sluggish compared to normal, but the same muscle memory that sent it searching for his rifle also registered the importance of a secondary weapon. With no vest or slung rifle, that hand dropped to his right thigh where the pistol sat at just the perfect height.

"*Whoa*!" Neil yelled, stepping in fast to clamp both hands hard around the barrel of the pistol. "Stop! *Stop*! No one's trying to hurt you!"

As diminished as Dan's mind was and as ravaged as his body had become by the fever, he still gripped the Glock hard enough that Neil couldn't twist it from his grip.

Neil hung on with every ounce of strength he had, desperately trying to prevent the slide from moving so the gun couldn't fire, just as Mitch joined him to clamp and twist the arm but still Dan wouldn't release the weapon.

Leah wrapped her right forearm around Dan's neck hard, locking it in with her left elbow and forcing the top of his head down. She flexed with everything she had; her eyes closed from the emotional pain and the gargantuan effort of trying to stop the blood flow to his brain and end this insane situation before someone got killed.

"*Stop! Stop! Stop!*" she hissed close to his ear, more of a desperate plea than an order.

He didn't stop. His entire body shook while everyone still shouted and fought for control of the gun. Both dogs were barking angrily, and Leah felt the hot pressure of Nemesis pressing her body into Leah's leg; every bark sending a sharp wave of vibration up her body.

She hung on, sinking the choke in as deep and tight as she could, summoning strength from places she didn't know existed until finally Dan began to falter.

The strength melted away from him, the Glock was wrested from his grip for Neil to fall away gasping, and Dan's hands lifted to try and pry her arm away.

His hands were weak, the fingers employing all the power of a baby as they fought desperately to free him, until eventually the brain had gone long enough without fresh oxygen and he went limp.

"On the bed! Get him on the bed!" Kate yelled, reaching for his boots to help Mitch lift him.

Leah struggled to hold the weight of Dan's upper body, and as the world around her began to swim back into her senses she felt Nemesis pressed hard against her left leg and still barking.

She looked down to see Ash – teeth bared and jaw snapping with each bark – fixed on Leah. Had anyone but her delivered the choke she was sure Ash would've attacked, but either his mixed loyalty to both her and Dan or the protective behaviour of her own dog held him back.

"Easy," she said to the dog, hand held out flat as she sank to the floor slowly on shaking legs. "Eeeeeeasyyyyy…"

She placed her left hand on Nemesis' back to soothe her, instantly quietening her barking at her sire in defence of her handler. Leah repeated the word gently as she reached Ash's level, making sure she kept her eyes on his and her confidence high.

She knew the dogs could sense more than just smells and sights, and she also knew somehow that the dog could still decide to go for her if she made a wrong move.

She ignored everything happening above her, just as Ash did, because he'd become so fixated on Leah hurting his handler that nothing else in the world existed.

Slowly she reached out to Ash, still saying soothing words, until at last the lips lowered to show almost no teeth. Ash seemed to shrink then, seemed to age five years and sag from the stress and effort of it all, and Leah's heart broke for him because he didn't understand what was happening.

She patted her thighs with both hands and Ash came to her. Nemesis, just as desperate for reassurance after the confusing incident came too, and she fussed both dogs and let them lick her face to feel safe and loved again.

"Kid, you good to go? I'll understand if you want to stay here wi—" Mitch began.

Leah stood.

"I'm coming," she said firmly.

She was frightened and upset, but she had an emotional charge she could put to good use on people who deserved everything they'd get.

Dan didn't move. This time it wasn't out of stubbornness or pride, but something far worse. The chaos had passed: the shouting, the barked orders, the barking of dogs, the sudden violence of bodies grappling in panic, and now there was only the rasp of his shallow, uneven breaths and the soft squeak of boots against the infirmary's tile floor.

Kate pressed the backs of her fingers to his throat and held them there for a moment, then nodded once.

Neil stood near the door, shoulders stiff, the Glock hanging from his hand like a dead weight. He stared at it as if it might confess something if he looked hard enough while his mouth worked silently, trying to form a sentence that never came.

Sweat slicked the grip. His eyes flickered from the pistol to Dan, then back again until he appeared to wake up and tucked it into the back of his waistband.

Kate had already turned away and was rifling through a battered, old medical kit with mechanical focus.

"We need fluids. Neil, I need you to squeeze the bag. Sera, help me find a line," she said, rattling off the separate items as one.

Dan's arm was deadweight when she took it, the skin waxy and far too warm.

"Shit! Can't find a bloody vein," Sera hissed.

"Loosen your tourniquet. His BP's too low, so hang his arm off the bed and let gravity fill it up until you can see one."

Sera didn't acknowledge the instructions verbally but followed them anyway, eventually seeing enough of a vein to slide the cannula in with practised hands. She secured it with tape, fast and ugly, then jabbed a finger toward Neil.

"Hold this up and squeeze but not too hard or you'll fill his lungs up and give him a pulmonary oedema. If he goes into shock or respiratory failure, we'll lose him."

"No pressure…" Neil muttered as he took the bag like it might detonate.

He began to squeeze gently, his hands trembling as the ridiculous severity of the situation finally dawned on him.

Sera hovered at the bedside, pale and wide-eyed, her gaze locked onto the fast, shallow rise and fall of Dan's chest. Sera and Kate locked eyes, communicating apparently through telepathy as they waited for some of the fluids to stabilise Dan's internal systems.

"Protect the airway?" Sera asked.

Kate glanced from the bag of saline squeezed in Neil's fist and back to Dan before nodding.

They rolled him over just far enough for his head to hang over the edge of the bed, mouth slack. Neil adjusted his legs to stop him rolling back before Kate wedged a carved block between his teeth to hold his mouth open and position a shallow dish on the floor beneath him.

Kate looked at the bag in Neil's hand, gauged the time to be right, then gave a nod to Sera. "Now. Do it."

Sera yanked the cap from a syringe and jabbed it into Dan's thigh.

"What's that?" Neil asked nervously.

"Some of the good stuff," Sera assured him.

"Watch his BP," Kate said without glancing up from watching Dan. "If it drops, we won't get him back."

Sera stepped away to return a second later with a blood pressure machine. Some supply of rechargeable batteries had been painstakingly preserved for the use of their medical team, and those now powered the little handheld electronic box that hummed to tighten the cuff around Dan's other arm.

"We need to lance the abscess and drain it," Kate said after leaning over to check the readout.

Sera moved to her desk and tore open a drawer, producing a squat, dusty bottle that she uncorked and sloshed a measure into a steel dish. She soaked gauze squares in it and returned to the bedside.

"Was that one of mine?" Neil asked, speaking from pure nervousness.

"One of your first batch," Sera responded absently. "Surprisingly good antiseptic actually."

Neil feigned a hurt look but his heart wasn't in it as Sera forced Dan's mouth open for the smell to hit him like a shovel like a shovel to the face.

"Oh! *Jesus...*"

Gagging, she shoved the booze-soaked gauze under his tongue and wiped her hands on her trousers, trying not to show how much they shook.

Kate was already assessing the bulge in Dan's jaw.

"Where are we doing it?" Sera asked

"Inside the mouth. Too much additional infection risk to go through the cheek," Kate said. "Neil, hang that up and help me move him."

Neil did as he was told, transferring the bag of saline to a metal stand attached to the bed and moving to help.

Kate passed a scalpel through flame until the blade glowed faintly, as Sera climbed halfway onto the bed to lean over Dan's hips and brace his shoulders, nodding at Neil to steady the head.

"Ready?" Kate asked, making the cut without waiting for a response.

The scalpel sank into the gum and pressure released with a sickening pop. A thick jet of pus burst from the wound, streaked with blood, splashing down Dan's chin and onto Kate, then into the dish below. The stench that filled the room was overpowering, sour, warm and rotting.

Sera staggered away and vomited into a bowl.

Kate dropped the scalpel, somehow immune to the sensory obliteration of the expelled infection, and pressed her thumbs into the swollen cheek. Another pocket gurgled and ruptured with a crack, releasing a second wave of foul fluid and blood.

Sera vomited again noisily, and Neil closed his eyes while leaning all of his weight onto Dan, but he was blissfully unaware of everything that happened.

Twice more she explored with her hands, finding another pressurised lump that needed to be sliced open, until the jellified mess and blood in the dish seemed like more fluid than Dan's face could've possibly held.

Kate grabbed a syringe of saltwater and began flushing his mouth, the tainted run-off spilling into the dish like slurry.

"Sera! I need more saltwater."

Still wiping her mouth, Sera staggered to the workbench, drew up more saltwater from a large jar, and passed syringes back one after the other. Kate flushed repeatedly, rinsing away blood and pus until the floor beneath them stank like a battlefield hospital.

Neil glanced at the drip. "Bag's empty!"

Sera connected a second as Kate extended her hand.

"I need syringes," Kate said, snapping her fingers hurriedly as she peered inside Dan's ruined mouth.

Sera passed over needles, one after the other. Kate jabbed into swollen tissue, withdrawing fluid pocket by pocket and each one crackled and oozed with another vile squelch.

Dan groaned and Neil stiffened. "He's stirring!"

Sera moved without prompting and administered another dose straight into his thigh.

"Now comes the really hard part," Kate said after she was satisfied the pus was cleaned away.

"Hard part?" Neil asked, face pale and eyes concerned.

In response Kate moved to a set of plastic organiser drawers and ran her finger down them until she found what she wanted. Pulling out a pair of chromed pliers she snapped them together twice and stepped back to Dan's side.

"Sera, I need you back to hold him. This might get...interesting."

Despite their fears Dan remained serenely ignorant of what came next. He never had to experience the chunks of swollen gum being sliced away to expose the tooth. Never had to know how hard his mouth was forced open until his lips cracked and bled. Never felt the pain of the pliers finally gaining purchase on the two halves of broken tooth that took five attempts to remove.

Dan remained unaware, but the three others would have to lie with it forever.

When they were done Dan was returned to his position leaning his head off the bed so the blood and unidentifiable gunk could drip down into the emptied tray.

Ash, silent the entire time, let out a low, uncertain whine from his post in the corner.

Neil crossed the room, dropped to his knees beside the dog, and wrapped his arms around him.

"He's alright, mate," he said quietly. "We've got him."

Marie chose that moment to come bursting into medical, face red and wet eyes wide as she took in the sight of her unconscious husband. She ran to him, calling his name and shaking his shoulder before Kate intercepted her and tried to pull her back.

"He's okay, he needs to rest!"

Marie ignored her and tried again to wake Dan, shouting his name and shoving him hard for a reaction.

"*MARIE!*" Kate barked, grabbing her friend by both shoulders and giving her a shake. "I said he's *okay*, but he won't be if you wake him up right now!"

Marie snapped out of her panic and stepped back, eyes scanning first the three faces in the room, then the mess of bloody gauze, then her face screwed up as the smell registered.

"Oh *God!* What happened?"

"The infection got too bad. He was delirious and I had to cut it to get it out," Kate told her.

Marie's hand lifted to her mouth as the shock of the words sunk in.

"But...*how?* I didn't see him last night because he was on duty, but...*how?*"

"Marie," Neil said gently. "There's more..."

She turned wide eyes on Neil who spoke fast, knowing she wasn't a woman to keep waiting for anything.

"A pigeon came warning about an attacking force near the farms. Mitch and Leah went with the QRF, but when they went to tell Dan he was..."

Neil trailed off, waving a hand at the unconscious, bloody man who was so important to all of them.

"He went a bit doolally...got all confused and...well he pulled a gun and—"

"He *WHAT?!*"

Neil held up both hands in an attempt to calm her that worked about as well as he expected it might.

"What the *fuck*, Neil?"

"He wasn't with it! Leah had to put him out, then we...you know...did the thing. He needs to rest and heal now."

Neil didn't say that Dan wasn't out of the woods yet, and neither Kate nor Sera chimed in to offer that opinion because all of them sensed it wasn't going to be remotely helpful at that point.

"Listen, I need to get to the wall," Neil told her. "You want me to take Ash with me or...?"

"I don't think you'll get him to leave this room any time soon," Marie said, scoffing a hint of laughter past her threatened tears.

Neil looked at the dog who looked right back at him, reckoning it was an "over my dead body" kind of scenario, so he left by himself to take charge of the defences.

COUNTERATTACK

Elías emptied his fourth or fifth magazine and dropped low behind the loose stone wall to reload. He was sweating despite the heat of the day not even coming close to reaching its peak yet.

After he'd sent the pigeon back to Sanctuary he'd wrestled with his emotions deciding what to do next. Eventually he decided that while he couldn't abandon his post to run back to the farms beyond the next rise, he could send a message.

That message was what caused him trouble, because while the oil-soaked barrel of logs would alert the other militia members and the farmers to the threat, it would also let these men from the east know that they'd been spotted.

He fought an internal battle over that decision for so long, cursing the man nominally in charge of the fighters deployed to protect the vulnerable region for not thinking about such an eventuality. Had there been two people on watch then at least one of them could've run back to raise the alarm, but that thought soured his gut because as he was the youngest and fittest of all of them, it would've been him who was volunteered to leave the hill and potentially miss his opportunity to prove his worth.

In the end, after most of an hour spent looking ahead into the valley and behind to see if anyone came his way, the enemy decided for him.

Bursting from the trees like some old cavalry charge, Elías found that his hammering heart and sweating hands no longer concerned him. An unexpected calm descended over him, allowing him to think faster than he ever had before. He waited until he knew his bullets would reach the enemy with enough force to kill, then with a generous adjustment upwards to aim over their heads, he opened fire.

He snapped off the first magazine in five shorts bursts, already seeing his enemy react by the third trigger pull. A horse tumbled, a rider fell backwards, and the attack was in disarray only moments after it had begun.

"*¡Vamos, cabrones!*" he yelled, striking a match and dropping it into the barrel before reaching for a second magazine.

~

The ride out was hard and fast, wheels skidding on gravel and banging hard over old potholes turned into craters by time and neglect. Leah rode shotgun, gripping the frame with Nemesis between her knees, her eyes scanning the horizon. In the back, nine militia held on to the truck's rails, faces grim. One whispered a prayer in Occitan, one muttered with eyes closed occasionally sketching the sign of the cross over his body, another checked her rifle's magazine three times in a row, and a quiet man near the back tapped his chest twice and kissed a silver medallion.

Nobody looked at each other, and nobody tried to speak over the rumble of the big tyres or the harsh whine of an engine pushed hard.

Mitch gripped the wheel hard, growling harsh promises of violent retribution on these men with horses who came to threaten their home.

The journey that took so long on horseback blasted by in a blur. Under other circumstances the journey would be enjoyable, with beautiful rolling landscapes to their east and the sharp rise of jagged peaks ahead and to their left, but now the outside world was irrelevant.

The smoke reached them first; a thin, dark ribbon rising vertically into the pale morning sky. The road dipped, then rose, then they crested the familiar ridge and saw the battlefield.

Men on foot approached the slope leading to the farms, running straight up the middle in a loose formation, ducking and dodging something unseen.

Muzzle flashes from maybe half a dozen rifles winked at them from the ridgeline while mounted men and women swept around the northern edge.

"Christ on a *bike!*" Mitch exclaimed angrily, but Leah pointed ahead at something he hadn't registered yet.

A wagon, machine gun mounted in the rear like some medieval technical, followed the infantry perhaps fifty paces behind.

Leah leaned forward and pointed again, this time towards the distant cavalry. "They're flanking!" she warned, seeing the precarious position of their few defenders on the ridgeline.

Mitch saw it too, understanding how this would end quickly and not in their favour unless they did something to break the enemy's rhythm.

"Mitch?" Leah asked when he didn't respond. "Mitch, they're flanking!"

"Aye, well they can fuckin' flank *this,*" Mitch snarled, banging a fist on the cab's roof and yelled loudly. "*Hold on tight!*"

"Hold on…? What's the plan here, Mitch?" Leah asked with deep concern evident in her tone.

"*Plan?* I'm makin' this shite up on the hoof!"

He rammed the accelerator down, aimed the big truck off the road and headed to intercept the heavy weapons wagon. The truck bucked over the terrain, suspension screaming, and yells of fright and annoyance came from behind.

Mitch didn't apologise. He was locked on target, thumbs moving to be outside the wheel, wearing a look of violent determination.

The impact was brutal.

Wood shattered, metal protested loudly and bodies scattered.

Mitch stood on the brakes, threw the truck into reverse, and went back over the wreckage while drawing a pistol and pointing it out of the window at a man staggering to his feet trying to figure what the hell just happened.

"*Bonjour*, ya fuckin' prick!" he said, pulling the trigger the second after the words registered.

He turned to Leah, but she was already out of the cab with her dog pressed to her side and her rifle ticked tightly into her shoulder. She advanced with fast, controlled steps, demonstrating the perfect firing stance on the move, and Mitch took a fraction of a second to appreciate her before he banged on the roof again and leaned out of the window.

"Six of you with her. Go! The rest stay with me and get those bloody gympies firing...and I need one o'you in here wi'me!"

Six of the militia volunteered themselves, leaping over the side of the truck to run after Leah and add the power of their rifles to hers. The older man climbed in beside Mitch and gave a nod, calm and collected which Mitch appreciated, and he selected drive again to set off in pursuit of the cavalry.

"Do me a favour, pal? There's two crates behind me. I need the one marked with the number eight, *comprend?*"

The man didn't answer, just twisted in his seat and climbed into the back to pop open the locking clasps on the case.

"*Sainte putain de merde sacrée!*" he breathed, hands fluttering at the silver medallion again.

Mitch caught enough of what he said to issue a filthy chuckle at the carnage he planned on unleashing.

~

Leah moved fast, scanning for enemies turning to see the danger she represented and dropping them with rapid pulls of her rifle's trigger. Militia joined her, and she yelled at them to spread out, not wanting to present a target that couldn't be missed when their enemy inevitably realised they fought a battle on two fronts.

They'd reached halfway up the slope now, close enough that the muzzle flashes and impacts of the defender's bullets held no pause between them.

She counted her shots, putting three into the back of a man moving too slow to stay with his comrades before she dropped out the spent magazine and slapped a full one home.

She resumed firing, putting two, three, four bullets into unsuspecting, unprotected backs until the inevitable happened and the attackers realised they were under attack.

Shouts rang out over the gunfire, faces turned, men and women panicked, but Leah reacted with a cool brutality.

"Down!" she yelled, dropping to one knee as Nemesis flattened herself into the grass beside her.

The militia followed her lead, one of them letting out a strangled, high-pitched cry as the thump of bullet striking flesh served as the percussion to the soprano solo.

335

"Rapid fire!" she yelled, flicking the safety catch all the way to fun before the strafed the barrel and her side sprayed the confused enemy with overwhelming firepower.

"Mop them up! *Acheves-les!*" she yelled, adding the order in French to remove any possible ambiguity.

They advanced, rifles snapping off shots at wounded attackers. One man, barely older than Leah herself, clutched at a bullet wound through his calf muscle with one hand and held up his right hand to plead for mercy. Leah stepped close, rifle aimed between his eyes, but her finger uncurled from the trigger.

"*Prenez-les vivants!*" she bawled, eyes still locked onto the young man crying for clemency.

Take them alive, she thought, because she knew when Dan got better he'd enjoy the opportunity to discuss their attack in detail.

"*Merci...pitié, mon Dieu...merci....*" the young man sobbed.

"Don't thank me yet," she snarled at him in English, seeing the confusion dawn on him before she lifted her right boot and broke his nose.

Shouts snatched her attention away. She turned to see a man running, one hand gripping a bleeping wound on his left arse cheek. She recognised him in an instant, felt mixed emotions competing inside her mind for the right course of action, and decided on what she was going to do.

Leah first gave the command for the militia to hold their fire, then let a wicked smile curl her mouth as she gave a command to Nemesis.

"*Get him, girl!*"

The machine gun roared into life over the truck's cab, sending out a screaming stutter of violence that chewed the air into ribbons. Brass spat from the feed port in a blistering stream, hot casings bouncing and clattering across the truck bed as the belt rattled through.

Mitch twisted the wheel hard and veered north, aiming for the cavalry assaulting the defended position on the ridge at an oblique angle, firing rifles from the saddle.

The GPMG gunner found his mark, carving a swathe of carnage through the three front runners to drop man and horse in bloody ruin, and as one the riders peeled off from their attack and headed down the slope right towards the truck.

Thirty riders at least, maybe more, thundering downhill with rifles raised and expressions carved from stone.

Mitch slammed on the brakes and the truck skidded sideways, calling out an insincere apology to the militia members banging around in the truck's bed.

Before the truck had even finished rocking, he was snapping his fingers at the man beside him, saying "gimme, gimme!"

The older man lifted a dull tube from the crate like it was liable to bite his fingers off, but Mitch snatched it away confidently.

He leapt down from the cab, launcher in hand, and climbed up into the back as rounds cracked past in sharp bursts.

One figure rode taller than the others, a sword raised above his head like a standard.

"What wanker brings a sword to a light anti-structure missile fight?" he asked rhetorically.

Mitch breathed out, slow and steady.

The rest of the world peeled away leaving just him, the launcher, and the bastard with the blade.

He flicked the safety off and rested his finger on the trigger. Aiming at the ground just ahead of the brave idiot, Mitch prepared to launch the rocket.

"Fight *this* wi' yer sword, ya stabby wee cu—"

~

Leah looked up as the truck bounced gently over the open ground towards her. The man Nemesis had brought down lay on the ground near her feet, writhing and crying out for the pain he suffered, but Leah was happy to watch that suffering. The man had caused more than enough personally, and what he felt now was only a fraction of what she felt he deserved.

The truck stopped nearby and Mitch jumped down, beaming a wicked smile from ear to ear.

"Did you see that?" he asked, evidently pleased with himself for the destruction he'd caused.

"Heard it, didn't see it," Leah answered, disappointing Mitch briefly, but his smile returned when he recognised the man on the ground.

"Well bugger me sideways with a deck chair! Why in the name of everything holy would *this* wanker come back?"

"I'm guessing," Leah said darkly, staring down at the man, "he thought he was going to take the farms and cut off our summer food supply...am I right?"

She kicked the wounded man to illicit a response to her apparently rhetorical question but only received a yell of fresh pain.

Beaulac growled like an animal, trying to resist the pain long enough to glare murderous intent up at the young woman, but his line of sight was broken by Nemesis sliding into view with bared teeth serving as a warning to forget whatever he was thinking.

"Any casualties?" Mitch asked softly.

"One. Not fatal but not great either. You?"

"None, thank God. How many prisoners did you take?" Mitch asked.

"Four," Leah replied before frowning in thought. "But I'm fairly certain one isn't going to make it."

"Best put him out of his misery now and be done wi'it," Mitch answered callously.

Leah knew he wasn't a heartless robot, as much as his words betrayed that. Mitch possessed one of the warmest souls she'd ever met – fiercely loyal and doggedly devoted to the safety of those he cared for – but he was a ruthless, pragmatic warrior when in pursuit of protecting his own.

Just as she was herself.

The prisoners were bound by the wrists and manhandled roughly into the back of the truck, including the two Mitch's half of the QRF had taken alive. Militia members worked to corral the panicked horses, gathering them as valuable resources not only for their use as transport but for the saddles and other equipment attached to them.

Others gathered weapons and ammunition from the dead, dragged the bodies of the enemy killed into one area, and set about scavenging anything useful from the horses that had been killed during the fight.

Nobody liked that fact, but it was a sad inevitability of riding animals into battle. Leah glanced at the front of the truck, seeing broken plastic and bent metal, but luckily the damage appeared to be limited to a purely cosmetic level.

Dan's not going to be happy about that, she thought. Then she stopped thinking about that because the part of her brain that turned everything into a fictional catastrophe was running on overdrive about the fate of her father.

Four militia descended the slop from the ridge, weapons slung, to join their people and recap what had happened.

"It is good you came when you did," the man sent to lead the farm contingent said sadly. "If you 'ad not, we would 'ave lost more than just one man."

Leah blinked in surprise, not saying anything before the man explained.

"That young Spanish boy who came from Andorra. Elías. 'e was killed at the very end when their 'orses got to the ridge."

Leah cast her eyes down as her memory banks were searched, but she couldn't picture the boy he was talking about.

"I'm sorry...was he...did he have any family?"

A sad, slow shake of the head was her only response, but she was saved having to speak more about it as Nadine arrived from the farm with three horse-drawn carts behind her. They were simple contraptions, tools for moving harvested crops around, but Leah was pleased that Nadine had thought to bring them.

They greeted, offered brief opinions about what had happened, and Leah accepted thanks again for arriving in time to prevent disaster.

Leah wasn't so sure any disaster had been fully prevented, but she gave a sad smile and a nod anyway.

"We will deal with this," Nadine said, waving a hand over the battlefield. "The dead deserve to be buried no matter what, and the 'orses...we won't be wasting the meat."

Leah nodded, turned when Mitch whistled for her attention, and headed back to the truck with their prisoners, three militia, and a heavy uncertainty as to what she would find when she got home.

BEHIND ENEMY LINES

Lucien stumbled through a doorway that he hadn't seen until the last second, dragged hard enough by the wrist that his feet scuffed on the floor and knocked something metal across stone. The object clattered away in the dark as he was shoved into a wall, the back of his shoulder striking cold stone and the sharp edge of a wooden crate. He gasped and spun, heart hammering, but the door slammed shut behind him and the light vanished with it.

Heavy silence filled the space as thick as the smell. Dust, old timber, dried meat, oil and sweat. It all felt airless, like the place had been sealed away from the world until then. Lucien's chest heaved, and the silence stretched so long that he wondered if he'd been left alone.

He still felt the reassuring weight of the Glock tucked inside his waistband, but something told him to leave it hidden, to not show his cards just yet, because this man had the air of someone who had saved him.

The sound of metal on stone came again. A match was struck, the brief flare of sulphur and flame revealing the shape of another man who used the tiny fire to light a lamp.

The glow grew slowly to fill the dark space, unkind and jaundiced, casting everything in a nicotine-stained hue. The room was square, windowless, and braced with old wood. Crates were stacked along the far wall, and a faded tarp hung over something large in the corner.

The space was bare except a single chair and a makeshift table. There were no signs of comfort, meaning it wasn't a room meant to be lived in but a place to wait.

Or disappear.

The man they had spoken to first bearing a clipboard and then cryptically over a beer stood in front of the door. His coat was gone, replaced with a loose shirt that clung under the arms. His face was the same, but stripped of the grey uniform and official posture he looked smaller somehow.

Wiry and less defined like he was just another man, only his eyes had lost none of their weight.

Lucien blinked at him, struggling to find words, but his throat was dry and his mind refused to settle long enough to produce speech. He opened his mouth, tried again, and shook his head.

Clipboard Man exhaled through his nose in an expression of tempered fury.

"You idiot," he said quietly, each syllable sharp and deliberate. "You absolute, reckless *idiot*."

Lucien flinched like he'd been struck. "I—I was spending the vouchers. I was doing what we agreed! Polly—"

"Polly?" the man interrupted. A single eyebrow rose, his head tilting ever so slightly. "I thought she was called Paulette?"

Lucien froze. The moment sat between them, prickling like static. His stomach lurched and Clipboard Man tutted sarcastically.

"Next you will tell me this *Polly* is not even your real mother! You weren't supposed to be noticed!"

He stepped forward, slowly, pointing with two fingers as if tracing blame through the air.

"You were supposed to blend in, you were supposed to wait, but now she is gone, you are in 'ere and there are soldiers out there searching for you."

He stopped just short of Lucien, and for a second neither moved.

"I...I didn't know she was going to do that," Lucien said.

His voice cracked, somewhere between defiance and grief.

"It wasn't part of the plan and she didn't tell me. I thought...I thought we were just gathering what we could and getting out."

Clipboard Man didn't speak. He turned away and kicked the leg of the table so hard it shifted and crates rattled.

"Do you think you are the only ones trying to keep people alive?" he snapped. "Do you think this is just some personal mission for a few romantic rebels on a cart with some pigeons and a pocket full of vouchers?"

Lucien shrank slightly under the weight of the words, the accusation hitting home even as he bristled with fear. "What's going to happen to her?"

The man didn't respond. He stood with both hands on the back of the chair, gripping it so tightly that his knuckles paled. The tendons in his forearms stood out like cables and for a moment he looked like he might lash out again, but instead he let out a breath and lowered his head.

"What did the note say?" he asked, without looking at Lucien.

Lucien hesitated, trying to read the question.

Was this an interrogation? A trap?

Lucien gave his best guess at the truth, seeing no other real alternative.

"I imagine she was warning home," he said. "The farms. They're going to hit them."

Clipboard Man turned his head slightly. "Then why didn't she *wait*? Why didn't you just spend your vouchers, get the *prévôt* to sign off on your trades, and leave with permission? It would 'ave taken you less than an hour!"

Lucien had no answer. He licked his lips, aware of how dry his mouth had become. His fingers fidgeted without permission, clenching and unclenching.

"I don't know. She just...she just acted, I suppose."

The man nodded once, the motion slow. Not in agreement, just simple acceptance of facts that he couldn't change.

"What's going to happen to her?" Lucien asked again.

Clipboard Man turned, his eyes falling on him like a weight. He looked older now, wearier, as if Polly's capture had drained something from him too.

"Nothing good, my friend," he said softly. "Nothing good."

"I want to know what will happen to her!" Lucien demanded angrily.

That anger was met with an equal and greater force as Clipboard Man shot towards him with a speed and intensity that made Lucien's hands come up instinctively.

"No!" the man said. "Trust me, you do *not* want to know!"

The words hit Lucien in the chest harder than a punch. He staggered back, hitting the crate again, then slumped down to sit on it, arms on knees and head hanging where his breath came shallow.

Outside, the world went on. The faint sounds of shouting had stopped, replaced by the hollow stillness of an occupied square. Someone laughed, sharp and false. A dog barked as the quiet trading resumed and the normality of it felt obscene.

Clipboard Man walked to a wall and opened a battered cabinet, revealing a bottle and two cups. He poured something that smelled faintly of aniseed.

He held one out.

Lucien stared.

"It will not 'elp," the man said, "but it will not 'urt you either."

Lucien took it and drank. It hit like fire and coiled in his gut, but the second swallow burned less.

Clipboard Man didn't sit. He walked the room's edge like a caged animal, always glancing at the door as though he expected someone to open it and end them both.

"She's strong," Lucien said eventually. "She'll survive."

The man didn't answer.

Lucien looked up. "Won't she?"

Clipboard Man didn't meet his eyes.

"She...may last longer than most. *If* she is as strong as you say she is," he said at last.

Lucien's stomach turned over. He stared into the dregs of his cup and saw nothing but failure.

TREASON

The cell door groaned on rusted hinges, the sound theatrical enough to be deliberate. Everything in that place felt like theatre now: crumbling stone walls, the insidious stink of damp, the oily flicker of lamplight in place of the hum of anything modern. Polly was flanked by silent guards, their movements stiff and ritualistic and their big hands gripping her upper arms tightly on each side, like actors playing executioners in some low-budget movie.

When the door hit the extremity of its path it bounced, creaking back towards her and vibrating to make it sound like a mouse laughing in some cartoon.

Polly, mentally detached from her situation and physical surroundings as if instinct took over to protect her, laughed also. That laugh earned her a hard shove in the back, propelling her into the room.

She staggered slightly under the push, her right eye swollen nearly shut, her upper lip split and puffed. Her hands had been bound behind her back for so long she could no longer feel her fingers, though the bones ached in rhythm with her heartbeat. When they unshackled her, she straightened. Not out of pride, but because surrender was a choice she refused to make.

Where she found this courage from, this defiance in the face of utter helplessness, she didn't know. Just as the laugh protected her from the ominous feeling of the room, the defiant pride armoured her against what might come next. What might come after the sly beating, after her "fall" down some steps that split her lip and after the very unsubtle punch in the face that closed her eye.

They led her into what had once been a courtroom.

The echoes of justice had long since died in that place, choked by banners and stale authority.

There was no jury, no observers, no defence.

There was no hope, just shadows, and two men who would decide whether she died today or lingered to suffer longer.

Le Maréchal sat elevated, high on a dais designed to dominate. His chair had been crafted to resemble a throne, all angles and carved intimidation, and he wore the expression of a man born to command; his eyes fixed on her like she was a problem to solve rather than a human being.

Standing to his right, Major Courbin shifted his weight with a twitchy unease that never left him. Thin and pale with sharp features, his grey eyes darted constantly as he glowered undisguised malice at her. His fingers moved without purpose, curling and releasing at his side like something was always just out of reach. Like he was subconsciously grasping for a power that would forever remain just beyond his grasp.

Le Maréchal said nothing at first, just simply watched her.

Polly met his gaze. The pain had become ambient now, a dull companion rather than a distraction as the prideful defiance took control and let her rest.

"Citizen," Le Maréchal said at last, the word wrapped in pomp. "You present yourself as a trader, yet you trespass 'ere to spy. You speak like an educated woman after 'iding your identity and you evade every attempt to seek the truth from you."

She gave him a half-smile, ruined by the tear in her lip.

"Is there a question in there?" Polly answered thickly, her busted lip distorting her words but not hiding her Quebecois accent.

Courbin looked like he was about to explode but Le Maréchal held a soft, deliberate hand out to still him. Polly cocked her head at the gesture, releasing another huff of amusement.

"Something is funny to you, *spy*?" Courbin snarled without the prerequisite depth to his voice that could make him in any way menacing.

"Funny? Yeah, actually. I know a guy who does that to stop his dog from running away," she said, jerking her chin at Courbin who remained locked in place by Le Maréchal's raised hand.

"Enough of your…your…" Courbin stammered, vibrating with rage so much that it robbed him of his ability to think of the right word.

"Your *insolence* is no defence, Citizen," Le Maréchal said, sounding pleased with himself for possessing the superior vocabulary. "You know, Caesar said 'If you must break the law, do it to seize power.' Is *that* why you are 'ere? Is that why you break our laws? To seize power?"

Polly twisted her body to show her bound hands and, in spite of the discomfort it caused her, called her fingertips together to make a weak noise but a strong show of mockery.

"Bra-*vo*. A Caesar quote! Who else do you idolise, Stalin? You got a poster of Pol Pot in your bathroom?"

Courbin looked like he was going to run at her but another subtle gesture from Le Maréchal and he stayed in his spot like a good boy. Polly half expected the man on the fake throne to toss the little guy a treat.

Seeing how far she could push, she said, "Tell me, *Maréchal*…Do you rehearse these little sermons, or do they just…kinda…spill out when you're playing dress-up?"

Courbin looked ninety-eight percent of the way to a full-blown coronary incident but Le Maréchal simply cocked his head. When he spoke, his voice was soft but cut like frost.

"You are only making this worse for yourself."

Polly laughed. She laughed hard, throwing back her head and belly laughing despite the pain in her ribs caused by being pushed down a dozen stone steps.

"Worse? How can it be any worse!" She laughed, then began dancing an odd, stiff-legged gait as she sang a word twice. "Jehovah! Jehovah!"

Courbin looked at Le Maréchal who didn't break character at all. Polly gave up and let her laughter subside into something sounding like embarrassment.

"Monty Python? No?" she said, dropping her shoulders to portray how disappointed she was in them.

"Careful," Courbin growled. "You might provoke your own execution."

Polly turned her face slowly toward him. "Am I supposed to be *afraid* of you?"

"You are supposed to tell us why you are 'ere and 'ho you are trying to send secret messages to! Your actions are a betrayal of France and everythi—"

"Except I'm not French."

Polly's interruption choked the words from Courbin's throat. "You are…not…French?"

"*Of course I am Frrronch*," Polly crowed in ridiculous parody of the man. "*Why do you sink I 'ave zis…outrrrrageous accent?*"

350

She laughed again, pleased with her own joke but secretly worried that her mind had fractured. She was quoting comedy from five decades before, having entirely forgotten about its existence until this moment, and she feared she was losing her grip on reality as a coping mechanism for what she knew would happen eventually.

The only thing she still felt in any control of was how she chose to meet that eventuality.

Le Maréchal chuckled. The sound was thin, practised and devoid of warmth.

"You are accused of treason. Of—"

"Except I'm not French," Polly interrupted, but she may as well have saved her breath.

"—of consorting with foreign agents. Of betraying the very order I bring to a fractured land."

"Order? You mean *control*. Men like you always call it something else. You hide behind words like discipline, stability...security. The only thing you're selling is fear."

Courbin stepped forward, no longer able to contain himself and, being given no counter order by his leader, he struck Polly hard with the back of his right hand across the bottom of her jaw. The blow rocked her, but it stung more than hurt. She righted herself to stand tall again, watching Courbin subtly shake the pain from his knuckles as he returned to Le Maréchal's heel like a loyal dog.

"We can keep you 'ere for as long as we choose," Courbin said. "And we...*cannot promise* your safety, you understand? Not from the...*men* outside. Not at every moment."

She didn't blink.

"Wow. *Really*? Using rape as policy? That worked well for Napoleon in Spain, didn't it?"

The line hit harder than the last blow she'd taken. Le Maréchal's mouth twitched like the anger he forcibly held within and came a split-second away from breaking out.

"Many of Boneparte's campaigns were chaos. I bring discipline, not indulgence."

Polly glared at him, waiting for the deadlock to break. Totally unaware of the battle of wills taking place, Courbin cleared his throat.

"The boy you arrived with. Where is 'e?"

Polly stayed still and silent. *He doesn't know. He doesn't have Lucien, oh thank you God!*

Le Maréchal's eyes narrowed, voice low and deliberate. "You think someone will come for you? You expect some 'ero to storm my gates?"

Her stomach clenched from the sick, taunting echo of hope.

She had pictured it. Dan kicking through the doors, wild with rage, Ash leaping through the air like a missile fired from a launch tube to tear out Courbin's throat while Dan advanced on the little man who begged and pleaded for his life.

She clung to that fantasy in the gloom, but she knew Dan wasn't coming so she said nothing.

Le Maréchal stepped down from his platform, each movement precise and careful to the point of being almost effeminate. His boots rang against the flagstones, echoing like the tolling of judgement until they stopped in front of her, close enough for her to see the tiny flecks of gold in his eyes.

"I could 'ave offered you a place in something eternal," he said softly.

Polly summoned the last of her courage to consider spitting in his face, but she opted for sarcasm, imagining that Leah might one day hear about it and smile.

"Hard pass," she said with a wide grin that split her swollen lip again and made it bleed.

Le Maréchal's smile fell. He turned away and spoke loudly, the clear, confident words echoing back to Polly as he walked purposefully towards his throne.

"You are defiant, Citizen, and I do not mean this in a good way. Caesar also said that 'defiance must not be met with outrage, but with instruction', did you know this?"

Polly said nothing, but her rolling eyes made her point well enough.

"'e also said, 'let the next man learn from the corpse of the first'."

Polly's blood ran cold despite knowing what would become of her. Part of her still hoped for a rescue, for a reprieve, maybe even for perpetual internment, but hope, as Dan once told her, was not a strategy.

Le Maréchal sat and arranged himself neatly before looking down on her again. "Victory decides truth. 'istory is written by power."

"Then history will call you a tyrant."

He smiled again, this time with teeth. "And 'istory will not remember you at all."

She took in a breath and squared her shoulders.

She didn't look away, staying locked in another battle of wills until Le Maréchal flicked the fingers of his right hand derisively.

Guards entered the room and hauled her back the way they'd come. Polly didn't resist, but a sharp word of command froze her progress at the heavy door.

"Wait!"

353

The guards turned her around to face Le Maréchal again.

"I will afford you one more chance to answer a simple question," he said flatly. "'ho were you sending that message to?"

Polly lifted her chin and angled her face so her one good eye bored a hole through Le Maréchal's forehead. "What message?"

The fingers flicked again and she was hauled way, more roughly this time. She was bounced off walls and doorways as her guards laughed like schoolboys to one another, and the suffering didn't stop until the cell door slammed behind her.

The light was weaker now. The damp had soaked further into the stone, and the stink of rot settled into her nose like it meant to stay. She sank down into the corner, her bones grinding against the wall, the air around her still and cruel.

History will remember me, she told herself, desperately needing to believe it. Needing to believe that this wasn't all for nothing.

She held on for as long as she could, biting down against the pressure that built in her throat, but it was inevitable. The first sob was silent. Her body trembled with the effort of making no sound, of keeping her grief as hidden as her secrets. Her sleeve came up to cover her mouth as more sobs came, bringing with them a symphony of pain she was too proud to let any of them hear.

Lucien, please…go. Just go.
Don't let them kill us both.

THE CORPSE OF THE FIRST

They called it a room.

It had a bed, a chair, a jug of water with no glass, but the metal bars on the one small window, the lock on the outside of the door, and the absence of a handle on the inside told the truth. It was a cell. A cell dressed up in polite language for an impolite purpose.

Lucien had been marched there without ceremony by the man with a mouth too tight to smile who avoided meeting his eye, and he hadn't explained a thing beyond what mattered.

"Do not be seen and do not try to leave. If you do, you will be shot."

He hadn't specified if he meant by the soldiers or himself, not that it mattered because the threat carried all the weight of certainty.

Now Lucien paced.

He paced for so long he didn't know how long he had been doing it, but his blood ran warm and his cheeks flushed pink with the continued effort that now made him want to sleep. He slumped on the bed, staring at the walls that didn't change. The light from the narrow window hadn't shifted enough to count time. His mouth was dry despite the untouched jug. His mind was a war zone of half-finished thoughts and the things he should've said and done, but mostly the things he couldn't stop seeing when he closed his eyes.

Exhaustion or stress must have overcome him because he opened his eyes to new shadows cast by the poor light from the covered window. He stood, body aching and clothing stiff from dried sweat to look out the window and see that a mob was gathering in the square below.

A knot of bodies at first, then hundreds, all pressed into the square with an energy that buzzed against the stone like hornets rattling a jar. From this angle he could see the scaffold being prepared, the thick beam arched like a ribcage pulled from the earth.

And the rope.

Coiled with the lazy menace of a snake that need not rattle because it knows it has already won.

Lucien gripped the edge of the sill as reality dawned on him.

No…no, no, no, no!

He stepped away from the window and reached for the non-existent door handle, growling in frustration as he tried to force his fingers into the door frame and pull it free. Falling back to the floor when his weak grip gave up he tried again, tried kicking it against the hinges, then grabbed the water jug and ran back to the window as panic rose sourly in his gut.

The sight of the bars stalled him, fearing that he wouldn't be able be force them loose, but he rebelled savagely against that weakness that stopped him from even trying.

He tipped the water out and used the jug like a hammer, smashing out the glass and breaking the jug on his first blow. He carried on, using the handle as a hand guard to break out the rest of the shards until he could reach through and test the strength of the bars.

They held devastatingly firm, not giving a millimetre no matter how much of his body weight he threw into trying to force them loose.

He gave up, allowing his legs to do the same and lower him to the floor like a child panicking and regressing into a foetal position before he caught himself slipping too far.

He stood, yanked on the bars again with no reward and tried the door again before frustration sent him back to the window to play out the very definition of insanity.

No sounds reached him clearly, but he saw the movement of soldiers and guards, rows of them, lining the square in full uniform. Faces fixed, rifles held across their bodies, they formed an impenetrable line between the crowd and the stage.

They seemed to Lucien to be expecting resistance in some form, their demeanour reminding people of what would happen if trouble did indeed surface.

Then they brought Polly out.

She'd been stripped of her clothes, now wearing a shirt too large for her and trousers rolled at the cuffs. Shackles on her wrists and ankles restricted her ability to move but she walked without stumbling. Her back was straight, her chin up in defiance, and it seemed for all the world to Lucien that she was not *acting* brave, she *was* brave.

Lucien could not breathe, but even from a distance he could see that Polly's eyes smiled past fresh blood from a split lip, and her mouth was gagged below one eye swollen shut.

He pressed his forehead to the bars and whispered a prayer, but no sound came out.

Below, the crowd stirred noisily. A shout, a call for names, a demand for answers.

Someone waved a bloodied bandage and screamed something that made three others grab his shoulders and pull him back. They wanted to know where their sons were, what had happened at the frontier, and what the silence meant.

Then a small, neat man stepped out and Lucien felt his stomach twist at the sight of him.

Immaculate, black hair combed to a precise wave and wearing leather gloves that shone when he lifted one hand. He did not smile, did not greet the people, he simply let the silence harden around him until the shouting slowed, then stopped.

~

Le Maréchal basked in that silence, loving every second of being the sole focus of his entire world as he scanned the faces of the crowd hovering beyond the reach of his line of soldiers. He dared them to say something, to challenge him to his face, but none did. None had the courage to repeat their opinions or questions when face with greatness.

He'd heard every word they shouted before, even made out who faces belonged to, which voices for Courbin or Armand to follow up with later, but now he had a job to do. He had a role to perform.

He had to meet their defiance not with outrage, but with *instruction*.

"Treason," he said clearly, feeling the last of the murmur vanish like the world held its breath when he spoke. "*Treason!*" he repeated, adding bile and hatred to the word to let the people know what they should rightly be angry about.

Then he turned his back on the crowd and paced, forcing every pair of eyes to follow his movement like the puppet master he believed himself to be.

"France lost 'er soul long before the collapse…She sold it, piece by piece. She gave it away in tiny little 'andfuls. She gave away 'er industry, 'er autonomy to foreign bullies, and she gave away 'er identity to immigrants and fools 'ho wanted cheap things – meaningless consumption and *for what*? For approval on the internet? For *virtue signalling*? Given away for free to people 'ho did not belong 'ere, 'ho did not bleed or die for France!"

Le Maréchal relaxed, stood tall again after his angry, impassioned words, and took on the character of a wise, thoughtful man.

"'Istory is filled with the sound of silken slippers going downstairs and wooden shoes coming up…now it is *our* time. Now it is for *France!*"

Le Maréchal didn't wait for any applause, not that any came, he simply turned to the executioner and nodded. The executioner did not hesitate, ushering Polly forward to stand on the right spot before lifting the waiting rope up and looping it over her head with the same reverent care a man might use to surprise a loved one with a necklace.

The executioner tightened the rope, adjusting the large knot to sit just under her left ear, then reached back for a sack which he prepared to pace over Polly's head.

He reeled away, recoiling like a man might from an animal. When he lifted a hand to wipe something from his cheek Lucien smiled despite the horror unfolding, silently urging Polly on for her defiance.

Polly did not struggle. She looked up like she was searching for a break in the clouds to see the sun one last time.

And she saw him.

Her eyes found his with the calm of someone who had already made peace with the end. She didn't cry, she didn't mouth anything, she just looked.

The executioner stepped into place beside the trapdoor, hands wrapped around the long-handled hammer. He waited, formal and still; a statue cast in meat and muscle.

Then a signal came from the raised platform behind her. Lucien saw Le Maréchal lower his arm, fingers flicked in an almost lazy gesture, judgment handed down like a king brushing crumbs from a table.

The hammer rose, paused at the top of the arc like a professional golfer about to tee off, then swung.

The sound of impact reached Lucien a moment late. A small but deep, blunt noise like a coffin lid slamming shut.

The trapdoor fell and Polly dropped.

An anguished, incomprehensible noise was torn from Lucien's throat as she fell four feet down into the open trapdoor, just far enough for the sudden stop to jerk her spine, but not enough to end it quickly. Everything but her head and shoulder vanished beneath the boards, her body yanked down like a puppet meeting its final cue.

Lucien sobbed, and Polly did not die cleanly.

Lucien's stomach clenched as he watched her jerk and twist. Her limbs moved in fits, chest heaving against the noose as she kicked once, then twice, but the rope held.

Her head tilted, jaw slackening, but the twitching continued as her eyes – her kind, shrewd, smiling eyes – bulged unnaturally from her head.

They made her dance, without even having the decency to make her barbaric death quick. The crowd watched without sound, as if breath itself had been taken from them.

No movement, and no mercy.

When it was finally over her body hung limp, gently swaying as if some breeze moved her like she weighed nothing at all. Her chin rested on her collarbone and bright, fresh blood trickled into her shirt from the broken skin beneath the rope.

Le Maréchal turned away without even a look back at the fruits of his leadership, but Lucien stayed fixed to the stage, unable to leave the room but unable to break his eyes away from the worst thing he had ever seen in his already eventful life.

He watched until the executioner stepped forward again, hauling on the rope to jerk her body back into view like she was some prize catch. He tied off the rope, restored the trapdoor and moved closer to place a hand on Polly's wrist and confirm what everyone already knew.

Dark patches stained the front of her clothing, running all the way to her bare feet to display her final indignity even after death, and Lucien blinked away tears at that shame he bore for her while below him the world below kept turning like she had never mattered.

But she had mattered. She *did* matter.

Lucien pulled back from the edge, heart hammering against his ribs like it wanted out to seek vengeance with or without the rest of his body. His hands trembled, cold and tight around the grip of the Glock he still had courtesy of the fool who had imprisoned him pretending to save his life.

Then the crowd began to stir. It began with a single shout, sharp as broken glass. Then another, then more.

They shouted accusations as questions.

"Where is my brother?"

"What happened at the frontier?"

"You said they were heroes, so why are we burying them in silence?"

Lucien heard the words clearly enough to know these people were unhappy enough to openly challenge a regime that executed people so easily, so he could only guess at the injustices they felt to be so emboldened.

361

A woman screamed the name of her son until her voice cracked and a man spat at the edge of the platform. Two others tried to push past the soldiers and were shoved back with the flat of a rifle. It was still controlled, but only just. The guards tightened their line as the noise of the crowd surged like bees exiting a hive to defend it.

Lucien gripped the windowsill, his fingers bloodless on the stone.

They were not mourning Polly, they were *angry*. Not angry at the execution but a flailing, unfocused rage of a mob that had deep roots to their unhappiness.

Below, Le Maréchal turned his back and continued to walk away, flanked by tall soldiers condensing to form a protective cocoon around him, but he kept his head up and kept walking as though the noise meant nothing.

Lucien saw the shift for what it was. The fear that had held them still, held him still, was cracking.

The rope had not silenced the people, but woken them up.

The shouting spread as the soldiers locked formation, their boots scuffing stone, orders snapped low and urgent. No shots were fired but the pushing intensified as though pressure was rising like steam behind a valve.

One soldier looked up just long enough to glance at the window.

Lucien ducked back instinctively, breath short, heart hammering.

By the time he looked again, the square was thinning. Not emptying as though they retreated, more that they were repositioning. As if every person who left was going to talk, to plan, to carry the heat somewhere else. As though the kindling had been soaked in flammable silence for too long.

Only Lucien remained behind, watching Polly's body sway in the breeze like a broken metronome keeping time for something that had not yet begun.

He stayed there long after the last of the crowd had gone and the soldiers gratefully followed their orders to march away, until the noise had drained from the square and only ghosts lingered.

Lucien did not cry so much as collapse.

It wasn't just grief for loss, it was knowing that what had just happened did not mark an end but a beginning.

BREAKING POINT

Mitch drove through the gates, the biodiesel growl of the truck echoing through the ancient stonework before the battered shape appeared. He came in hot, the front grill dented and streaked with dried blood and the broken bumper smeared by fresh blood. The gates were pulled open just enough to let him through before slamming shut again behind him.

When Mitch killed the engine Leah dropped down from the passenger side, her face unreadable. There was blood on her sleeves, none of it hers, just as the blood staining Nemesis' face had similarly been earned in combat.

She walked to the rear of the truck and dropped the tailgate, waving the prisoners forward while the militia riding with them helped with orders and pushing. With hands bound behind their backs and eyes wide with the silence of people who had seen death and understood how close it had passed, they climbed down uncertain of their fate.

One of them had a limp that worsened with every step while another had a blackened, swollen eye. The last one of them was Beaulac, blood-soaked from hip to ankle, a field dressing wrapped tight around his ribs and another on his left calf.

Nemesis trotted behind them all, silent and watchful like a hungry shark posting sentry on a sinking boat.

Neil waited, rifle slung over one shoulder and eyes as wide as the prisoners' were.

Leah stalked across the stones with the purposeful stride of someone holding back something dangerous behind her eyes.

"Prisoners," she said, as though their injured state and bound hands weren't obvious indicators.

Neil squinted at the tallest of them before his eyes shot wide again and he turned a horrified, surprised look on her. "Is that Beaulac?!"

"In the flesh," Leah answered sharply, still clearly amped up from the fight. "Bastard needs a medic or a bullet."

"When Dan wakes up a bullet would be kinder," Neil groused.

Leah's eyes searched his, the question urgent and obvious but unspoken.

"He's okay...it, ahh...it wasn't pretty, but the infection's been flushed out. Let's just hope he doesn't catch sepsis."

Leah's expression didn't change but something about her vibrated with anger or fear.

Mitch climbed down from the truck, looked around for a moment before he spotted Neil then walked straight over, boots crunching gravel, and stood in front of him like a soldier reporting in.

Blood was spattered across his vest, and one of his hands was curled in a fist.

"We hit the bastards *hard*! They had a bloody horse-drawn technical if you can believe that shite! Running a MAG-fifty-eight on a tripod setup!"

Neil's clever eyes flickered, like he just internally drew up plans for something better. When he opened his mouth Mitch spoke again and dashed his hopes.

"No, I drove right through the fucker," he said, gesturing back towards the battered front end of the truck. "The MAG survived but the mount was all fucked up. Saved the gun and a few belts of seven-six-two."

Neil closed his mouth and deflated a little. "So they weren't pissing about then?" he asked.

"They most definitely were *not*," Leah answered darkly. "Small infantry force and what? Twenty cavalry?"

The request for clarification was aimed at Mitch, and the old soldier nodded sagely before answering. "Thirty of the horsey wankers...One hoofin' great twat tried tae charge me wi'a *sword*!"

Leah's eyes rolled and Mitch grinned, telling Neil that not only was there more to that story, but that Leah had heard it more than once already.

"So I sent a rocket up his arse and told him, fi—"

"They had horses, we found supply carts in the woodland, and a couple of heavy weapons so no, they weren't messing around," she said, popping the fun bubble Mitch was inflating.

"How's the auld man?" Mitch asked, dropping his mood instantly.

"Banged up but alive," Neil said darkly, eyeballing Beaulac with a look bordering on murderous. "Now come on...we need to get this lot locked up before someone does something drastic."

~

Lucien sat on the edge of the bed, shoulders hunched, eyes fixed on the same blank patch of wall he'd stared at for hours. The room smelled of damp stone and old sweat, the kind of air that clung to skin and made everything feel closer than it was. When the door creaked open he slowly emerged from the state of catatonia he'd slipped into and breathed out slowly.

He was expecting Clipboard Man again, expecting his questions to be met with no answers, but the footsteps weren't alone this time.

Two soldiers filed in behind the man he recognised, boots clomping heavily on the floorboards, followed by a man who moved with unsettling grace.

It was as though he didn't have to prove anything to anyone, and Lucien's spine straightened a fraction knowing this was no routine visit.

Clipboard Man gave a curt nod after fleetingly meeting his eye.

Lucien's gut coiled, cold and tight, as it finally dawned on him that his rescue was not rescue at all.

The calm, graceful man stepped further into the room and regarded Lucien as if he were something under glass. He was dry despite the rain outside, hair neatly parted, coat sharp enough to suggest he'd never been caught in anything so uncivilised as weather. His smile was thin and practised, like he'd worn it often and never meant it once.

He took the chair, turned it around, and straddled it like it was a throne.

"Please. Sit."

Despite the firm order dressed up in frilly manners Lucien stayed still, heat building in his jaw.

"Come now," the man said affably with a faint smile teasing his lips. "If I wanted you dead, you would be hanging beside your friend down there."

He nodded his head slowly back over one shoulder towards the door that one guard closed quietly. There was no remorse in his words, no indication that he disapproved of such unwarranted barbarism, so Lucien stayed stubbornly standing in defiance.

"My name is Armand. *Capitaine* Alexis Armand," he said, gesturing once again for Lucien to sit on the bed.

Armand's voice was too even. Too calm. It wasn't the voice of a torturer but it felt somehow worse.

It was the voice of a man who made things happen and let others do the screaming.

Lucien's stomach twisted but he sat, seeing no sense in further defiance until he knew what he was facing.

Armand laced his fingers over the top of the chair. "Now, tell me…what is your real name?"

Lucien met his eyes, hard. "My real name is *va te faire foutre.*"

A pause, then a sigh of disappointment, as though Armand fully expected to be told to "go fuck" himself but was still hoping for his conversational partner to show some decorum.

"Charming. Now, permit me to tell you what I believe…I believe that you work for the man from the south, and you come from the place they call *Sanctuaire.* I know the message your friend tried to send was to warn your people of the attack on their farms, but it so 'appens such a warning was not needed. Tell me, your leader…your *warlord*… 'ho is he really?"

No answer. Just Lucien's silence, thick and coiled with rage. Armand watched him, waiting, amused by the defiance.

"You are not very cooperative," he said at last. "I suppose we can work on that, if it is only violence you understand, of course, but I was 'oping you were more brains than brawn."

Lucien's fingers twitched.

The Glock was still there, tucked behind his back and missed by Clipboard Man when they'd moved him. It sat now like a secret promise against his kidneys like a reassuring presence he could feel as much as he could still feel Polly's weight hanging from that rope.

"No? Per'aps I should tell *you* what 'appened," Armand went on. "There *was* an attack, only your people defeated it."

Armand laughed mirthlessly when Lucien's face betrayed everything by the fleeting ghost of a smile.

"*There* 'e is, huh, Jean?" Armand said, twisting to smile at Clipboard Man – Jean – who mirrored the gesture only to drop it and resume his glare aimed at Lucien the second Armand looked away.

He's smart, Lucien thought. *He doesn't trust me.*

"Yes, your people own a decisive victory, it seems. Only a few of our people made it back to tell of what 'appened."

Lucien said nothing and just tried to keep a gloating look off his features.

"So…now that I am certain of where you come from, and seeing as 'ow you do not want to tell me anything useful, I find myself unsure of what to do with you…"

Lucien stiffened and his lips began to move before his brain could filter the impulsive words he spoke.

"Why don't you string me up like a piece of meat to please the mob? I see Polly's death made them so *very* 'appy!"

Armand smiled, having already gathered intelligence by sparking Lucien's emotions.

"So… 'er name was Polly, was it? You know, I 'ave a friend – my superior officer in truth, but 'e is my friend nonetheless – and 'e told me of a woman called Polly."

"You mean that piece of shit Beaulac?" Lucien spat, knowing the truth was already out there but unspoken.

"*Colonel* Claude Beaulac, yes. A very resilient man. A *brave* man, only I fear for 'is life now because 'e led the attack and 'e 'as not yet returned…"

Lucien smiled again, imagining his militia gunning down Beaulac and his soldiers. He imagined his young wife leading them, and the dog who silently fought him for space in their bed each night by her side.

That moment of connection broke him, and the anger threatened to transform into tears.

Lucien bowed his head to fight the growing collapse of will.

"But no," Armand said, speaking as though they were friends. "I do not think your death in such a...*public* manner would appease anyone, but this does not mean you are not of value to me. You will stay 'ere as insurance, because I rather suspect your warlord will want to pay us a visit in the future."

Lucien kept his eyes down and squeezed them closed. He felt his blood pumping harder. Felt his pulse quicken and his heart bang a war drum in his chest demanding action, demanding a statement be made, compelling him to do something that would ripple outwards.

He could still hear the breathless silence of the crowd. Still taste the bile in his throat.

A coward's death, he told himself. *Or—*

He moved. The Glock came up fast, smooth from the shadows beneath his shirt. Two shots cracked through the room and the soldiers dropped before their rifles even shifted.

Lucien turned the pistol on Jean, seeing that the man had reacted far quicker than Lucien expected, but he never got a third shot off.

Because Armand didn't hesitate. He rose, grabbed the chair, and swung it with full force. The legs hit Lucien square in the ribs with a splintering crunch, sending him sprawling into the wall. Air fled his lungs and Jean was on him in a flash, grabbing the gun and twisting it violently so Lucien heard the pop of his knuckle dislocating before the shock of pain hit him.

Lucien fought through the fog, his body remembering what to do, so an elbow drove into Jean's sternum, a left hook curved up toward his jaw, a knee snapped forward towards flesh, but Jean was faster than he looked.

He came in close, drove his forehead into Lucien's face with a sickening thud, and followed it up with a brutal downward swing of the stolen gun so the butt cracked Lucien hard over the eye.

Stars exploded in Lucien's vision and forced him unwillingly to his knees, hot blood already pouring from the gash opened up on his brow.

His hands were wrenched behind him and steel clamped around his wrists.

He tasted blood, felt it drip from his nose and run warm down his lip as the entire universe tilted suddenly off its axis.

He heard Armand breathing through his teeth, not winded but adrenalized to activate the calm, collected rage he hid just under the suave surface that disguised one thing Lucien learned too late.

The man was a killer.

"Next time," Armand growled, brushing dust from his sleeve, "search 'im *properly.*"

Jean wiped his mouth with the back of his hand. "You want me to get rid of 'im, *Capitaine?*"

Armand looked down at Lucien like a man eyeing a faulty clock. "Not yet, just lock 'im up somewhere quiet. 'e is still useful insurance."

Jean grunted his compliance and shifted his weight to look down at Lucien with pure hatred in his eyes. He shook his head once, admonishing Lucien for not seeing the obvious truth the man himself believed, and cocked back a fist to slam Lucien's skull into the floorboards.

Lucien's vision swam.

His heartbeat thundered in his ears, drowning out everything else, but he wasn't fully out yet. Jean must've recognised that, grunted something about a hard head, and hit him again.

This time the darkness was instant and absolute.

RARELY PROUD WHEN ALONE

Inside the old garrison hall, a converted meeting room now dressed in candlelight and damp smoke, a half-dozen officers snapped to attention as the door opened. Le Maréchal entered without speaking, shedding his soaked cloak to one of the aides who scurried forward to gather it with the reverence of a fan at a rock concert catching a thrown drumstick. Armand followed clutching a leather folder to his side, silent and unreadable as ever, though even he looked drawn at the edges.

Had anyone in the room known his true nature they would have seen that the outward appearance was a front; a faked air designed to destabilise others.

The smell of burnt oil and damp wool clung to everything in the room. A map dominated the central table where it had once been rolled out with pride, every contour line and ridge traced with care, but now it was stabbed with pins and dirtied by the soot-blackened fingers of men who no longer planned victories but delays.

"Gentlemen," Le Maréchal said with feigned dignity in spite of the terrible news. "Explain to me what 'appened."

"The scouts who fled said they struck at the rear to cut off the attack," Armand said, speaking confidently before anyone else could try to set the tone. "Routed the vanguard, destroyed the assault and took prisoners."

Le Maréchal was still for a long time staring at the map and at nothing at all before he exploded in an uncharacteristic display of emotion by slamming a fist down hard onto the table.

"*Merde*! 'ho is this bastard that leads them, ah? Why did we not know of 'im already?"

Nobody answered, so Armand cleared his throat and spoke respectfully. "Colonel Beaulac said 'e is a very capable man, and I suspect we knew nothing of 'im because 'is other adversaries did not survive to spread word," he said, changing his tone to something darker, more accusatory. "Allow me to point out, sir, that we only learned what happened because the reserves chose to flee instead of fight."

Le Maréchal snapped his head up to fix Armand with a deathly glare. The room collectively held its breath expecting an order for them to be imprisoned or shot for cowardice, but no such order came as he forcibly calmed himself and stood to begin pacing around the room, hands clasped behind his back to prevent them from fidgeting.

"And Beaulac?" he asked. "What word of 'im?"

"Gone," Armand intoned flatly. "At best 'e is a prisoner, and at worst…dead."

A long silence settled, like dust after demolition. Then a quiet chuckle came from the far end of the room.

Le Maréchal stopped dead, turning slowly to fix his beady gaze on the man who had made the sound. "Something *amuses* you, General Moreau?"

Le Maréchal's tone was coldly inquisitive, and it carried the full weight of consequence for the next words spoken out loud.

"N-no, *mon Maréchal*, I just…Beaulac was an ambitious man, and ambition 'as a way of getting a man killed."

"*Ambition*, General, is the virtue that made Caesar cross the Rubicon. That made Voltaire question kings, and Bonaparte crown himself. It is the appetite of *empire*…I only ask that *you* show some ambition and not seek pleasure in the failures of other men."

Moreau bowed his head and mumbled something that sounded apologetic, while others tried to hide their chagrin at seeing the senior man chastised like an impertinent boy.

"So…" Le Maréchal said, clearly attempting to get his own thoughts back on track. "We 'ave suffered losses, but we 'ave not been defeated. Losing one battle does not mean our cause is lost or that it is not just, but we must now learn caution. We must not seek to engage this Englishman in small skirmishes. Boneparte 'imself warned us that we must not fight too often with one enemy, or we will teach 'im all our art of war."

More silence followed, as it often did when Le Maréchal quoted something obscure that only he understood.

"Am I to believe, sir, that you wish to bring this man to battle once and destroy 'im?" Duval enquired.

"I wish to do nothing about this Englishman, Duval! *Nothing*."

Le Maréchal's sudden flare of anger – the second such breaking of character in as many minutes – spoke volumes for his grip on self-control. It signalled something unspoken in the room, and everyone shifted uncomfortably save for Armand.

"May I suggest, Maréchal, that we deploy more scouts?" Renaud said with all the confidence of a frightened orphan.

Le Maréchal ignored the suggestion, telling everyone what he thought of weakness and a lack of confidence, to resume his pacing.

"And what of the people earlier? What was that…*vulgarity*?" Le Maréchal asked, speaking of the mob's reaction to the public hanging.

General Moreau harrumphed loudly enough to wobble his jowls, stirring himself to voice his own indignation.

"Peasants act like peasants, sir. It has always been so and shall alwa—"

"Do not speak of your fellow citizens in this manner in my presence," Le Maréchal said quietly, the weight of his soft tone spelling disaster for the next person to displease him. "Are you yourself not a citizen, General? Or do you think of yourself as *better* than the people? Tell me, do you sit yourself atop a pyramid of society?"

"Forgive me for misspeaking, *mon Maréchal*, I simply meant that they are not educated in the way we ourselves are. I—"

"Duval, you are charged with keeping the peace within our walls," Le Maréchal said, cutting Moreau off abruptly. "Tell me why they acted this way?"

"The people are restless," Duval said instantly, showing little courtesy and too much honesty. "Our 'old weakens by the 'our and there are fights in the streets almost every day, and there 'ave been attacks on soldiers guarding supplies and the gates. They are angry that the people we sent out 'ave not returned and they 'ave not been told why...but it is not just 'ere. The Castres barracks 'ad to be retaken after guards turned on each other, and this—"

"I know of this, Duval, I asked you only why the people acted this way and you told me. I did *not* ask your opinions on our vision for France unravelling."

Courbin, ever the eager toady to Le Maréchal, glared at Duval as if his weak chin and rodent eyes could force the man to show more respect.

"No sir, I apologise," Duval said, finally showing signs of self-preservation that had nothing to do with Courbin's attempts to intimidate. "I merely meant to say that the people are un'appy. Our vision for France is *not* unravelling."

"No," Le Maréchal said softly. "Not yet it is not."

He walked to the map in the following silence and studied it. His hand hovered over Sanctuary, then traced the route north towards the mountains.

"The farms were vital," Armand said. "We 'oped to cut their food supply, but I fear we simply gave them 'orses and 'ostages."

"They broke a tooth, Armand," Le Maréchal said distractedly, "not the jaw."

Armand tilted his head. "Maréchal, I understand you are angered by this loss, but—"

Le Maréchal's eyes burned with something cold and constant. "This is not anger, Capitaine, this is inevitability...So, tell me again why I cannot besiege this man in 'is 'ome and starve 'im out?"

A small noise sounded from one end of the table where Second Lieutenant Bellier tried to clear his throat confidently, yet the resulting sound was more of a squeak. He adjusted his ledger and summarised the facts given by Beaulac.

"Because they 'ave walls as strong as our own, they 'ave access to the sea and a fleet of fishing boats, they 'ave weapons and ammunition—"

"And nobody confirmed this, did they?" Courbin snapped. "Beaulac failed to gain access to their armoury, so we don't know if they even 'ave enough bullets to stop us walking right up to their gates and—"

"Per'aps, Courbin," Armand said pleasantly, "you wish to test your theory personally?"

377

Snickers of amusement were quickly stifled when Le Maréchal spun around, annoyed at the bickering between jealous children competing over an inheritance.

Luckily for Bellier the interruption saved him from suffering anyone's wrath for having spoken after being expressly forbidden from doing so.

"So, the question remains...what to do about this Englishman?" Le Maréchal said, speaking as if to himself.

He stepped toward the window, looking out at the flickering torches lighting the square.

"Let them believe they 'ave won something...Soil must be soaked before anything can grow."

He turned back to the room. "And some things only grow in blood...you are all dismissed."

Chairs scraped as the senior officers all departed, but Armand lingered at the doorway until he was the last to remain before he cleared his throat.

"There is another matter I wish to bring to your attention, Maréchal."

Le Maréchal turned back to the window, peering into the distance at the approaching rumble of angry clouds. "Speak."

Armand closed the door and walked back to the table, taking the time to pour himself a glass of red wine before he made his play. "Courbin."

That name brought a shift in the room even though Le Maréchal didn't move a muscle.

Armand continued, his tone so casual it bordered on disinterested. "I 'ave spoken with several individuals – both soldiers and civilians – and all of them prepared to swear under oath that Courbin has been consolidating 'is own command. Of course I did not believe this at first, but I felt compelled to check before bringing it to your attention."

"And tell me," Le Maréchal said after a pause so long Armand began to believe he'd made a grave error. "What did you find?"

"That Courbin 'as been reassigning men loyal to 'imself and re-writing supply ledgers to 'ide stored weapons. I regret to say this, Maréchal, but Courbin is preparing something."

Le Maréchal turned slowly, his gaze dark under a deep frown. "If this is true, 'e would not be the first to mistake my mercy for weakness."

Armand allowed himself the faintest shrug. "The man 'as made promises to more than one officer, quietly, of course, but 'e 'as escaped notice. 'e forgets, sir, that others 'ave eyes and ears in places 'e assumes loyal to 'im."

Pre-empting being ordered to produce this evidence, Armand withdrew a heavy sheaf of papers from the leather folder and placed them on the table. Each document had been carefully curated, the signatory of each either a dead man with a statement backdated to before their demise or attributed by a living witness who had been coached to say precisely the right thing if their account was questioned.

Jean had been invaluable in compiling this meticulous weight of falsified evidence, but the risk, the effort and the time it had taken were all worth it to remove the one person Armand suspected had seen him coming a mile away.

And it took a true schemer to recognise one of their own, so Courbin had to go.

There was another long pause before Le Maréchal spoke. "Treachery, Armand, is older than loyalty. Caesar learned that at the

379

base of Pompey's statue, as did Napoleon at Fontainebleau, but I find Voltaire most honest on the matter. 'e said, 'We are rarely proud when we are alone'."

He turned now, facing Armand fully. "What do you propose we do?"

Armand met his gaze without flinching. "With your permission, Maréchal, I will deal with him. *Quietly.* There will be no scandal, no noise, 'e will simply…*cease.*"

Le Maréchal studied him. Slowly, he nodded.

"But I also wish to ensure 'is betrayal 'as not infected anyone else."

"Do what you must…" Le Maréchal intoned, turning to look Armand directly in the eyes. "You are a loyal citizen, Alexis. A true 'ero of France…Capitaine Armand, the loss of Beaulac leaves a void in my command structure, as such you are promoted to full colonel effective immediately."

Armand bowed his head, simply extending an exaggerated nod to show deference to a man he saw as a joke, but Armand's game was, and always had been, a long one.

He left the room, nodding to Jean who fell in stride beside him as they paced down the torch-lit corridor. "Did it work?" he asked quietly.

"It did. You know what to do."

The two men peeled off in different directions, and the torches burned lower as the storm moved closer.

THE FRUIT OF QUIET SEEDS

The room had no name. If it ever served a purpose beyond storage and silence, no one remembered it. Its stone walls were marked with scuffs and old nail holes, damp patches high up in the corners like permanent shadows. A single lantern burned near the door, its oil low, casting a flicker that never quite reached the far walls. A sour tang of something unpleasant lingering in the still air.

Courbin sat in the centre on a plain chair facing away from the door. His coat was gone, boots muddy, shirt clinging where the fabric had soaked through. He sat unmoving, hands resting in his lap. His grey eyes were unblinking as he stared at a fixed point on the floor as though it might offer him the words he needed to escape.

He thought no fear showed in him, and no false front either, just a steady, unnatural calm that made the quiet crackle of the lantern feel louder than it should. He strived for that aura, but the man leaning against the wall in his blind spot could smell his fear.

He felt it every time he shifted position and the little man tensed, waiting for another strike, because as hard as he might pretend to be calm there was no way to disguise his true, flinching nature.

Armand had been watching him from the shadows for five full minutes before stepping into view, prompting a jolt of shock, visible fear, then a hateful malice to descend on Courbin's features.

"*You*," Courbin spat.

"Ah, yes…*me*," Armand replied with gleeful threat.

He began to walk a slow circle around Courbin, daring him to twist and keep him in sight, walking with the patient steps of a man who had already decided the outcome.

He moved like still water, and Courbin sat unable to hide the trembling in his body.

Armand didn't ask questions. The questions had come hours ago, back when the unspeaking thug stopped staring blankly at him, and Courbin was confused at first. He believed there was a genuine misunderstanding, that Le Maréchal had ordered his detention and questioning, but when Armand stepped into view the truth he thought he understood vanished like smoke in a breeze.

"Armand? What is the meaning of this! Release me at once!"

Armand stopped pacing and smiled down at Courbin with genuine amusement.

"Tell me, why would I listen to any order given by you?" Armand asked, genuinely wishing to understand.

"Le Maréchal will 'ear of this, and 'e wi—"

"Le Maréchal *ordered* your arrest, Courbin. 'e is done with your lies," Armand interrupted.

"My *lies*?!"

"Yes. Le Maréchal 'as proof of your plot to take control. 'e 'as evidence going back months, Courbin, *months*. Evidence of 'ow you forged supply ledgers, 'ow you manoeuvred people loyal to you into prominent positions of authority, 'ow you schemed for almost a year to remove your rivals and place yourself in a position to take over. You 'ave been found out, Courbin, and now you must face the consequences of your betrayal of France."

Courbin's jaw flapped as he was utterly lost for words. Unable to respond, he watched Armand glare at him until he could no longer contain himself.

Armand laughed. The man in Courbin's blind spot laughed too, and Courbin finally found his voice.

"This is a lie! I 'ave *never* plotted against Le Maréchal! I am loyal! To Le Maréchal, to France, I..."

Courbin trailed off, finally seeing the whole picture. His gut turned to acid and he thought for a fleeting moment he might void his bowels on the spot. "You...you are the one...you are framing *me*...?"

Armand stopped laughing and wiped a finger under each eye. "*Merci*, Courbin. I truly mean that. I 'ave not laughed so 'ard in too long...but yes, I am the one with a plot and you are very 'elpfully going to disappear so my tracks are covered. So again, *merci*."

Courbin broke. He began yelling, bawling orders for guards to come, for Armand to be arrested, for Le Maréchal to be summoned, and when he finally summoned the courage to stand up Armand reacted fast.

Courbin doubled over, unable to breathe or speak from the savagery of the gut punch that folded him in two, and unable to resist when he was shoved unceremoniously back into the chair where he croaked to try and force air into his starving lungs.

Armand drew a cord from his pocket and stepped fast to stand behind the chair. He paused, not for drama, but certainty. His voice, when it came, was soft enough that it might have been for Courbin's ears alone.

"Don't worry," he muttered. "This is entirely personal, not business."

The ligature was smooth. Armand slipped it into place with a steady grip making Courbin flinch and clutch with desperate fingers at his throat.

There was such violence in the action, so much pressure exerted with so much raw, emotional energy that Courbin was rendered utterly helpless.

Still unable to breathe from the punch, and seeing stars as his brain fought for blood to stay alert, Courbin fought back with the kind of ferocity only a dying person could summon as the body took over from the mind.

Courbin fought for his life and Armand held on tight to extinguish it, but the result was as inevitable as the sunset.

Courbin's heels jerked one last time on the stone, then settled. His body resisted for a moment longer before it slackened, but Armand didn't let go.

He waited and watched. He counted the beats behind his eyes, and when he was satisfied it was done, he straightened, rolling the cord neatly back into his pocket before stepping away to dust himself off.

Jean leaned on the doorframe like a man who hadn't seen a thing.

"That felt better than I expected," Armand said, smoothing his sleeves and still breathing heavily from the exertion.

Armand glanced back at Courbin's lifeless body then back at Jean.

"Get rid of 'im. Quietly. No mistakes."

Jean nodded and stepped in to deal with the body as Armand left without so much as a single look back.

⁓

The wall was slick underfoot after rain had fallen in that annoying, misting drizzle for hours. It was the kind that didn't soak through clothing but clung to it, making everything feel damp and close.

He found Duval speaking to someone near the western parapet; voice low, hands folded behind his back like a man pretending at patience while Armand knew he affected the posture to mimic Le Maréchal. The moment Armand stepped up onto the rampart, the other figure peeled away and vanished down the steps without even a nod.

Duval turned, too late to hide the twitch in his expression.

"Good evening, *Capitaine*," he said, a little too brightly. "I did not expect to see you up 'ere at this late 'our."

Armand stopped a few paces short, letting the silence sit a moment.

"I came to tell you that Courbin is dead," Armand said conversationally. "And it is *Colonel*, now."

Duval's eyebrows lifted. He pulled a face as if weighing the appropriate reaction, then settled on a smile that didn't touch his eyes.

"Congratulations, *Colonel*...Very efficient of you to dispose of Courbin, although if I am being *truly* honest, I 'eard whispers it might be *you* 'ho vanished first."

Duval gave a short laugh, sounding like a man trying to bluff his way through dangerous waters.

Armand stepped closer – too close - then reached up slowly to brush something invisible from Duval's shoulder in a gesture that looked casual and perfunctory, but both men knew it wasn't.

The push was quick, combining with the slick stones underfoot and the weight shift of a man too used to standing his ground. Duval's foot slipped, his balance tipped, and he managed only to release a startled gasp like people made when the world dropped out from beneath them.

Armand stepped closer to the parapet and leaned over, just in time to hear the body hit the stone below with a dull thump and a wet crack.

Armand adjusted the collar of his coat, turned back into the wind and walked.

"You should be more careful with your words, Duval."

SILENCE ON THE WIND

Leah entered the medical ward fast, still amped from the fight as though she hadn't fully expended the rage she'd loaded ready for it. Kate and Marie both jumped with a start when she burst in, the doors hitting walls when she'd opened them harder than intended.

Nemesis loped in behind her, heading straight for Ash who still stood sentry in the corner beside Dan's bed and fussed at him until Ash growled, then relented to lick the blood from his daughter's face.

Muttering an apology she stepped over to Marie who stood to wrap her up in a tight squeeze that risked crushing her if she wasn't wearing body armour.

"Careful, I've got blood on me," Leah said through a face full of Marie's clothing.

Marie released her and pushed her back, holding her at arm's length to inspect her before Leah ended her concern.

"Didn't say it was *my* blood."

Marie slapped a hand lightly on Leah's vest in admonishment before she turned back to Dan.

"Just like your bloody father," she muttered, making Leah wince at the graphical accuracy of her words.

Dan *was* bloody. Blood sheeted his chest, soaked the bed, and had splashed a fair amount onto the floor for good measure.

Leah gasped at the sight of him. He was unconscious, broken and weak, looking more vulnerable than she had ever seen him in her life. He suddenly looked so old to her, no longer the indomitable fighter she knew, and her heart broke into pieces just seeing him brought so low.

Tears pricked her eyes that she tried to blink away, but her running nose forced her to sniff until Marie wrapped her arms around her again.

The second she uttered a comforting sound Leah's resolve shattered, and she burst out in tears.

Marie held her for a long time, her own tears adding to the sound, but all the while she tried to reassure her girl and take away the burden of emotional pain, just as she always did.

"He's going to be fine," she whispered.

Marie kissed Leah's hair after each time she spoke the words that sounded more like she was trying to will it to be true more than assure someone it was.

They stayed like that for a minute longer, before the anger Leah bottled up inside overtook the shock of grief, and she straightened herself so Marie let go. She hardened her heart in that moment, armoured herself against the possible outcome like she was already following Dan's last instructions.

Wanting to hear it directly from the expert, Leah turned to fix Kate with a stern look. "Tell me."

"I had to cut the infection and drain it," Kate said. "No other way. Neil said he'd been taking out-of-date antibiotics, and that's probably what made him...you know..."

Leah did know, because she'd been the one to choke Dan out only three feet behind her.

"We managed to get the broken tooth out too, and now we just need to keep him hydrated and keep flushing out the wound," Kate finished.

"What about sepsis?" Leah asked, proving to Kate that the little girl she'd taught how to bandage a cut hadn't forgotten a damn thing.

"I...I—"

"We don't know," Sera said, entering the room behind Leah having evidently heard everything. "Simple truth is that there's no way *to* know yet, so we do everything we can and we wait."

Leah nodded, accepting the prognosis even though she didn't like it at all. Not one single bit of it.

"We wait," she echoed, snapping her finger and thumb for Nemesis' attention.

The dog came to heel obediently, but Leah stayed staring at Ash who blinked guiltily and turned his head away.

"How long's he been here?" Leah asked.

"Since you brought Dan in," Kate said. "Every time someone tries to make him leave he growls and shows his teeth."

Leah stared at Ash before letting out a huff through her nose that carried an unmistakable tone of, "Right then, you little fucker".

She stepped closer to Ash and called him to heel. Ash ignored her and kept his head turned away, so Leah stepped closer again, adding some snarl to her voice when she ordered the dog to fall in. Still Ash ignored her, twisting his body so he physically couldn't see Leah as though that excused his stubborn refusals to obey.

Leh stepped closer and reached a hand down, only this time Ash went from stubborn refusal to active resistance, snapping his teeth at her hand and unleashing a savage, rippling snarl of warning.

Marie flinched and Kate yelped before placing herself on the other side of the substantial wooden desk, while Sera watched impassively.

Leah's hand didn't move, even when Ash snapped again, coming so close that Leah felt the hot wetness on her skin.

"Just leave him," Marie tried. "He's not doing any ha—"

"And when he can't hold it in anymore and pisses all over the floor?" Leah asked, directing some of her hostility at Marie for what she perceived in that moment to be weakness.

Marie didn't answer, making it clear she was butting out and whatever happened to Leah next was entirely on her.

Leah leaned closer, staring Ash in the eyes and showing her own teeth as the dog rose up to try and intimidate her. Leah intensified the emotions radiating outward, knowing it would sound ridiculous to anyone who didn't operate as a partnership with a dangerous dog would and could never comprehend it.

Leah leaned over him, forcing him to roll half onto his back in reluctant submission but still he showed his teeth, still snarled, and Leah snarled back until she finally snapped one word of command at him.

"OUT!"

Ash streaked low for the door, not looking back even as Leah and Nemesis followed him.

Leah followed Ash all the way outside, having to jog to keep up while Ash increased his own pace to stay ahead of her.

Outside, literally feet from the doors, he stopped to cock a leg at the first appropriate spot and unleash a hot stream he'd evidently been holding for so long it had grown painful.

Leah sat on the steps nearby and waited for him to finish, then before he could slink back inside she snapped his name and brought him back to her where he sat just beyond her reach.

"No, come here," Leah said, her tone softer and loving now.

Ash shuffled closer, putting in apparent maximum effort to move his body an entire inch at a time until he was close enough that she could reach out and stroke him.

Ash's stubborn resolve folded like paper, and he rolled into her body to soak up the physical reassurance he so desperately needed. He turned full puppy, rolling over and contorting to try and get as much of it as he could which made Nemesis feel jealous enough to get involved so the three of them ended up rolling around at the top of the steps until Leah felt it was time to get serious again.

She stood, adjusted her rifle sling, and headed back to the walls in search of Neil. In search of news of her husband and daughter, because right then she felt very alone and needed them more than ever.

~

"What do you mean?"

Neil blinked at Leah, wondering how his words could possibly have been misconstrued.

"I mean there hasn't been a pigeon since the day before yester-day…sorry…"

"But…what does that mean?" Leah asked, desperately trying to wrap her head around this latest crushing blow.

"It means they haven't sent a pigeon, that's all…it might even mean they have, but it got taken by a sparrowhawk or a falcon. Leah, it's not the end of the world. We expected them to go quiet when they got there, so you need to not wind yourself up about it, okay?"

Leah eyed hum suspiciously while Neil rooted in a pocket for a scrap of paper that he handed over. She read it twice, wishing Rafi spoke French or she spoke Spanish instead of having to decipher his written command of English.

"Kids are fine, no activity on the border," Neil summarised for her.

She ignored him and read it again, needing to see it directly rather than trust the word of someone who just told her she shouldn't worry about her husband.

Satisfied that he hadn't glossed over anything she handed the note back and turned away, flanked by a dog on each side, to head back down the stairs in search of Mitch for a second opinion that agreed with her growing sense of impending doom.

~

The stairwell stank of cold sea water, like the underground parts of Sanctuary wanted to remind anyone down there that the sea was right outside the walls.

Leah took each step with purpose, boots striking the stone loud enough to announce her mood as well as her presence. Ash padded at her right heel, silent but alert, while Nemesis stalked the other side with her usual low-slung, casual menace. The narrow passage twisted once and opened into a low-ceilinged corridor where iron rings still protruded from the walls. Water dripped steadily from somewhere out of sight, echoing down the line of rust-streaked doors.

She found Mitch down there, sat on a chair in front of the nearest cell with a cup of something steaming balanced on his knee. The prisoners inside sat slumped or cross-legged, eyes dull and faces drawn with hunger and uncertainty. One of them watched Mitch with something like contempt while another looked like he'd already given up. The youngest of them flinched when Leah stepped into view, flanked by two sets of eyes far more dangerous than her own.

Mitch didn't look up. "Didn't think *you'd* come down here."

"Yeah, well, I needed to go somewhere where people didn't smile at me like they're pretending everything's fine."

"So you've come to see Uncle Mitch for the low-down on doom and gloom," he said, not expecting a response and not receiving one.

He reached for the cup, sipped, then offered it to her without turning but she didn't take it, so he retracted the offer and settled it back onto his knee.

"You get anything out of them?" Leah asked, folding her arms and glaring through the bars.

"Names. Lies. The usual."

The young prisoner glanced up again, then looked away quickly when Leah's eyes pinned him. She let the silence stretch before speaking again.

"You think they're worth keeping?"

"Depends on what you mean by *worth*," Mitch answered with a shrug.

"I mean, do they *know* anything, or are they just mushrooms?"

The man closest to the bars shifted uncomfortably. Ash responded with a low rumbling growl that sent him further back into the shadows.

"They know enough to be scared of you," Mitch said. "That proves they're not all dumb as a haggis wi' no legs."

Leah stepped closer, just enough for the boy to back up until his shoulders hit the rear wall. She tilted her head slightly, inspecting him like she was weighing up meat cuts. Her tone, when she spoke, was almost casual. "Which one pissed himself during the fight?"

Mitch made a sound that might have been a suppressed laugh and pointed at the cowardly culprit. "Don't think he's recovered from it yet."

She didn't laugh. Her mind had already shifted to another room at the far end of the corridor, where Beaulac sat alone in reinforced confinement. He hadn't said a word since they'd dragged him in, and somehow that made her want to kill him more. It wasn't just rage; it was fear, and simply acknowledging that made her very angry.

Fear that he knew things she didn't, that Lucien was already dead and this bastard was just waiting for the moment to tell her.

Or worse, to let her find out another way.

Leah turned back to Mitch. "What about Beaulac?"

"What about him?" Mitch asked.

"Well he's clearly not kept in the dark and fed bullshit. I say we question him."

"Aye, and by 'question' him you mean you want to hurt the bastard even more than y'already have…"

"I *want* to kill him," she said, without a shred of hesitation. "Like…right now. Today."

Mitch met her eyes. "I know, lassie, but tha's no' your call and well you know it."

She hated how calm he sounded. How he didn't flinch or argue or tell her to take a breath. Just sat there, steady as ever, like a bastard rock in the tide.

"I know I can't," she said, dropping her voice and uttering the words she dreaded to hear out loud. "Not until we know Lucien's still alive."

Mitch nodded once. "You're right, but there's more to it than just that. Don't get me wrong, I'm very fond of the lad, but we're talkin' about things over both our heads now."

Leah paced, not far, just enough to move the energy through her legs before she exploded. Ash and Nemesis moved with her, perfectly in sync, like two shadows ready to pounce if she gave the word.

"Mitch…If they've hurt him…I swear to fucking *God* if he's dead, then Beaulac doesn't get a clean bullet. I'll make him *suffer*. I'll turn him into a piece of fucking *art*."

"You will," Mitch agreed, still maddeningly calm, "and when that day comes I'll hold the bastard still for ye, but not today."

The boy in the cell was watching again, eyes wide now. Leah turned toward him and he shrank back into the dark like a kicked dog.

"You still rattled?" Mitch asked, softly this time.

"*Of course I'm fucking rattled*!" she exploded.

The echo of her voice bounced down the corridor, and the prisoners all looked away. Ash stood like a statue, his eyes fixed on the bars, while Nemesis sat beside Leah with her hackles barely raised.

"No bird?" Mitch said.

She shook her head, not daring to speak in case the tears came again to render her weak.

"Still could be nothing."

"And it still could be *everything*," she snapped back.

Mitch held up his hands in mock surrender. "I'm no' askin' ye tae play pretend, I'm askin' ye not tae crack before all the pieces are on the board."

Leah gave a bitter smile. "Too late."

Mitch gave her a sad smile and stood to grab her close for a hug she tried to resist at first. He didn't linger, just patted her hard on the back and propelled her back towards the stairs.

"Come on, let's get out'a here. Place bloody stinks."

Leah started up the stairs as Mitch glanced back at Beaulac's door which had stayed firmly closed. He'd heard about the lack of news from Lucien when Leah was still in medical, and had promptly ordered a militia member to find him a cup of tea and bring it back down to the cells, where he waited knowing full well Leah would find her way down there and likely do something stupid if her Uncle Mitch wasn't around to stop her.

Back at surface level Leah leaned against the wall with her head back and her eyes closed, just letting the sun soak into her skin as though it might revive her.

Mitch stood nearby, letting her have the silence and space he thought she needed while remaining close enough to the doorway to block her path if she decided she didn't want to wait any longer to transform Beaulac into modern art.

When she sucked in a sharp breath and walked away, Mitch turned and gave a subtle nod at two militia guards. They stepped forward, obviously awaiting orders that Mitch gave.

"One outside, one inside. Nobody comes in or out unless it's me or the medical people. *Nobody else*, y'understand me?"

The militiamen, one French and one Spanish, nodded eagerly. They understood the words but more than that they understood the *tone*, and that tone said Mitch would be very unhappy with anyone who let him down.

Catching up to Leah and her akimbo-canines, Mitch slowed to walk with her back in the direction of the main keep – the heart of their fortified home – when a figure came running out of the main doors. That figure looked around, head whipping left and right, before easily recognising Leah from the four-legged fur missiles flanking her. Arms began to wave and shouting reached them, but too faint to make out.

"What's that mad bastard sayin'?"

"*Shhh!*"

Mitch followed orders when the shout came again, and Leah's eyes went wide moments before she broke into a dead run.

"*Il est reveille!*" came the shout that Mitch understood this time.

Dan was awake.

THERE IS *ALWAYS* A CATCH

The word "awake" was a technicality. Dan was conscious but not fully lucid, and he blinked constantly like a drunk waking up in a ditch long before the booze had left his system sufficiently to revive him.

He vomited, unable to keep his head up so the bloody bile ran in two thick streams that clung stubbornly to his nostrils until Marie wiped them away. Kate had been quick but not quick enough, meaning that the bowl she rushed to his side caught only half of the first hot, stinking expulsion he spewed out.

Luckily he hadn't been able to eat much for days before the situation became critical, so after the third round of uncontrollable heaving there was nothing left in the tank.

He groaned, spat into the bowl so weakly that it just caught on the chin of his beard and hung there until Ash raised himself up on the side of the bed and licked it away to a chorus of disgusted noises.

Exhausted, Dan flopped back on the bed and screwed his eyes shut.

"Dan? Dan, I need you to keep your head tilted to one side. Can you do that for me?" Kate said, reverting to her paramedic roots instantly.

"What's wrong? Why is he throwing up?" Leah asked, her voice loud and higher than usual.

"I jabbed him with a couple of shots of pethidine, so…yyyeah…he's gonna feel a little rough after that," Sera said, not sounding as "sorry, not sorry" as she usually would.

"Farms," Dan mumbled wetly. "Farms!"

"The farms are fine," Leah told him, summing everything up as fast as she could to stop him from trying to speak more and interrogate her.

"They attacked with mixed infantry and cavalry, the militia held the high ground but were going to be overrun, Mitch drove your truck through a horse-drawn technical and I mopped up the infantry while he fucked up the cavalry with a rocket. When you're better I'm sure he'd *love* to tell you about his one-liner."

Dan stared at her and blinked rapidly again like an eighties computer trying to parse a sequence of input codes.

"Aye, it was *epic*," Mitch added proudly.

Dan's brow knitted in an obvious "What the fuck?" expression and Leah nodded.

"Yeah, you heard all that correctly. And we have pr—"

Dan lurched over again, dry heaving noisily into the bowl and turning the stomach of most people in the room.

"Everyone out!" Kate barked. "Too many of you in the way and he needs to sleep off the rest of the drugs. Now! Out!"

They shuffled from the room but Ash took the opportunity to resume his post.

Three days passed with Dan sleeping through much of it, and every day brought word from Andorra but of Carcassonne and Lucien there was nothing but ominous silence.

By day five Dan had recovered enough to walk, although slowly. He'd learned of Beaulac's capture on the third day and only the threat of more pethidine being jabbed into his thigh made him stay in bed.

Talking came with effort, his voice thick and low, and the salt-water rinse he swilled through his torn mouth every half hour made him feel constantly sick. He did enjoy one of the treatments, though, and that was to have raw honey drizzled onto the wounds inside his mouth. Sera told him it was a natural antibacterial, but he just liked the taste.

There was also a strict regimen of naproxen and paracetamol to keep the swelling and fever away, but of any surviving antibiotics there was no sign so caution was the name of the game. If at any moment he dropped into a fever or fainted, Kate and Sera wanted him back on the bed where they could watch him closely.

Walking slowly through the town he found that the people of Sanctuary greeted him like the old days, with nods of respect and quiet greetings. A few clasped hands on his shoulder and he acknowledged them with curt nods, grateful but guarded.

Fickle buggers, he thought. *They'd follow a squirrel if it looked like it knew what it was doing.*

The bitterness caught him off guard. It was harsh, he admitted to himself. Too harsh, and guilt followed in its wake.

He found Neil near the pigeon loft, feeding the birds. "Any word?"

"Nothing," Neil responded with a shake his head.

Dan nodded, lips tightening. "I should've done more."

No reply came from Neil, just the rustle of wings, so Dan walked away feeling every ounce of shame and regret. He'd been avoiding Leah who had stopped coming to see him multiple times a day, and instead of seeking her out he stayed out of her way.

Marie told him that their daughter needed his support, needed to let her be heard, but Dan's only way to fix a problem was to attack it headlong, and in his current state he could barely fix himself a sandwich.

"I'll do more," he growled to himself, but at that moment he didn't exactly know what.

On the sixth day he made his way toward the old fort and the prison cells beneath it. The air changed as he descended; it was stale and cold but with something new now. Something that made him imagine decay.

The rot of festering wounds and damp stone clung to his skin as he neared the bottom of the stairs just as Kate came up them. She paused beside him, her face taut and tired.

"They're healing," she said. "Most of them. One might lose his leg if he keeps ignoring my instructions."

"Beaulac?" Dan asked.

"No. Someone else."

"Won't be a problem for much longer."

Kate's eyes narrowed in suspicion. "What are you going to do with them?" she asked, accusation heavily implied with every syllable.

Dan met her gaze unwaveringly. "I'm going to let them go," he told her in his best flat "no bullshit" tone

"Seriously?"

"Well I'm not going to just kill them, if that's what you're asking."

"I wasn't, but if that was the plan I'm just saying I didn't need to waste a load of my time and medical supplies treating them!" Kate said sharply before moving past him in search of fresh air.

Outside the cells he found Mitch with two other guards. They looked wrecked, with red-rimmed eyes and hollow cheeks, betraying the weight of too many nights without proper sleep.

"I need Bollock," Dan said, gesturing at the cells. "Alone."

Mitch eyed him for a few seconds, just long enough to annoy Dan but not quite long enough to spark a reaction, then he stepped away and unlocked the correct door.

"On your feet," he barked into the gloom.

Beaulac limped forward, stiff and pale. Sweat clung to him like a second skin and he moved like every step cost him, but he didn't flinch on seeing Dan and Ash. He didn't beg. He looked far from broken despite the injuries as pride held what little dignity he had left.

"I'm letting you go," Dan told him bluntly.

Beaulac stared at him, caught between disbelief and suspicion. "What's the catch?"

"No catch. You even get a ride home."

Beaulac didn't say anything and neither did Dan. The silence just lingered as they stared at one another.

"There is *always* a catch," Beaulac said, staggering and leaning a hand against a wall as his ravaged leg gave out on him.

Dan waited until he steadied himself and took a step closer, almost daring the man to make a move. As weakened as he was, Beaulac looked in worse shape than Dan did and he wanted his enemy to see that. To know it and believe he had no choice other than the one he was given.

Dan stunned his adversary with the stark truth, pinning Beaulac's eyes wide.

"Two of my people are in Carcassonne spying on your Marshal and I want them to come home, so we're going to exchange you for their safe return," Dan said, facing Mitch before turning his back to Beaulac like the man no longer posed any credible threat to him.

"Put him back. I'm done with him," he said, walking away to find Leah and tell her what plan he'd come up with to get her husband back.

Two trucks rolled north at daybreak, engines grumbling over broken roads as they took the direct route to Carcassonne.

Leah drove the lead truck with Dan sitting beside her, map unfolded across his lap and two dogs fighting for space among the gear bags behind them.

Their battered second truck followed, hurriedly patched with tape and zip ties by Neil after Mitch's recent joyride through enemy ranks.

Dan pointed occasionally, giving directions with curt words and brief nods. Leah acknowledged the instructions, but the feelings inside her were in a perpetual state of war and so confused that her mind seemed to display a firework show every minute she was awake. Dan, although dressed for war including the brutal, short-barrelled shotgun he hadn't taken out in months resting on the wide dashboard, was a shadow of the man she knew.

He looked like Dan, mostly walked and talked like Dan, but part of him seemed hollow. Diminished somehow, and not just physically.

Leah might've had the time to find out what it was that left him that way, only her heart was being torn in multiple directions that always ended up with her imagining never seeing Lucien again or even finding out what happened to him, and Adalene growing up never knowing her father.

With their heads full of their own internal turmoil, they drove steady onward until they reached their target.

They stopped short of Carcassonne, angling the truck to block the road but enabling them to drive back in the direction they'd come from in a hurry if needed.

They parked far enough away to stay safe from the range of any conventional weapon but more than close enough to be seen.

Dan climbed out, teeth clenched as he reached for a smoke and thought better of it. Restoring the rolled cigarette to the tin he raised the flare gun taken from the group he and Mitch had made disappear, aimed high, and fired.

A faint red bloom lit the sunny sky, arcing away for the flare to fall near the walls.

"Now what?" Leah asked from beside him.

Dan watched the smoke trail fade.

"Now we wait."

Five soldiers approached, their formation loose and swaggering with false confidence. They were young, armed, and clearly trying to appear braver than they felt. One wore a grin that didn't reach his eyes while another bore the twitchy stance of a man ready to shoot but simultaneously terrified that he might have to.

404

Dan stepped forward slowly, expression flat and unimpressed. Ash stayed at his side, ears back, hackles stiff.

One man raised a hand and called out a friendly yet confused greeting.

"Bonjour," Dan responded affably. "Now fuck off!"

Confused glances were exchanged. One of them opened his mouth to protest.

Dan cut him off, butchered French rolling from his tongue with all the grace of a sledgehammer.

"*Fous le camp!*" Dan said loudly, waving his arms to shoo them away as insignificant creatures.

They hesitated a moment longer, so Dan lifted the slung rifle casually and stitched a line of suppress, automatic gunfire into the grass verge close enough for them to jump.

They didn't flee as such, but their retreat was what Mitch called *hasty*.

A while passed. Dan lit a cigarette, winced at the sting in his mouth, and spat blood into the dust. Leah said nothing and the dogs watched the horizon, as if they knew it wasn't game time just yet.

A larger group arrived next. More organised and better armed, and at its head walked a man Dan didn't recognise but knew immediately.

The man was composed, clean, confident and dangerously calm. This was a man worth talking to if he wanted to get something done, Dan knew, so he met him halfway.

"You in charge?"

The man smiled easily. "I suppose that depends on what you need. If I knew what your people came 'ere to discuss, I might present a better case."

Dan threw his head back and growled his frustration like a teen-ager asked to clear up their own mess, confusing his composed greeter.

"*Monsieur*, I do not underst—"

"Mate, you've been here ten seconds and you're already fucking boring me!"

Dan's boorishness was intentional, finding it the fastest way to break through false manners and ceremony.

"You know full fucking well who I am and you know full fucking well who *we* are, so go get your big boss and stop wasting my time."

"I am afraid I do not understa—"

"I want the organ grinder, chap. Not the monkey."

The man paused, frowning as a smile crept over his features. "I 'ave not 'eard this one before, but I think you mean to say you will not speak to a…a…*sous-fifre?* 'ow you say, a 'nobody'?"

Dan snapped his fingers and turned the gesture into a finger pointed at the man's face.

"Bingo. See? Nowhere near as dumb as you look, now off ya fuck and get m—"

"Allow me to start again. My name is Alexis Armand, and I am a *Colonel* of the forces 'ere."

"Right. And you report directly to your Marshal, do you? So be a good lad and go fetch the fucker."

Armand smiled, unconcerned at the deliberate hostility which implied to Dan he knew it was false. Dan dropped the act and told him straight.

"I want to have a word with your boss, so go and fetch him."

Armand smiled again, a hint of unoffensive laughter in his re-sponse. "*Monsieur,* I'm sure you understand I cannot simply 'go fetch' a *Maréchal* of France. 'e must know at least something of the subjects you wish to discuss, no?"

Dan dropped his cigarette and crushed it underfoot. Turning to the second truck he held up a hand, giving the agreed signal for Beaulac to be hauled to his feet and the gag pulled from his mouth. Dan turned back to watch Armand's reaction, and as hard as the sharp, young man tried he couldn't hide the stab of recognition.

Dan leaned closer and spoke in a low tone that invited no argument.

"Go get your *Maréchal*. Tell him I have prisoners, and tell the bastard that unless he wants me to blow the fuckers up in sight of his pretty walls that he should get his fat arse out here and talk to me face to face."

He leaned back and saw Armand's expression flicker, betraying the presence of a competent killer hiding behind a catalogue model's smile and exquisite manners.

"As you so cleverly pointed out, *Monsieur*, we do 'ave walls. Why should *le Maréchal* step foot outside them?"

"Because we've got walls too, and we've also got plenty of shit that'll bring down someone else's."

He held up a hand again, this time giving Mitch his own prearranged signal to show off the goodies.

Mitch ducked down to retrieve something he'd been saving ever since their little slice of the world was threatened by pirates. He only had two additional reloads for it, and he knew there were better weapons by just about every standard, but anyone who'd ever been lucky enough to watch TV or had access to the internet recognised an RPG launcher.

It was as ubiquitous the world over as an AK-47, and the very sight of it was enough to make their point crystal clear.

"*Armand*, was it? Thing is, Armand, your big, pretty walls were designed to resist fire and big rocks being lobbed at them a few hundred years ago…Not eighty-five-millimetre high-explosive anti-tank rockets that can cut through about a metre of reinforced concrete and knock a tank out if you're good enough to know where to aim. My guys know where to aim, just in case you're wondering…Question is, just how much damage are they likely do to your gates and old stone walls?"

Armand drew himself up and nodded stiffly. "I will pass on your…*regards*…to *le Maréchal*."

Armand turned and left, waving an irritated hand at the soldiers flanking him.

PRISONER EXCHANGE

When Le Maréchal came, he brought a crowd. More soldiers, more noise, more posture all marching in time like a miniature French column.

"Fuck me, it's the auld guard!" Mitch commented from above and behind Dan.

He ignored the comment, as accurate as it may have been, and turned to speak quietly to Leah. "I want you up on that gympy."

Leah opened her mouth to argue, but Dan shot her a look that wiped away any sense she might still be harbouring of his temporary weakness. She closed her mouth and walked away to comply, leaving only Dan and Ash standing isolated and unafraid ahead of their people.

Ash looked back at Leah and Nemesis – one stomping fast to her position and the other loping alongside obediently – then back at Dan wearing a questioning look.

"She's too emotional," Dan told his dog quietly.

Dan was right to send her away because as Le Maréchal's people halted the very air felt like it shifted. A fight was possible, that much was blatantly apparent, and one mistake could turn conversation into chaos.

Mitch stood tall on the truck bed with his rocket-propelled grenade launcher at the ready, while Leah crouched behind the mounted GPMG, eyes hidden behind mirrored lenses.

Le Maréchal approached alone, his very normal-looking face un-readable.

He extended a hand, as if this were a meeting between equals. Dan looked down at it for a second then ignored it, looking back at the man who seemed nothing like a ruthless leader. He didn't yet know if the book was unjustly judged by its cover or if the man used proxies for his dirty work.

"Walk with me," Le Maréchal said in English, turning away as if the very notion of being disobeyed was unconscionable.

Dan followed, Ash pressed to his left thigh, stopping just far enough to be out of easy hearing.

"This is better," Le Maréchal said as though they'd just found a pleasant, solitary spot by a river to cast their lines.

"Better than what?"

Le Maréchal glanced back at his own people who, although not aiming their weapons at Dan's, seemed ready to do just that if pro-voked. Dan glanced back also, seeing that half the eyes of both fac-tions were on them and not the opposing forces.

"Better than being over'eard, yes?"

Dan laid it out. "Fine. You stay away from Sanctuary, from An-dorra and from my whole region. You want to go conquer some-thing, go north. There's plenty of space up there."

Le Maréchal smiled thinly. "Are you familiar with Voltaire, Dan?" he asked, both proving Dan's suspicion that they knew exactly who he was, and simultaneously annoying him by wanting to speak in riddles instead of being honest and blunt.

Le Maréchal didn't wait for an answer or recognition, and Dan suspected the man liked the sound of his own voice a little too much, but he let it play out.

"Voltaire said that men demand liberty, then beg to be ruled the moment it costs them comfort."

"Well *this* man calls bullshit."

The smile faded but Dan kept his eyes fixed on his smaller opponent's.

"Your attempt to take over Sanctuary failed. I killed your reinforcements, the sleepers you left in Andorra are dead, and my people wrecked your attack on the farms. That's where we took your people and now I want mine back."

"You suggest an exchange? Are they to offer their *parole* also? Are they agreed not to bear arms against you for the duration of our conflict?"

He spoke mockingly, using the tone Dan had heard from so many others who believed their book learning made them superior to him as a simple brute.

"I suggest you get your people back, I get mine, and we agree to stay the fuck away from each other. That way nobody has to get killed."

"Tell me," Le Maréchal said, ignoring the response. "Do you 'ave any notion of what I am doing for all of France? A unified nation, under one banner, seeking one goal of liberty, equality and brother'ood?"

Dan stared at him, wondering just what the man had been sniffing to think in such grandiose terms when as far as he believed people wanted security, a good harvest, a warm bed and for someone else to keep the wolves away.

"Just *think* about it...*one* France, under *one* rule, for *one* purpose! Do you not see 'ow this will save lives? 'ow it will improve the quality of life for *everyone* and not just those 'ho 'ave been fortunate?"

411

"You think I was born with a silver spoon up my arse?" Dan bit back. "You think we're *lucky* to have what we have? No. We *built* it. We *bled* for it, so we're not going to just hand it over and go under the thumb of anyone, especially not some jumped-up twat who thinks quoting bloody Voltaire makes him smarter than everyone else."

Le Maréchal betrayed a flash of anger behind his calm exterior, giving Dan the sense that belief in his vision wasn't something universally enjoyed within the walls of Carcassonne.

"So you are not interested in peaceful negotiations," Le Maréchal stated flatly, his voice suddenly deeper as if drawing a metaphorical line in the sand.

"Peaceful?! What's peaceful about sending a covert force to take over a town? What's peaceful about murder, about attacking farmers?"

"What is the English phrase? You must break eggs to 'ave an omelette?"

"Yeah, and I prefer to break skulls to have autonomy."

The retort left Le Maréchal silent for a while, and breaking his own rule Dan spoke first to fill that silence.

"What I'm suggesting is a non-aggression pact. You leave us alone, we leave you alone...and as a gesture of good faith I'm willing to trade prisoners. You'll see they've been given medical care and food, because while we might not follow your delusion we aren't animals."

"What you suggest 'as 'istorical precedent," Le Maréchal said after a thoughtful pause. "Joseph Boneparte 'imself signed a treaty with your own General Lord Cornwallis in 1802."

He smiled at Dan, looking as though he'd manipulated him into a blind alley.

412

Dan smiled back. He'd taken the opportunity while he healed sufficiently to make the journey to consult with the apologetic, sheepish man residing in the highest part of Sanctuary's main town and suffered a long lecture about the subject. He didn't know at the time, and he was even more surprised to realise the relevant knowledge had stuck, but the history lesson came in handy.

"And Old Boney broke that treaty a year later, so maybe your analogy isn't the best one to use?"

Le Maréchal's brow furrowed, not in anger, but in consternation that this man he clearly believed to be an uneducated brute possessed knowledge he kept hidden. This was Dan's play, because if his opponent misjudged him from the start he'd now be worrying about what else Dan knows.

"Five for two," Dan said, indicating the trucks behind him. "That's more than a fair trade."

Le Maréchal's eye twitched, and try as he might he was unable to hide the discomfort he felt.

"You *do* have my people, don't you?" Dan asked in a low, menacing tone. "A young man and an older woman?"

"I…we…we did not know the woman was yours. She did not…she would not speak. She was caught sending a message, which is treason and—"

"*Treason?*" Dan asked, his voice like an icicle pushed slowly into Le Maréchal's neck.

"Yes, she w—"

"She *was…?* Where is she? Right now?"

Le Maréchal's mouth dropped open with a wet pop but nothing came out of it. Dan stepped closer, sensing the hum of activity as weapons on both sides were raised but he ignored the outside world, fixing his hateful glare down into the smaller man's eyes as Ash, sensing the shift in mood also, began to growl.

"The woman…the woman was…was executed as a traitor."

The words came softly, like a child admitting they'd done wrong because the punishment for dishonesty would be far worse than their original crime.

Dan said nothing, but the cold drop in his chest was forced upwards by the rising fire in his gut. He wanted to kill him on the spot, to rip his beady little eyes out of his arrogant skull in front of everyone, but he forced himself to remain calm.

Picking up the invisible cue Ash growled louder forcing Le Maréchal to take an involuntary step back.

"How?" he asked quietly.

Le Maréchal swallowed, terrified now but trying so desperately to display a strength and resolve he clearly didn't feel.

"She…she 'ung."

Dan's heart broke into pieces, all of them sharp enough to tear from his chest and stab the fussy little man with.

"You hanged a woman you didn't know, with no proof, all because she tried to send a message," Dan said, not asking him, just reiterating the facts so Le Maréchal could comprehend just how much of a bastard that made him.

"It was treason," he said weakly, his voice barely audible now.

"Treason…" Dan said again, scornfully this time. "She was Canadian you fucking moron. You murdered her."

Le Maréchal had no idea how to respond, but Dan rammed the momentum he'd gathered down the man's throat.

"And the other? Young man with a shaved head?" Dan asked slowly.

Le Maréchal blinked with unfeigned ignorance. "I-I am...I am unaware of this person."

Dan's voice dropped to a growl as he leaned close enough to whisper in Le Maréchal's ear, "Then go find out. *Now.*"

Le Maréchal returned to his entourage, doing his best not to hurry as all eyes fixed on his failing grip on dignity. Words were exchanged, Armand spoke to another officer, then three soldiers ran for the gate.

They waited, every hand on a weapon and every finger near a trigger, until the soldiers returned minutes later, escorting a figure who stumbled more than walked.

Leah gasped, clearly audible from far away, and Dan fought the urge to bend double and rest in his knees in pure relief.

He watched them march Lucien closer, seeing swollen eyes and split lips, and the way he walked indicated someone had done their best to break his ribs, but he was still alive.

He heard Leah raise her voice at someone to take over her weapon, and Dan hoped he'd be able to contain her. He caught Lucien's eye, offering him a subtle nod, then turned away to intercept his daughter.

Leah was barely holding it together, and Dan rightly worried that she was seconds away from starting a gunfight unless he got through to her. Risking that lethal gunfight on a hunch, he blocked her way and shook his head.

"Not yet," he growled, seeing that she had every intention of ignoring him so he pulled the trigger on that hunch. "They killed Polly."

Leah stopped dead and rotated her head to face Dan. She wore a look of shock, but it was being pushed away by the volcanic eruption of grief-fuelled rage he knew she was about to unleash.

She tried to sidestep him but Dan moved to block her again, grabbing her arm hard with his left hand. "*Not. Yet.*"

It was the dynamic of two fighters who'd gone into combat so many times together that they'd developed their own language. They knew each other so well that Leah understood Dan was never going to let that brutality, nor the violence inflicted on Lucien, go unanswered, and that was the only reason she brought herself back under control.

With a shaky breath released through her nostrils and her eyes fixed on her battered husband, Leah gave Dan a curt nod that he similarly understood to speak more than words could.

Le Maréchal straightened his coat and marched back to Dan with some regained sense of formality, like he'd gone away and reminded himself he was in charge.

"You want your people now?" Dan asked.

Le Maréchal nodded. "We 'ave *standards*. We 'ave *rules*. The treatment of prisoners of war is cl—"

"Your people were injured in a fight, and we gave them medical care," Dan said, cutting him off with a finger raised at Lucien. "*He* didn't arrive looking like that, so fuck your rules you piece of shit."

"I...did not know that this man was in our custody," Le Maréchal said carefully, coming close to admitting he wasn't in full control of his people's actions.

Dan glared at him, daring him to say more, then abruptly turned and waved a hand.

"Let the bastards go!"

Leah hissed something at him angrily, but he turned and glared at her, hoping to communicate without being understood by Le Maréchal, who clearly had superior language skill. He considered using Spanish, but his educated guess told him the man would decode his attempt far more easily than using British military slang.

"Gimpy, now! And take Ash."

Leah hesitated, so tense she vibrated, until Dan's orders were processed in her mind. The fact that he wanted Ash off the board and away from the bullets that were about to fly told her everything she needed to know.

She turned and ran back to the truck pausing only to glare at Beaulac long enough for him to know he was incredibly lucky to be alive.

Dan watched as a few militia urged the prisoners towards their own side, but Dan held up a hand to stop them.

"Send him," he called out, waiting as Lucien was unbound and propelled away.

He walked tall – as tall as he could with battered ribs on his left side forcing him to lean over in sympathy for them – and he moved slowly, with a defiant pride that mocked his tormentors.

Dan waved Le Maréchal's people onward, falling in step behind Beaulac. The man looked over his shoulder but said nothing as the prisoners parted to allow Lucien space to limp through the middle of them.

When he passed Dan he muttered urgently in English, "They murdered Polly! Strung her up like a p—"

"I *know*," Dan snarled. "Get on the fucking truck and keep your head down."

Beaulac looked back again and frowned, but Dan was looking ahead.

"Marshal…You got any Voltaire quotes about an eye for an eye?"

Le Maréchal opened his mouth to speak but never got the chance. Dan drew his sidearm, pressed it to the back of Beaulac's head, and fired.

Beaulac went down like a sack of water and blood sprayed across Le Maréchal's face, stunning him long enough for Dan to grab him, yank him forward with a handful of his fancy coat, and spin him around. Dan felt the world grow close, go slower as the adrenaline hit hard, and savoured every moment of Beaulac's dead body hitting the roadway with a satisfying thud.

The pistol, muzzle still warm from the round that killed Beaulac, twisted into the skin of Le Maréchal's neck and made him cry out in fear and pain which Dan enjoyed just as much as killing Beaulac.

Guns raised fast but Armand, his voice slicing through the panic, barked a massive order for calm.

Dan backed toward the truck, Le Maréchal a shield in front of him.

He fixed his eyes on Armand, suspecting he might've miscalculated because there was no fear in those eyes. Armand almost looked ready to shoot his leader personally, so Dan moved fast before he summoned the good sense and courage to do just that.

He climbed up, shoved him inside, and felt a stab of panic because his driver was still on the roof.

"LEAH!"

The door opened and she threw herself behind the wheel, leading the way south fast.

Dan moved the gun, shoving it into the man's mouth and feeling the muzzle grate sickeningly over teeth. A glance in the side mirror showed Mitch still standing tall, leaning on the truck's side in the rearmost vehicle still with the RPG aimed. Satisfied that they weren't about to be engaged he turned his full attention on Le Maréchal's panic-stricken eyes.

"If you or your people come near us again, and you're not waving a *massive* fucking white flag, I will come back and end every last one of you. Do you understand me?"

Le Maréchal nodded, trembling.

Dan pulled the gun free. "Say it."

"I-i-if any of m-my people come to you...a-and they are not under a flag of truce, they w-will be shot," he whispered.

"No," Dan said, moving the muzzle hard up under his chin to force him against the window. "Repeat my words back to me so I know you understand!"

Le Maréchal hesitated before he spoke with great difficulty for the pressure of the pistol under his chin.

"If I or any of my people come near you again and we are not waving a massive fucking white flag, you will come back and end every last one of us."

"*Louder.*"

He repeated it.

Dan flipped open the door release and forced the muzzle harder, sending him out into mid-air with a panicked yelp.

He leaned out and shut the door, settling back into his seat and breathing hard to control himself before holstering the pistol on his leg with a shaking hand. He sat there, eyes closed just breathing and willing his hands to stop shaking, until Leah spoke.

"You okay?"

"Yeah," Dan said, knowing he was anything but.

He expected more from her. Expected blame or criticism, but she stayed silent for another few miles until someone else took over the driving and she climbed into the back to be with her husband.

EPILOGUE

It was late summer, the kind that made your skin prickle with salt even when you hadn't been near the water. The mercury had hit thirty-two the day before, and with a squinted glance up at a clear, blue sky Dan suspected the same again that day.

Sanctuary moved at its usual pace, the quiet churn of life in the aftermath of war as people returned to their own version of normal. Children's voices carried on the breeze and somewhere, someone was hammering something wooden. Chickens chatted in their pens about whatever it was chickens discussed and it all felt...normal.

Dan sat beside Ben on the worn sea wall, legs dangling over the edge as they hauled hand lines back from the glittering shallows. The boy's brow furrowed in focus, tongue peeking out between his lips like a little engineer as he jerked the line to tease a shape gliding beneath the surface. Dan baited another hook with the practiced ease of someone who never quite learned patience, and tried not to think about how good it felt to sit still for once.

Then came the shout. Sharp and urgent, but distant. Dan tensed like an old dog who'd heard a tone too many times before, and held his breath until the words reached him clearly.

People approaching the gate.

His first instinct was dread. His second instinct was to replay his memory to check if anyone was due to arrive that day, and when he recalled no such planned visits he returned to dread.

The sea, the wall, his son beside him; none of it felt real anymore. Just a dream interrupted by the harsh reality of his life.

He turned to Ben, voice low. "Pack up. Go find your mum."

Ben didn't argue. He just looked at his dad for one long second, nodded, and began to reel in the line, all notions of battling the fish he stalked vanished like Dan's own contentment.

Dan ran, body still stiff but capable now. Ash kept pace like a shadow, silent and coiled with anticipation. When he reached the repaired stretch of wall above the gate, he paused just long enough to rest a hand against the stone, grounding himself.

Then he raised his rifle, not to shoot but to see, and recognition electrified his body with natural chemicals preparing him for action.

Armand stood alone on the roadway, arms spread wide and a ridiculously large white flag clutched in one hand.

Not a flag but a double bedsheet. It billowed in the breeze like a stage curtain, theatrical and just on the edge of mockery.

Dan sighed and lowered the rifle, retreating from the top of the wall and waving to the guards below.

"Open it. Shut it after me," he ordered.

Leah's voice came from behind him as he waited for the gates to creak open. "You're not going without me."

She was already striding towards him flanked by Nemesis, hair tied back and rifle in both hands, wearing an expression like tempered steel.

"Wouldn't dream of it," he answered.

Both dogs fell in beside them as they crossed the threshold and walked down the road, meeting Armand halfway, who had dropped the sheet and offered a faintly amused smirk to Dan along with a hand to shake.

He took it, feeling the perfectly measured grip strength that displayed prowess without turning the greeting into a competition.

"*Bonjour,* Dan," he said, nodding to Leah as an afterthought that Dan could tell pissed her off.

The man was as polite and immaculate as Dan remembered, with that same faint air of smugness that made him want to wash his hands.

"What the fuck do you want?" he replied, likely presenting to Armand the same way as when they first met.

Armand smiled as if Dan had just greeted him with an invitation to dinner.

"To talk. Man to man," he said in better English than Dan recalled him using.

His eyes flicked to Leah, lingering just long enough to ask the silent question.

She stared him down with a cold appraisal, letting her gaze crawl from his polished boots to the neat comb of his hair like she was checking livestock for signs of disease.

"Still waiting to see the evidence of the second part," she said, her tone bored.

"*Madame,* it would be impolite of me to show you such evidence."

Leah fought the rising colour in her cheeks and Dan smirked despite himself.

"You're such a man you like to torture," Leah spat back. "Or are you not even man enough to do it yourself?"

Dan held out a hand to settle Leah, and to prove to Armand that he was still very much in charge.

"She has a point," Dan said.

"I regret the actions my predecessor's people took against your own," Armand said with the careful, political tone of a born liar. "I do not condone this, and it was done without my knowledge…now, may we speak?"

Dan glanced between Armand and Leah, gauging if she could control her feelings long enough to do business, but she seemed calm. She looked to him like a leader.

"Man to man and woman," he told Armand, indicating that they should walk to a large boulder nearby with a jerk of his chin.

They walked uphill, away from the walls. Armand carried himself with relaxed arrogance, displaying none of the arrogance of Le Maréchal, with his hands clasped behind his back like a schoolmaster about to deliver a lecture.

They stopped at a low rise overlooking the wall and beyond that, the glinting Mediterranean stretching into forever, and Dan gestured to the boulder. Armand sat on the flat stone, reached into a pocket and pulled out a thin tin. Opening it he offered Dan a view of the contents like they held a secret.

"Smoke?"

Dan took two, wedging one behind his ear just to annoy Armand, and Leah gave a huff of amusement from where she remained standing.

Both dogs loitered, subdued by the heat in their thick coats but wary and alert of the stranger.

Armand chuckled softly, touching a flame to his own and puffing slowly before offering the lighter to Dan and waiting while he lit his own.

"I come bearing news I wished to share with you personally," Armand said, eyes on the horizon. "There 'as been a…a change of leadership at Carcassonne."

Dan raised a brow. "Interesting...What happened to the last guy?"

Armand shrugged, as if discussing a failed harvest. "His senior men – at least those loyal to 'is cause, suffered what you might call...misfortune? Unfortunate accidents, maybe. Eventually, 'is failures became too obvious to ignore so the people demanded change. And now..."

He spread his arms like a magician revealing the final trick. "I am in charge."

Dan nodded slowly. He couldn't claim he'd seen it coming, but he felt no surprise. "And?"

"I 'ave come to reaffirm our agreement. Of non-aggression. Of 'ow you say...a mutual disinterest? I propose the same terms, unchanged."

Dan didn't respond right away. He watched a gull dive into the sea, imagined a shoal of fish scattering, then vanish.

"I'm not interested in fighting over causes," he muttered.

Armand turned to him, smiling faintly. "But this is where you're wrong! You *do* fight for a cause; you just do not name it. Stability. Community. Order...These are causes, even if you cloak them in survival."

"You rehearse that in the mirror much?" Leah snorted.

Armand didn't rise to it, defusing her mockery with more directed at himself. "For almost an 'our, yes!" he said lightly before turning back to Dan.

"I still believe in a unified France, but I 'ave come to believe fighting battles over borders are the acts of desperate men. France 'as already lost so many sons and daughters that I fear a war over territory would only 'arm 'er more...no...*Diplomacy*, 'owever...diplomacy leaves something be'ind. It leaves a *legacy*."

He looked out across the water, posture softening just slightly to betray the fact he fully believed his own lines.

"Per'aps not for us, but for our children and their children after."

Dan didn't argue. He didn't necessarily agree, but neither did he walk away.

"You stay away from Sanctuary," he said, "and from the places who trade with us. You keep your people behind your walls and I won't come looking to add a second fortified town to my patch."

Armand smiled, with genuine satisfaction. "Then we are agreed."

Dan nodded, once. "Where you headed next?"

Armand sighed, theatrically wistful. "I thought per'aps Andorra. I visited once as a boy, you know…from what I remember it is very beautiful."

Dan tilted his head, expression flat. "I wouldn't bother, pal. I've got Andorra's proxy, and they're under the same agreement."

Armand nodded, no offence taken. "Of course. Then I will go home."

He began to walk away, then stopped, turning back with one hand extended.

"We should, ahhh, *seal the deal,* no? Like gentlemen."

Dan looked at the offered hand, then at Armand's smug face.

For a long moment his knuckles itched. He imagined punching him square in the throat, just to see if smugness could survive blunt trauma. When that urge subsided he considered spitting in the palm of his hand just for vulgarity, but eventually he just shook the offered hand.

Leah stood watching beside him as Armand walked back to his escort.

"You know, for a second there it looked like you were about to smack his jaw off."

"Crossed my mind," Dan grunted. "Only he's the HMIC now."

"Yep…wait, what?"

"He's now the head motherfucker in charge, kid."

"So it's done? You believe him?"

Dan thought for a long moment before he breathed his reply. "For now."

They stood watching the man disappear into the heat shimmer of the road.

"You believe he doesn't want a war over territory?"

"I believe him when he says that's the act of a desperate man, but something tells me he's far too bloody clever to be desperate."

"So, what? We just leave him out there to come back when he's stronger? We just…let some warlord gain power?"

Dan turned to look at her, half suspecting she might take a shot now and end the future war she feared was coming.

"That door swings both ways," he told her, feeling older and wiser without having noticed any transition. "From his perspective he's leaving a warlord here to grow stronger."

"Maybe," Leah allowed cautiously.

"But I'm no warlord," Dan muttered. "The thing about warlords is they're only important when there's a war."

ABOUT THE AUTHOR

Devon C Ford is from the UK and lives in the Midlands. His career in public services started in his teens and has provided a wealth of experiences, both good and some very bad, which form the basis of the books ideas that cause regular insomnia.

Facebook: @decvoncfordofficial
Twitter: @DevonFordAuthor
Website: www.devoncford.com